FATAL
EQUITY

Neal Sanders

The Hardington Press

Fatal Equity is a work of fiction. The characters and events described are entirely the product of the author's imagination.

Also by Neal Sanders

Murder Imperfect
The Garden Club Gang
The Accidental Spy
A Murder in the Garden Club
Murder for a Worthy Cause
Deal Killer
Deadly Deeds
A Murder at the Flower Show
Murder in Negative Space
How to Murder Your Contractor
A Whiff of Revenge

A brief description of each of these books can be found beginning on page 289.

For Betty, once again

FATAL EQUITY

Chapter One
Tuesday evening

Alice Beauchamp had no idea she was about to save someone's life when she answered her phone on a Tuesday evening in August. It was the voice of a dear, old friend with a benign request.

"I'm flying out to see Jeannie in the morning but can't find anyone to look in on Cleo and Franny. Would you stop by tomorrow and Friday and make certain they have seed and water?"

Alice readily agreed to the task. The conversation had taken less than a minute. The two parakeets had been the principal sources of joy and comfort for Rebecca Cooper since the death of her husband two months earlier. Being asked to watch over them for a day or two was an honor.

But Alice's phone was barely back in its cradle when the gnawing feeling something wasn't right began to intrude on her thoughts.

Rebecca's daughter lived in New Mexico. Including changing planes, flying from Boston to Albuquerque consumed the better part of a day in each direction. Yet Rebecca had asked that Alice come by for just two days. Only one day with her daughter? That made no sense.

And at Frank's wake, Jeannie Cooper had spoken of the stress from practically commuting between Albuquerque and Denver; never knowing which city she would awaken in on any given day. Her employer, she said, seemed to take pleasure in keeping her guessing where she would next be needed.

Also, the trip seemed to come out of the blue. Spur-of-the-moment travel had never been part of Frank and Rebecca's lifestyle in the thirty years Alice had known them. To the contrary, even a weekend jaunt to Vermont required poring over maps and multiple consultations of guide books.

Ten minutes after the call and five minutes after gathering her purse and car keys, Alice pulled into the driveway at 217 Metacomet Road. It was a house Alice knew well, part of a Hardington subdivision built in the early 1970s near the home where she once lived. Sited on a now-densely-wooded acre of land, the split-level structure had been Frank and Rebecca's brand-new dream home when they moved into it in 1973. They had raised two children here. And, for the past four years, it had been the convalescent space where Rebecca cared for her invalid husband as his health declined.

There were no lights on in the front of the house, but that was not unusual. The large, seldom-used formal living and dining rooms were to the left and right of the front door. Rebecca would be in one of the three rooms at the back of the house that had come to be the perimeter of her existence in the final months of Frank's illness.

Alice rang the doorbell but heard no response from inside. She tried the front door and, not surprisingly, found it unlocked. Crime was rare in Hardington and neighbors watched over one another's homes.

"Becky?" Alice said, announcing herself as she stepped into the darkness. She heard only the sound of the two parakeets coming from the family room, from which also emanated a dim light. Unwilling to turn on lamps that were not her own, Alice slowly followed the light to its source.

In its heyday, the spacious room had been the center of family life. Jeannie and Gregory had been popular student athletes. It was not uncommon to come to the house in the afternoon to find a lacrosse scrimmage on the front lawn and the hockey team in the family room sprawled across chairs and sofas, engaged in a group study session.

But that was 25 years earlier. Frank's diagnosis of Multiple Sclerosis had progressed from an inconvenience to a forced retirement. Five years ago, Rebecca and Frank were faced with the reality that, because of the progression and severity of the disease, he would not live to see 75 and, within a year, he would be unable to care for himself. Unwilling to place her husband in a nursing home, Rebecca instead engaged a team of home health aides. The family room was converted to an infirmary and she saw to her husband's needs until the end.

Alice entered the family room. Frank's bed and the ancillary equipment required for his care were no longer in evidence, but neither had the displaced furnishings been returned from storage. The room now was empty except for a large birdcage, a writing desk and a chair.

At the desk, wearing a bathrobe and a towel around her head, sat Rebecca Cooper. In front of her were several sheets of writing paper; in her hand, a pen. On the edge of the desk was a short stack of what looked like business papers and correspondence. Only a desk lamp illuminated the room.

She and Alice were the same age – seventy-two. Osteoporosis had shrunk Rebecca's frame to about five feet six inches. Always slender, she was now gaunt; the years of providing for all of her husband's care had caused Rebecca to neglect her own. Oddly, she wore carefully applied makeup.

"Are you all right, Becky?" Alice asked.

Rebecca turned her head toward Alice. "Why are you here this evening?" she asked querulously. "You're not supposed to come until tomorrow."

Alice crossed the room and placed her hand on Rebecca's shoulder. "I'm here because I think you need me."

Rebecca slowly shook her head. "Tomorrow. You should be

here tomorrow. I should have put you further down the list but I couldn't be certain what time you went to bed."

Alice did not respond. Instead, peering over Rebecca's shoulder, she read the list on the desk. Rebecca made no effort to cover it. Most of the items were crossed off – tasks apparently completed – but the last two items were neatly written:

> *Write explanatory note*
> *Take pills*

"Why?" Alice asked in a soft voice. There was no need to expand the question.

Rebecca slowly reached for and pulled to the center of the desk a quarter-inch-thick stack of papers, on top of which was multi-page letter on the letterhead of a law firm. She fumbled with the pages, finally finding the one she wanted.

"They're going to foreclose on my house," she said, her voice a monotone. "They're going to sell it. They promised I could stay here for the rest of my life. But now I have to leave. I have no money and no place to go." She added, with a shrug of her shoulder, "And I'm not certain I have anything left to live for."

Alice tried to make sense of the letter but it was all legalese. It might as well have been written in Latin. Returning it to the desk, she said in a firm voice, "You, Cleo and Franny are coming home with me for tonight. Tomorrow, we'll sort this out."

The two women spoke little on the short drive home. Alice's head, though, swirled with thoughts of what almost certainly would have happened had she not driven to Metacomet Road when she did. Tomorrow, she would have come to feed two parakeets only to instead discover her friend dead of an overdose of whatever pain medications remained from Frank's final illness. She would have found the note Rebecca intended to leave, and it would have fallen to her to locate Jeannie and Gregory and break the horrific news to them.

Alice also wondered if the call to her was a final plea for help;

made to the one person in a position to intervene. As the relatively small gathering for Frank's wake and funeral attested, most of the couple's friends had long since moved away. Once a town where even people of modest means could afford to live, Hardington had moved decidedly 'upscale' in the past few decades. Taxes were high to provide the kinds of services affluent residents expected. Small homes were sold for the inflated value of their land; their owners took the proceeds and moved to the Cape or to Florida.

What Alice knew above all was she was not equipped to help Rebecca solve the problem that had nearly caused her to take her life. Alice could provide friendship and comforting, but it would take a group of resourceful people to parse the letter she had received and find a way to undo Rebecca's pending eviction.

Tomorrow morning, she would call them.

Chapter Two
Wednesday morning

Samantha Ayers fumed as she re-read the letter and its supporting document.   *Bloodsuckers*, she mumbled to herself. *Thieves, crooks and charlatans.*

Samantha was a tall, attractive woman who looked younger than her 28 years. At 20 she had been the third generation of her family to join the Worcester Police Department but, after five years, she determined that while race was no longer a barrier to advancement (her father was a Lieutenant, and likely to be made a Captain before the year was out), sexism still ran rampant. After enduring an endless stream of assignments as a decoy high school student, collegiate drug buyer, and prostitute, she resigned.

Over the past three years she had found her niche as an investigator for Massachusetts Casualty Insurance Company. In the past twelve months Samantha had solved a high-profile theft at the Brookfield Fair and, in the process, uncovered municipal corruption in the town. She had brought down a chain of automotive dealerships that solved its cash flow problems by torching unsaleable cars. In doing so, she also unmasked the patriarch of that organization as the head of a counterfeit auto parts ring.

They met in Alice's Hardington townhouse. Alice felt no need to explain to Rebecca the close relationship she and three of her close friends had with Samantha. How they had banded together a year earlier to form 'the Garden Club Gang' and that Samantha had saved Alice's life (and spared 'the gang' from a likely stay in prison for robbery). She simply introduced Samantha as, "my friend, and someone who knows something about these things."

Samantha put down the papers and slowly shook her head.

"Mrs. Cooper, start at the beginning. And please don't think that something is too trivial to mention."

Rebecca Cooper did not flinch from the request. "Frank and I had a pact. We made it when we were, I think, about sixty-five. We would never put one another in a nursing home. We hated them. We hated what they did to people's spirits. We would take care of one another and, if things went too far downhill, we would help the incapacitated person to die peacefully."

Rebecca leaned forward in the dining room chair in which she sat. "Then Frank was diagnosed with MS. Not the easy kind like Jed Bartlet had on *The West Wing*; not that any MS diagnosis is easy. Frank was ultimately diagnosed with an aggressive form of Progressive-Relapsing MS. There were never periods of remission. Every month seemed to bring a fresh symptom. He couldn't walk for the last two years and couldn't swallow for the last few months."

"Frank and I were hardly well-to-do; he was the Hardington Postmaster and I taught third grade. He had a good pension with good medical benefits. But do you know what the annual cost is for a drug like Tysabri? More than $60,000 and the insurance company made us pay half. And that's just one drug."

Rebecca leaned back in her chair. "We had just about exhausted our savings when we got one of those letters. 'Is a reverse mortgage right for you?' I went to an 'informational luncheon' and there was a nice young man sitting right next to me. I told him about Frank's deteriorating condition. He made all the right sympathetic noises, then asked where we lived. When I told him, he said, 'Hardington! Your home has got to be worth a fortune!' I said we didn't live in one of 'those' houses and he just waved aside what I said. 'I'll bet your home is worth a half million or more,' he said. 'You won't have to pay it back. And they can never make you move out of your home. It's yours for life.'"

Samantha glanced down at the paperwork. "So this 'nice young man' was with Senior Equity Lending Services?"

Rebecca shook her head. "No, he said he was a 'reverse mortgage consultant' and told me he would find Frank and me the best deal from among all the companies he dealt with. He said his services wouldn't cost us anything. He kept saying the mortgage would be insured; and stressing we wouldn't have to pay back anything."

"Did you hire a lawyer?" Samantha asked.

Rebecca again shook her head. "A lawyer would have cost us several thousand dollars. We wouldn't *have* that kind of money until we had a mortgage. Bryce – that was the young man's name – got us a meeting with Chad, the Company's President. I remember that meeting so well… the first thing Chad asked me was, 'Who is your favorite actor of all time?' It didn't take me two seconds to answer. 'Angela Lansbury,' I said. 'I always loved *Murder, She Wrote.*' Chad let out this 'Whoop!' and clapped his hands. 'So you've seen our commercials? Angela is our celebrity endorser. She has brought us more customers than I can count. Oh, my gosh. Wait until I tell everyone.' Of course, I had never seen those commercials, but I didn't want to sound stupid. So I just nodded. But he kept going on about 'Angela this' and 'Angela that' and promised he would introduce me the next time she was in Boston."

Samantha had been tapping her phone for a few seconds. She shook her head. "Angela Lansbury has never endorsed any reverse mortgage product." She turned the screen to show Rebecca.

Rebecca nodded. "I figured that out eventually. But he had me believing I had seen her commercials dozens of times. He asked me whether I liked the one better of her in the floor-length silver gown or whether she looked like she had just come in from working in the garden. I chose the gardening one because I am – or was – a gardener. He even told me she used plants from her own garden when they were filming." She shook her head. "I was a fool."

Samantha leafed through the paperwork. "You signed loan origination agreements, inspection agreements, title insurance, waivers to claim... even one that said you understood you were not reviewing materials with your own attorney..."

Rebecca again nodded. "They kept telling me about getting the funds to keep Frank at home. Of course, the 'half million' number disappeared almost immediately. Our house is assessed by the town at more than $600,000 but *their* appraiser said the number wasn't realistic because it was a split-level and no one wants our kind of house any more. Also, we had modified it for a wheelchair ramp and to set up Frank's infirmary. In the end, they said it was worth..."

"Three hundred and thirteen thousand," Samantha said, reading from the document. "And they would give you seventy percent of that less an origination fee of four percent and enough other fees to get your total available funds to $202,600."

"Which kept Frank at home for another eighteen months," Rebecca said, sighing. "And the last of the funds paid for his funeral. Frank's pension ended with his death. I still have my social security. It isn't much but, combined with being able to stay in my home, I thought it would be enough."

"And then you received the foreclosure notice," Samantha said. "I can only imagine what kind of shock it was."

"It was the amount that puzzled me," Rebecca said. "So much more than they gave me."

Samantha turned a page. "You drew out the full $202,600. Then they wanted back all their fees. That was $26,500. And, they wanted interest on what they considered a loan. That was another $31,337. And they want a 'termination fee' of $30,000. So, from their perspective, you need to pay them $290,437; otherwise, they have every right to sell your house out from underneath you."

"But why can't I stay in the house?" Rebecca said. "They promised."

"That's what we need to understand," Samantha said. "You added your son's name to your home's deed. What prompted you to do that?"

Rebecca was silent for a moment. "When it became apparent Frank had just a few weeks to live, I went back to see Chad. I explained to him Frank was failing and it might be better if I sold my home and moved into an apartment. I explained all the money they had given me had gone to Frank's care, and I thought I had enough to cover his final expenses. Chad expressed his sympathy and asked that I wait in the reception area while he found all my files."

"That was when I met Margaret. Margaret was a woman who said she was seventy-five, though she looked a great deal younger. I told her about Frank, and she said her own husband died just three weeks earlier, and she was so glad she had added her sister to the deed to her home because now both she and her sister were protected. Her sister was just sixty and longevity runs in the family. She said if I added my son or my daughter to the deed, then they would also be able to remain in the house after I passed. She said it was the secret that all these reverse mortgage companies didn't want you to know about."

"We chatted a few more minutes and then Chad came out to say he could meet with me again. He listened to my plan to sell the house and said I shouldn't act hastily, because many of the worst decisions were made under emotional duress."

"That was the extent of it?" Samantha asked. "You went to the Registry of Deeds and added your son to your home deed?"

Rebecca shook her head. "No. I thought about it, but it sounded, well, unethical. Like I was taking advantage of the arrangement. I was grateful for what Senior Equity had done. They gave me another eighteen months with Frank, and I was able to keep my promise to him. What happened was, three days later I was at the Roche Brothers in Hardington and I literally ran into

Margaret's cart or, rather, she ran into mine. She said she didn't know I lived in Hardington and what a surprise it was to see me again."

"Did she say she lived here?" Samantha asked.

Rebecca again shook her head. "She said she lived 'a few towns over' but there wasn't a Roche Brothers near her and so she shopped here. She offered to buy me coffee and a pastry. Neither of us had much of anything in our carts, so we just went next door to the Silver Spoon. After about five minutes of chit-chatting, she asked if I had added either of my children to the deed. I explained that, while it was a good idea, it was cheating on the agreement, and I didn't want anyone to be angry with me when they found out."

"How did Margaret react?" Samantha asked.

"She laughed," Rebecca said. "She said these reverse mortgage companies gets tens of millions of dollars from the government to make these loans possible. She said when she told Chad about the fact she had added her sister, he was delighted and said it showed she had 'learned how to game the system' – I think those were the words she used. Then she said it was so simple and explained how to do it."

"Could you recognize her if you saw her again?" Samantha asked.

"I did see her again," Rebecca replied. "Two days later. I was at the CVS picking up something. And there was Margaret again. This time I thought it a little odd because every town around here has either a CVS or something just like it, so she surely couldn't have driven to Hardington from wherever she lives just to go to our drugstore."

"Did it occur to you these meetings weren't just an accident?" Samantha asked.

"Not until it was too late," Rebecca said, a rueful tone to her voice. "This time there were hardly any cordialities. She said I owed it to Frank and to my family. That as soon as I passed, the house would go to the highest bidder and they would immediately tear it down. She said it was a disservice to Frank's memory. But if my son was in the house, all those memories would live on for decades to come. She said she knew my daughter lived too far away, but Gregory was close enough by that he could commute. I didn't remember telling Margaret the names of my children, but I may have."

"And so you went to the County Registry of Deeds," Samantha said.

"Margaret even offered to drive me," Rebecca said, regret in her voice. "I said I could drive myself. I went that afternoon."

"And you never saw Margaret again," Samantha said.

Rebecca just shook her head.

"But you'd recognize her."

"Without a doubt," Rebecca said.

"Do you remember the dates you saw her?"

Rebecca thought for a second. "I save all my receipts for my taxes. The dates will be on those."

Samantha jotted a note. "How long was it after you added Gregory's name you were notified by Senior Equity that adding someone's name to the deed to your home placed you in default of the terms of the reverse mortgage?"

Rebecca's eyes moistened for the first time. "Frank was failing so quickly. We all knew it was a matter of days. My mind wasn't on bills so I just let mail stack up unopened on the desk. I didn't read any letters until a week after the funeral. As soon as I read the first one, I opened all the others and was shocked. I called Chad's office but was told my 'account' was now in the hands of their law firm. All my calls to that law firm went to voice mail, where I was informed communications had to be by registered letter."

Alice passed Rebecca a box of tissues. Rebecca took one and dabbed at her eyes. "Which was when I realized what a fool I had been; and began to understand I had been swindled." She paused.

"And I started to understand I was probably better off just going to join Frank."

Alice and Samantha were silent while Rebecca composed herself. After a minute, Rebecca said, "Alice, I owe you an apology. I was going to put you in a horrible position. No person should ever have to find…"

Alice reached across the table and took her friend's hands. "The important thing is you're here with us now." Alice turned to look at Samantha. "And can we do something about it?"

Samantha nodded slowly. "This is fraud. That's for certain. I have a lot of things to check into before I can offer any suggestions. It's clear 'Margaret' is working with those people. No one 'just happens' to be sitting outside an office like that. And she was effectively stalking Rebecca – showing up at a supermarket and a drug store a few minutes after Rebecca did the same. Nothing like that happens in a vacuum. Which means, I'll bet, Rebecca isn't the first person to find themselves with a foreclosure notice from these folks. By the end of today I'll have a better picture."

Addressing herself to Rebecca, Samantha said, "I need to take photos of these letters so I can find out more about 'Senior Equity Lending Services' and 'Chad' and all the other cast of characters. In the meantime, you need to see an attorney. You need legal advice and you need it in a hurry."

"But I can't afford…" Rebecca started to say.

"We'll talk to someone today," Alice said.

* * * * *

"You've been dealing with the scum of the earth. The worst kind of criminals – people who prey on the elderly. And who hide behind the law."

The person speaking these blunt words was Diane Terwilliger. She was a woman somewhere in her sixties who looked as though she might have been an athlete in her younger years. She was of medium height, but there was a muscular feel beneath the skirted suit she wore. Her short, gray hair was offset by large, round glasses with thick, black rims. The immediate visual impression she sent was she was not to be trifled with.

Terwilliger was seated in the same chair at the small dining room table Samantha Ayers had occupied a few hours earlier. An attorney with her primary practice in Hardington, Terwilliger knew Alice Beauchamp only slightly; she had created a trust that owned the townhouse in which Alice now resided. But Terwilliger was well known to a woman named Paula Winters. A call from Alice to Paula resulted in Terwilliger shuffling an appointment in order to meet with Alice and Rebecca on less than an hour's notice.

Terwilliger leafed through the sheaf of papers, laying out the various forms Rebecca Cooper has signed.

"The first thing you need to know is this isn't an HECM-compliant mortgage," she said. "A Home Equity Conversion Mortgage caps the origination fee at something like $6,000 and has all manner of cooling-off periods where a senior can change his or her mind without penalty. There's a specific prohibition against termination fees. There's mandatory counseling before the mortgage is issued along with other assurances that protect the borrower. The problem is, with HECM-compliant mortgages, the table is tilted so heavily toward the borrower that most banks have gotten out of the business because there's too little money to be made. As such, the groups that are doing HECMs are non-profits and they're hard to find. That's what leaves the door open for sharks like Senior Equity."

Terwilliger began laying documents across the dining room table. "And look what these guys have done to protect themselves," she said, pointing at the first sheet of paper.

"They had you sign an affidavit acknowledging you were making these decisions without having had consulted an attorney," Terwilliger said. "They were covering their collective asses three ways from Sunday." She pointed to a second document. "This is their own affidavit they had advised you to seek an attorney's opinion, and they then had you initial their affidavit acknowledging you concurred." Terwilliger looked at Rebecca. "Do you remember any of this?"

Bewildered, Rebecca shook her head. "I just signed whatever papers they put in front of me."

"Of course you did," Terwilliger said, bitterness in her voice. "And you also initialed you were in full agreement with their ridiculous lowball appraisal. And here's a good one: you specifically acknowledged to them that, if you repay the mortgage, you will reimburse Senior Equity for all of their expense involved with originating the instrument, as well as a hefty termination fee."

"I did?" Rebecca asked.

Terwilliger nodded. "That's how they do it. They just start putting sheets of paper in front of you and telling you to sign." She gave a wry smile as she held up another sheet. "This one says you have three days to change your mind about the mortgage. I'll bet they never explained that one to you."

Rebecca shook her head. No, they had not.

"And then you signed this one," Terwilliger said, holding the sheet in the air. "It says you acknowledge they explained all of the other forms to you, and you understood each of them."

"I had no idea," Rebecca said softly.

"Of course you didn't," Terwilliger replied. "That's the whole idea. And then 'Margaret' comes along and says you ought to do something to violate the terms of the mortgage. That way, their money is tied up for maybe two years, after which they have an asset worth at least twice what they paid you."

"What can Rebecca do?" Alice asked.

Terwilliger was silent for a moment. "Legally, almost nothing. Senior Equity has the law on their side. This file is papered with proof they followed the letter of the law and you agreed with everything they did. It's only when you throw in 'Margaret' and the fact they just happened to be performing a 'routine title search' after Rebecca's husband's death that it all begins to smell like what it is: a scam."

Terwilliger began placing the papers into a folder. "I'm just a suburban attorney," she said. "I do cut-and-dried wills and probate, divorces, separation agreements, and whatever else comes across the transom. I get idiot kids out of jams those kids would never have gotten into except their parents were too busy to notice. I'm here because Paula is one of the few people in this town for whom I will drop everything to be of help."

Terwilliger placed the last sheet into the folder. "We can file an injunction. We can ask for a stay of the foreclosure while you seek the highest price for your house. But that isn't going to solve the underlying problem these people have their claws into you for almost $90,000 more than you received from them, or it was their underhanded tactics that caused you to violate the loan."

"You are going to need a shark to get out of this," Terwilliger continued. "These people are slick and they've already thought about the angles, which tells me they've been doing this for a while. They'll play a delaying game that can last for years, and time is never on the side of the elderly. You should also lodge a complaint with the state Attorney General's office and the Consumer Financial Protection Bureau. They're supposed to be a consumer advocate and look at things like this. But I suspect they're only interested in big fish. Beating Senior Equity would take too much time and energy."

Terwilliger rose from the chair and slipped on her jacket. "As much as I hate to say it, with people like this, hiring an attorney might be throwing good money after bad. There has to be some kind of a back-door solution." She gestured to the room around her. "I created the 'GCG Trust' last year at Paula's request. The trust exists for one reason: to own this exceptionally nice townhouse condominium you live in. I didn't ask Paula where all that money came from. It isn't my business and, as an officer of the court, there are things about which I'm much better off not knowing."

"But I know wherever that money came from, it went to good use. I'm going to suggest to Paula she put on her thinking cap and get creative." With those final words, Diane Terwilliger shook hands with Rebecca and Alice, collected her briefcase, and said her goodbyes.

Chapter Three
Wednesday

"How did it go?"

Charles 'Chad' Pannett glared up from his desk at the slouching person in the doorway who asked the question.

The two men were in a large office on the third floor of a building that had once housed the corporate headquarters of a formerly-high-flying company that had crashed and burned when, like many businesses, it discovered its market niche could be filled by a smartphone app. The imprudent company had tied up tens of millions of dollars on the long-term lease and tasteful furnishing of this building. One product of the company's Chapter 10 bankruptcy filing was the availability of 160,000 square feet of elegant, fully equipped office space at bargain-basement rates to anyone willing to live with the uncertainty of having to move on thirty days' notice should a more suitable tenant appear.

Senior Equity Lending Services LLP had no such qualms about squatting in temporary quarters. The Framingham office building the firm called its home was actually its third such transitory abode in as many years. The beauty of the current set-up was that, because they were the building's only tenant, prospective customers could be paraded past dozens of offices supposedly housing Senior Equity employees. In reality, the company occupied just seven offices totaling 1500 square feet.

"How did it '*go*?'" Pannett parroted back at the man in the doorway. "I don't think it's going to '*go*' at all," he said with gritted teeth.

Pannett pushed himself back from the mahogany desk and rose to his six-foot-one-inch height which, to anyone who had ever seen him in his stocking feet, was in reality three inches short of that figure. His hair was a glossy jet black; his suit a hand-tailored Zenga, his tie a jacquard silk Brioni. At age 34, Pannett had mastered the art of exuding charm, concern, and understanding to people twice his age. Now, in the privacy of his office, he seethed anger.

Pannett plucked a red file folder from the desktop and opened it. "Let's start with your name," he said. "I called you 'Bryce'. Mrs. Berry thinks you're 'Carl' so, of course, she was mightily confused when I kept saying wonderful things about 'Bryce'. We have a rule: you attach the right business card to the file so I don't look stupid in front of the money."

"I won't forget to attach the right card in the future," the man said contritely. In reality, his name was neither 'Bryce' nor 'Carl' but, rather, 'Dustin'. However, because 'Dustin Payne' had accumulated a lengthy rap sheet in the 31 years since his entrance into the world, both of his birth names had been retired in favor of a revolving list of aliases.

"Let's see what else you got wrong," Pannett said, turning pages. "She isn't certain she owns her home outright and her daughter may already be the co-owner..."

"I checked carefully," Dustin said. "The title search showed no encumbrances and no co-owners. I think she's just starting to have cognitive issues. She's perfect."

"And is the house in Med*field* or Med*ford*?" Pannett asked, pulling out two sheets. "We seem to be trying to have it both ways."

"That's a typing error," Dustin said. "I'm certain the house is in Medford. Her husband was a professor at Tufts. She told me several times. I've screened her thoroughly."

"Really?" Pannett asked. "And while you were performing this thorough screening, did she also tell you how much she loves opera? I asked her about her favorite actor of all time. Do you know what she told me?" In a falsetto voice of a well-bred woman,

Pannett said, "'Oh, I really don't bother much with film or television. They're rather boring. Give me an hour with Plácido Domingo and I'm in heaven.' Was I supposed to ask her if she preferred the ad where he's dressed for *Il Rigoletto* or *Aida*? And if she doesn't watch television, where did that ad she saw run?"

Pannett slammed the folder down on the desk. "It's your job to make certain these people are ready to deal. They need the money *now*. I also asked Mrs. Berry what she planned to do with the proceeds. 'Oh, I'm thinking about going to Venice,' she said. 'A cruise.'" He paused to allow the words sink in. "Unless she's thinking she needs to buy the cruise ship, she's not a candidate. She isn't going to sign and, if she does, she'll have her lawyer with her."

"We have a sweet business," Pannett said, removing his suit jacket and carefully hanging it over a burgundy sofa left by the previous tenant. "It's also a simple business. Little old ladies. House rich, cash poor, and a need for ready money. *Gullible* little old ladies who don't ask a lot of questions and don't have sons and daughters that are lawyers. And, if they have health issues, that's perfection. New England is *crawling* with women like that. Your job is to find them. My job is to close them. Bree's job is to get them to make a mistake. The lawyers do the rest. This is a money machine. But it produces money only if everyone does their job. And so far this morning, you aren't doing yours."

Dustin was silent. He knew when it was time to keep quiet and take his punishment.

"You cost me sixty minutes," Pannett said, turning to a window overlooking the tops of trees. "We should be closing forty mortgages a week. That's ten bona-fide clients through my door every day because we set aside Fridays for closings. Last week we did just thirty. Well, we just lost one more opportunity. I hope the hell you vetted your other five pigeons better than you did Mrs. Berry…"

"The next one is out in the waiting area," Dustin said. "I

guarantee you she's prime. Eighty-one and scraping by on social security and a two-bit annuity, but with a house in Weston with 'tear down' written all over it."

Pannett shook his head and retrieved his jacket, inspecting it for errant lint or hairs. "This had better be good. And let's start by telling me what name you used when you roped her in..."

* * * * *

Paula Winters reclined, half asleep, in a chaise lounge on the deck overlooking her back garden. A glass of iced tea was at her side. The mid-August sun was warm, the humidity low, and a soft breeze blew from the north. It was a perfect day in a life that had bestowed too many horrific ones over the past few years.

Four years earlier, Paula's husband had returned from a business trip to announce he wanted a divorce. Weeks after the divorce was final, he married a woman only a few years older than their daughter. Six months later, Paula was diagnosed with breast cancer. A lumpectomy seemed to take care of the problem but after eighteen months of clean tests – a year ago, now – there was a recurrence and the lone question was how far the cancer had metastasized. It was the low point of Paula's life, and the diagnosis left her with the sobering realization she had led an unmemorable existence that could only be characterized as 'safe and dull'.

That epiphany had led to the formation of 'the Garden Club Gang' and an adventure that in hindsight was as dangerous as it was reckless. But out of it also came a new reason for living and a second set of exploits no less satisfying than the first.

And out of all of that had come the most unexpected but welcome of results: a widower, a detective, a sensitive and caring man named Martin Hoffman. Two months earlier on their first vacation together; needing to be honest with him but fearing the truth would drive him away, she confessed everything. She was the ringleader of the group that robbed the Brookfield Fair in broad daylight. The Massachusetts State Police had arrested, and juries had convicted, the wrong people. Those men were guilty of many crimes, but not the one that had sent them to prison. And, while she was coming clean, Paula admitted her sudden decision earlier in the year to take a night nursing position in an upscale retirement community was not a desire to return to her one-time profession but, rather, to investigate the death of a garden club member.

Paula was launching into her role at Pokrovsky Motors when Martin gently placed a finger over her lips.

"I figured it out," he said, softly.

"How?" Paula asked, astonished.

"I'm a detective," he replied. "It's what I do for a living."

"But I lied to you," Paula said.

Martin nodded imperceptibly. "People lie for lots of reasons. You seem to have had a fairly benign motive. Well, except for the money you didn't give back. How much was that again?"

Paula gulped. "Three hundred and fifty thousand dollars."

Martin again nodded. "Which I suspect helped buy that townhouse Alice Beauchamp lives in."

It was Paula's turn to nod.

"And the money you didn't give back was part of a Selectman's bribe."

Paula again nodded.

"Yeah," Martin said. "I figured it out. And the Cavendish Woods thing did kind of make me a hero. I handed the state police a serial killer. That's a once-in-a-career sort of thing."

"You should have arrested me once you figured it out," Paula said.

"I make it a point not to arrest the woman I love," Martin replied.

Those words were etched in Paula's memory.

Which is when the ringing of a telephone brought her back to the present. She opened a glass sliding door and reached for the telephone.

"Paula, I think I need your expertise," Alice said.

* * * * *

An hour later, Paula had heard the story of Senior Equity Lending Services and had asked and been provided with answers to most of her questions. There was no question in her mind but that Rebecca Cooper had fallen prey to a financial scam. The most chilling part of the story was the implication the frail, elderly woman sitting opposite her at Alice's dining room table had been within minutes of taking her own life.

"You're thinking we should do something," Paula said to Alice. "Go undercover. Something like that."

"Samantha said she had to do a lot of checking," Alice replied. "But the more I think about this, the angrier I get. There must be dozens – maybe hundreds – of people who have gone through what Becky is living with right now."

"Have you forgotten how close you came to... not being with us?" Paula asked.

Alice involuntarily closed the fingers of her right hand around her left wrist and rubbed it. There was still intermittent pain; the product of having had her wrist smashed by a Thermos bottle... one filled with poisoned tea.

"Becky has been my friend for three decades," Alice said. "She was there for me when I lost John. I owe it to her."

Paula chose her words carefully. "What would happen if someone simply loaned Rebecca the money to repay these people. She could then change back her deed and apply for a new reverse mortgage with a reputable lender; this time getting what her house is really worth."

Alice looked down at her notes and then back at Paula with horror. "And pay those people almost a hundred thousand in 'interest, fees and expenses'? Plus having to pay a new set of fees?"

"We had luck on our side," Paula said. "We were incredibly fortunate. We could just as well all be in jail right now. Rebecca can also sue. This is fraud."

"Which Diane Terwilliger says could take years to prove, and this group could just disappear, taking everyone's money with them," Alice retorted. "Would you help me?"

Paula was silent as she thought. Finally, she said, "We'd need a house. It can't be mine – I'm still ten years too young to apply for a reverse mortgage." She gestured at the walls around her. "You're the right age, but you're technically a tenant. The last I heard, Jean was still un-tangling the legal morass her husband created for her. That leaves Eleanor, and I don't know if she is ready to do something like this again. Phil's death was a blessing in its own way, but it was exceptionally hard on her."

"But we can ask Eleanor," Alice said. "And if she says 'no', we can try to recruit someone else."

Paula looked at Alice, seeing her mix of determination and pain.

"We can ask Eleanor," Paula said. "But not until we hear back from Samantha." After a moment, she added with a sigh, "And I suspect Jean will be interested as well."

Chapter Four
Thursday evening

It was the evening of the following day when Samantha Ayers, bearing a thick file folder, appeared in Paula Winters' 'great room'. On chairs and sofas were assembled Alice, Paula, Eleanor and Jean; the four women who had first called themselves 'The Garden Club Gang' eleven months earlier. Also present was Rebecca Cooper, who was still absorbing the fact that Alice, her quiet and retiring friend, was part of such an enterprise.

"Lucy McClellan is an extraordinarily resourceful woman to know," Samantha said. Speaking to Rebecca, Samantha added, "Paula and I met her in California back in February. She is a senior executive at a large high tech company in Silicon Valley, and she was grateful we were able to shed light on the circumstances of her mother's death at Cavendish Woods. She offered to assist us in the future, and I feel like I cashed one of those chits yesterday when I asked her if there was a way to get security footage from the drug store and supermarket where Rebecca encountered 'Margaret'. All I had to go on was the date and time code on Rebecca's sales receipts."

Samantha opened the folder and removed a series of photographs. "I didn't ask Lucy what strings she pulled to get this but, this morning, I received a dozen or so video clips from the drug store, all showing conversations between any elderly women and a somewhat younger one in the store in the ten minutes before Rebecca made her purchases. There were half a dozen possibilities."

Samantha showed the first photo and handed it to Rebecca. "Is this the woman you knew as 'Margaret'?" The photo, taken from a ceiling camera, showed two women conversing.

It took Rebecca only an instant to say, "Yes." She then began crying.

Samantha nodded and removed four more photos. "Here is the best frame of the series," she said. "It isn't perfect; security cameras are set up to look for shoplifting. But this is the woman who convinced Rebecca to alter her deed. I believe she told Rebecca she was 75; I'd say she's not even 50. Has anyone ever seen her around Hardington?"

Everyone looked at their copy of the photo and at one another. They all shook their heads.

"The store's exterior camera doesn't film continuously," Samantha said. "Instead, it snaps a frame every seven seconds." She handed out another set of three photos. "This is 'Margaret' coming into and leaving the store immediately after talking with Rebecca – empty-handed, I might add, which pretty much proves she followed Rebecca to the store for the sole purpose of convincing her to change her deed. The camera's field of view doesn't capture all of the parking lot, but this frame may capture 'Margaret' leaving in a late-model Camry. I didn't find anything except the side view, so there's no license plate to trace." Samantha sighed, "That would have been too easy."

"As to Senior Equity, they're a limited liability partnership." Samantha saw the blank look on several faces. "They're almost impossible to sue. Each partner's financial liability is limited to what they have invested in the firm. The firm has virtually no assets."

Samantha continued. "To get at these guys through legal channels, you have to catch them in a criminal act. And, apart from 'Margaret', everything they do is strictly legal; though everything they do is also as unethical as the day is long."

Samantha picked up a clipped-together sheaf of papers. "They've been in business for a little over three years. They've initiated about 550 reverse mortgages – half of them in the last year." She paused. "Two-thirds of those mortgages have gone into foreclosure, some in as little as three months. Most homeowners buy their way out, paying whatever ransom Senior Equity demands to settle. But to date, 91 properties have been seized. When they do, Senior Equity takes over and flips the house, always for just a bit more or less than the foreclosure amount. Then, a month later, the house is re-sold – always for a much higher figure. The average profit on that second sale is around $250,000."

"There's one other thing you need to know," Samantha said, lowering her voice and speaking to each of the women in turn. "Out of those seized properties, almost half of the homeowners died within months of receiving those notices. I didn't check on causes of death; I just noticed 43 were marked, 'deceased' and settled out of Probate Court."

The five women were stunned. Finally, Jean asked, "Why can't the law stop them?"

Samantha paused before answering. "They've thought this whole thing out quite carefully. They don't pretend to be offering an HECM-compliant mortgage. They even say so in boldface type. They just don't explain the difference. They're depending on their customers – and I apologize to Rebecca for saying this – being too polite to ask hard questions."

"What sets them apart from run-of-the-mill scammers is they're using the law as protection. Most outfits like this just ignore the law and hope they don't get caught. Senior Equity more or less dares the law to find a loophole in what they're doing. But they're also cautious: they keep moving around. They never stay in one office for more than a year. Also, the man Rebecca knew as 'Carl' goes by at least three other names."

Samantha closed her dossier. "I earned a fair amount of respect from the state Attorney General's office for turning over the documents on Pokrovsky Motors. As a result, my contact there was a lot more candid than she needed to be. She told me Senior

Equity has been on their radar. They've had complaints. But every time they investigate, the firm has all of its paperwork in order."

"I'm a little confused," Jean said. "When you take out one of these reverse mortgages, you get money you're not obligated to pay back in your lifetime. Where does the money come from?"

Samantha pondered the question. "Mortgage companies aren't required to disclose their funding source but most reverse mortgages are usually funded by 'patient' money from investors with a time horizon measured in a decade or longer. Pension funds, for example. They're willing to pay out millions knowing for the first ten years, they'll be getting what you call a 'paper' return but no cash. After those ten years or so, enough customers are either dying or have repaid their mortgages that there is a steady flow of income to balance the money paid to new reverse mortgagees. What Senior Equity is doing is pushing people into foreclosure to speed up the cash coming in."

"So, there's nothing we can do," Paula said.

"I didn't say that," Samantha replied. I'm just saying it won't be easy. The AG's office says if we can find 'Margaret' or some other 'smoking gun', they'll jump in. They also said – strictly off the record and with a promise they would deny ever having said it – if a trove of records like the ones I brought them on Pokrovsky ever surfaced, they'd be thrilled."

"You have a plan," Eleanor said. "I can tell."

Samantha allowed herself a smile. "Yes. I have a plan. Let me tell you what I think we can do."

Chapter Five
Friday afternoon

Paula noted the real estate agent – a forty-something woman named Leslie Mullen and whose name tag said she was a member of her firm's 'Million Dollar Movers Club' – could barely contain her glee. An immediate lease for a small space, with more than a hint something much larger was in the offing after the first of the year. Yet an hour after seeing the space, negotiations were still underway. Something was holding back an acceptable conclusion. Ms. Mullen, for whatever reason, wasn't completely convinced.

Of course, it was highly unusual two women would walk into a commercial real estate office on a Friday afternoon, ask for a broker by name, request a quick tour of a 160,000-square-foot office building called One Broadmoor Hill, and say on the spot they were interested in leasing space in it.

Perhaps the issue was credibility. All right, Paula was prepared to offer credibility in spades.

They were back in the broker's office; three women seated at a small conference table. Paula opened a large briefcase and removed two items from it. The realtor's eyes bulged with disbelief.

"This is why we can't run this out of my home any longer," Paula had explained. "There are three of us now and we need a place to meet customers. Starbucks was fine for the first few months, but it's time we recognize this is a serious business opportunity…"

Mullen was hardly listening. Instead, she was fingering a napkin and placemat, feeling the smooth polished cotton, marveling at the perfect stitching, and wondering at the intricate swirls of colors and repeating designs.

"These are French?" she asked.

"From Provence," Paula replied. "These particular ones were block-printed in Avignon and stitched in Carpentras. I'm their primary sales agent in the Northeast. But I won't be for long if I can't get orders processed, and I don't have the time to look at twenty places and then go leasing furniture…"

"Where can I buy these?" Mullen asked. Paula noticed for the first time the agent wore expensive-appearing rings on three fingers of each hand.

Exasperated, Paula said, "I will *give* you a complete service for eight right now if you can put us in that office building for three months starting Monday morning. That will give me time to figure out staffing and space requirements for next year."

"We're trying to lease the entire building," Mullen said, trying to seize the upper negotiating hand. "You're looking for an office suite in a building in a desirable location. We need to be talking at least twenty dollars a foot…"

"And no one seems to want that entire building right now," Paula countered. "And if you started negotiations for a lease tomorrow, nothing would be signed for three or four months. Meanwhile, the owner is getting nothing toward the building's maintenance and utilities…"

"I don't know…" Mullen said, both wavering and stroking the placemat.

"We also need to know about building security," Paula pressed. "With just two tenants, how do we get into the building on weekends? How do we open up in the morning and lock up at night?

Mullen had a prompt response. "The central security system powers off at seven each morning, unlocks the main entrance, and activates the elevators. The cleaning crew re-arms it when they leave at night. If you need after-hours entry, you'll have a front entry key and a proximity card to activate the elevator." Mullen added, "But I can't go less than fourteen a square foot." She also did not stop feeling the napkin's texture.

"Paula turned to Jean, who had sat in muted admiration throughout the conversation. "Jean, you liked the building on Speen Street better, and it's ten bucks triple net. Let's go with your first choice."

"I think we can match that," Mullen said hurriedly.

An hour later, Paula packed her Provençal samples, minus eight napkins and placemats swirled in yellows, rusts, and golds.

Step one, Paula thought.

It had been an extraordinary 24 hours. They needed a business that sounded plausible and would *look* plausible. Two hours of brainstorming had yielded a dozen ideas, none of them good enough to pass what Samantha called 'a sniff test'.

That five-way conversation had been held at Paula's home on the deck overlooking her garden. What kind of business could cause a small group of women to have need of a suite of furnished offices for a few months? They were despairing of ideas when Samantha picked up one of Paula's Provençal napkins on the table in front of her and idly noted, "Mass Casualty has an entire container load of these waiting to be destroyed. Chinese knockoffs, seized by Customs at the Port of Boston."

Eleanor snapped to attention. "Chinese knockoffs of French linens?"

"Yes," Samantha said, still resting her chin in her hand, turning over the napkin with her other hand. "Ten or fifteen thousand pieces. Everybody in the office was talking about them. Beautifully done, right down the '*Fabrique en Provence*' tags, but produced in Shaoxing. They're beautiful. No one wants to make the decision to destroy them."

Samantha suddenly noticed four pair of eyes were on her. "Someone has an idea…"

"We import beautiful French linens directly from the manufacturers," Eleanor said. "Or we appear to do so. We've been in business less than a year and our business is exploding…"

"We need a place to see customers and do order fulfillment," Paula added excitedly. "It's the perfect kind of business everyone would expect to see. It explains itself." Paula held up her own napkin. "I bought these at a pop-up sale at the Hardington Community Center. I spoke to the woman who organized it and she said her problem was getting stock…"

"We'll need business cards and some sort of incorporation papers…" Eleanor said.

"A room where we pack up boxes to take to UPS every afternoon," Jean offered. "And every evening, we unpack them and start over…"

"We'd need to borrow some of that inventory," Paula said to Samantha. "How hard would that be?"

Samantha, used to being the person who came up with the perfect idea, could only respond, "I think I could make that happen…"

By nightfall, through the miracle of online incorporation, 'Provençal Home Décor of New England' had been born. That evening, Paula's laser printer created suitable temporary business cards for everyone. Over the weekend, a Hewlett-Packard vendor who owed many favors to Lucy McClellan created a website that purveyed Provençal Home Décor of New England's wonderful line of handcrafted products. And, Monday morning, a delivery truck from Mass Casualty dropped off three large cartons of counterfeit napkins, placemats and table runners to One Broadmoor Hill.

Chapter Six
Monday

Chad Pannett was born to be a con man. Possessed of the evil twin assets of good, youthful looks and no fixed moral compass, he had skated through his teen years pocketing twenty-dollar bills proffered from elderly ladies for a variety of goods and services he neither delivered nor performed. In his college years, he sold pot heavily leavened with whatever vegetative matter was at hand to students eager for a high. In his early twenties, he apprenticed in pump-and-dump boiler rooms and high-return Caribbean promissory notes.

At 27, Chad launched his own scam, a day-trader 'starter kit' that promised staggering returns in exchange for a modest ($2,500) up-front investment. To finance his scheme, Chad tapped the same network of investors who funded the promissory note swindle. After 30 months of increasing scrutiny by the Securities and Exchange Commission, Chad closed down the business. To his surprise, he found his recent success generated funding offers from other sources that had become aware of his 'Midas touch', and a few of which offered to finance a larger con.

Restless after folding his day-trading firm, he used his fresh-faced charm to launch an affinity fraud aimed at Mormons. While moderately successful, he had trouble being noticed above the din of competing phony offers because he found the field so crowded with scam artists targeting the same audience.

Eager for a monumental score he could call his own, for the first time in his life, Chad buckled down and studied. He looked for a fraud with prospects for a high rate of return and few competitors. He found it in reverse mortgages.

The reverse mortgage industry's reputation, never stellar to begin with, had been tarnished by years of media reports of the elderly losing their homes to fraudsters. Government agencies swept in and promised a clean-up of the business. New rules were promulgated. Existing players were rooted out or fined heavily for making false claims.

A new kind of heavily regulated, government-approved reverse mortgage was created. It offered all manner of protection to seniors. It severely limited the profits lenders could make. It was so tightly controlled and offered such meager returns that banks and credit unions weren't interested in underwriting them. In fact, only a handful of do-good organizations did so, and those that did limited the number they issued because they found the product to be a drain on their finite resources. As for banks, when a senior came in inquiring about a reverse mortgage, they were quickly steered by most lending representatives to a sensible and highly profitable line of credit based on the senior's equity in their home.

The first remarkable thing Chad discovered was 'non-compliant' reverse mortgages were still legal. It was assumed by government agencies 'bad' reverse mortgages would wither away for lack of demand. The second remarkable thing – and this was an inspiration that was truly an epiphany – was no person with an ounce of sense would choose a reverse mortgage as their preferred means of generating cash to live on. If you owned a nice big house but you were starting to run out of money, the logical thing to do was to *sell* the house and move; buy a condo or rent an apartment and pocket the untaxed capital gain. If for whatever reason you felt some absurd need to hang onto your too-large house, get a home equity loan.

In short, if someone wanted a reverse mortgage, there was an above-average chance the person wasn't especially smart.

As Chad began to hone his idea, he wrote down what would become his mantra: *Your job as the originator of a reverse mortgage is to paint the golden picture: it all boils down to Free Money. We will give you hundreds of thousands of dollars with no up-front cost to you. You get to live in your house for as long as you live. And you never have to repay a penny of the money we give you.*

Of course there were a few catches. That money we gave you? We didn't really give it to you. You *borrowed* it at a hefty compounded interest rate. And there are tens of thousands of dollars of up-front fees, many of them phony and all of them jacked up to absurd levels. You just don't see them because we rolled them into the loan. And if your kids want to pay off the mortgage, their heads are going to hurt with all fees and accumulated interest we piled on. And if you slip up and forget to pay your taxes, we can foreclose even though you were still living there.

Is America a great country or what?

So Chad hatched his idea and put together a business plan. He started calling his network of funding sources, including the ones who said they would be interested in something 'big'. Whoever backed him would be a silent partner, reaping rewards for years to come.

'Big' is what Chad knew he needed. If you loan ten old codgers $200,000 each, you need two million bucks up front. Sure, the two million should at least double, but you have to wait for the old folks to buy the farm. If you loan a *hundred* senior citizens the same $200,000, you need $20 million to seed the pot. Twenty million will eventually turn into forty million, but you need to have patience.

Most of Chad's contacts balked at the idea of putting up a million dollars – or any amount of money – that might be tied up for a decade or longer, regardless of the rate of return.

But one prospective funder wanted to hear more.

Chad first met Vinnie Malone in a suite at the Four Seasons in Boston. Vinnie, who looked to be about forty, moved like the kind of person who routinely inhabited the concierge floor of Four Seasons properties. He was suntanned and handsome with just a bit of a paunch (surely a sign of good living), wore a custom suit, and sipped small-batch Bourbon as they spoke. He listened intently as Chad pitched his idea.

Vinnie understood instantly and slapped Chad on the back for coming up with such a brilliant concept. *Of course* the group for which he managed money was interested and could supply *all* the cash needed to make the business a roaring success.

With one or two modest tweaks.

The first such tweak concerned silent partners. Vinnie didn't want to be one. He would be one of the two public faces of Senior Equity. He would host the seminars to bring in the old codgers. He would glad-hand them and soften them up for the next stage of the scheme.

"I'm also a little bothered by the timing. What if some old lady lives to a hundred?" Vinnie said. "We wait twenty years to see any return on investment and, after inflation, we get out less than we put in. My funding source is going to be awfully unhappy."

Chad started to explain about spreading risk by establishing actuarial pools. Vinnie clapped him on the shoulder and shook his head. "There is no need to lose money on *any* mortgage," he said. "We're going to specialize in selling these reverse mortgages to people who, in addition to being unsophisticated and unlikely to run a contract by their own lawyer, are in poor health."

Vinnie added, "Oh, and while it isn't your problem, you should probably want to know all my funding starts as cash, and whenever we can pay bills in cash, we'll want to do so."

That was when Chad realized his new venture was going to be funded with drug money.

Drugs generate an obscene amount of cash. The cash has to be laundered – legally deposited into a seemingly legitimate business for reasonable purposes. Mortgages were made to order for such a purpose. Moreover, while most money-laundering operations meant losing some fraction of the amount as overhead, reverse mortgages would be a profitable business. Just wait a few years and the profits would start rolling in.

If Chad realized he was in well over his head, he did not mention anything to Vinnie.

When he left the Four Seasons suite, Chad took with him a mandate to generate lots of reverse mortgages. His initial pool of capital was $50 million. At an average loan of $250,000, all he needed to do was find two hundred trusting senior citizens who needed money and had a short life expectancy.

* * * * *

On Monday morning, Chad immediately noted the three cars in the parking lot, not the least because one was parked in the spot he thought of as being reserved for himself. Two of the cars were nondescript sedans and he gave them no further thought. The third, the one parked in his space, was a red Tesla Model S. This annoyed him because he coveted this particular model and color but had been told by Vinnie it 'attracted too much attention'. That was the same 'inconspicuous' Vinnie who had recently bought a $185,000 metallic silver Audi convertible and sported a diamond pinkie ring a Kardashian would be proud to wear.

Chad was even more annoyed when he encountered a rather well-designed sign adjacent to the elevator reading, 'Provençal Home Décor of New England – Third Floor'. Not only did it mean Chad could no longer imply Senior Equity occupied this entire building; it became obvious he was not even the sole tenant of the third floor.

At the third-floor landing, another sign pointing to the offices of the interlopers, coupled with voices in the distance, made it also clear the idiot real estate firm had placed this decorating firm in the offices adjacent to his own. He made a mental note to employ just the right level of outrage when he called the broker.

He paused as he walked by the open door. Two women were lining up desks in a conference room. Both were in jeans and sweatshirts. One was pixyish and in her mid-sixties with silver hair, though she had enough upper arm strength to successfully wrestle tables into place. The other was around fifty, with chestnut hair, and reasonably good looking for someone her age. Her baggy clothing hung loosely around her slender body.

The older woman was the first to notice him.

"Paula, we have our first visitor," the woman said.

The slender woman, apparently Paula, shifted a table three feet to her right before pausing to turn around.

"We're not really set up for visitors," the slender woman said. Then, she stopped and cocked her head. She spoke, as though to herself. "Wait a second. This address isn't even on the website yet." She turned to the diminutive woman. "Jean, take a break. I'll join you in a minute or two."

Chad made the assumption 'Paula' was in charge. Her voice sounded authoritative, even addressing someone more than a decade her senior.

Paula approached him and held out her hand. "Hi, I'm Paula Winters. And you are…? She let the question trail off.

Chad offered his own hand and smiled. "Chad Pannett. I wasn't aware anyone else was moving in the building. My understanding was the building manager would give us say over the location of any new tenant." The statement was a bald lie, but he wanted to see the effect.

Winters shrugged. "I imagine it keeps down maintenance expense to cluster us together. This is just temporary for us. If this flies, we'll need something with warehouse space before the end of the year."

Chad gestured with his head in the direction of the elevator. "I saw your sign. You're a decorator?"

Winters laughed. "Home décor, decorator. I can see how someone could mix up the two. No, we import French linens. Beautiful, high quality, block printed and hand sewn in Provence.

It's a high-end market and most of my companies don't have much of a North American presence."

Chad listened carefully. "You said, 'if this flies'. I don't understand."

Winters shrugged. "This business is three months old. I've been running it out of my home until this morning. We shot out of the gate with lots of orders and I'm not certain I know how to manage them all. So far I have two employees. I don't know if I need two more or ten more." She laughed. "If you come in here one morning and find there's nothing but a hole in the ground, you'll know it didn't work out. But for now, it's fun and a challenge."

Chad noticed the absence of a wedding ring. "So this isn't 'a hobby to keep the wife happy' sort of thing."

Winters shook her head and laughed again. "Divorced four years now, and the kids are grown and gainfully employed. Well, one of them is gainfully employed. The other is still 'finding himself'." She added finger quotes to the last statement. "No, this is serious, and I have a fair amount of money sunk into inventory and payroll. But I have a feeling this could be a real business. Either way, we'll be out of your hair before the end of the year, and probably before Thanksgiving."

Then she added, "How about you? The real estate agent said you're a private equity service or senior something. I didn't see a sign on the entrance."

It was Chad's turn to smile. "We didn't need one until now. We were the only tenant, which was fine with us. The business is 'Senior Equity Lending Services'. We do reverse mortgages."

Winters nodded. "Tom Selleck. I've seen the ads. They're quite…" She seemed at a loss for words as she fluttered her hands.

Chad shook his head. "Right idea, wrong company. We're more locally focused. Say, within a hundred miles. That's plenty enough market for us." He added a slight smile.

"You got to ask me all the personal questions," Winters said. "What about you? Married? Two kids with another on the way?"

Chad felt vaguely uncomfortable for the first time. He seldom talked about himself, and then only to lie. But this woman seemed to be trying to establish a connection. He held up and waggled his left hand. "Never been successfully tied down," he said. "Close once or twice, but I enjoy playing the field." He added, "And as for kids, not really interested."

"You sound like my son," Winters said. "But, based on your suit, I have a suspicion you're not living in your parent's basement."

Chad self-consciously looked down at his suit jacket. "People expect me to dress a certain way."

Winters laughed and pulled at the midriff of her sweatshirt. "And all I have to do is sound like I'm wearing couture clothing when the phone rings." The she sighed. "Except now we're going to have a real showroom." She paused. "Well, I have the clothes. If they still fit."

"You don't look like you've gained weight," Chad said.

"Other way around," Winters said with a forced smile. "Cancer survivor."

Chad was at a loss for words. He had really put his foot in it. "Well, I'll try to stay out of your way." He smiled. "Welcome to the building."

Winters returned the smile. "We're the ones who will try to stay out of *your* way." She reached into her jeans pocket and pulled out a business card, then looked at it and sighed. She held out the card to him. "These are officially obsolete as of this morning, so take all you want. One more thing for the to-do-list."

Chad took the card, then quickly shook her hand and turned around to leave. He stopped at the door, turned, and asked, "By the way. How did you end up in this particular building?"

Winters smiled and chuckled. "Where else could you get a month-to-month, thirty-day-out agreement for eleven bucks a square foot, fully furnished?" She gestured to the walls around her. "This is exactly what we wanted – and needed. Instant office, instant furniture. Instant credibility for buyers."

Chad nodded and smiled. "See you around."

* * * * *

Five minutes later, Chad was playing back the recording he had made on his phone, writing down all salient information. He opened his computer and typed in the company's web address from the business card. He found pages of colorful placemats and a photo of Winters listed as 'Founder and President'. *Check*, he thought.

The business card showed an address in Hardington. He Googled it. It was a real address and Winters was shown as living there. He refined the search to ownership records. She owned the property. He did a Google Maps search. The house was imposing. Yes, three people could easily have worked there. *Check*, he thought.

He did one other search. 'Paula Winters' and 'divorce records'. He found a four-year-old entry. *Check*, he thought and, only then did he begin to relax.

For much of his adult life Chad had taken nothing at face value. He took it as an article of faith there were no coincidences, no serendipity, and no 'fortunate chance encounters'. He assumed everyone who called was with a regulatory or law enforcement agency and their intention was to bring down whatever con game he happened to be running.

His skepticism had been validated on multiple occasions. Since founding Senior Equity, several couples in their seventies had shown up at seminars, eager to take out a reverse mortgage. On the surface, all were ideal candidates waiting to be fleeced. And, also on the surface, their stories were plausible.

But some digging revealed the truth. They were well-coached actors or retired agents. They weren't married and the homes they claimed to own were not their own. There were always two of them because one could back up the other's sworn testimony. Bit by bit, Chad chipped away at the façade to uncover the true story. And, once he did, Chad put on his best smile and told the visitors they were making a decision based on too little information and without having explored all the options. He told them a home equity line of credit was a more suitable way to supplement their retirement savings. He offered them the names of banks and credit unions offering special terms to seniors. He shook their hands, smiled, and wished them luck.

He left them with nothing to take back to their government handlers. Not only did they go away empty-handed; they created a record of a scrupulously honest business. But turning away customers didn't help him meet his weekly quota. It only wasted his time. And Vinnie Malone made it quietly clear even five million a week was unacceptable performance. His 'people' were looking for ten million and, to achieve it, Chad needed to close at least 40 mortgages every week.

He put the old ladies out of his mind for the moment and turned his attention to two thick documents. The first was a printout showing the pipeline of pending and prospective applicants. There were ample sheep out there waiting to be fleeced; more than a hundred were listed in twenty dense pages. Almost all of those candidates came from seminars – 'Your Home Is Your Pension Plan' – held around the region.

At those seminars, attendees were sized up for their suitability as Senior Equity candidates. Pannett's goal was to sign up only the ones meeting the criteria of having a home worth at least $500,000 and be over 70 years old with one spouse facing severe medical needs. Those over 75 got a special push, and a widow living alone was ideal.

Ninety-three such opportunities were starred in red. Their homes had been visited and found to be in desirable locations and in good repair. Chad read the notes on each prospect. He crossed out several where both husband and wife reported their health was excellent. He needed at least one to be in failing health. The applicants needed a reason to tap – and spend – a large percentage of their home equity as soon as their mortgage was approved. They needed to be in a position where they could not easily repay what they had borrowed. Getting back inflated fees and a year's interest was not what this enterprise was about.

The second printout – showing the status of 218 existing mortgages – received the bulk of his attention. Here was the gold ready to be mined. Fourteen customers were delinquent on their property taxes by between one and five months. Chad had found out the hard way courts were generally understanding of seniors being late by up to six months when foreclosure notices were filed.

At seven months, though, attitudes began to change in favor of the lender. A Notice of Default could be filed. If unchallenged (and keeping an eye on customer mailboxes played an outsized role in ensuring mortgagees had no idea of the filing until it was too late), a lender could move for immediate repayment. If the judge was especially lender-friendly, the house could be seized in lieu of repayment, with any 'surplus' being remitted to the former homeowner. It was amazing how often the sale of the house managed to just barely cover the demand amount.

Another sixteen customers had now been away from their property for nine months or more. The magic number was a year and a day. Some were in nursing or rehabilitation facilities; others were at second homes in Florida. The goal was to keep them away exactly the number of days to quality for 'no longer in residence' status. The beauty of these clients was they weren't around to receive the bad news.

'Material property impairment' watches were on 20 mortgagees. It was a relatively simple idea. Note the name of their landscape service. As soon as the landscaper left, call them and say their services were no longer needed. Watch the grass grow and take lots of photos. It wasn't Senior Equity's fault its customers couldn't keep track of who was maintaining the property, or the lack of care was causing the price of the home to erode.

The most satisfying list in the document was of 'unauthorized changes to title'. There were just twelve of them in this report, but they were the lowest-hanging fruit. A customer who tried to add a son or daughter to the ownership record of the property didn't have a legal leg to stand on. They were toast; it was automatic default. How dare a greedy senior try to sneak something past the lender to keep the property in the family for another 30 or 40 years?

As soon as a title search showed the change, Chad instructed his lawyers to file for a declaratory judgment. Can't come up with the money you owe? Fine. We'll take your house.

The two reports were the product of the first of Chad's 'secret weapons'. Jordan Wells had been well on his way to a career in computers. He majored in Business and Information Technology at UMASS – Lowell and was within ten credits of graduating when an unfortunate encounter with the Massachusetts State Police left him unable to explain why he was in possession of 50 tablets of MDMA, better known as Exstasy, and also had more than a thousand dollars in cash in his pocket.

Jordan's defense – that someone other than he was the person in the surveillance video at an Alpha Sigma Tau fraternity party shown selling the drug to several attendees – proved unpersuasive in court. While he received a suspended sentence as a first offender, the University of Massachusetts understandably asked him to continue his studies elsewhere.

Two years later, Jordan's sentence was overturned when it was learned the laboratory technician who testified the seized substance was 3,4-Methylenedioxymethamphetamine routinely took radical shortcuts in testing police-produced drug samples. Jordan's record was expunged, but his IT career aspirations were a distant memory.

He had moved on to identity fraud, a much more lucrative vocation.

When Chad put out the word he needed someone with computer and research skills (and, unspoken, a flexible definition of 'right' and 'wrong') for a continuing but part-time role in Senior Equity, Jordan's name was one of first to surface.

The young man continually queried databases for changes in deeds, missed property tax payments, changes of address, and any other evidence mortgage terms had been violated. All of these were entered into an impressive database. As new mortgage candidates surfaced, Jordan quickly verified the value of properties and bona fides of prospects, including verifying adult children were in appropriately remote locations. He spoke weekly with the six 'wranglers' who brought in prospects; updating every file of every prospect. Once mortgages were issued, those same wranglers were pressed to send photos of houses to document any deterioration in maintenance.

Jordan Wells was a gem, Chad recognized. He visited the office only once a week – on Saturday morning – to deliver his report and collect his all-cash $2,000 fee. Chad went through the twelve properties. All gems. All great towns. Little Compton, Needham, Hardington, Winchester…

Chad also thought about the red Tesla in front of the building. Vinnie had no business telling him what to drive. Hell, Vinnie had just bought an $180,000 sports car.

Chapter Seven

Summer Copeland was a fidgeter. Though she stood just five-foot-three, her knees perpetually bumped against the underside of her desk as she worked. She twirled pencils and pens while she spoke. Her mother told her it was nervous energy. Summer knew it was restlessness born of being five steps ahead of every conversation, game, or project of which she was a part.

She was a brilliant web designer, mentally writing code even as a project was described to her by a client. Her bosses found it unnerving at first. Then, they saw the finished product and they learned to forewarn those clients 'Summer's brain works differently – and faster'.

Summer was just 25, but she already had an office with a window; something normally reserved for managers and account executives. Like many web designers, hours and days blurred for her. Saturdays, Sundays, and holidays were inconvenient labels to be ignored when there was interesting code to write.

Yesterday in mid-afternoon, the president of Austinplex walked into her office and closed the door, ensuring this Sunday would be memorable. Usually, Summer saw the head of the firm only in meetings or in awkward encounters in the break room.

"If I say 'Lucy McClellan', do you know who I'm talking about?"

"Sure," Summer said. She's what you called our 'bread and butter'. She's a senior vice president for…"

"Exactly. I just got off the phone with her. She needs a personal favor. It isn't an HP project; this is house billing. But I want you to treat it as though it is the most critical project you've ever handled. Lucy is counting on us, and I'm counting on you."

Summer stopped twirling the pen in her hand. Her knees also

came to rest.

"By tomorrow morning, she needs a full-featured website. In all likelihood, only one person will ever visit the site but, when they do – and it will almost certainly be on Monday morning – the site has to look to the person like it belongs to a well-established business…"

For fifteen minutes, Summer made notes. By the time Austinplex's president left her office, Summer had a vision in her head. The best part was she wasn't bound by the third-rate graphics and text most clients insisted be included. She could borrow or invent everything beyond the general subject matter, company president photo, and a few details McClellan wanted salted into the site.

For the next few hours, Summer delved into Provençal fabrics and culture. She grabbed images and wove a story of centuries-old artistic traditions being preserved in glorious, one-hundred-square-inch time capsules. She found the perfect fonts. Sometime after 10 p.m., Summer began writing copy. At two o'clock she cobbled together her test site and found it wanting. She re-wrote, changed formats, and added music and a video. Feeling more was needed, she added web ordering protocols and ardent customer testimonials.

At 5 a.m., Summer pronounced herself satisfied with her effort. She pointed to the new site from an established, high-traffic Austinplex-managed one. With the tap of a key, the site went live. Now, Summer thought about visibility. Would this lone person know the address or use a search engine? Austinplex had accrued hundreds of thousands of Google Ad Dollars. For a few thousand of those dollars the site would top search results in a dozen key words for a week. She added the words and debited Austinplex's account.

Summer then went out for breakfast and home to shower and change.

At 8 a.m., she was back in her office. She logged onto the admin page of her newly created site. Sure enough, just shy of an hour earlier, Provençal Home Décor of New England had its first hits. The first, oddly, was from France and the visitor was still on the site. The second, from Framingham, Massachusetts, had spent six minutes on the site. As she watched, a third visitor, this one also from Framingham, found the site.

Summer twirled around twice in her chair and allowed herself a moment of satisfaction.

Then, she opened her home screen and started on her next project.

* * * * *

Leslie Mullen arrived at her office more than an hour earlier than her usual ten o'clock. Though agents might be on the phone or at their home computer at six, 'office hours' were a kind of compulsory three-day-a-week throwback to a different time, and a relic of another century.

On a different day, Leslie might have spent the drive to her office fuming at her manager's stone-faced intransigence concerning mandatory 'face time'.

Today was quite different. She had an idea.

Nine months earlier, Leslie had won what she thought was a plum assignment to anchor her IRA nest egg. A company had gone belly up leaving behind a nearly new, fully furnished, six-story office building atop a hill. Her extensive network of contacts got her the exclusive sale or leasing rights.

All One Broadmoor Hill needed, Leslie reasoned, was to be noticed by the perfect client looking for 160,000 square feet of Class A space. It might be Google or Amazon. Or some older, cash-rich company with a hankering for a prestigious building to call their own. She had invested in print ads in all the right publications. The lone requirement was to catch the eye of the right decision maker.

Six months later, Leslie Mullen knew she had a turkey on her hands. The hot companies were expanding in Boston, all right. But they were going to Kendall Square or the Seaport District. Framingham and MetroWest was so far off the radar they didn't even register as a blip. Worse, every time she opened the business section of the *Globe*, there were even more depressing articles about suburban companies decamping for more glamorous digs in the city.

The money she had spent on marketing was measured in the tens of thousands, and it was real, out-of-pocket cash. Instead of feathering her nest, it was being lined with bills.

Needing to be cheered up, Leslie had friends over for dinner the previous evening. She chose to use the new placemats and napkins given to her by Paula Winters. She served Baking Day Chicken and a good Chablis, turning the event into a celebration of all things French.

Although Leslie was a more than competent cook, all her guests could do was talk about the placemats. Where did she get them? What did they cost? Could she get more? For two hours, she fielded variations of those same three questions.

At 3 a.m., she awakened with an idea. Two relatively young and growing businesses had moved into the building. Both had cited 'fully furnished' and 'room to expand' as key factors in their decision.

One Broadmoor Hill should be a services industry business incubator targeting women entrepreneurs. It should be filled with small companies seeking a 'good' address clients would find appealing and would burnish the images of the organizations making it their home.

Leslie's activities for the day included attending the MetroWest Women's Club. Usually, she went primarily to listen for interesting real estate prospects and to have lunch and drinks with old friends.

Today, she was going with quite a different purpose: to sell an idea.

* * * * *

Marie Deveraux had never shared her co-workers' habit of taking two-hour luncheon breaks. For the most part, it was a matter of expense - €25 for a midday meal for five days each week would consume €125 a week and €500 each month – the same as her rent. She could have a decent place to live and good clothes, or she could join everyone for not-so-special repast at one of the dozen or so 'business' restaurants clustered in the center of Salon-de-Provence.

She would much rather be in Paris. Of course, everyone in the world would much rather be in Paris, where she would get paid a decent wage and not have to resort to the internet to find stylish clothes. But a few minutes into every job interview Marie secured in Marseille or even Montpellier, the person conducting the interview would cock his or her head, smile, compliment Marie on her 'charming' accent and attempt to place 'the musical lilt' of her voice.

And while the interview might go on for another hour, Marie knew no job offer would be forthcoming. Her voice betrayed she was 'country', and there was no demand for rustic office staff when everyone was hell-bent on pretending they were just slumming in the 'secondary' cities of France while their new office in La Defense was being outfitted. When she sought employment with businesses where everyone spoke Provençal-tinged French, no one cared she had two years of business courses and was moderately fluent in English, Spanish and German. What mattered was she knew how to type and use a computer.

Instead of dining out, Marie spent the hours from twelve to two each working day visiting the world beyond the lethargic town of Salon-de-Provence and her position as Office Administrator of the equally sleepy *Conseil de Commerce des Tissus Provençaux,* or Provençal Fabrics Trade Council. She vicariously visited Osaka and Beijing, New York, Buenos Aires and San Francisco. She longed to visit Montreal, a Francophone city in the New World.

Promptly at two, Marie turned her attention to the task she performed every week: finding cheaters. The 62 members of the trade council were obliged to report each month on their sales and unit shipments of products and, for each piece sold, the Council received a modest fee. Because almost all of the members were family-run businesses, the bookkeeping was haphazard and the temptation to under-report sales was strong.

It was not merely greed causing firms to fudge their numbers. There was also the quite real perception the trade council did nothing for its cut of their livelihood except have a booth at shows in Aix and Nice and send its *Directeur Général* on boondoggle trips to Paris and London where he invariably stayed in the most lavish hotels and dined at outlandishly expensive restaurants. All of which was true.

Marie's task was to look for rogue distribution sites. The easiest way to cheat on sales was to establish a new distributor without informing Salon-de-Provence. Every Monday she typed keywords into her computer to find the websites of companies around the world selling Provençal fabrics. She then went through the site picking out products from specific suppliers. After four years, Marie could instantly match almost every napkin, placemat, tablecloth, and runner to the correct workshop. For outliers, she could consult two thick books of product samples.

Since coming to work for the Council, Marie had more than paid for her place in the organization by spotting hundreds of previously unknown and un-reported outlets. Each month turned up at least one and, a year earlier, she had spotted a distributor in Moscow handling the products from at least six workshops.

Less than a minute after entering her search terms, Marie had her first catch. In fact, it was at the top of her search results. A website called 'Provençal Home Décor of New England' offered the wares of at least twenty of the 62 members of the trade council.

This was an enormous breach of both trust and fiduciary duty on the part of members, and clearly had required workshops to covertly work together to get around the Council's reporting requirements.

Marie quickly jotted down the names of workshops whose products she recognized. Provence Soleil and La Cigale Jacquard were apparently selling their entire line through the American company. She quickly filled a page, and then a second.

The website, she noted, was beautiful. Workshops had lent their best photos of artisans engaged in their trade. Whoever built the website had also found and used vintage images from the Wesserling Park Textile Museum in Alsace as well as from the Louvre. Visually at least, this unknown American importer had done a better job of enticing people to purchase Provençal textiles than did the Council's own admittedly mediocre site.

The Managing Director was in London and, this being August, he would be gone all week. His second in command, the *Liaison des Associations*, who worked with individual workshops, was on maternity leave. There were only four people in the office for the week; herself, two secretaries and the association's bookkeeper. The other three had now been gone for nearly three hours; a strong indication they might not return at all.

For the past four years, upon showing the Managing Director the wares from an unauthorized distributor, Marie had been instructed to send screen shots of the textiles for sale on the site to the responsible workshops, together with a request the manufacturer supply a spreadsheet showing shipments to the sales outlet and resulting revenues. Marie could do so with this one, though the task would take her much of the remaining work day.

The Managing Director routinely composed a letter to the rogue distributor 'welcoming' them to the Council's family of sales outlets and explained their responsibilities to report quarterly unit product line shipments from each workshop. The purpose of the letter was to ensure the distributor knew they were on the Council's radar, and the vendor with which they were dealing had tried to circumvent established protocols. Most distributors went on selling the same products, though with the Council now collecting its proper commission. In turn, devious workshop owners went looking for the next off-the-books sales outlet.

Because the Managing Director was not a man of great imagination, the letter seldom varied in content or tone. Marie always thought she could write a much better letter, but her responsibility ended at finding the best email address and sending it off.

This afternoon, though, Marie was faced with a dilemma. She was alone in the office and her official title was *Administrateur de Bureau*. She could attempt to track down her boss, though he never answered his cell phone and was seldom at the location shown on his itinerary. His return calls could come in a few hours or might not be returned at all. The last time she had called the Associations Liaison, Marie had been the subject of a five-minute-long screaming tirade of the need of mothers and their infants for adequate sleep. It was a mistake Marie was not going to repeat.

And so Marie composed a letter to Madame Paula Winters, the President of Provençal Home Décor of New England. She had always found her boss's letters rather stuffy and formal. Moreover, because she was addressing a woman, Marie felt a lighter and more feminine touch might be just what the situation needed. Finally, because Marie had frequently been complimented on her conversational English, she composed her letter in that language rather than using Google's document translation service. She thought Google was superb at individual words and phrases, but frequently failed to capture the context of sentences and paragraphs.

An hour later, the email was dispatched and Marie went on to the arduous task of capturing screen shots of the individual products. By the trade council's closing time of 6 p.m., twenty-two workshops had been sent hard evidence they had once again tried to circumvent their responsibility.

When the last photo-laden email was sent off, Marie Deveraux smiled and congratulated herself on having done her job superbly well and with great initiative. She would have shared her accomplishment with her co-workers, except none of them had returned from lunch.

* * * * *

Leslie Mullen felt elated. The MetroWest Women's Club had listened politely to the beginning of her presentation. Then they saw the placemats and napkins, and it was like a feeding frenzy. Armed with her dinner experiences from the previous evening, Leslie kept the discussion on topic. *How many women do you know with 'kitchen table' businesses who could turn their avocation into something a lot more serious with a 'real' office suite amid other, similarly driven entrepreneurs?*

Leslie answered the question using photos of the building and of suites in it, all ready for immediate occupancy. The space was priced below market because the building's owner was in bankruptcy. Best of all, no long-term commitment was needed. If the business took off, then stay and expand. If the business didn't catch fire, only the current month's rent was owed. Paula Winters was the perfect prototype: suburban empty-nester (Leslie even played on the divorce angle) with a great idea, trying to run a business out of her home. In one simple action, Paula Winters was going to turn a hobby started with a few friends into a powerhouse business. Leslie told them Paula had already asked her to start looking for a warehouse.

The *pièce de résistance* was showing the group Paula's website. Paula hadn't even mentioned it on her visit to the real estate office. It was only after arriving at her office Leslie thought of looking for a Provençal Home Décor website. And there it was in all its polychrome glory: page after page of beautiful linens. It was one of the most beautiful websites Leslie had ever seen. At the meeting, Leslie projected them onto a wall. Each new page got a fresh set of *oooh's*.

By this evening, forty women would be calling their friends and their friends' friends.

One Broadmoor Hill was about to get a lot of lights in those dark offices.

Even better, as the luncheon ended, a young woman Leslie barely remembered ever seeing before came up and introduced herself as both a relatively new club member and as a stringer for WGBH, the local National Public Radio affiliate. She thought she could sell her news director on the idea of an incubator for women-owned businesses. Could Leslie put the writer in touch with this Paula Winters? Of course, Leslie would be credited with coming up with the concept.

Leslie, of course, said she'd be delighted. For the rest of the day, she thought of promotional campaigns and other media she might interest in the story. If NPR was on board, why not the television network affiliates?

Suddenly, the possibilities seemed endless.

* * * * *

At 3 p.m. in Austin, Summer Copeland was getting ready to call an end to what had turned out to be the longest 'day' of her working career. It had started the previous morning at 9 a.m. Including an hour's nap in her office, it had run thirty hours. Not since college had she pulled an all-nighter like this one.

Tired but curious about whether any other visitor had gone to the site since this morning, she opened the admin page for the Provençal Home Décor of New England website.

"Holy crap," she said loud enough so she immediately looked around to see if anyone outside her office had heard her.

At 7:08 a.m. CDT, a visitor from France logged on, viewed

every page multiple times, and stayed on the site for nearly four hours.

There was the one visitor from Framingham, Massachusetts at 7:52 a.m. CDT. Whoever logged on stayed with the site for six minutes and viewed four pages.

Eight minutes later another visitor from Framingham found the site and stayed twelve minutes, looking at all ten pages.

Then there was a lull until 11:45 a.m., when someone from Natick, Massachusetts visited the site and stayed on it ten minutes. All ten pages were viewed.

After which all hell broke loose.

Since noon, the site had been visited 121 times with more than 40 of those viewing the site logging onto it from France and the balance from Massachusetts, with a few from New York and New Hampshire. Most stayed at least ten minutes. A few stayed more than an hour. Fifty visitors were looking at the site right now.

Well, she thought to herself, *Lucy McClellan wanted a real-looking website. This one looks so real people are visiting it from two continents.*

Chapter Eight
Tuesday

Paula Winters re-read the email for the third time.

Dear Madame Winters,

Hello from beautiful France and sunny Salon-de-Provence. I am writing to you on this letter to tell you we have just today discover your excellent website Provençal Home Décor of New England. It is of superb quality for words and illustrations.

I am Paul Tanguay, General Director of CCTP which in English is the Council of Commerce of Provençal Fabrics. We are the official association of more than 60 manufacturing company here in sunny and picturesque Provence.

I notice your beautiful website contain pages with 22 of our associates. Their products can be detected by their distinct façade and manifestation. I am attaching a file of names.

When you become the distributor for Provençal fabrics, manufacturing companies must tell you of correct necessities for telling numbers and types of fabric units you sell on your website or retail. These files are supply every month. My apology if you are only learn now of this requirement.

We wish you to vend many fabric pieces to your American customers for many years. We hope you profit well from this association with CCTP. If you have question do not delay to call or email our office. My Officer Administrator Marie Deveraux will help in my time off.

Yours most truly,

Paul Tanguay

The letter made sense only in the most holistic sense, Paula thought. In a place called Salon-de-Provence there was an organization called CCTP representing the real products her make-believe company showed on its make-believe website. And, in pretending those real products were for sale on the make-believe website, Paula had run afoul of a real trade group's reporting requirements.

How could she tell this Paul Tanguay it was all a hoax; that the website had to look real enough to convince one person the company next door wasn't there to spy on him?

Paula wasn't even certain how the website had come into being. She knew only Samantha had called Lucy McClellan and asked a favor. Eighteen hours later, a fully functioning website was apparently up and running – though Paula had not yet seen it – and it looked real enough to fool people in France.

Dear God, what have I gotten myself into? she thought.

* * * * *

In the village of Aubignan, part of the Vaucluse department of Provence, Alain Duperon stared in consternation at the email from the CCTP. Duperon was distrustful of computers. Part of it was being 82 years old and distinctly remembering a better, happier time when there was no internet or iPhones or instant messaging. He put on his detested reading glasses. *Ce vieux bâtard, Paul Tanguay, thinks he has caught le renard sauvage in the act of cheating,* Duperon thought. Yes, of course he cheated. With the Council raking ten cents off the sale of every damned table cloth he sold and five cents off napkins and place mats, Duperon had to cheat just to stay in business. He reported less than half the sales from his workshop in a good year and, even then, he barely broke even. Well, broke even if you took into account supporting an extended family of children and grandchildren who considered work to be beneath their dignity and who married and divorced with a frequency rivaling movie stars.

Tanguay, though, had really outdone himself this time. Tanguay was under the delusion *Tissus du Aubignan* was selling through some outfit in America. *Nice try,* Duperon thought. *I do my illegal sales in Japan, where your damned search engine doesn't do you a bit of good because they don't translate the catalog.*

Duperon considered ignoring the message. The CCTP was

absolutely wrong on this one and, if Tanguay tried to make an issue of it, Duperon could prove he did not export to America and never had. Idly, he clicked to the site where his wares were reportedly for sale. And furrowed his brow. Those were indeed his napkins and placemats. Either some *fils de pute* was counterfeiting his best products or else this American outfit had a wholesale source he didn't know about. Duperon enlarged the photos of his placemats and examined them carefully. He knew every stitch. These were his, all right.

He checked the pricing. Mentally translating hated dollars to equally reviled euros, he determined the price was about what it ought to be for a retail outlet. He racked his brain for someone who would try to undercut him and could come up with no one who disliked him that much.

He went through the rest of the website and was surprised to see many of his friends were also selling though this site. Why hadn't they told him about it? Everyone knew what he thought of Americans, but business was business. The presentation was excellent. The background stories were wonderfully illustrated. This business was run by someone who understood they were dealing with craftsmen and artists.

Duperon went to the 'About Us' page and had Google translate it. Paula Winters did not look like she had an ounce of French blood coursing through her veins. But she knew quality goods. He cracked his knuckles and pulled the keyboard to him. He wrote:
Chère madame Winters,

Je viens de jeter un coup d'œil à votre site Web et j'ai constaté que quelqu'un vous vendait en gros les produits de votre entreprise (Tissus du Aubignan). Pourquoi ne pas nous traiter directement? Je suis prêt à vous vendre ma ligne complète à mon meilleur prix de gros si vous ne m'occuperez que de moi et dites-moi le nom du grossiste qui vous a approché. Permettez-moi de vous entendre dès que possible.

He added his name and briefly considered putting it though a translation website. He scowled and thought, *let this American woman figure it out for herself.*

* * * * *

By 4 p.m., Paula had stopped translating the emails. She already knew what they were going to say. There were twelve of them so far and she had no doubt more would arrive in the hours ahead.

She had put the first message through three different translation sites just to be certain there was no room for error. It had read, *"Dear Madam Winters, I've just taken a good look at your website and found someone is wholesaling you my company's (Tissus du Aubignan) products. Why don't we deal with one another directly? I am prepared to sell you my full line at my best wholesale price if you will deal with only me and tell me the name of the wholesaler who approached you. Let me hear from you as soon as possible. Alain Duperon.*

The next one offered to absorb shipping and the third one invited her to tour the factory and have a 'real Provençal meal' on her next buying trip.

This is spiraling out of control, Paula thought.

She had spent the afternoon with Jean and Alice. Working in the glass conference room so everything they did was visible to passersby, the three women placed the counterfeit napkins, tablecloths and placemats into boxes of varying size. The boxes were taped and mailing labels affixed to them. There were two goals: first to ensure any Senior Equity employee passing by saw a 'real' business had moved into the adjacent suite.

The second goal was to see who went in and out of Senior Equity's offices and, especially, to look for 'Margaret' – the woman who had convinced Rebecca Cooper to add a name to her home's deed. If any woman matching Rebecca's description were to come though the building, either Jean or Alice would drop whatever they were doing. They would ride down the elevator with her and one of them would use her phone to photograph both the woman and her car.

Thus far, two men who were apparently Senior Equity employees or freelancers had appeared in the hallway several times. They were always in the company of an elderly man or woman, escorting them in or out. The men were solicitous of their charges; smiling and holding the women's arms.

While the prospective customers were in with Pannett – who apparently always met alone with them – the men lounged in the hallways. They glanced with varying levels of curiosity into the newly occupied showroom but made no move to enter. After about forty-five minutes they made their way back to Senior Equity's offices.

The way they came out was the 'tell'. If their client had taken the bait, the men were all smiles. They were overtly courteous and walked at the same slow pace as the people whose money they were about to steal. Conversely, if the meeting had not gone well (there was apparently some kind of non-verbal signal exchanged), there was a decided aloofness to their demeanor. No touching and conversation was perfunctory. It was intended as a message to the elderly: *I will no longer be your friend.*

At 5:30, roughly ten minutes after meeting with the last client – one ending in smiles – Pannett walked down the hallway. He knocked politely on the glass door before entering.

Paula, Jean, and Alice sat at the conference table, each with a bottle of water. The sweat and exhaustion was real. Stacked up in the conference room were fifty boxes of varying sizes. Each had a UPS mailing label.

Paula watched Pannett take in the room. This was an important moment.

"Not quite bankers' hours," Paula said.

"Even bankers don't keep bankers' hours anymore," Pannett replied, still looking at the piles of boxes.

"Allow me to introduce my staff," Paula said, rising from the table but gesturing for the others to remain seated. "Alice

Beauchamp and Jean Sullivan. They're still my friends, though another week of this much work may turn them into sworn enemies. Ladies, this is Chad…" Paula paused, her mouth open. "Bennett? That doesn't sound right."

"Pannett," he replied. "Tough name to remember."

He walked over to one of the piles of boxes and picked it up. "This is one day's shipments?"

Paula nodded. "And not even a heavy day. You should see Fridays."

The women murmured their agreement.

"Why not let Amazon do your fulfillment?" Pannett asked, lightly tossing the box, probably to make certain it felt like fabrics.

"Because then I'd pay Amazon's stocking charges and fulfillment fees," Jean said quickly. "And if I wanted my products to be part of Amazon Prime, I'd pay yet another fee. Every one of these packages is going within New England; most of them within fifty miles. Right now, I can pack and ship on the same day. UPS can get it to a home in no more than forty-eight hours. You do the math."

Pannett nodded appreciatively but said nothing. He looked at other boxes, then said, "Duxbury, Swampscott, Greenwich, Wellesley, Marblehead, Weston… You've got the right customer base all right."

"And my average order is over two hundred dollars," Paula replied. "You should take a look at our website. Of course, perpetual bachelors don't need fancy French tablecloths." To Jean and Alice, Paula added, "Mr. Pannett says he has 'never been caught'."

Pannett smiled and returned the box to its pile. "I hope your day ends soon."

"It ends when the UPS guy gets here," Paula replied.

They watched as Pannett turned the corner for the elevator. Waiting thirty seconds after the elevator 'ding', the three women went to a window overlooking the front of the building. They saw the lights flash on Pannett's car, watched him enter the car and, with their eyes, followed the car as it pulled out of the parking lot.

Only after the car disappeared from view did Paula say, "OK. I think we passed inspection. Let's get everything unboxed. Then we can go home."

An hour later, with Alice and Jean gone, Paula went on her first reconnaissance of Senior Equity's offices. The office suite's door was unlocked and Paula entered. She looked to see if any security cameras were in evidence and saw none.

There was a reception and waiting area though, apparently, no receptionist. Down a short hallway were five offices and a storage area. Three interior offices had been configured identically as small conference rooms: a round table with four chairs, and two side tables. There was no desk or 'executive' chair and no adornments on the walls. Paula concluded these rooms were for meetings with clients or would-be clients.

The storage area held little of interest; paper goods, copier paper, and office supplies. Two filing cabinets held nothing but never-used folders.

Which left two offices. To judge from the length of corridor space they occupied, they were 'executive offices' and of comparable size. One door was locked, the other closed but unlocked.

The unlocked office was relatively formal with a large desk and ergonomic chair on a plastic floor protector. To judge by the lack of wear on the floor protector, this office was used infrequently. There was also a comfortable sofa, coffee table, two upholstered side chairs, and a long credenza. Paula went through each drawer and found no evidence of human occupation.

The locked door did not yield to a nail file or pushing and, after several minutes, Paula gave up. By process of elimination this was Pannett's office. Being locked meant it held information he wanted hidden.

Paula left the office suite empty-handed and frustrated. She had been Senior Equity's neighbor for two days now. Apart from observing the routine of an almost hourly round of elderly visitors escorted by four different men and two women, she knew nothing of what went on inside their offices. She had met Pannett, but nothing more.

Thus far, her record as a sleuth was atrocious.

Chapter Nine
Wednesday

Eleanor Strong's irritation showed with every correction. Samantha Ayers, no less frustrated, kept ticking the realities with her fingers.

"They're not interested in someone with vague plans to spruce up their house or take a trip," Samantha said. "They need to be confident you'll draw down the money quickly. Without some certainty, they're going to cross you off their prospect list."

For forty-five minutes, the two women had discussed what Eleanor would say at noon when she attended a 'Your Home Is Your Pension Plan' seminar sponsored by Senior Equity.

Seven months earlier, Eleanor had gone through a comparable ritual. Then, her goal was to make herself 'Medicaid Ready' so she would no longer have to pay her husband's nursing home bill. She had never intended to go through with the complex legal transaction. Her goal, then, was to see whether a certain firm might have been complicit in her friend's death.

In the process, though, she discovered the elderly were easy prey for organizations promising financial relief. Scare tactics were common, as were high fees for dubious services. But Phil had been dead now for six months. While Eleanor missed her late husband, his passing had been a relief in so many ways. Alzheimer's had robbed him of everything that had made him a wonderful man, leaving behind an empty shell.

Now 62, Eleanor was entering a new phase of her life after living in a shadowland during the four years Phil's cognitive decline went from absent-mindedness to late-stage dementia. She had a network of friends, especially in Hardington and chief among them were the other three members of the Garden Club Gang. Apart from Phil, she now knew Paula, Jean, and Alice more intimately than anyone in her life. The four of them had found their lives in peril on multiple occasions over the past year. The fear cemented a bond which was made all the stronger by their willingness to help one another.

And this woman seated with her in her living room, Samantha Ayers, was in many ways the glue holding them together. Samantha was smart, tough, and insightful. Though still in her twenties, Samantha possessed a maturity and sense of purpose Eleanor could only have imagined in her own youth.

Now, Samantha was attempting to make her friend ready for an audition lasting under two minutes.

"You're at the bottom end of the range for reverse mortgages," Samantha said for what was possibly the third time. "You can take less money out of your home. Also, your face doesn't show the wear and tear of someone losing their mental sharpness." She sighed. "But you're also our only chance to get inside the place."

Eleanor had an idea. "What if I know I have a fatal disease."

"Like what?" Samantha asked.

"I'll think of something," Eleanor replied. "But what if I plan to fight this thing and, if I lose, I'm going to go down swinging. I know it will cost a fortune because it's all experimental and not approved by insurance plans. Or maybe I need to go out of the country for treatment…"

"Pancreatic cancer," Samantha quickly said.

Eleanor nodded. "That's what killed Steve Jobs."

Samantha took out her smartphone. Soon she was quickly tapping the screen, alternately shaking her head or nodding. After several minutes, she looked up. "You have Stage Four pancreatic cancer. You weren't even diagnosed until three months ago. But your cancer has a high level of sugar called hyaluronic acid squeezing down the diameter of veins so drugs are less effective. You're 'HA-HIGH'. You're taking the two standard drugs but you were turned down for the clinical trials…"

"So I'm going to a clinic in South America or Europe offering the same drugs…"

Samantha nodded. "And you need a fast quarter of a million dollars."

"Wow," Eleanor said. "I think I could pull it off."

* * * * *

Before 9 a.m., Paula had printed out the last of the emails from France and wondered if calling the trade group in Salon-de-Provence was wise. What would she say? She wasn't really running a business? No one would believe her. But she had to do something…

Paula's thoughts were interrupted by Jean, who was standing in the doorway of her office.

"What do I do with the orders?" Jean asked.

Paula shrugged. "We'll start re-boxing in an hour or so, I need to…"

"I mean real orders," Jean interrupted. She held out a dozen sheets of paper to show Paula.

"New orders?" Paula said, incredulous. "How on earth did we get new orders?"

It was Jean's turn to shrug. "I just turned on my computer and there they were. One of them is for almost a hundred pieces. Six services for eight – placemats and napkins. All different styles."

"Let me see them," Paula said, crossing to the door. She took the sheets from Jean and flipped through them. "Dear God," she said. "These people have paid for products we don't have."

"Can we ship them what we have here?" Jean asked. "They look a lot alike."

Paula shook her head. "Samantha would kill me. Those are all counterfeit."

"What about the ones you gave the realtor?" Jean asked.

"I bought those at a store in Cavendish," Paula said. "I paid a fortune for them, but I needed to make a good impression." She went through the sheets of paper again. "These are all more or less local… Natick, Wellesley, Ashland, Southborough… I wonder if our Ms. Mullen showed these to her friends, and…. Oh no."

Paula closed her eyes and breathed slowly, trying to calm herself. She put down the sheets of paper and held her hands stretched wide in front of her.

We have to find a way to fill these orders, Paula thought. *If we can't fill them, Leslie Mullen knows this is just a front and she'll tell Chad…. Think!*

Jean watched in amazement. She had never seen her friend look like this before.

After a minute, Paula said, "Jean, I want you to get on the computer. Get Alice to help you. Whoever created our website had to have grabbed pages from other sites. Google all the names of the styles in these orders and see how much they want… and let's all pray the person who put together the site didn't decide to put in absurdly low prices. Let me know what you've come up with in an hour."

Jean nodded and was gone. Paula heard her speaking excitedly with, presumably, Alice. They were smart and motivated, Paula thought. They'll do what they need to do.

With her heart pounding, Paula sat down at her own computer and typed into Google, '*What is required to import something from France for resale in the United States?*'

She held her breath and crossed her fingers.

Twenty minutes later, she thought she saw a chance… a slim chance. The incorporation papers creating 'Provençal Home Décor of New England' included a Tax ID number. Commercial invoice forms were available on line. Under US-EEC agreement, there were no import duties on fabric products. And – for a price – customs brokers could expedite getting Provençal napkins and table cloths cleared through Logan.

This just might work…

It also occurred to Paula people had paid via the website for products, but where was the money going?

A half an hour later, a perplexed but exceptionally helpful branch manager at Rockland Trust in Hardington had opened a business account for her. Having banked at the branch for more than a decade helped get past some of the niceties, such as signatures and starting balances.

"You know, most companies open the account before customers start sending them money," the manager said.

"You don't know the half of it," Paula said.

At 10 a.m., Paula met with Jean and Alice. "Please tell me you can find all these products," Paula said.

Jean produced two sheets of paper. "Fortunately, when the web designer copied pages, he or she also copied the prices." Jean smiled and looked at Paula to see if she smiled back. What she saw was a look of relief.

"How fast can we get these products?" Paula asked.

"How do you feel about overnight shipping?" was Jean's response.

Paula shook her head. "This is going to cost us a fortune. Yes. Pay the premium."

Jean paused before speaking, uncertain of the response. "Do you want me to order a few more pieces – just to give us a cushion?"

Paula threw up her hands. "Why not? Now, I've got to see if I can get some inventory from the people who actually make these things."

"I'll need a credit card…" Jean started to say.

"I'll get mine," Paula said with resignation.

With the first crisis of the morning averted, Paula looked at the time on her phone. *If it's 10:15 a.m. on the East Coast, it's 4:15 p.m. in France…*

Google provided the telephone number of the CCTP, including the country code for France. Paula had a suspicion her carrier's calling plan did not include unlimited international calls.

"Puis-je parler avec madame Deveraux? Je m'appelle de l'Amérique…" Two years of high school and college French passed before Paula's eyes – and promptly vanished.

* * * * *

"This is Marie Deveraux. How may I help you?"

"Well, for a start, do you mind if we speak in English? My French is atrocious."

Marie barely suppressed a laugh. "This is Madame Winters?"

"I am. One and the same. International lawbreaker."

Marie understood the first sentence. The rest made no sense. "Perhaps we must speak in more simple words."

Marie heard a laugh from the other end of the line. "I looked it up. *'Contre-loi internationale.'* I set up accounts with members of your Council. If I do not *faire amende honorable*, I will go to prison. I think 'prison' is the same in French as in English."

Marie liked this woman. "Yes, it the same. But the problem is here. Some of our members… they do not like to report all their business."

"Ah," Winters said. *"Triche d'impôt.* I just looked it up on Google. We have those here as well."

This time, Marie did not stifle her laugh. "Then we must *travailler ensemble* to keep them *honnête*. Is it the same in English?"

"Honest," Winters replied. "I suspect they both have Latin roots."

Honest, Marie repeated the word under her breath. A good word to have.

Winters continued, speaking slowly, "I am contacting each vendor today to tell them I will report all sales to you. Please keep in mind this business is *trés noveau*. We just launched…" she paused for a moment. "…*Lancé* our website. Surprisingly, we already have orders."

"Your website," Marie said, "It is *fantastique*. *Trés* beautiful. It is designed by a woman? It is very... feminine and also *informatif*."

"I was wondering that myself," Winters replied. "It was the gift of a friend. *Le cadeau d'un ami*, if I remember French 101."

"Your friend has much talent," Marie said. "And is *très généreux*."

"Marie Deveraux, it has been a pleasure speaking with you," Winters said. "*Merci pour votre temps*."

Marie could not help but smile. "Next time, we speak English only. *Au revoir*."

Marie replaced the phone in its cradle. She could not have been more pleased with herself. She had spotted a new importer who was not aware of the reporting rules and had successfully negotiated with the importer to ensure future compliance. She had done all of this using her own initiative. Paul Tanguay could not have done more and, in achieving the same result, he would have made threats and, in the process, also enemies.

It had indeed been an exceptional day.

* * * * *

At a few minutes before noon, Eleanor walked into a wide hallway flanked by a series of function rooms of the Westford Regency Inn and Conference Center. Ahead of her was a lone table positioned to prevent unwanted guests from strolling into one of those function rooms.

She knew she was walking into a meeting for which she was not registered and doing so almost fifty miles from her home. Both actions were certain to raise red flags, and she and Samantha had talked through possible answers to the inevitable questions. The key was arriving just before the seminar was to begin.

A young woman smiled up at Eleanor from the desk. There were just four name badges unclaimed on the table.

"Hi," the woman said. "What's your name?" One of her hands was already moving toward the unclaimed badges.

"Eleanor Strong," she replied. "And I'm afraid I'm not registered. I hope I can sit in, though."

"Oh," the woman said, her smile turning to a look of concern. "Let me talk to someone." She quickly rose from her chair and disappeared into the room. A few seconds later, she returned. Behind her was a man in his mid-thirties dressed in a suit and tie.

Eleanor felt herself being quickly appraised. Samantha had suggested a summer-weight skirt and blouse. She also suggested Eleanor 'go easy' on the makeup so as to look both a little older and a little more desperate.

"May I help you?" the man asked. His tone was courteous.

"I received a letter a few months back inviting me to one of your seminars. At the time, I wasn't interested and threw it away. I'm in a position where I think I ought to be looking at a reverse mortgage. I read on your website you were having one today…"

"Then please come in and join us," the man said. "I see we may have one or two no-shows, so it's their loss and your gain. We're about to start… may I have your name?"

"Eleanor Strong."

It was a small room, with just four tables of six and a podium. The man led her to a table where a man and two women – all well over seventy – were already seated. Eleanor took an empty seat and the man reclaimed what was likely the chair from which he had been summoned.

A moment later, an elderly woman – silver hair worn shoulder length in a classic style, sensibly dressed in a yellow tailored skirted suit, stepped to the podium. "Good afternoon," she said. "My name is Betsy Metcalf, and I want to tell you a true story."

She spoke without notes. "Elizabeth and Roy were married right after he got out of the service. She was a bank teller for a time but stopped working when the kids came. They raised two wonderful daughters in Winchester. One would go on to teach elementary school, the other went into nursing.

"Roy had a good job with Raytheon. They owned a fine home and took a family vacation every year. Roy retired after the girls got out of college and, for the next ten years, the two of them had a dream life, doing all the things they had planned over the decades: traveling, being with friends, becoming grandparents."

"Then, in the eleventh year of Roy's retirement, he had a stroke. He had never smoked. and he certainly wasn't overweight. His recovery took about six months, and all seemed well until, a year later, he suffered an incapacitating stroke leaving him unable to care for himself, and the task quickly became beyond Elizabeth's capabilities. Love could only do so much."

"Roy spent two years in a nursing home until his passing. He still recognized Elizabeth up until the end, and she was with him part of every day."

"After the funeral, Elizabeth had to face the grim reality Roy's strokes had decimated their nest egg. His pension ended with his death, and she had only his life insurance and a small amount from Social Security upon which to live. Her daughters offered her their homes, but one lived in Colorado and the other, unfortunately divorced, in Vermont."

"She knew her home was her principal asset. Her financial advisor urged her to sell and move into a retirement community. Elizabeth visited several such communities. There were people her age and enough activities to keep her busy, but she understood two things: first, her happiest memories were attached to her home and, second, her greatest joy during Roy's long illness was puttering in her garden. If she moved, she would lose both of those things."

"She had heard about home equity loans and so Elizabeth went to her local bank where she had done business for more than thirty years. Or, at least, it was the same building where she had banked. Her local bank had long since been swallowed up by a larger one, which merged with a still larger one until now she was never certain who owned it. And she spoke with a loan officer who didn't know her from Adam. The loan officer agreed Elizabeth's home was a fine one with a great deal of equity."

"But he explained the size of a home equity loan would be based less on the equity she had built up in her home and more on her ability to repay it. And, unfortunately, she had only her Social Security. He valued her home at more than $600,000. But, without a source of income to guarantee repayment – and he told her she would have to start repaying the home equity loan thirty days after she received the funds – his hands were tied. He offered her $65,000 and said the amount was generous because she had been a bank customer for so long."

Elizabeth knew there must be a third choice. She heard about what was then a brand-new company called Senior Equity Lending Services. It was a local company and she met with its president. Two weeks later, he handed her a check for $450,000. With that money plus Roy's insurance, she finally achieved peace of mind."

"Some of the money is in a bank – and, by the way, she changed banks – the balance is invested. She pays her property taxes and homeowners' insurance every year, which are a tiny fraction of what an apartment in a retirement community would cost. She gets her hair done every week and, when she leaves her hairdresser, she has lunch with the friends she has known since she was a young mother. She flies out twice a year to see her daughter and grandchildren in Colorado. She goes to the same church she has known since she moved to Winchester, and she volunteers regularly at the school her children attended."

The woman paused and took a deep breath. "You might be wondering by now how it is I come to know so much about Elizabeth and Roy. It's simple: I go by 'Betsy' but my given name is Elizabeth, and Roy was my beloved husband for forty-two years. Every so often, my friends at Senior Equity invite me to tell my tale. I love telling true stories with happy endings."

She left the podium to a standing ovation.

Eleanor felt the tears spilling down her cheeks as she, too, stood and applauded. She and this woman were kindred spirits. Both had cared for spouses through adversity, only to lose them in the end.

A minute later, a second woman, this one blond and in her forties wearing a red, severely tailored suit, came to the podium.

"You are contemplating a life-changing financial decision," she started. "You are faced with alternatives. This seminar is designed to help you navigate those choices…"

For half an hour, she spoke of risk factors and caveats. Fat folders were passed out with thick stapled-together sheets of paper printed on both sides. Slides flashed by on a screen showing mortality tables, inflation trends, and bond yields. Like the four women at the table, Eleanor opened the folder and flipped through the contents, pausing to look at bewildering graphs of seasonally-adjusted home sales by region, liquidity and volatility tables, and property tax rates by town.

In her head, she tuned out the woman's droning voice and instead went back to Betsy's re-building of her life after Roy's death, and she now had her hair done every week before having lunch with friends.

The woman in the red suit concluded her presentation to a sparse sprinkling of applause. A man came to the podium. He gripped its sides with his hands. He exuded purpose and energy. He looked to be in his early forties, a little on the heavy side, but impeccably dressed in a dark suit, white shirt, and blue tie.

"Your home is your pension plan," he began. "Decades ago, you bought a home and raised a family in it. You probably paid twenty or thirty thousand dollars. It was a huge investment at the time – perhaps twice your family income. Over the years you cared for it, expanded it, gave it a new roof and a more efficient furnace."

"All the while, you never gave a second thought to the idea you were doing this thing called 'building equity'. This was where you lived. This was home. Perhaps you thought your children might want to live there one day."

"Then two things happened," he continued. "Inflation sent the price of new housing rocketing through the stratosphere. Land prices soared. People started building out farther and farther from Boston, Providence, Portland... And your charming little house in its modest suburban setting became something everyone wanted. The second thing? Pension plans disappeared. Stocks gyrated from boom to bust. Interest... interest just disappeared. Banks which once offered you six or seven percent on a one-year certificate of deposit dropped to *one* percent, and then only if you left it with them for six or seven years."

"You didn't know it, but you made the smartest decision of your life when you bought your Cape or Colonial way back when. Because today, it is your pension plan and your biggest asset. The question is, how do you turn your asset into an income stream?"

"You can sell it. Yes, you can sell it. And take the after-tax proceeds and either buy something somewhere else or rent something somewhere else. You see these ads for these retirement communities. They want $600,000 for a house functionally identical to the one you just sold. You can afford to buy it, sure. But it just took every dollar of the profit you made on the sale of your house, and now you're stuck somewhere sixty miles from your friends and ten miles from the nearest grocery store. And where is the money for the association fee and the taxes going to come from?"

"Or, you can rent. Sure, you can rent. Twenty-five hundred dollars a month. Three thousand dollars a month. That's $36,000 a year. You're watching your nest egg evaporate before your eyes. And you're living somewhere out in the boonies, losing touch with the people you've called friends for decades."

"Or you can keep your home and try to borrow against its value – it's called a Home Equity Line of Credit. You heard Betsy's story.

Banks just want to get repaid. With interest. With lots and lots of interest. Remember your CD at the bank? The one where they're paying you one percent? Well, they'll loan your money right back to you… for five or six percent. And they don't care about your other assets. They want to know how much you get in Social Security. And that, plus the pathetic one percent on your CD, together with whatever dividends you may be getting from your nest egg – and boy, have those yields dropped – *that* constitutes your income stream. So, your $600,000 home, as far as they're concerned, qualifies you for a fifty- or sixty-thousand-dollar loan. For which they'll charge you six percent and *on* which you have to make a payment every month."

The man collected his breath. "There's one other option. A Reverse Equity Home Mortgage. Your home is the collateral. Not your Social Security check or your jewelry. Just your home. The U.S. Government dictates what percentage of your home's value we can give you. The older you are, the higher the percentage. You tell us whether you want your money given to you as a monthly payment, or as a lump sum. That's all there is to it. You can pay it back if you choose, but there's no requirement to do so. If you live to a hundred, then God bless you. Just keep up with the taxes and insurance and stay in your home."

"By the way, I'm Vincent Malone. I helped found Senior Equity three years ago. Betsy was one of the first people I helped. I've helped a lot of people since then. I hope you'll choose to be one of them. And enjoy lunch on us."

He, too, went back to his table to strong applause. Waiters appeared and salads were placed in front of each attendee.

The thirty-something man who had brought Eleanor into the room said, "I'd like to introduce myself. I'm Andrew Douglas. I'm an independent Accredited Retirement Financial Planner. I don't work for Senior Equity but they let me come to some of these to answer questions." He looked at the name badges of the four people at the table. "You're Mr. and Mrs. Teague, and you're Mary Hames." He paused at Eleanor. "And you're our mystery guest." He smiled.

"Eleanor Strong," she said, with only a hint of a smile and nod of the head. She added, "Uninvited Guest." She noted Douglas wrote her name on a pad of paper in front of him.

"Did everyone get something out of the presentation?" he asked.

Everyone nodded.

"Mrs. Hames, did you have any specific questions that weren't covered?" he asked.

Hames was a grey-haired woman, likely in her late sixties. She was well-dressed and her curly hair showed signs of a recent permanent. "My children have been telling me it's time to sell my home," Hames said. "I thought it would be good to hear about other ideas before I make a decision."

Douglas nodded agreement. "Where do your children live, Mrs. Hames?"

Hames answered quickly. "My daughter's in Concord. My son is about a mile away from me."

"And where is that, Mrs. Hames?"

"Oh, Acton. My daughter assumes she would get the listing, even though she's one town over and has always said real estate agents who try to sell in another town never get the best price."

Douglas nodded his understanding. But Eleanor could see he had already lost interest in Mary Hames. "Mrs. Strong, you seem a little young to be thinking about a reverse mortgage."

"I'm sixty-two," Eleanor said. "I believe I qualify."

"And why do you think a reverse mortgage would be right for you?" Douglas asked.

"You asked a rather personal question," Eleanor said. "But I buried my husband earlier this year after what is called 'a lengthy illness'. A reverse mortgage may be the only solution to a problem

I have only recently discovered I need to solve."

Everyone at the table looked at Eleanor. The two women murmured they were 'sorry for your loss'. Douglas, on the other hand, only studied Eleanor's face more intently.

"Is it something you would be willing to discuss in a more private setting?" he asked, a look of concern on his face.

Thirty minutes later, Eleanor and Douglas sat in the now-empty meeting room. She began her carefully rehearsed story.

"My husband died earlier this year of Alzheimer's," she said. "His decline began almost four years ago and, for the final year, he was institutionalized. We carried long-term care insurance but it still left me with a substantial co-payment every month. His disease made a fairly serious dent in the funds we planned to last us for the rest of our lives. But I didn't worry about it."

"Then, three months ago, I went in for my annual physical and got some terrible news. I had been feeling tired and didn't have much of an appetite, but I put it down to depression after my husband's death. My blood work came back with some strange results and, to make a long story short, I was diagnosed with late-stage pancreatic cancer. Part of me said, 'well, that's it, time to go join Phil.' But another part of me said I'm not ready to die."

"I was put on the two drugs that seem to slow the progress of the cancer, but they weren't as effective on me as on most people. It turns out I have a blood sugar issue narrowing my veins. It stops the drugs from getting to the cancer cells. There are clinical trials going on to test the effectiveness of a drug for people with a hyaluronic complication."

Eleanor took a deep breath. "I was told the trials are full. I can apply for the next round, except, by then, I'll be either dead or on death's door." She blotted tears on her cheek. "That was four weeks ago. Which is when I read about the Hirslanden Clinic in Lausanne. They have access to the new drugs, but they're outside the clinical trial. They're reputable, they get results, and they have openings. They're also not cheap."

Douglas, who until now had only listened and nodded, finally spoke. "What about your children? Are they in a position to help?"

Eleanor shook her head. "Phil and I never had children." She waved her hand and shook her head as if to preempt any questions on the subject. "There were medical issues on my part. So, no one is guiding me on this decision. My house is assessed at more than $700,000. Selling it would take too long, and I got the same answer as Betsy when I applied for a home equity loan."

"The way I figure it, there's a chance the drugs won't work and, in a year or less, I'll be dead. But, if I don't do anything – if I just say, 'OK, put me down for the next trial', I will certainly be dead in less than a year. If the drugs work, I'd like to have a home to come back to."

"Do you have any idea what treatment at the clinic will cost?" Douglas asked.

Eleanor nodded. "About $250,000. I told you it wasn't cheap."

Douglas looked Eleanor directly in her eyes. "I think I can find someone to help you."

* * * * *

By 2 p.m. – and by studiously copying the examples from the Department of Commerce website – Paula had created twenty-three commercial order forms and emailed them to the workshops of all of the companies whose products were featured on the Provençal Home Décor of New England website. She requested a quote and terms for expedited delivery. She guessed at quantities based on pure instinct.

She also looked at the spreadsheet in front of her. Alice had tallied the expected cost if all of the workshops shipped the products Paula had requested. Provençal Home Décor of New England had just committed itself to paying $47,284. And, since the business's income stream amounted to less than a thousand dollars, Paula felt with some certainty she was going to have to pay those bills out of her own pocket.

Tell me again why I'm doing this, she thought.

* * * * *

At 3 p.m. Austin time, Summer Copeland idly logged into the admin site for her Provençal Home Décor site. She looked at the 'views' tab and blinked. There were now more than a hundred hits on the site from France. And the U.S. counter showed more than two thousand clicks. The hits were initially from Massachusetts. Now, they were coming from ten northeastern states.

Just as interesting, the visitors lingered. Some were on the site for more than an hour.

Wasn't this supposed to be for the benefit of one person? she asked herself.

After a few minutes of gathering statistics, Summer shrugged, put on her headphones, and opened the tab for a new project.

* * * * *

Andrew Douglas closed his computer and let out a sigh of relief. Eleanor Strong was the real deal. There was an obituary for Philip Strong from February listing Eleanor as his surviving spouse and with no mention of children. There was a photo of Eleanor from last year in an archived copy of the *Hardington Chronicle* having to do with a garden club event. Town records showed a home in Hardington in her name with an assessed value of $714,000 and no mortgage lien.

He had also found the private clinic in Switzerland to which she had alluded, and he found information on pancreatic cancer listing medications comparable to the ones she said she was taking. The condition causing narrowed veins was real and there were ongoing clinical trials for medications to solve the issue.

In short, Eleanor Strong was the ideal pigeon. She was desperate. She would blow through the money in three or four months. If she croaked, Senior Equity would have title to a

$714,000 house (and homes in Hardington usually sold for about 110% of assessed value) for $250,000 plus expenses. That would be more than a half-million-dollar profit in a year or less.

He had held out hope he might have a twofer. The other widow at the table – Mary something – she looked like she was ready. But then she brought up the kids. One of them a real estate agent and the other living just down the street. They'd never let Mom go through with this kind of a reverse mortgage. They'd be all over the paperwork in a heartbeat because this was part of their inheritance. He had wished her well and went onto real prospects.

He had dismissed the elderly couple at the table out of hand. First, there were two of them. Second, they looked healthy: no canes or walkers. They were both going to live for another ten or twenty years. Third, the man had what might have been a phone in his top pocket and, if so, he might have been recording everything for posterity. Chad had warned him the state Attorney General's office had been snooping around again.

Well, everything he had done, and everything in the meeting, had been by the books. Betsy's story was perfectly true. Hell, she didn't even know she was part of the plan; she did this for free, or so Chad said. Clarice was perfect. She stood up there at the front of the room and rattled off everything that could go wrong, and she did it in such a way no one in the room paid the least bit of attention. And Vinnie. Oh, man, Vinnie was smooth. He was the closer with a two-minute spiel setting up the process. He was the guy who made the sale process so smooth you didn't even know you were buying anything until you looked in your wallet and saw it was empty.

But he had to move quickly on Eleanor. She said she had already been to see a bank. She might well stumble onto one of those goody-two-shoes outfits with a conforming reverse mortgages. She wasn't dumb, but she was, in her own words, desperate.

And desperate people were ripe for the plucking.

* * * * *

Chad was relaxing in the Jacuzzi, a half-consumed gin and tonic on the side of the tub. At the other end of the swirling foam was Bree. Bree the chameleon, who said she was twenty-eight but who, with a wig and five minutes in front of a mirror could pass for sixty-five.

Chad suspected Bree was fudging her age. He distinctly remembered she had said she was twenty-seven when they met three years earlier. But whatever her age, she was luscious. And she was driven. She could spot a mark and tailor a heart-rending sob story in the blink of an eye.

She was also tenacious. There were marks – clients, if you must – who looked as though they were going to find a way to repay their loans. Chad gave up on them and was willing to settle for the outlandish fees coming his way. But Bree always found a way. She befriended the suckers and left them somehow missing the crucial hearing or misplacing the important documents.

And Bree was utterly without scruples or remorse. She did everything she did knowing full well some of the women – and it was invariably women – gave up and… died. Last week when he told her a client facing foreclosure had overdosed on heart medication, she had shown no emotion; she had merely tilted her head and nodded. Afterward, she said, "Yeah, I figured her way out would be pills."

Bree was his kind of woman.

She spoke little of her past. She said she was from Texas, though nothing in her voice betrayed southwestern roots. She never spoke of college or even high school. If she had parents or siblings, they went unmentioned. Apart from sharing an occasional line or two of cocaine, she didn't do drugs. And, while she enjoyed wine and cocktails, he had never seen her get drunk. What she did enjoy was uninhibited sex, which she frequently initiated.

Bree had almost certainly put away a substantial bankroll in the past three years. By Chad's estimate, she had received nearly two million dollars in payments for her services. She never asked for a larger cut and she never volunteered how or where those funds were deposited. She had a condo in the South End, or at least he assumed it was a condo. He had never been there.

Three years earlier, she had shown up at P.F. Chang's where he was dining. He was in the process of putting together the funding for what would become Senior Equity. She sat down across from Chad, told him her name, and said, simply, "You're going to need someone like me."

Playing along because an attractive woman had initiated a conversation with him, Chad smiled and asked, "Why?"

Bree had replied, "Because everyone – and especially the elderly – make mistakes. Waiting them out takes time and patience. You need to *help* them make mistakes on a timetable you choose. Otherwise, all you're doing is giving them money and waiting for a break in the laws of probability."

Chad was speechless. Bree knew his plan, so she had obviously spoken with one or more of the people whom Chad had approached.

After almost a minute, Chad asked, "Who sent you?"

"I sent myself," was Bree's reply. "You're setting up a brilliant con. But you need someone – and it has to be a woman – to shave the dice, one mark at a time. I'm going to be that woman. I'm going to be the person who makes sure you win, not just some of the time, but all of the time."

"And what do you get out of it?" Chad asked.

"I get ten percent," Bree replied, never blinking. "What I'll do is worth more – a lot more, in fact – but I'm not greedy and ten percent of thirty or forty million dollars is fine with me."

When Chad said he would need to speak with some of the people with whom she had worked, Bree supplied two names.

Neither was anyone he had approached for funding, though both were aware of his plan. Bree, obviously, was someone well connected in the con artist world.

Their relationship had been sexual from the start. After dinner, Chad had asked, "So. what do we do next?" Bree's immediate response had been, "Let's see if you look as good out of those clothes as you do in them."

She seldom stayed the night and she left no clothing or toiletries at his condo. It was, in Chad's mind, the ultimate 'no-strings' relationship except they were business partners in all but the binding legal sense. Bree could choose to leave at any time and, after three years, Chad knew the void her departure would create could take months or years to fill.

As happened many evenings, they talked business as they soaked in the tub.

"We sent out formal notices of foreclosure on three houses today," Chad said, taking another sip of his gin and tonic.

"Which ones?" Bree asked.

"Andover, Grafton, and Quincy."

"Which one in Quincy?" Bree asked.

"Lorraine Higgins. Dartmouth Street."

Bree nodded. "Non-payment of taxes?"

"Yep," Chad said. "Missed two in a row. Slam dunk."

"I have her figured for the head-in-the-oven type," Bree said. "She's got some kind of heart condition. I figure she'll break when she gets the news." She finished her glass. "Do you think she needs consoling?"

Chad shook his head. "You've got bigger fish. Andrew thinks he landed a big one today. Lady in Hardington with a seven-hundred-plus house, husband died this year, and she needs to get a cancer treatment in Switzerland, though even she calls it a crap-shoot."

"What does the lady need?" Bree asked.

"A quarter gets her on a plane and into treatment."

"So, we could turn a quick five hundred." Bree splashed a little water onto her neck. "What do you need from me?"

"Andrew did her background based on what she told him at the seminar. The assessment checks out, the death notice on the husband is real, and he found a newspaper photo of her. There are no kids looking over her shoulder. So, she is who she says she is. But Andrew says she's smart and practical. She knows exactly what she's getting into. She's just betting the treatment will work – pancreatic cancer – and she'll have a place to come home to."

"I don't hear a problem," Bree said.

"Andrew's fear is she is going to do a Google search and find Salem Five or People's Bank; and then she'll see words like 'conforming' and 'FHA insured'."

"So, she needs reassurance."

Chad nodded. "Betsy was on top of her game. Had the whole audience crying, including Andrew's mark. But a one-on-one would probably seal the deal."

"Is she coming in for 'the talk'?"

Chad again nodded. "Andrew is pushing for tomorrow."

"I'll call him and get set up," Bree said with a smile. She held up her glass. "Can I freshen yours, too?"

She rose from the tub, water glistening on her perfect skin, and Chad looked on admiringly.

* * * * *

Paula Winters was exhausted. Maybe even beyond exhausted if there was such a thing. She had dealt with twenty vendors who pretended they had never even heard of the English language. She had interviewed three customs brokers and wondered what they would do for her that she couldn't do for herself and save thousands of dollars. She had explained to American Express there might be a few unusual charges in the next day or so – more than $40,000 of such charges. She had personally packed fifty-something cartons. In twelve hours they would need to be unpacked. She had been confronted by Alice with two dozen additional orders for products she did not have and was not certain she could get. She had paid yet another fruitless visit to Senior Equity's offices. This time, she got back to her own rooms just as she heard the clattering of a cleaning crew coming from the elevator.

And Martin Hoffman was due in ten minutes.

The logical thing to do would be to call Martin and beg off for the evening. The *sane* thing would be to tell him she needed a week off; maybe even a month to get past this project. Because she certainly didn't want to get him involved in it.

But the only reason she had kept her sanity today was the knowledge he was coming over. The lone saving grace to the most hellacious day she had endured since she couldn't remember was the man she loved was coming over to see her.

And to have dinner.

Paula slumped into the sofa in the Great Room. She had done nothing toward dinner. She hadn't given it a single thought. She wasn't even certain if there was a bottle of wine in the refrigerator. Maybe she could talk him into going out to dinner….

The doorbell rang.

She pulled herself to a sitting position and then willed herself to stand. She got as far as the half-bath midway between the Great Room and the front door. She went into the bath, turned on the light and looked at herself in the mirror.

I look ghastly, she thought. There were deep circles under her eyes, her lipstick was long gone and her hair had frizzed in the heat. *He is going to take one look at me and run screaming.*

Paula tugged at the blouse she had worn all day, which now bore visible sweat marks. She shook her head. It was hopeless. She went to the door and opened it.

There stood Martin Hoffman. In one hand, a bouquet of

flowers. In the other, a shopping bag overflowing with food containers.

She began to cry. But they were tears of joy.

"I had a call from Jean," Martin said. "She said you might be, in her words, 'way beyond cooking dinner'. So, I stopped and picked up something. And I'm willing to listen to what I suspect is a fascinating story."

Paula shook her head. She had no words. She gestured him in and retreated back to the bathroom for a handful of tissues.

* * * * *

A year earlier – almost to the day – Brookfield Town Detective Martin Hoffman had shown up in her driveway. He was investigating the daring daylight robbery of his town's fair. Paula and Eleanor had been docents at the flower show in the building nearest to where the robbery had taken place and, given the building opened onto the crime scene, they might have been unwitting eyewitnesses to the event.

What Detective Hoffman did not know at the time was he was interrupting Paula's cutting the money bags from the robbery into four-inch squares.

After a few minutes of questioning, Martin was satisfied Paula had nothing to offer by way of leads. But then he did something he had not done in five years since the death of his wife.

He asked a woman – Paula – if after all this was over, she might want to go out for lunch.

Forty-eight hours later, the Massachusetts State Police solved the crime and made a series of arrests and recovered the $127,834 Fair officials said had been stolen.

Six months later and a few months into a more serious relationship, Paula had inexplicably taken a position as a night nurse at an upscale retirement community. Two weeks later, through Paula, Martin had been handed the opportunity to expose a serial killer who had taken the lives of dozens of nursing home residents across several states.

It took a while for Martin to deduce Paula's true role in the Brookfield Fair heist, the undoing of the Pokrovsky auto empire, and the 'undercover' nature of her return to nursing. His conclusion was everything she had done had been for noble purposes.

The woman before him now, though, looked as though she had been run over by a truck.

He carried the flowers and bag of food to the kitchen. He found a vase, cut the ends of the flowers, placed them in the vase, and filled the vase with sufficient water to ensure they did not dry out.

He found placemats, flatware, and plates, and set the small table on the deck overlooking the back garden. When Paula came in the kitchen, having applied a modicum of makeup and repaired her mascara, she found dinner waiting for her. This time she did not cry. She instead sat down in the chair he held out for her.

"Maybe you want to start at the beginning," Martin said.

"We haven't done anything illegal," Paula said.

"That's a hopeful start. Who do you mean by, 'we'?" Martin asked.

"The usual suspects," Paula replied. "Alice, Eleanor, Jean, Samantha. A friend of Alice, Rebecca – Becky – Cooper. She got involved with a sleazy reverse mortgage company, Senior Equity Lending Services. They're about to foreclose on her house. I came up with this brilliant idea of moving in next door to them. We're supposedly importing French linens. The problem is, people think we really *are* importing them. We've got orders. I've got to line up suppliers. I'm going to have an American Express bill of close to $45,000 and my French sucks."

"What is getting close to this company going to do?" Martin asked.

"The head of Senior Equity, Chad Pannett, seems to be at the heart of it. He fairly oozes charm, except he was checking us out every step of the way yesterday. He was lifting boxes to see if they really had placemats and napkins in them…"

"I thought you said you needed to line up suppliers?" Martin asked.

"The boxes contained counterfeit linens," Paula sighed. "That's a different story. I felt like Chad was going to go back to his office and verify everything we said."

"How did people know you supposedly had these linens?"

"Samantha called Lucy McClellan – the daughter of Margaret McClellan, one of the women who died at Cavendish Woods – and she called in a favor. Provençal Home Décor of New England has the most charming website you've ever seen."

"I take it Provençal… whatever – is your fictitious company," Martin said.

"It isn't fictitious," Paula said. "That's the problem. There's a woman who works for Chad who dogged Becky – convinced her to add her son to the deed for her house, which violated the loan covenant. We need to find her. Being next door to Senior Equity is the only way to do it."

Martin nodded. "It's a good plan, all things considered. Find the mystery woman, have Becky ID her. Have Samantha turn it over to – who? – the state Attorney General?"

Paula nodded. "That's the idea."

"Can I help?" Martin asked.

Paula shook her head vigorously. "This should all be over in a week or two. I will survive this."

"You didn't look that way a few minutes ago."

Paula smiled. "That was before you brought me dinner and flowers."

Chapter Ten
Thursday

Bree Fleming's habit was to check her brokerage account every morning. And, every morning, she was amazed at how far she had come.

She had been born Candace Lockhart in Sioux City, Iowa and, until the age of nine, her life was unremarkable. Then, in rapid succession her parents divorced, and her mother re-married a man whom she had known as 'Uncle Bill'. She and her mother moved into Uncle Bill's house six miles away. Suddenly, she was in a new school. Things quieted down for about three years. That was when Uncle Bill began giving her a good night kiss on her forehead when he tucked her in at night.

One night when she was twelve, Uncle Bill's hand brushed her breast after her good night kiss – and those kisses were now on her cheek and moving inextricably toward her lips. Between her middle school health class and afterschool television shows, Candace knew exactly what was going on, and she wanted no part of it. Instead of telling her mother or her teacher, Candace took a paring knife from the kitchen and placed it under her pillow. The next night, Uncle Bill again allowed his hand to come to rest on her breast. Candace reached under her pillow and stabbed Uncle Bill in his arm.

Uncle Bill's scream brought Candace's mother into the bedroom. Uncle Bill was seated on the edge of Candace's bed, his arm bleeding profusely, with blood all over the bedsheets and Candace.

The following week, Candace was shipped two hundred miles northeast to her grandmother's and great aunt's home in Mason City.

For the next six years, Candace lived under the continuing suspicion she had 'led on' Uncle Bill. Every boy who called was offered as proof of her wickedness (her mother's subsequent divorce from Uncle Bill notwithstanding). At eighteen, Candace graduated high school having acquired a vitriolic hatred of her grandmother and great aunt and, by association, any woman over the age of sixty.

Two years at Iowa Central Community College instilled in her a love of the theater and an awareness she was a natural on stage. She appeared in six plays and became part of a summer stock company touring the Midwest. She earned excellent reviews, with writers extolling both her 'fresh, good looks' and how she 'disappeared into the part'.

At a film festival in Omaha, Candace saw the film *Klute*. That night, she became 'Bree'. 'Fleming' was an afterthought because one reviewer had called Candace's 'ravishing good looks' a 'modern Rhonda Fleming'.

Bree went to Chicago and found acting work which, coupled with trade shows, allowed her to scrape by. But by the age of 30, Bree knew she was 'aging out' of the theater world. It wasn't her appearance that cost her auditions, it was the length of her résumé. So she re-positioned herself as being 26 and trimmed her credentials accordingly. It worked. Bree Fleming got cast in commercials and even went on national tours.

Then, at the age of 35, she went on a casting call and found herself in a suite at the Hyatt Regency Chicago with two men and two women. All appeared to be in their mid-thirties. They were dressed smartly. 'Sam Jones' said he had seen her at the previous week's Chicago Auto Show and said her 'poise' working the Mercedes-Benz exhibit was exceptional. "You didn't stick to your script," he said. "You continually improved on it. You improvised and, even when you fudged the specs, you never batted an eye."

A woman who identified herself only as 'Cassie' said, "You

kept everyone's eyes on you, right up until the time it was right for them to focus on the car." For 30 minutes, Bree was by turn flattered and peppered with probing questions.

'Sam Jones' was the first to broach the real purpose of the interview. "We need someone who can be a distraction. Different locations every day. If it works out, this is a long-term gig, and the money will be excellent."

Bree became the fifth member of a group preying on gullible people with money who had the mistaken impression they were smarter than everyone around them. She replaced someone who had elected to marry one of her marks.

For three years, Bree bounced between in Chicago, New York, Miami, Las Vegas, and Boston – all places where the newly wealthy congregated to display their success to one another. She worked short and long cons. In her best year, she netted more than half a million dollars; a considerable sum considering the group's high operating expenses. She parted company with the group only after two members of the ring drew the unwanted attention of law enforcement officials in Chicago.

Bree examined several opportunities before targeting Chad Pannett and his reverse mortgage scheme. Pannett was sure of himself to the point of being cocky. But he had an excellent idea and a high likelihood of finding the start-up funding he needed. And Boston was a city she already knew well.

Now, after three years, she knew she had made the right decision. The account balance on her computer screen showed more than $3 million under professional management. In addition, she owned the second-floor apartment of this South End brownstone (where her neighbors knew her as 'Emily Colwin'). She could look forward to million-dollar-a-year payouts for as long as Senior Equity remained in business.

Bree logged out of her account with a sense of satisfaction. She had a long day ahead of her. Starting it off by knowing she didn't *have* to go to work made it all tolerable.

* * * * *

Martin, too, began this day by examining his finances. With bills from the electric and cable companies in front of him on his kitchen table, he was all set to write checks for his utilities, but found they had been deducted from his bank account the previous week. He had no earthly idea his bills were paid automatically or how he had given authorization for such an intrusion. But tiny print on both bills stated an appropriate amount had already been debited. He closed his checkbook in exasperation.

Martin lived simply. His home (to the extent it could be called a home) was a one-bedroom apartment on the second floor of an extremely large apartment complex along Route 9 on the western edge of Framingham. While the names were different – Jefferson Hills, Chapel Hill, Waterview Terrace – the half-mile-long expanse of buildings were functionally identical.

Martin, now 56, had moved here five years earlier. It was a few months after the death of his wife in a senseless traffic accident. Not wanting to live with daily, painful reminders of his loss, he sold his home in Cambridge and gave the furniture to his children (who dutifully each selected a few pieces that soon became the property of Goodwill). On his 25th service anniversary with the Cambridge Police Department, he took his pension and 'retired' to become the sole detective for the town of Brookfield, roughly ten miles northwest of where he now lived.

His apartment was anonymous by design. Back then, Martin had assumed the 'good' part of his life was now over. He had his one true love and soul mate, and she had been taken from him. His goal was to keep busy and to accumulate funds to pass down to his children. And, for four years, that is how it had worked. He did his job competently, he passed his evenings watching whatever sport was in season.

Then, a year earlier on a Sunday afternoon in August, he got the call the Brookfield Fair had just been robbed. There were 15,000 people at the fair, yet no one witnessed a robbery of the van collecting the Fair's daily cash receipts. He had begun investigating but, the next morning, the Massachusetts State Police exercised their prerogative to take over the case. Why? Because the people who committed the robbery had chosen the slowest news day on the slowest news month of the year. Their robbery was the lead news story at every media outlet in New England... and the Massachusetts State Police saw an opportunity to ride that publicity wave.

But, in the course of his day of investigating, Martin had driven down to Hardington to speak with a possible eyewitness. And when he saw Paula Winters, he sensed something he had not felt in five years: interest in a woman.

Forty-eight hours later the crime was 'solved' by the state police and a cast of bad actors were under arrest. Martin met Paula for lunch and then dinner, which became the kind of cautious romance entered into by two people in their fifties.

Six months later came what Martin still thought of as 'the revelation'. Paula had inexplicably taken a short-term position as a night nurse at a high-end retirement community. Then she flew to San Francisco in the afternoon only to return, exhausted, the next morning. But she had with her a folder of emails and memos about an employee of the retirement community who was almost certainly responsible for the deaths of several of its residents, and links to deaths at half a dozen nursing homes in other states.

Paula had left it to Martin to 'do what needed to be done' with the information. He immediately shared it with a friend in the state police who would act on it rather than moving it up the chain of command. The employee was arrested and readily confessed.

Several things baffled Martin. One of the emails given to him by Paula bore a time stamp just hours old, though Paula had not been back to the retirement community. And, even as state police were making their arrest, one of Paula's friends – apparently temporarily living in the retirement community – was assaulted by another employee, who then took her own life.

It took Martin several weeks to put together all the disparate pieces. And, when he did, he realized Paula was the leader of a gang. She had masterminded the robbery of the Brookfield Fair and, along with insurance investigator Samantha Ayers, had devised the way to 'solve' the crime in such a way no suspicion fell on them. Her brief nursing stint at the retirement community had been one facet of the 'gang's' plan to determine whether an elderly member of her garden club had died of natural causes or at the hand of someone in the facility. They had found not one, but two, murderers.

Martin's surprise was that, when he worked out the truth, he was not angry. Rather, he was in awe of Paula's skills and determination to do what she thought of as 'the right thing'. It was at that point he acknowledged to himself he was in love with Paula Winters.

Two months later they took their first vacation together. On the night they arrived, Paula – without any prompting on his part – told him everything. She said she wanted no secrets between them. And he told her the truth: he had figured it out.

Not everything. The business with 'Smilin' Al' Pokrovsky had completely escaped him. That these four women had gone undercover to aid Samantha Ayers and had exposed the largest counterfeit auto parts operations in the region was a shock.

And now she and her 'gang' were clearly up to something else. She said it wasn't dangerous and she didn't need any help. She said it would take as little as a few days but no more than a week or two. It was to help a friend and, yes, to right an injustice. She also said, with just a hint of sarcasm, the operation might leave her in poverty.

Martin awakened with the realization that, whether or not he had been asked, he intended to make certain no harm came to Paula.

* * * * *

Eleanor's phone rang at exactly 8:30.

"Eleanor, this is Andrew. I've got some wonderful news for you,"

Before she responded, Eleanor clicked the button to activate the recording device attached to her phone. Non-consensual recordings were not admissible in court in Massachusetts, but they nevertheless played a crucial role in establishing which side was telling the truth in civil litigation.

"I'm sorry," Eleanor said, "Who is this, again?"

"Andrew Douglas, Mrs. Strong. We met yesterday at the luncheon."

"Oh, yes," Eleanor replied. "I didn't expect to hear from you so quickly."

"You made it clear time was of the essence, Eleanor. I spent most of yesterday afternoon speaking with five different reverse mortgage originators. Without using your name, I outlined your requirements to see what reaction I would get."

"You didn't use my name," Eleanor repeated.

"No, ma'am," Andrew said. "I described you as a widow, age 62, living in a 'good' Boston suburb. I used a home value of $700,000 which, based on the way you described it, is certainly in the ballpark. I asked about a timeline to take $250,000 in equity out of the house to pay for specialized medical procedures."

"You did all that in one afternoon?" Eleanor asked.

"I did what I said I'd do," Andrew replied. "You told me your treatment can't wait. Two of the five companies – and I spoke directly with people on the underwriting desk – gave me a timeline of four or five months."

Eleanor gasped. "I could be dead by then."

"Once I heard their timeline, I cut those conversations short,

Eleanor," Andrew said. "One said they could push something through in a month. I said it was too long. Another said as little as two weeks. I liked the sound of that until I pressed them. They said they'd have to get approval from Dubai – Dubai! – to expedite a mortgage. And, because you're just 62, they would limit your payout to thirty percent of the home's value. Which means that, unless your home appraised for something around $900,000, you'd come up short."

"Then there's no hope," Eleanor said.

"I said I spoke with five originators, Eleanor. The fifth one listened carefully, asked a lot of questions in return – including whether I thought you were an honest person – and they came back with a better answer than I could have dreamed of. They'll write you a check for up to half of your home's value. And you can have a check next week."

"Oh, my stars," Eleanor said. "Where did you find this company?"

"*You* found them, Eleanor." Andrew replied. "The good news came from Senior Equity. They're smart, they believe in what they're doing, and they're responsive. Oh! And talk about the stars lining up: their CEO was supposed to be on vacation this week. His wife threw her back out playing tennis so he's in the office. Could you meet with him this afternoon?"

"The head of the company?" Eleanor exclaimed. "Oh, no, that would be…"

"Relax, Eleanor," Andrew said, his voice soothing. "Chad Pannett meets every applicant before a check gets written. This is a local company, not the Chase Manhattan Bank. He wants to be able to say he knows every customer. Granted, we're kind of putting the cart before the horse. He usually meets the client after all the approvals are in place. But I have a suspicion this one is going to sail through without a hiccup. You're an exceptional case."

"What do I wear?" Eleanor said.

Andrew laughed. "You just be yourself. And be sure to ask about his wife's back. What if I pick you up at, say, three o'clock? You can meet with him at 3:30."

Ten minutes later, Eleanor was playing the recording for Samantha over the telephone. When it was finished, Samantha said, "There's a lot of pressure coming from somewhere to close business."

"I told Andrew I needed treatment right away," Eleanor offered.

"No," Samantha said. "This is something different. First, it means they have a money source that can come up with a quarter of a million dollars in a week. And, if they're closing thirty or more mortgages a week, that's a funding source that has $7 million sitting around in petty cash."

"Well, how does an honest firm do it?" Eleanor asked.

"They have a couple of deep pockets. Pension funds, mostly. Outfits that buy zero coupon bonds. They have long horizon and what they're looking for are stable returns. These guys are trying to shovel money out the door. Now, we know their goal is to steal your house and double their money in a year or so, but they still need a lot of up-front operating capital."

"Could it be Mafia money?" Eleanor asked.

"The Mafia isn't what it used to be," Samantha replied. "Just take a look at Tony Soprano. No, this is drug money or a rogue arm of a sovereign wealth fund. I'd like to poke around a little bit."

"Do I go to the meeting?"

Samantha laughed. "Oh, please go. That gets us inside. That gets us evidence. And be certain to ask about Mrs. Pannett's poor, aching back."

* * * * *

Paula was the first to arrive at the office, and she was relieved to see eight large cartons stacked up by the front door. They all read, 'express overnight' and she cringed at the probable cost of having FedEx deliver products to her she would turn around and ship this evening. At least for today, Provençal Home Décor of New England was a running business. Albeit a deeply unprofitable one. One by one, she pushed the cartons inside her company's 'headquarters'. It wouldn't do to have Chad wondering why one retailer was buying its inventory from another store.

At the desk she had decided was her 'office' she opened her computer. Yes, she could have done this in her kitchen ninety minutes ago, but she wanted to preserve her sanity and her blood pressure.

And she wanted to savor the previous evening before she slipped into her Paula Winters, Phony Company Executive costume.

When Martin showed up at her door with dinner in hand, it made her cry. For 25 years, she had spent much of her waking hours anticipating her husband's needs, making certain his home life always went smoothly. Her reward was to be dumped for a younger woman.

Last night, she had walked into her home, prepared to put aside the tensions of her day and put on a smile, all to please a man. And the man had done the most unexpected thing... he had instead anticipated her needs.

She was in love with Martin. She knew it without reservation. She knew she had fallen in love with a man who had once found that 'true love' of his life, and then had lost her in a horrible accident. She, on the other hand, could no longer be certain she had ever really been in love with Dan. They were married, lived together, and had children. But Dan was in his own world and she was... the mother of his children and the administrator of his non-working life. Or at least the part where he wasn't sleeping with a woman just two years older than their daughter.

Paula shook her head to get rid of the negative energy.

There was Martin, standing in the front door, a goofy smile on his face, bearing dinner in brown paper bags. It was the most welcome sight she could remember. She took the bags from him, set them on the ground, and threw her arms around him. And cried.

For two hours, he listened. He asked questions when they seemed appropriate but, mostly, he genuinely listened. When, afterward, they made love, it was with a tenderness she could never remember with Dan.

Paula was jolted from her memory by the sound of 'good morning' from Alice as she walked through the door. Paula left her office to join Alice in the conference room.

"I couldn't wait to see what kind of orders we were going to get," Alice said, a broad smile on her face. "Since I was up at five, I decided to log into the account."

Paula looked at Alice's smile and did not know whether to be pleased or terrified. "What did you find?" she asked.

Alice put down her purse on the conference room table. "Brace yourself," she said. "One hundred and thirteen new orders. Nine hundred and seventy pieces. Just shy of $10,000. And that's just since six last evening."

Paula looked up at the ceiling. "Tell me we ordered the right things from those other websites. Tell me those boxes I just brought in have what we need to fulfill those orders."

Alice cocked her head. "Do you want the truth, or do you want me to tell you something that will make you feel good for a little while?"

Paula found a chair and slumped into it. She shook her head. "How bad is it?"

Alice shrugged her shoulders. "I can tell you more in an hour, but I'm guessing we can fill about half of the orders and partial-ship most of the others. The rest? We're starting from scratch."

Paula place her hands on her face and rubbed. "Alice, I'm out of my depth here."

"We could tell Samantha to tell whoever put up the website to take it down," Alice offered.

Paula shook her head. "No. We take down the site and Chad will know he has a stakeout going on next door." She added, "And I'll be out about $50,000."

Paula rose from the chair. "Time to be grown-ups. Print me out an inventory and match it to the orders. I'm going to see what our friends in France were up to overnight."

* * * * *

Summer Copeland logged into the admin account on the Provençal Home Décor of New England website. She blinked. A hundred overnight hits in France. Three hundred in Massachusetts and as many more from the five other New England states.

And the hits were creeping west and south. Two hundred from New York and almost as many from around Washington and Baltimore. Two dozen hits from Chicago.

Summer left her office and went to the other side of the floor to the office of Joyce O'Quinn, the President of Austinplex. She tapped on the door.

"I'm trying to decide if I'm doing too much of a good thing," Summer said. "You know the website you asked me to do for Lucy McClellan? It's getting an awful lot of hits."

Joyce turned to her computer. "Give me the IP address."

Summer provided it.

A few keystrokes later, the two women were looking at the site's home page.

"How are you promoting it?" Joyce asked.

"Google Ad Dollars," Summer replied. "I've got more of them than I know what to do with."

Joyce scrolled through the home page. "We have no more important account than HP," she said, "and making Lucy happy is the most important thing I do around here. Here's what I want you to do. Lucy said the person needed to know the site belonged to an established and successful company. What you've done proves it's established. Let's prove it's successful." Joyce pointed to an area on the screen. "Put a traffic counter here. Underneath it, show a geographic feed. And throw some more of Google's money at it. Let's make Lucy ecstatic."

* * * * *

Bree paused outside the door of Provençal Home Décor of New England. She recalled Chad saying something about it last evening. He was initially annoyed but, on further reflection, concluded the company's presence demonstrated the building's otherwise empty parking lot must be deceptive.

The placemats, napkins, and runners on the wall were certainly attractive. Well, she hadn't promised Chad she would be here at a specific time. She went inside.

A pixyish woman in her sixties poked her head around the corner. "Can I help you?"

"Just looking," Bree said and flashed a smile.

"We're online only," the woman said. "But please look around."

"They're beautiful," Bree said, moving from design to design.

"Hand-made in Provence," the woman said, pride in her voice. "Paula – she's the company's president – goes to France twice a year to look for new designs and check up on the workshops."

Bree nodded. "They're stunning. She has a great eye."

The woman disappeared around the corner and reappeared with a business card in her hand. "This still has the address from when we were working out of our president's kitchen, but the website is correct. When you get ready to order, here's the information you'll need."

Bree accepted the card and placed it in her purse. "This is quite helpful," she said.

* * * * *

"Who was that," Paula asked.

Jean shrugged. "It wasn't our old lady. Just someone in the building. Oh, and for the record, if anyone asks, you fly to France twice a year to spot new designs and make certain all those workshops are humming away."

"Did you tell her where I stay?" Paula asked, amused. "I hope it's someplace exquisite."

"I'll do some research and get back to you." Jean replied. Then she added, "Funny thing about that woman. When I first saw her, I thought, 'late twenties'. You know, the sort of clothes those millennials wear and the right kind of hair style and makeup. Nice complexion, too. But her hands…"

"What about her hands?" Paula asked.

Jean again shrugged. "When I gave her our card, I noticed her hands. They were an older woman's hands. Forty at least. Well, not my problem. My hands don't even remember 40."

Paula drummed her fingers on the desk. "There are just two businesses in this building, and no one just wanders around an empty office complex. The only visitors are little old ladies being escorted in and out by Chad's feeder sharks. She has to be part of Senior Equity."

"Do this," Paula continued. "Have your phone somewhere it isn't obvious. If you see her walk by again, ask her to come in and tell her I'd like to say hello. While we're together, find a way to get a photo. We need a 'rogue's gallery' of Chad's people."

Jean snapped a salute. "I'll do it, boss."

Paula nodded toward the storeroom. "Now go help Alice get those orders together."

When Jean was out of sight, Paula allowed the smile to fade from her face. On her desk was a sight that would have thrilled any business owner: consumers clamoring for product and suppliers eager to ship their products to her at advantageous prices.

The problem was she was only pretending to be a business

owner.

Her proposals to the Provençal manufacturers had been met with enthusiasm and swift approval (except for one which deigned to reply only in a version of French that Google Translate could only throw up its figurative hands and say, 'phrase not found'). A customs broker was ready to expedite shipments at a special, 'get-acquainted' rate. UPS was making an actual pickup of outgoing orders this afternoon. She had two hardworking employees who thought this was great fun.

The complexity lay in timing. Even with expedited air freight and quick customs clearance, she was unlikely to see product from French suppliers until next week. Alice's report showed the mismatch between her overnight orders and what she had purchased from other internet vendors was, while not terrible, also not enough to meet existing orders. And, if the online vendors from which she was finding her supplies discovered they were selling to a competitor, they would either raise their prices or cut her off.

Oh, and fifteen additional orders had come this morning.

Paula could have frozen with indecision. She could have thrown her hands up, walked out and admitted defeat. She could have laid her head on the desk and sobbed.

She did none of those things. In the time-honored tradition of good managers everywhere, she decided to take care of one item, complete it, and then move on to the next one. From the pile of emails and notes, she plucked the nearly indecipherable letter from Alain Duperon, the head of *Tissus du Aubignan*. She copied it into an email and sent it to Marie Deveraux with a request to help with a translation. She noted the time in France would be just after 2 p.m.

Two minutes later, she placed a call to the *Conseil de Commerce des Tissus Provençaux*. As she hoped, Marie answered the phone.

"I just sent you an email," Paula said.

"I have just opened it," Marie said excitedly. "This is from Monsieur Duperon. He is one of our most... I do not have the word... *irascible* members."

Paula laughed. "I think the word is the same in English as in French, except we pronounce it 'irascible'. It means difficult to work with. Hard headed."

Paula heard typing on the other end of the line. "Ah, *têtu*. Yes, Monsieur Duperon is also most hard headed. He had written you entirely in the *Provençal*, even using some words that are unique to his village. He says he accepts your terms and will ship as soon as you send a certified guarantee of payment." She paused. "He also says he has a good-for-nothing son who is not married whom he will send to America to marry you, provided you have a sufficient.... *dot*. I do not have that word..."

"Dirt?" Paula asked.

"*Dot*. D-O-T," was the reply.

Paula typed the word and laughed. "Dowry," she said. "His son will marry me but wants to make certain I'm wealthy."

"I told you he is *irascible*," Marie said.

"Well, fortunately for me, I will be too poor for Monsieur Duperon's son after I order all these *tissus*. My biggest problem is trying to coordinate shipment from so many factories."

"*Pardon*?" Marie said. "You wish to *consolider* – consolidate many shipments? We can do that. We used to do many more... before the *chinois* began to steal our *modèles*. Our special Provencal pattern. Perhaps I should not be so open, but we have lost most customers in *Russie* and *Amérique du sud*. They buy... *contrefaçon*."

Paula typed furiously. On her third try she got a translation. *Knockoff.*

"You mean Chinese knock-offs. Can't you stop them?" Paula asked.

"We cannot find the factory," Marie said, her voice rising. "And the EU tells us this is not *prioritié* as long as they are not sold into EU countries. Our fear is the *chinois* will try to sell to the big American internet *à prix réduit* sites."

"Ah-pree…?" Paula repeated.

"*Pas cher*, cheap," Marie explained. "In America you have internet companies selling things people know are knockoff but are so cheap you do not care."

Paula thought about Samantha's container load of counterfeit goods. She had never asked how they came into the hands of Mass Casualty. She would certainly call Samantha and ask.

"Marie, if someone could document the name and location of the Chinese factories making these *contrefaçon*, could you stop them?"

"It would be the best news ever," Marie replied. "Each year we see more knockoff. But that is our problem. You have the problem of *consolider* for your order. I can have your order picked at our *entrepôt* in Salon de Provence…"

"*Entrepôt* is…" Paula asked.

"How do you say… houseware?" Marie offered.

"Warehouse!" Paula exclaimed.

"Yes," Marie continued. "I can have your order picked from our warehouse here in Salon de Provence this afternoon. You send me agreements with the workshops and I have container at Marseilles Airport for shipment to Boston tomorrow morning."

"You can do that?" Paula asked, trying not to let the incredulity – or the relief – show in her voice.

"*Bien sûr*. That is my pleasure." Marie paused and added, "It is also how we keep people like Monsieur Duperon *honnête*."

Paula laughed. "Do you know you've just saved me an entire day's work?"

"Then you should reward yourself with a long lunch," Marie said. "Like my *collègues de bureau*. They do not think they must come back from lunch if our boss is not here."

Paula ended the call with more thanks, then placed her head

face down on her desk. *What I don't know about business will probably kill me*, she thought. *I had been about to arrange more than two dozen separate shipments...*

Her thought was interrupted by a tap on the door frame. It was Alice.

"There's someone here who would like to see you," Alice said.

Paula lifted her head. "Do I get to know who it is?"

Alice came through the door and gingerly handed Paula a business card. "You looked like you didn't want to be disturbed. Are you all right?"

Paula shook her head. "I am going insane. I am also going broke. I don't know which is worse." She looked at the card. "National Public Radio?"

Alice nodded. "She says she heard about you at a women's club meeting."

Paula stared at the card again. "Sure. Why not? What could possibly go wrong?"

A minute later, a young woman with long, black hair and glowing skin fairly bounded into Paula's office, her hand outstretched.

"Ms. Winters, it's an honor to meet you," the woman said. "I'm Adriane Miranda, and I'm a stringer for NPR. I heard about you a few days ago and my editor..."

Paula held up her hand. "Wait a second, Adriane... You heard about me from.... Who?"

"Leslie Mullen," Adriane said. "At the MetroWest Women's Club. About your scaling up from a 'kitchen-table' business to be the first tenant in a Women's Empowerment Zone. My editor said to get an interview. I couldn't wait!"

Paula tried to parse each word. Leslie had rented her this suite of office in One Broadmoor Hill. Somehow, an almost-empty office building had been transformed into a 'Women's Empowerment Zone'.

Paula decided she would strangle Leslie Mullen at a time of her own choosing.

"Could we do this interview tomorrow morning?" Paula asked. "Right now, I'm trying to get several dozen vendors' orders consolidated from France."

"Sure," Adriane said. "Are they by any chance women-owned companies?"

Paula thought of Monsieur Alain Duperon. "You know, I've never asked. But there's a wonderful lady at the trade council office in Provence…"

"Perfect!" Adriane said. "I'll be here with a crew at nine tomorrow morning…"

"Crew?" Paula asked.

Adriane nodded. "Well, my Producer, of course. And some video and sound people. These are great visuals…"

"Your card says 'National Public *Radio*," Paula said, pointing to the card. "The last time I looked, radio didn't require cameras…"

Adriane gave Paula a look that reminded Paula of the ones her daughter, Julie, gave her every time Paula said something betraying technological or cultural ignorance.

"Radio is just the tip of the media iceberg," Adriane explained. "At minimum, in addition to the radio story, this will be on our website as a podcast and an extended video interview, and the PRX people loved the pitch."

"'Loved the pitch,' Paula repeated, and wondered what kind of 'pitch' had been made and to whom. "Sure. Tomorrow morning."

Paula shook Adriane's hand, and the young woman bounced out of the room, 'ooh'ing at the samples on the wall. Alice came back in when the visitor had been seen safely back to the elevator.

"Alice," Paula said, "I'm going to forward all these vendor term sheets to a wonderful lady in France. And after that, I am going to take a walk. If anyone comes with an arrest warrant for me, I should be back before noon."

* * * * *

Chad leaned back in his chair and cracked his knuckles. "I have a feeling we're going to close eight mortgages today."

Bree looked askance at him. "And how many mortgages are you going to call?"

Chad looked at Bree. "That's your department," he said, breaking into a grin.

Bree shook her head. "I can nudge them. I can line them up. You and your crack legal team have to pull the rug out from underneath them."

Chad shrugged. "They're doing OK work."

Bree crossed to Chad's desk and opened a folder of papers. "Here are at least two dozen marks whom you've notified their mortgages have been called, but you haven't taken action." She waved the folder in Chad's face.

Chad looked annoyed. "As you have so delicately pointed out, a certain percentage of these people resolve the matter by buying the farm."

"So, I have to do all the work," Bree said. "God, you're a terrific businessman."

"You know and I know it isn't that simple," Chad said. "If we move *too* quickly, we end up with a judge starting to look at the paperwork."

Bree opened the folder. "Let's look at this one. Rebecca Cooper. *I* got her to add her son to the deed. Took me three tries and, by the time I did, I was fresh out of coincidences. But that was a month ago. Her husband is dead and buried. She doesn't have a legal leg to stand on and she hasn't responded to the notices. You're going to turn at least 300K on that property."

"And you'll get your share when we flip it," Chad said, smiling.

"No, Chad. You're waiting for her to swallow a bottle of sleeping pills so you don't have to spend money on lawyers and court costs. I'm saying, you clear these files so we can get some cash flow around this place. This is a business; not a charity."

Chad grinned. "I love it when you get mad."

Bree returned his look with a cold stare. "And I hate it when you start getting cheap and sentimental."

Chapter Eleven

At 2:15, Andrew Douglas rang Eleanor Strong's doorbell. This was his first time seeing the property in person. He noted the well-tended shrubs and lawn with nothing overgrown. High-quality siding had been painted in the past two or three years and there were no obvious flaws or cracks. The gutters were clear of debris. The house would show exceptionally well.

The inner door opened and Eleanor stood there, looking nervous. That, too was good. She was off-balance, a necessary condition of making a sale. She opened the outer screen door.

"May I come in for just a second?" Andrew asked.

"Don't we have to be there at three?" Eleanor asked.

"We'll make it there with time to spare," Andrew said. "I'm just looking for a glass of water. I tend to get dehydrated."

Eleanor appeared to accept the reason and quickly disappeared into what Andrew assumed was the kitchen. He likely had less than a minute to assess the interior of the house.

He liked what he saw. The layout was clean; there was no wallpaper to contend with. It wasn't overstuffed with furniture or bric-a-brac. There were a lot of photos, but that could easily be rectified. He rated the house a B-plus. On the open market, and especially in Hardington, it would easily sell in the sevens. He could wholeheartedly recommend giving her the quarter million.

The calculus was as simple as it was cold. Mrs. Strong would go to Europe for her treatment. She would spend the money at a clinic. The treatment would fail and, in six months, she would be dead. Not only dead, but dead without children or a husband to complicate things. The two-step sale would first wipe out the debt owed to Senior Equity, and then line the pockets of everyone involved.

In six months, the serendipity of Mrs. Strong showing up for a luncheon uninvited would put at least $21,000 in his pocket. Life was good.

The trick was to close her before she had time to think, much less to research alternatives.

Eleanor returned with a glass of water. Andrew drank it and thanked her profusely. Three minutes later – two of them spent looking for her purse – they were on their way to a meeting with Chad.

On the way there, Andrew launched into his pitch.

"I can't begin to tell you how fortunate you are," he said. "The government just proposed a whole new set of rules about reverse mortgages. They want to lower the percentage of your home's value you can take as a lump sum, and they want to raise fees."

"Why would they do that?" Eleanor asked. She had, of course, activated the recorder in her purse.

"Greed, Eleanor," he said. "Reverse mortgage companies are clamoring for more profits. They have lobbyists. The lobbyists have the ear of the folks who write the rules. Right now it's just a proposed rules change. In anywhere from a few days to a few weeks, it will be law."

"Does it affect me?" Eleanor asked, nervousness in her voice.

Andrew shook his head vigorously. "No, ma'am. As long as your application is in and approved, you get the current maximum and the lower fees. And, after your treatment, you'll still have your house to come back to for as long as you live." He added, "And I hope that's for a long, long time."

"That's reassuring," Eleanor said. She was silent for several moments, then asked, "Pardon my asking, but you're being so generous with your time. You said you were an independent… something. Shouldn't I be paying you for your time?"

Andrew laughed. "I'm an independent Accredited Retirement Financial Planner. I'm exceptionally proud of that title. And I'm proud of the work I've done for you. But you don't have to worry about me. I got into the stock market back when things were really tough. I had a good feeling about where the economy was going, I was right, and I made a lot of money. If you want the truth, what I'm doing now is my way of giving back."

"So, you're doing all this for free? That isn't right."

Andrew laughed again. "No, I don't do it for free. There are government programs to help people like you, and people like me can get a stipend to provide you with unbiased information. But I'm certainly not starving, and what I can tell you is I've never had more professional satisfaction than I'm having now, including being with you today."

He ended with a broad smile and kept glancing over to see how Eleanor was reacting. After two or three seconds, he was rewarded with a peaceful smile and dreamy look on her part. She had swallowed it all. She was the smartest girl in the world because she had chosen just the right moment to place her financial affairs in the hands of the one person who could navigate the murky waters of high finance.

This is shooting fish in a barrel, Andrew thought. *You're picking their pocket and they're thanking you for it.*

* * * * *

Eleanor saw the look of smug, self-satisfaction on Andrew's face. She had seen such a look a few times in her life. Most recently it had been on the face of another con artist, but one moonlighting as an accountant and financial advisor. Was he unemployed now? Probably not. For bottom-feeders who preyed on the elderly, there was no dearth of opportunity. She could not remember his name, but he might even be peddling reverse mortgages right now.

His patter was smooth and well-rehearsed. There was careful phrasing in everything he said. Yes, he was an 'independent Accredited Retirement Financial Planner'. It was a title with absolutely no meaning. He could have filled out a one-page multiple-choice test on the Internet, paid a hundred dollars, and been sent a certificate. Or, he could have invented his own certification and skipped paying anyone anything.

Was he in the stock market at its bottom? The implication was he was a professional investor, but he could have held a single share of AT&T and the statement would be literally true. More likely he was working in a boiler room somewhere, peddling worthless stocks to gullible seniors.

And are there government programs to help guide people through the reverse mortgage process? Almost certainly. Except he didn't say he was part of such a program; only it existed. Slick.

And the information about changing rules for reverse mortgages? Maybe true, maybe something gleaned from a headline months ago. But it made no difference. The reverse mortgage being pushed by Senior Equity was part of no officially sanctioned government program. It was all simply part of an 'act now before it's too late' strategy.

She would have liked to catch him in an impossible-to-slip-through lie, but maintaining her aura of complete gullibility was more important. Any pointed question on her part might begin to raise questions.

They were both actors in this automobile, driving to play out yet another scene of an unfolding drama. Each of them knew he or she was an actor and had rehearsed his or her part. The wonderful thing about this drama – and it was what brought that peaceful smile to her face – was that only *one* of the two people in the car realized *both* of them were actors.

And then they were pulling into the parking lot at One Broadmoor Hill. The lot and adjacent garage would easily accommodate two hundred cars, yet there were just a handful of vehicles, all clustered by the main entrance. Eleanor spotted Paula's distinctive red Tesla. It was comforting to know she had friends and allies in the building.

Rebecca Cooper said she had been told Senior Equity occupied the entire building. How could she have fallen for such an obvious fabrication when the parking lot offered such obvious proof otherwise? Was it old age, or just the willingness to trust in the words of someone who claimed to be your friend?

They were parked. Andrew rushed around the car to open her door, smiling as he beckoned her outward.

"The start of an adventure," he said. "I'm pleased to be along for this part of it."

He's trying to make it all seem like fun, Eleanor thought. *What a stupid thing to do.*

"This is not an adventure," Eleanor said. "This is a decision I must make if I am to have any chance to stay alive."

She saw Andrew start to say something, then think better of it.

Because the building had been designed as a corporate headquarters, there was no expansive lobby or other public area; this was a utilitarian structure. Two banks of facing elevators were within twenty feet of the main entrance, with a pair of darkened glass doors beyond the elevators.

They rode to the third floor in silence, Andrew still apparently stung by her comment. At the third-floor landing, Andrew said simply, "Turn right here."

Eleanor saw the placard for 'Provençal Home Décor of New England' and smiled inwardly. It must have annoyed everyone at Senior Equity to have it so visibly demonstrated not only was this not Senior Equity's building, but they even shared the floor.

As they walked by Paula's 'headquarters', Eleanor saw Alice and Jean placing linens into boxes. Both glanced up quickly, then went back to their work.

"I'm going to let Chad know you're here," Andrew said. "We're right on time so it should be just a minute or two. I'll ask you to stay in the waiting area where you'll be comfortable."

Two glass doors opened onto a reception area with light grey walls and dark grey carpeting. Polished aluminum letters illuminated by pin spots proudly proclaimed this was the home of Senior Equity Lending Services. There was no receptionist at the dark wood desk beneath the sign.

The area could have seated eight visitors around two groupings consisting of a small sofa and two large, boxy chairs. Eleanor was surprised to see one of the sofas was occupied by a woman in her late twenties. She was attired in a skirted suit, a good leather purse at her side and a briefcase at her feet. She looked up when the glass doors opened, then back down at a tablet computer.

"This shouldn't take more than a few minutes," Andrew said.

Eleanor saw the look of disappointment on the woman's face. When Andrew had disappeared around the corner, the woman said, "You must be Chad's three o'clock appointment." She sighed.

"I guess I must be," Eleanor said. Because the woman had started a conversation, Eleanor felt bound to sit in one of the chairs across from the sofa.

"I know I should have made an appointment," the woman said, chastising herself. "But I owe Chad an update and I wanted to do it in person."

"What kind of an update?" Eleanor asked.

"On my Mom," the woman said, and a smile broke out across her face. "I just heard from her this morning. She's been told she's going to make a full recovery."

"Recovery?" Eleanor said, leaning forward. "What kind of recovery?"

The woman looked left and right, as though she was leery of being overheard. Eleanor began to notice things about her. Shiny, shoulder-length dark brown hair cut quite well and also recently. Gold hoop earrings. A thin gold chain around her neck, from which dangled a cross. A minimum of makeup and pale pink lipstick. She was every woman's successful daughter.

"Ovarian cancer," she said in a low voice. She shook her head.

"Six months ago, Mom was calling us kids together, asking who wanted what from the house. It was so sad, but Mom was brave about it." The woman took a tissue from her purse and dabbed at her eyes.

"How old is your mother?" Eleanor asked.

"Sixty-three next week," the woman said. "She was diagnosed two years ago. She went to all the best specialists in Boston, but there came a day when they said, 'Mrs. Malone, we've bought you all the time we can'."

The woman dabbed again at her eyes and sniffled. "My Mom is a fighter. She went through all the chemo rounds. She lost her hair twice. But she also did her own research. She found out about ONX-0801 and the clinical trial in Britain. She brought it to her doctors' attention at Dana Farber. They all said it was too early – Phase One stuff; the kind of thing too many times looks promising but then either has terrible side effects or stops working. They said it was unorthodox. Mom went to her insurance company. They said they wouldn't pay for it even if Mom could talk her way into a trial. 'Too small a chance of success', they said."

"She flew to England. Went straight to the Institute for Cancer Research. They told her about a private group doing their own clinical trials with ONX-0801. She went to them and said, 'I don't care what it costs, I want in.' They looked at her charts. They said, 'OK, but it's an infusion every two weeks for three months with daily monitoring'."

"And now, she had to find a way to pay for it," Eleanor said, nodding. "What did your father say?"

The woman shook her head. "Dad died while I was in college. Mom had the house and his insurance but not much else. We – my older brother and I – offered to pay as much as we could. She said she wouldn't hear of it. She thought she could get a line of credit from her bank based on her home equity. *Pfft*. No income, no loan. She went to a real estate agent – a woman she had known all her adult life. Her friend told her the truth: everyone would know it was an emergency sale and she would get hosed. And it would still take six months before she closed. So she went the reverse mortgage route. Four companies, four salesmen without an ounce of compassion between them explaining she was barely over the age limit to get one, they couldn't give her as much as she needed, and it would take two months to close."

"Then she came here," Eleanor said.

"Chad listened," the woman said, nodding. "He bent the rules. That was four months ago. Mom got the treatments. Her tumors responded. She stayed an extra month for follow-up care. Chad advanced the money. Yesterday, Mom called with her doctor on the line with her. The tumors aren't gone, but they're 'under control'. She's flying home this weekend."

Tears were flowing down the woman's cheeks.

"I want to tell Chad personally. He deserves…" The woman stopped talking and looked up.

Eleanor heard Andrew clearing his throat.

Speaking to the woman, Andrew said, "Chad asked if you can wait until after his last two appointments. If not, he can see you at eight o'clock tomorrow morning."

The woman looked at her tablet. She was still crying. "I guess this will have to keep overnight. But I'll be here at eight sharp." She placed the tablet in her briefcase, gathered her purse, and rose to leave.

Eleanor interjected, "That is ridiculous."

Andrew and the woman both froze. They stared at Eleanor.

"This woman has been waiting to speak with Mr. Pannett. What's a few minutes of my time compared with the news she wants to share?"

The two looked at one another. Andrew said, "But Eleanor, your appointment is for three, which is right now."

"And when I have a doctor's appointment for noon, I can

know with absolute certainty I won't be seen by the doctor at that exact time," Eleanor countered. "If someone calls in with an emergency, they're going to be squeezed in. We have to be flexible because one of these days, it's us who need to see the doctor right away. This young lady has a story to tell, and if it means I'm here an extra fifteen minutes, then so be it."

Andrew's mouth was open, ready to speak. Eleanor saw the woman give him an almost imperceptible shake of her head.

"Eleanor, that's quite generous of you," she said. She turned to Andrew and said, "Andrew, could I see Chad now? I'll be just a few minutes." Her voice had just the right pleading note, Eleanor thought.

"Well, it's not policy, but…" Andrew was cut off by the woman grabbing his arm.

A moment later, the pair had disappeared around the corner and Eleanor could barely suppress her laughter. *What a farce*, she thought. *I'm left alone with a woman who just happens to have a mother with a life-threatening medical condition similar to the one I'm supposed to have. And she just happened to pop in this afternoon with wonderful news she wants to share with the man I'm supposed to see. As soon as she told me her story, she was supposed to disappear, stage right. Except I disrupted the story line.*

Now, the three of them are in there, together, trying to figure out how long it should take for this woman to share her wonderful news. And they'll have to invent a reason why Andrew went in with her. Oh, and why she knew his name was 'Andrew'.

I played my part straight. I listened attentively to every word. I asked the right questions. I never showed any hint of doubt. So, now they're figuring out how to incorporate her story into the next act of the play.

Ten minutes later, Andrew and the woman reappeared. She thanked him effusively and then she thanked Eleanor. Eleanor concluded she was a gifted improvisational actress, thrown in with a second-rate bit player.

Eleanor also noticed she wasn't in her late twenties as she

implied. If "Mom" was sixty-two, having a daughter within a year or two of thirty made perfect sense. The woman's youthful makeup was skillfully applied. Her dress was that of a young professional. Her hair retained that youthful sheen. But her neck and her hands belonged to someone at least ten years older, which coupled with her having referenced an 'older brother', meant "Mom" had given birth in her late teens or around twenty.

"I never got your name," Eleanor said.

"Oh, I'm sorry. "Ashley. Ashley Moore." The woman smiled and proffered her hand, which Eleanor took with both her own.

"That was an inspiring story, Ashley," Eleanor said, exuding warmth. "It meant a great deal to me."

'Ashley' returned Eleanor's smile. "And you were so generous."

A minute later, Andrew and Eleanor were in Chad's office. Like the reception area it, too, was decorated in grey on grey tones, with a large desk at its center. Eleanor's first task was to memorize the office. Were there filing cabinets? Closets? She made the necessary mental notes.

"Eleanor," Andrew said, "this is where I leave you for now. I want to introduce you to Chad Pannett, the founder and President of Senior Equity. I'll take you home when you've finished your talk."

Chad rose from his desk and came around to greet Eleanor. He offered his hand and then gestured toward a large sofa along one wall. "I think we can dispense with the formalities of you sitting on one side of a desk and me on the other," Chad said. To Andrew, he said, "I'll call you when we're done." Andrew promptly and discreetly left the room.

When they were seated, Chad asked, "May I call you 'Eleanor' or do you prefer 'Mrs. Strong'?"

"Eleanor will be fine."

"Then I wish you'd call me 'Chad'. He sank back into the sofa, one arm across its back. "Andrew told me about your, well, plans. I must say you are the healthiest looking cancer survivor I know."

"I haven't survived it," Eleanor said. "That's just the point. And pancreatic cancer is called the 'invisible' cancer for good reason. People get to Stage Four and all they have is some lower back pain. Three months later, they're dead. I'm trying to avoid being part of that statistic."

"And there is no treatment in the U.S.?" Chad asked.

"There are different forms of pancreatic cancer," Eleanor replied. "There's a relatively benign form for which there's a 'cocktail' of drugs that keeps it under control. Mine, unfortunately, is not that kind. The more aggressive cancers also come in several variations. I have a complication called 'HA-HIGH' which makes the newer treatments ineffective. There is a new drug to work around being HA-HIGH currently in trial. To get into the trial in the U.S., you enter a lottery. I entered. I was told to try again in three months. I went looking elsewhere and found a clinic in Switzerland running private trials that conform to the highest European standards. I can buy my way in. With your help, I will do so."

Chad seemed taken aback at her cool logic. Eleanor suspected he had been primed for something more emotional.

"But if this works, you'll be cured," Chad said.

Eleanor shook her head. "It means I won't be dead in three months. It says nothing about six months or a year, let alone five years. I'm buying time, hoping science catches up to my cancer."

"You sound remarkably…" Chad searched for the right word. "…resigned to all of this."

Eleanor shook her head. "No, I am not resigned. I am realistic. Mr. Pannett, I buried my husband this year. I loved him with all my heart, but love was not enough to overcome the horrible disease that took his mind without taking his body first. I had time to say 'goodbye' and to mourn his loss. I have looked at death. I do not fear it, but I'm not ready to die. I have friends, I have causes. I enjoy living."

Chad was silent, his mind absorbing Eleanor's words.

"Andrew said you were at one of our seminars earlier this week," he said after several moments.

"Betsy Metcalf gave an inspiring talk," Eleanor said. "I liked her."

"But you also heard Clarice Lindstrom?"

"The thin blonde in the red suit?" Eleanor replied. "She lost me after about a minute. I didn't understand anything she said and so I just stopped listening."

"But you also received the packet of materials," Chad said, a look of concern on his face.

"Which I did not read and have no intention of reading," Eleanor said emphatically. "I understand the basic proposition. You will give me a percentage of the value of my home. If what Andrew says is true, that amount will be enough for me to get treatment in Lausanne and still have some money to live on while I see what the future brings. I have no children. If I did not do this, when I died my estate would be inherited by a sister I haven't seen in more than a decade, and who didn't even bother to come to my husband's funeral."

"Wow," Chad said. "Andrew didn't say anything about your being so blunt."

"Andrew is a nice young man and a salesman," Eleanor said. "I treated him the way nice young men expect to be treated by older ladies. You, on the other hand, are a businessman and I am treating you accordingly. I expect a fair valuation for my home. I expect your fees to be reasonable. And I expect you to understand that, for me, every day we dawdle is a day that decreases my chance of being alive at the end of my treatment. That isn't being blunt; that is being honest."

"Speed is of the essence," Chad said.

Eleanor nodded. "I would gladly close this afternoon."

"I will see just how quickly I can move this along," Chad replied.

* * * * *

An hour late, Samantha and Eleanor listened to the recordings made that afternoon.

"You are one amazing operative," Samantha said, shaking her head. "You have the head of a company freely acknowledging you told him you haven't read the materials and don't intend to read them. Yet he is going to put paperwork in front of you saying you did, knowing full well you are making a fraudulent statement. This kind of blunder sends people to prison."

"Can you use this in court?" Eleanor asked.

"Yes and no," Samantha replied. "Under Massachusetts law, recordings made without both parties' consent are ordinarily inadmissible unless there is a court-approved exception such as a wiretap. And, if a law enforcement agency had asked or encouraged you to make a recording like this, it would never see the light of day. But there's an exception: if a private citizen uncovers an illegal act and takes that evidence to a law enforcement agency, it may be used as the basis for further action, such as a wiretap."

"You've done this on your own," Samantha continued. "You're not an officer of the court and neither am I. I can take this to the Attorney General's office and play it for them. Senior Equity has always had this 'I dare you to try to prove anything' attitude. This might change the equation."

"Our primary goal still ought to be to track down 'Margaret'," Samantha said. "She's the weak link in all this."

"Are you certain we haven't?" Eleanor asked.

"What do you mean?" Samantha replied.

"This afternoon, I saw a woman who is at least 40 playing the role of someone in her late twenties. If, with makeup and wigs and acting skills, someone can look ten or fifteen years younger, would it be too much of a stretch for that person to play someone in her sixties? If I recall correctly, Rebecca said 'Margaret' somehow seemed younger than the age she claimed to be."

"An actress playing multiple roles," Samantha said, starting to think aloud. "I assumed Pannett has a stable of cohorts ready to push his clients into doing something that would allow Senior Equity to call the mortgage. 'Ashley Moore' and 'Margaret' could potentially be the same person. She'd probably be working for a percentage of the profit they make on every house."

Samantha cocked her head, considering possibilities. After a moment she said, "Eleanor, you're a genius."

* * * * *

As Samantha and Eleanor were having their debriefing of Eleanor's meetings at Senior Equity, Alice, Paula and Jean were hastily packing boxes and creating mailing labels. The three women were sweating profusely despite having turned the air conditioning to 'Max Cool'.

"Does anyone have anything from Tissus Toselli?" Alice asked plaintively. "I'm short two Lavender Bouquet Yellow napkins on a $500 order."

Paula grabbed a printout. "I saw those," she said. Turning pages, she found what she was looking for and stabbed the page in the air with her finger. "Alicia McFadden in Albuquerque. Just six…" Paula sighed. "False alarm. It's Tissus Toselli, but it's Ramatuelle Yellow and Blue. Sorry."

The sorting and boxing had been going on for three hours. Yesterday, the outgoing packages had all been fabrications; counterfeit linens in boxes addressed to Paula's Christmas card list. The boxes sat in full view for Chad to see as he walked by at the of the day, then were brought back to be recycled. Today, though, more than sixty genuine orders were in various stages of completion.

The problem was each of the sixty orders would go out at a loss. The linens had been purchased from other retailers at full price, plus tax and overnight shipping charges. Paula's back-of-the-envelope calculation was every hundred dollars of merchandise she shipped was costing her twenty dollars.

At 3:30, they had watched as Eleanor and one of Senior Equity's 'vultures' (as they started calling the young men who accompanied would-be clients) pass by on their way to a meeting with Chad. Ten minutes later, the young woman who had stopped in during the morning walked by. However, Alice did not notice the woman until she was almost to the turn for the elevator. It would seem odd to chase after her, so the three accepted it was an opportunity lost and vowed to be on the lookout for her tomorrow.

Then, a few minutes after five, there was a commotion from the direction of the elevator; voices, all feminine, and many of them laughing. The three women looked up and at one another, the same puzzled look on each of their faces.

A moment later, a group of eight woman appeared in the hallway. At their center was Leslie Mullen.

"These are the pioneers," Leslie said proudly to her group as they reached the glass office doors. "Provençal Home Décor of New England, owned and operated by Paula Winters. Last week, she and her employees were working out of Paula's home, literally sorting napkins on the dining room table. This week, they became the first tenants of the Women's Empowerment Zone. By the end of the year, they'll likely have graduated to a facility with its own warehouse space. But this will be their spiritual home, because they'll be surrounded by like-minded entrepreneurs."

As Leslie beamed, Paula felt her anger rise. Leslie had barged in, unannounced. She had picked the worst possible time to be here. She and Alice and Jean were exhausted, yet they had another hour's worth of work to do before incurring yet another cost for a 'late pickup' from UPS.

Paula was on the verge of yelling, *'Get the hell out of here!'* when, out of the corner of her eye, she saw Chad. The crowd of women had not noticed him and he stood behind them, trying to stay out of their sight line. He was carrying a briefcase, so it was apparently the end of his business day. He must have wondered why eight women were gathered at the entrance to the building's only other business, so he thought he would stop and listen.

Instead, Paula smiled and said, "Ladies, welcome to my dream, which was born of a nightmare. Four years ago, my husband decided to trade me in on a younger model. His timing was perfect: the kids were out of college and his career was flying high. She was 26 with an MBA from Wharton. He was 52 and ready for a trophy to demonstrate what a successful guy he was."

"The only good news was I had a smart lawyer. I couldn't stop him from walking out. I couldn't stop him from re-marrying. But I could squeeze him for half our assets. And he had just enough guilt to not try hiding those assets – plus he was in a hurry to start his new life. So, six months after he came home and broke the news I was past my expiration date, I had a nest egg large enough I didn't have to worry about property taxes or the cost of gasoline."

"What I didn't have was something fulfilling to do with my time. I had given up a career in nursing almost before it began in order to raise two children and run a household. I had good taste, but then so do a lot of people. And then one day I was in a store on Newbury Street looking at place mats and napkins. A woman in her early twenties – my daughter's age – came over and asked if she could help me. I asked about the provenance of a particular napkin's design."

"The woman looked at me strangely and explained the napkins were from Provence, not 'Provenance'. And that was when I realized I undoubtedly knew more about French fabrics than anyone in that store. All those trips to France turned out to have been tax-deductible. Who knew?"

There were smiles of appreciation from the assembled women.

Paula continued. "It took a year. It took a year to build up my courage. It took a year to teach myself what I would need to do to go into business. And it took money. I needed inventory, I needed a staff even when they weren't fully occupied. I needed a website because I had a feeling I could do a lot more business online than I'd ever get at a shop of Newbury Street – which, by the way, is now a tea shop."

"I outgrew my kitchen table six months ago, but it took Leslie to show me I could turn some corporation's bad planning into an asset for me: high quality space for a fraction of the going rate. What she promised me, though, was neighbors. She promised me there would be other women-owned businesses here. She said she would fill the building with them. We could learn from one another and not have to worry about being laughed at for asking questions. She talked about a gym and a coffee shop run by and catering to women. She waxed enthusiastic about bringing in business consultants."

"I have just one question for Ms. Mullen. I've been here four whole days. When am I going to get some company?"

The crowd burst into a combination of laughter and applause. Most important, she saw Chad grin before turning to head for the elevator.

The talk was mostly spontaneous. But Paula realized she had been thinking about what she would say to the NPR reporter in the morning. From the reporter's comments this morning, Paula had a reasonably good outline of what Leslie had said to the women's club. Now, Paula was parroting it back, but giving Leslie credit for having steered Paula to the building rather than the other way around.

The group of women was now inside the showroom, handling samples. Alice and Jean slapped the hands of three women who tried to unpack partially filled boxes to see what was inside.

A half an hour later, Alice, Jean and Paula had their workroom to themselves. Paula asked the two women to stay for a few minutes. She disappeared into her office and came back with a bottle of Champagne and three plastic glasses. She opened the bottle and poured. They had finished packing the last of the order they could fill. That was the good news. The bad news was they were effectively out of inventory and Paula had made the 'executive decision' not to order another cache of inventory from other websites.

"It would raise red flags," Paula explained. "The last thing we want is for anyone to know we've been in business for just a few days. So, tomorrow, we pack dummy products like we did that first day."

"You know we received more than a hundred orders today," Alice said.

Paula nodded. "And I had an email from France saying the container will be loaded at Marseilles tomorrow morning. I've also hired a customs broker. There is a slim chance we can have real product early next week."

"We also had more than a thousand hits on the website today," Alice reported.

"Then we should thank our lucky stars they were just looking and not ordering," Paula said with a smile. "Remember, though, we're here to snoop. Chad locks his office at night. Does he lock it if he goes out to lunch? We need to find out. Eleanor should have memorized the office layout. She should already have met with Samantha and relayed that information and I'll speak with Samantha this evening. Tomorrow, we make certain we get a photo of the woman who was in with Chad today. Oh, and NPR is coming to interview us."

She poured everyone a second glass of Champagne.

"I am weary down to my bones right now," Paula said. "But I feel we're on the right track. There's a group of people next door doing horrible things. They're telling elderly people – mostly women – they can give them money for their homes while still allowing them to live in those homes for the rest of their lives. Except as soon as these people can, they do their best to steal the house out from under those elderly people. Rebecca Cooper is just one example."

"You heard Samantha say the Attorney General can't prove anything because Chad and his crew hide their methods so well. Today, Eleanor placed herself in harm's way by going in for that interview, and it's up to us to watch her back. I think we passed Chad's final 'sniff test' and, from here on in, he's going to see us as a bunch of old ladies with some stupid decoration business."

* * * * *

Martin was still at his desk long after his shift ended. As the Town of Brookfield's lone detective, he was fairly well left alone to set his own direction. And, because Brookfield was a town with a low crime rate, there was seldom an urgent need for his services. And, because everyone in the Department knew – completely unofficially but with complete certainty – that Martin had helped the state police catch a serial killer in a nursing home, he was accorded the kind of respectful distance good detectives were deemed to need.

In truth, Martin had spent almost all day researching the subject of reverse mortgages and Senior Equity. While he could hardly be considered an expert on the subject after ten hours, he knew enough to know the industry was littered with bad actors, and no one should enter into one without considerable planning and expert guidance.

He had two calls to make. The first was to the branch manager of a bank in Brookfield. The manager and Martin were on cordial terms; a product of Martin having caught the bored teenagers who had bashed her mailbox three months earlier. The four boys had made the mistake of tying a rope to one box containing mail and dragging it and the attached post a distance of a quarter mile, thus entering the rarefied air of committing the federal crime of mail theft. It had taken just two days of listening for hallway boasting to identify the culprits who, upon being told their alternative was to negotiate with federal marshals, apologized and installed new mailboxes.

"Michelle, why doesn't your bank offer reverse mortgages?"

Michelle Ramos, recognizing the voice and not used to having people ask negative questions, laughed. "Because they're a lose-lose proposition. And hello to you, too, Detective Hoffman."

"Humor me," Martin said. "Walk me through the rationale."

Michelle paused for a moment. "OK, first, the mortgages are just barely profitable. And, second, they're a PR nightmare if something goes wrong. It isn't just our bank that made that realization. I don't think there are five commercial banks in the state willing to wade into the product."

"Explain the 'PR nightmare'," Martin asked.

"We issue a reverse mortgage to Mrs. McGillicutty," Michelle said. "Mrs. McGillicutty gets $723 a month from us. After a year, Mrs. McGillicutty stops paying her property taxes. The town calls us to ask what's going on. We call Mrs. McGillicutty. We also call her son and daughter, one of whom lives in Florida and the other who lives at home but is usually high. Oh, and the grass around Mrs. McGillicutty's house is getting to be a foot high. What can we do? Let's see, we can start deducting the property taxes from the amount we're sending Mrs. McGillicutty. And we can send around a lawn service and deduct that, too. Or, we can call the loan."

"Whatever we do, the PR nightmare begins," Michelle continued. Because now the son and the daughter are out in front of the house saying the mean bank is withholding Mom's money or, worse, wants to put her out on the street. The *Globe* sends out its most compassionate reporter. Channel 4 sends out a camera crew. Neighbors with iPhones put the whole thing on YouTube. And everyone shows up here demanding to know why we're so heartless."

"I get the idea," Martin said. "Is there some halfway point?"

"It's called selling the house and getting an apartment," Michelle said. "These people are sitting on gold mines. They can cash out tax free, but they're convinced they'll run out of money and they'll never see their friends again. Or, the kids agree to help out Mom and Dad. Fat chance of that."

Martin laughed. "You've been extraordinarily helpful."

"Is this a general police kind of query, or are you investigating something?" Michelle asked.

Martin replied cautiously. "What makes you ask that?"

"I'm working with a family here in town," Michelle said. "Long-time bank customers. A lady took out a lump sum to defray her grandkid's tuition. That was a year and a half ago. Then, she met this other lady who convinced her property insurance is the lender's responsibility. After it lapsed, the lender foreclosed with the court's blessing. The lender wants astronomical fees on top of repayment, and her kids are beside themselves with guilt, because the money's gone. It all went for tuition. She told them it was an annuity she cashed in. It's an unholy mess and I don't think we can save the house."

"Is the lender an outfit called 'Senior Equity...'" Martin started to say.

"Senior Equity Lending Services," Michelle said. "How did you know?"

"I know of another family that has a problem with the same lender," Martin said. "I said I'd make some calls."

"Well, these guys are piranhas," Michelle said. "It's all by the book, but it stinks."

"Could you give me the name of your customer?" Martin asked.

There was a pause. "This gets into client confidentiality," Michelle said. "I'll raise it with her kids, but their feelings are kind of raw right now."

Martin pondered the call for a few minutes. The circumstances were so similar to what Paula had told him a coincidence was out of the question. Senior Equity was an outfit preying on the elderly.

His second call was to the same Massachusetts State Police investigator to whom he had entrusted the email trail from Cavendish Woods. The investigator's quick action resulted in the arrest of a serial killer and no small amount of fame for everyone involved in making the arrest.

"I need some advice," Martin said. "This is white-collar crime territory. I've got two instances of a private lender running a scam built around reverse mortgages. They're encouraging borrowers to do things that cause their loans to be in default." Martin was surprised by how much of the industry language he had absorbed in a few hours of work.

"This sounds like a call to Maura Healey," his contact said. "The Attorney General looks at things like that, not the State Police."

"As I understand it, her office has inquired, but never found anything concrete," Martin said. "Their paperwork is always in order. Their outer defenses are tight. It's just that the results are always the same. I'm looking for their soft underbelly."

"Soft underbelly," his contact repeated. "It's usually someone who knows they're breaking the law, isn't getting paid the big bucks, and who knows he or she will be the fall guy if everything goes south. Lawyers and accountants are the places to start."

"That's great advice," Martin said. "I think I'll take it."

"Can we help?" his contact said.

"When the time comes," Martin replied.

Martin re-dialed Michelle. "Please say it's not part of client confidentiality to divulge the name of the attorney or law firm handing the mortgage lien for Senior Equity."

He heard the sound of shuffling paper. "Not a problem," Michelle said. "It's The Walpole Law Group. The attorney is Ryan Herndon."

"And do you have the paperwork for the firm that initiated the mortgage?" Martin asked.

"I'm a step ahead of you," Michelle replied. "Same firm. Same guy. So, do I at least get to ask why it's so important?"

"Call it the search for the soft underbelly."

Martin quickly Googled 'The Walpole Law Group' and found its address. He plugged the address into Streetview.

"Bingo," he said to himself.

Chapter Twelve

Ryan Herndon graduated from Western New England Law School with modest expectations. He never aspired to join the ranks of one of the national law firms; he knew they drew their associates strictly from the top-ranked schools. Nor was he expecting an offer from a major corporation. They did not make recruiting trips to Springfield and he assumed his résumé would end up in some electronic waste basket.

Ryan's goal was to work for the government. He saw episodes of JAG as a kid and the idea of appearing in court in a terrific uniform while working with Catherine Bell was glamor of the highest order. However, the armed services didn't want green lawyers fresh out of school. Neither did any of the New England states. Their rosters were already filled with men and women who considered civil service to be a lifetime sinecure and were in no hurry to leave their cushy berths.

Which pretty much left the cesspool of private practice.

Ryan was smart, and his education had been sound. He passed the Massachusetts and Connecticut bar exams on his first try. It was just that he had gone to a third-tier school at a time when lawyers were quickly becoming a glut on the market.

And so he wisely returned to his hometown of Walpole, Massachusetts, a suburb of Boston known principally as the home of two state prisons. Faced with student loans gathering interest at an alarming rate, he cobbled together a living doing whatever legal work he could find, most notably real estate closings.

Along the way he gathered two partners – graduates of other unknown or unappreciated law schools – and formed 'The Walpole Law Group'. They rented an old frame house and the three attorneys hustled business wherever it was to be found.

Then, at age 27, Ryan Herndon's life changed in the blink of an eye. A well-dressed man opened the front door of the frame house. As there was no receptionist, he was inside the building for five minutes before anyone noticed him. He said his name was Chad Pannett, and he was starting a mortgage company.

He asked if anyone knew of some exceptionally smart and ravenously hungry lawyers.

Chad's pitch was simplicity itself. His new firm expected to write a lot of reverse mortgages. He needed a detail-oriented firm capable of delivering quickly. He would pay $300 for complete, letter-perfect 'doc set' and another $300 for filing with all state and federal agencies and for notary services. The selected firm would need to be able to guarantee speed and accuracy. The first time the firm failed to deliver, they would be history.

Chad would be The Walpole Law Group's salvation. Closing document sets – 'doc sets' – were downloadable from the internet for about $25. A laptop computer's global search and replace allowed multiple copies of a completed package of as many as 50 individual documents to be created in under an hour. Filing fees for mortgages with the Registry of Deeds was $175, which left $125 to cover travel and overhead.

If Chad's company originated five mortgages a day, that was $3,000 of income against maybe a thousand dollars of out-of-pocket expense. Each week would bring $10,000 of gross profits. It would not only pay the rent and keep the lights on, it would allow them to pay... salaries.

From the beginning, Chad routinely expected extra services without paying extra fees. The first surprise was all closings took place one day a week at Senior Equity's offices rather than, as tradition dictated, at the law firm's offices. This meant travel time and the loss of one day a week for all three attorneys. Granted, Senior Equity's offices were more attractive, but the deal effectively meant the attorneys were billing their time at about $50 at hour.

The second surprise was Chad paid them in cash. He never explained his rationale for doing so, and depositing the funds was an annoyance. Still, prudence dictated you did not tell your primary benefactor you were miffed with his way of paying you.

The third, and largest, surprise was after a few months of doing business normally, Senior Equity began consistently low-balling appraisals and adding questionable fees to its mortgage originations. Either because Ryan was inexperienced in such matters or chose to believe this was how all mortgage companies operated, he chose to keep quiet about what he saw.

While The Walpole Law Group did not exactly prosper, it did reasonably well. The frame building was acquired by the Group and its exterior was re-done to be pleasing to those who drove by. A receptionist/admin was hired to free the attorneys to be more productive. In the second year of association with Senior Equity, each partner took home $60,000.

Fourteen months after Chad first walked in the door, Ryan was asked to stay after the last closing.

"I'm afraid we've had our first default," Chad explained, sadness in his voice. He related the circumstances: an elderly woman had inexplicably added her daughter to her home's deed in direct contravention of the mortgage's term. "I'd like your firm to handle the legal notifications, filings and any court appearances."

The agreed-upon fee would be a flat $2,000, paid in cash. The paperwork was not as cut-and-dried, but it took just ten hours of Ryan's time and expenses were nominal.

Two weeks later, Chad said a second mortgage needed to be called. The homeowner had moved to Ft. Myers, violating the 'primary residence' clause of her loan. Within a month, The Walpole Law Group was filing as many as ten 'called mortgage' actions each week.

There was now considerably more court time as judges mulled objections. Chad, though, was adamant the agreement was for

$2,000 per foreclosure action.

By the end of the second year, Ryan and his partners fully understood they were part of a scam. And, not just part of it; theirs were the signatures and stamps lending a veneer of legality to the enterprise. They notarized every document and filed every mortgage. They attested every reverse mortgage applicant had read and understood the myriad documents placed in front of them. Then, in sometimes as little as six months, they again attested mortgagees had willfully violated the terms of a binding contract.

The worst part was, at the end of the third year, the firm's billings were at an all-time high, yet their take-home pay had not budged. Senior Equity consumed all of the firm's time; they had no ability to pursue other, more profitable clients. And, the $2,000 they were paid for each foreclosed mortgage was frequently insufficient to cover all filing fees and court costs. Admins seldom stayed more than a month because their primary responsibility was to take calls from Senior Equity customers who either screamed profanities or cried incessantly.

Six months earlier, Ryan had taken his dilemma to Chad. "You're killing us," Ryan said. "We need to agree on an amount allowing us to make a living."

"I'm not unsympathetic," Chad said. "But try to see it from my point of view. If I say, 'OK, I'll pay you $500 over and above court fees and expenses', you have no incentive to be efficient. You'll let cases drag on and I'll watch my legal budget spiral out of control. If I say, 'OK, I'll bump up your fixed fee $2500', you'll be back here in six months saying you need three thousand."

Chad leaned back in his chair. "I need for The Walpole Law Group to be as invested in this as I am. These people made a legal commitment, and I gave them a big chunk of cash. Then, they took it into their heads they no longer needed to pay homeowners' insurance, or they decided Florida was a great place to live twelve months of the year. They willingly violated the terms of their loan.

They took my money and, now, after they spent my money, they act surprised I want them to pay it back."

Ryan countered, "If we go back eighteen months, two-thirds of the mortgages we issued either have been foreclosed or are in litigation. That's so far outside the law of probabilities as to be impossible to justify."

Chad smiled and placed his hands behind his head, rocking in his chair. "Yet, every single one of those mortgages includes paperwork from you or your partners attesting – swearing, if you will – that these people knew exactly what they were getting into. If you're insinuating fraud, you and your partners' fingerprints are everywhere. It could be argued the three of you perpetuated that fraud. You get paid regardless of what happens. I, on the other hand, can lose everything if I can't unload a house."

"Then why do I keep getting paid in cash?" Ryan asked.

Chad stopped smiling. "With cash, you get to decide how much income you declare." He shrugged. "And it was your idea."

"It was never my idea," Ryan said, raising his voice.

Chad shrugged again. "That's not the way I remember it. And that's not the way I memorialized it in my memorandum to my partners."

Ryan was speechless. He was being set up. Finally, he asked, "How much longer will this go on?"

Chad looked up at the overhead light in his office, as though pondering the question. "Not too much longer. When I lose interest, certainly. Also, if things get complicated." He nodded. "That's when it ends."

"Complicated?" Ryan asked, incredulous. "Complicated how?"

Chad sighed. "You keep doing your job. Keep doing it exceptionally well and keep looking for ways to save money. The law can make you wealthy."

Then Chad rose from his chair, an indication the meeting was over. His last words were, "Disbarment, on the other hand, would be a lifelong handicap from which you would likely never recover."

* * * * *

Samantha Ayers ate another slice of reheated pizza as she reviewed her notes. She lived in a 'good' apartment – meaning one her parents approved of – and she was surrounded by comfortable furnishings of her own choosing. Though she had not stayed in law enforcement as her father and grandfather had hoped, she had a well-paying job and was living independently while a noticeable percentage of her high school friends were still ensconced in their childhood bedrooms.

There was no steady man in her life. Samantha was attractive, but she was also too tall, too thin, and too smart; and she had yet to meet a man who was looking for that combination in a woman. And especially a woman who was a Police Academy graduate. Samantha refused to stoop to Tinder, and her few forays to bars told her they were unlikely venues to meet someone interested in a long-term relationship.

Instead, she threw herself into her work. Mass Casualty considered her an amazing asset. She resolved even the most complex investigations, and almost always to the insurance company's advantage. Her bonuses far eclipsed her salary, and two of those bonuses had been handed to her by Mass Casualty's Chairman at all-employee meetings.

It was her work with the Garden Club Gang, though, that gave Samantha her greatest sense of accomplishment. Being assigned to investigate the Brookfield Fair heist had been the luckiest day of her life because it brought her into contact with Alice, Paula, Jean, and Eleanor. Because of them, Samantha now had credibility at the state Attorney General's office. When and if she was able to document what was going on inside Senior Equity, she would have a ready audience.

While she was not yet close to that point, Samantha knew

without reservation Chad Pannett was running a heartless scam that had cost hundreds of innocent people their homes. Eleanor's meeting this afternoon had provided the first hard evidence Chad would willingly agree to issue a mortgage to someone who pointedly said she did not understand the repercussions of the legal documents she was signing.

The largest unknown was the financing for all this. Con men could not invent the tens of millions of dollars it took to get Senior Equity off the ground. It required a funding source and, in all likelihood, the money came from people who were well acquainted with Senior Equity's ultimate goal of foreclosing on as many homes as possible.

The key to the case, Samantha felt, was 'turning' the woman who worked alongside Chad. Getting her to switch sides was a matter of showing her that working with law enforcement would mean little or no jail time and an opportunity to rebuild her life.

It would all be in the selling.

* * * * *

Bree instinctively knew something was wrong.

Chad had called, inviting her to come over. When Bree said she needed an evening alone, Chad launched into the story of his conversation with that Eleanor Strong woman. Strong, he had said, had done a complete about-face in his office. She wasn't some weak-willed widow frightened by her cancer. She knew exactly what she was doing – including the risks – and was going through with the mortgage because it was the fastest way to get the money she needed.

"Get this, Bree," Chad said. "She said Andrew is a salesman, and she treated him the way young sales guys think old ladies treat handsome young men. But because I'm a CEO, she's going to treat me differently. She told me she wants to close as soon as possible."

How did this Eleanor Strong woman know Andrew was a salesman? Bree thought.

Andrew was an idiot but, because he had played his role enough times, he had the part down pat. He knew his lines. He knew what to say, how to behave, and never break character.

He wasn't supposed to behave like, let alone be perceived as, a salesman. He was an independent advisor with no attachment to Senior Equity.

"Are you certain Strong used the word, 'salesman'?"

"That's what she said," Chad said. "I thought it was hilarious."

"And that doesn't bother you?"

"Bree, she was giving it to me straight," Chad replied. "She says if she doesn't get the money for this pancreatic cancer treatment, she's dead in a couple of months. And the treatment isn't any guarantee she gets better."

"And Andrew checked out her story?"

"It's definitely her house, her husband really died a few months back, she has no kids, and the treatment center in Switzerland is a legit place." Chad sighed. "She's real, Bree. Don't get paranoid."

"Give me Andrew's number," Bree snapped. "I want to hear it from the horse's ass."

"C'mon, Bree, you know I keep everyone..." Chad started to say.

"Give... me... his... number..." Bree said in a cold voice.

Chad gave her Andrew's phone number.

The conversation had ended, but not the doubts. Bree thought back on her own encounter with Strong. The woman didn't seem ill with a terminal disease. She had walked in with Andrew, passively accepted she should remain in the lobby, listened intently to 'Ashley Moore's' heartwarming tale of her mother's recovery, and then insisted 'Ashley' should be given an immediate audience with Chad... and Andrew should accompany her into Chad's office.

That was the first time in three years anything like that had ever happened. No one *ever* gave up their place in line. Andrew had been so flustered he didn't know what to say and needed to be rescued.

If Eleanor Strong saw through Andrew, did she also see through 'Ashley Moore'?

I mean, how convenient was it there just happened to be a woman in the lobby waiting to tell a tale of her mother's miraculous recovery from a similar cancer? What were the chances of that? One in ten thousand? One in a billion?

She called Andrew.

"Tell me everything you know about Eleanor Strong," Bree said.

"I'm on a date here," Andrew said, annoyed. "Can't this keep until morning?"

"Guys like you date women who rent by the hour," Bree sneered. "Tell her she's off the clock for a few minutes. Where did you meet Strong? How was she referred?"

"She was a walk-in to a seminar," Andrew said. "Showed up just before it started…"

"So, how did she know about it?"

Andrew thought for a moment. "She said she had thrown away an invitation to an earlier one, but her circumstances…"

Bree cut him off. "Which seminar did she go to?"

"Westford, two days ago."

"And she lives in Hardington," Bree snapped. "She drove forty miles to come to *our* seminar."

"Bree, we've had people who drove more than a hundred miles to come to *our* seminar, and they were perfect marks."

"Yes, and they lived in East Overshoe, Maine," Bree replied. "And you really checked her credentials? I mean, *seriously* checked them."

"Yes, Bree," Andrew replied, a note of sarcasm in the words. "I know she owns her home. I know her husband died in a nursing home and he wasn't on Medicaid. I was at the house today. Seven-fifty easy, and she's looking for…"

"I know, I know," Bree said. "And she presented to you as some dithering old lady."

"If by dithering you mean she spent five minutes looking for her purse, then yeah," Andrew countered.

"Did you see her medical records?" Bree asked. "Did she volunteer to show them to you?"

"We've *never* asked for medical records," Andrew shot back. "But I looked up her diagnosis. Everything she said was consistent with what I read."

"Then why did she call you a 'salesman' in front of Chad?"

There was silence for a moment. "She said that?"

"Chad was quoting her," Bree said. "He thought it was hilarious. I think it sets off alarms."

"Maybe I overdid it," Andrew said in a contrite voice. "I was feeling cocky. She was so easy. She offered to pay me."

"Pay you?" Bree pushed.

"Yeah, she said I had been so helpful. We were on our way to see Chad. She said she ought to be paying me for my time because I shouldn't be doing all this good work for free. I gave her the song and dance about government payments. I know the script."

"But it took her five minutes to find her purse?" Bree asked.

"Yeah, she had put it in a different drawer than usual."

"Giving you an extra five minutes to size up the place," Bree said.

"I used it to good advantage," Andrew said defensively. "Photos of her with her husband taken over a twenty or thirty-year period. No evidence of kids in any of them."

"Any evidence of medical paraphernalia?" Bree asked. "Pills, pamphlets? Guides to Switzerland?"

"It was her living room, Bree. Old ladies keep them for show. They don't live in them."

Bree tried to reconcile the idea of a woman not being able to locate her purse yet spotting a selling job. Yes, Andrew could have 'overdone it'. He was that stupid. But Chad wasn't. And Chad had been delighted at her directness.

And it could hardly have been a legal probe. 'Eleanor Strong' was using her real name and her own life story insofar as the freshly deceased husband was concerned. Bree felt a little less on edge.

"Give me her address," Bree said. "I may want to check up on her. Then you can go back to your hooker."

* * * * *

Paula poured a third glass of wine and noted less than a quarter of the bottle remained. It had been a year since she drank alone though, until a year ago, she could sometimes drink an entire bottle every night.

Back then it was out of loneliness. Back then, it helped ease the fear of an uncertain prognosis. Back then, she drank so she would not think about her former husband and his 27-year-old wife.

For the past year, her drinks had always been in the company of friends; like the bottle of Champagne she had surprised everyone with a few hours earlier. She drank to share happiness and camaraderie.

Tonight, the bottle of wine – an everyday white of no special significance – was to help her clarify her thinking. She was trying to focus on something she had felt just about the time she gave her extemporaneous speech to the women Leslie Mullen had assembled.

The feeling was this: she was physically exhausted by the past few days of creating and running this supposed fabric importation company. She was mentally drained by dealing with hourly crises. She was so fatigued by today's schedule she had no energy to make dinner. Instead, she had scrounged through the refrigerator, grateful Martin had brought so much food.

But what she was thinking was this: she had never been more exhilarated in her life. Each new crisis was a challenge, and she was using every synapse and neuron in her brain to meet those challenges.

She was, in short, being challenged and, in being challenged, she was having fun.

Paula had set aside her career aspirations to be a wife and mother. Dan had seldom asked her opinion on anything business-related and seemed annoyed when she offered to read something he had written. But she did read the copies of the *Wall Street Journal* he brought home in his briefcase and she listened in on any business-oriented conversations. She had competently managed all of the family expenses for more than two decades.

She knew she was intelligent and a quick learner. She also knew how to treat people fairly and with dignity.

And so, the wine this evening was helping her distill an idea that had formed in her head: 'Provençal Home Décor of New England' might have a life beyond the few days or weeks it took to bring Chad to justice. Whether or not it was a practical idea was another question that would take time to answer.

Isn't life strange? she thought to herself. *A week ago, none of this was even a blip on the horizon. Now, I'm contemplating a career...*

Chapter Thirteen
Friday

Marie Deveraux eagerly pressed the 'refresh' button on the 'AF-KL MyCargo' screen. She had never expressed any interest in any other freight shipment, but then she had never had such a personal investment in one. At 6:45 a.m., an Air France freighter had lifted off on time from Marseilles Provence Airport on its eight-hour trip to Boston. The aircraft had long since cleared French airspace and was smoothly cruising the North Atlantic.

Marie had pestered and cajoled every hand touching the special parcel it carried. She made the head of the crew picking the order read back every item as it was fitted into two large wooden crates. She spoke with the *inspecteur des doanes* to ensure the oafish crew had properly labeled the parcel with the name of the Boston customs broker who would receive it. When his accent betrayed its Provençal origins, she gladly lapsed into a patois that instantly bonded them as kindred spirits. She excitedly explained this was the Trade Council's largest new account in years and the new beachhead against the hated Chinese forgeries that left so many workshops on the verge of penury.

In turn, the customs inspector said he would make certain this proud handiwork of the region would be in the first compartment bay to be offloaded at Logan Airport, and would carry the special *'expédtier immédiatement'* instructions reserved for the highest value and time-sensitive cargo. He could do this because the Air France *chef de fret* for Marseilles just happened to be his brother-in-law.

With the six-hour time difference between France and the east coast of America, Marie felt no urgency to send the emails she had composed to the customs broker and to Madame Winters; those could wait until lunchtime. But she nevertheless felt a joy at being part of something that was not merely the everyday clerical duties for which she had been hired. She was *helping* someone whom she liked even as she created orders for the workshops the Council ostensibly served.

One more refresh, she thought, and pushed the computer key. The tiny plane on the screen had moved a perceptible fraction of an inch on its path across the ocean.

* * * * *

At Senior Equity, Fridays were set aside as 'closing day'. Three conference rooms were set up for simultaneous closings, with an hour allotted for each transaction. Fifteen minutes were allocated to arrange documents before the next client was ushered in.

Ryan and his two partners were at One Broadmoor Hill at 7:30 a.m., a full hour before the first three closings were scheduled. In turn, they had spent much of the previous day printing out, proofing and organizing 27 doc sets.

At almost any other law firm, such work would have been done by an admin, and the closings would have been the responsibility of a paralegal. However, the most recent admin had left in tears three weeks earlier, and no paralegal had responded to the ads the firm placed on dozens of job sites. The two previous paralegals had both provided devastating online reviews of The Walpole Law Group to 'glassdoor', a website where employees could post frank opinions about their employers. One called it a "place where no one wanted to answer the phone because the person on the other end would either be issuing death threats or begging for intervention." The other said it was a "one-client, one-product, lowest-common denominator law firm where careers went to die." Neither would 'recommend the firm to a friend'.

As a result, three lawyers served as their own admins and paralegals. Working in the small supply room commandeered for the purpose, they set up inch-thick folders with the name of the mortgage applicant, the time, and the conference room where the closing would take place. After each closing, each document set would be quickly reviewed to ensure each signature line was properly filled in.

With 27 closings, the process was guaranteed to take until at least 7:30 p.m., after which the three lawyers would be too exhausted to do anything other than pick up takeout and go home. And, of course, Ryan would need to stay an extra half hour to collect the firm's payment: 162 one-hundred-dollar bills in a large manila envelope.

For its part, Senior Equity's two officers made brief appearances at each closing to present checks or show evidence of wire transfers, but otherwise stayed aloof of the proceedings. Instead, the 'handholding' was the province of the seven independent contractors who steered the elderly applicants to Senior Equity. Variously called 'sheep dogs', 'pilot fish', and 'shepherds', their role on closing days was to collect the applicants at their homes, ensure they were mentally alert, drive them to One Broadmoor Hill, calm them as dozens of papers were placed in front of them for their signature, ensure those signatures conformed to specimens, and whisk the client away as soon as the deal was done. As a shepherd might have as many as four clients on closing day, they scrambled to rid themselves of one client in order to pick up the next one for the trip to Framingham, often with as little as an hour and fifteen minutes between closings.

The payment for the sheep dog was the choice of either three percent of the value of the reverse equity mortgage, or a two-step payment of a flat $5,000 upon closing plus three percent of the ultimate sale value of the home after foreclosure less the value of the mortgage.

The value of patience was compelling. Assume a home with a true value of $600,000 was at stake. Through chicanery and outright lies, the homeowner agreed to an assessed value of $400,000 against which the borrower received $250,000. If the runner took the up-front three percent, he or she received an immediate payment of $7,500. If the runner took the option of the two-step payment, the prospective reward was $5,000 immediately plus an additional $13,500 in twelve to eighteen months. It was no wonder the men and women who brought their 'clients' to these closings were so giddy: assuming they brought in four clients each week, they were earning at least $30,000 for their week's work, and possibly as much as $100,000.

Bree, whose interactions with clients began only after the mortgages were issued, steered clear of One Broadmoor Hill on closing days. She took ten percent of the sale of every home where there was a 'premature' foreclosure, or $60,000 on that hypothetical $600,000 house.

Those paydays paled to the take for Chad and Vinnie. They each immediately pocketed $5,000 for each reverse mortgage issued, but the real payday came when the foreclosure was completed. In return for fronting $250,000, their investor received $300,000 – a twenty percent return on investment for a twelve-to-eighteen month waiting period. Payments to Bree and the shepherds totaled roughly $80,000. That left $220,000 to divide on every home that ultimately went into foreclosure. Even after the expense of seminars, advertising, office rent, legal expenses (a rounding error, really), and realtor commissions, Chad and Vinnie could each ultimately expect to clear almost $100,000 per mortgage, or $2.7 million this week.

There were more lucrative cons – a penny stock scheme could generate a $5 million per week profit – but they required a much larger sales force and hundreds of fresh 'investors' every week. Moreover, such schemes also had the full attention of the Securities and Exchange Commission: 'Pump and Dump' scams seldom lasted more than a few months.

The beauty of the reverse mortgage was it was all above-board except for Bree's 'interventions'. In its three years of operation, Senior Equity had responded to six queries from Massachusetts government agencies. All had come in response to complaints concerning foreclosures. In each case, a detailed chronology and complete paperwork was promptly provided to the requesting agency and there was no follow-up.

* * * * *

Andrew Douglas collected Mamie McCoy at exactly 7:45 a.m. From his previous interactions with her, he surmised she was in early-to-middle stage dementia. She could not remember his name and getting her out of the house was, at minimum, a fifteen-minute process. Further, in the twenty-minute drive from Westborough to Framingham, she twice told him what she had for breakfast and how much she appreciated his driving her.

Occurring so early in the day, an ethical person would have seen this conversation as a sign Mamie was not competent to enter into a contract. Fortunately, Andrew was willing to set ethics aside because Mamie, a widow, owned a small house on nine acres in a town that was one of Boston's 'up and coming' desirable suburbs. Her home – a modest frame house from the 1950s, was nothing special. But her lot had three hundred feet of frontage on a street with town water and sewer.

Mamie had come to a 'Your Home Is Your Pension Plan' seminar three weeks earlier and Andrew had been assigned to her table. Andrew guessed her age to be close to eighty, and she fell asleep during the presentation. But afterward, she asked if a reverse mortgage could be used to pay for college tuition. Andrew went on high alert: an opportunity to sell a lump-sum payout.

Andrew visited Mamie the next day and learned she worried her son was not keen on paying for his daughter's college education. Andrew also inspected Mamie's property, assessed by the town at $400,000, and judged it to be worth at least double that amount based on subdividing it into between three and six building lots.

"You can give Hannah four years of college," Andrew told

Mamie. "You can even prepay it so the cost of her tuition, room and board are locked in until she graduates. It would be the best birthday present any grandparent ever gave, and one that will live in her heart forever."

Using the town's assessment and Mamie's age, Andrew promised her $275,000. "She can go to any college in the country and even spend her junior year abroad," he said. "Think about the tears of joy you'll see. It's a selfless act."

When they reached One Broadmoor Hill, Andrew helped her out of the passenger seat and held her arm as they walked to the entrance. It was, he thought, a perfect execution on his part. Her son and daughter knew nothing of this, of course, but the funds would be wired to the Hannah McCoy Irrevocable Trust he had set up through a mammoth bank that cared only about the fee it collected for setting up such a trust.

At 8:30 a.m., Andrew and Mamie were seated in a small but comfortable conference room. Pots of coffee and tea were on a side table together with a plate of fruit Danish. Mamie immediately reached for a cherry Danish.

A moment later, they were joined by Ryan. Andrew introduced Ryan as 'the attorney who will walk you through the paperwork and make certain everything being done is in your interest.'

Mamie asked Ryan to repeat his name and she began looking for a pen and paper to write it on. "I have such trouble with names these days," she said.

Andrew and Ryan exchanged a look.

"Let's get started," Ryan said. "If you forget my name, just ask me."

For the next 45 minutes, Ryan placed documents in front of Mamie, explaining the purpose of each one. For most of them, Mamie would in turn look at Andrew, who would nod and smile. "It's an important one," he would say. "Important and necessary."

Toward the end, Andrew noted Mamie's signature began to

waver.

"Let's take a five-minute coffee break," he suggested. "Let's have a Danish. These last papers are the most important ones, and you want to make Hannah proud."

Mamie drank her sweetened coffee and obediently consumed another Danish. Her blood sugar rose, making her more alert.

At 9:25 a.m., the last paper was signed. As if on cue, there was a knock at the door. Vinnie Malone came in, attired in a charcoal gray suit and blue tie. He was grinning from ear to ear.

"Why, I remember you!" he said, taking Mamie's hand. "Mamie from Westborough with the world's smartest granddaughter!"

Mamie beamed. She did not remember this man, but he looked important.

"I have something for you," Vinnie said. From his jacket pocket he extracted and opened an envelope and from it took out a sheet of paper. "This says we have just wired the sum of $275,000 into your granddaughter's college account. You have just given her the finest present a young woman could ever receive."

Mamie took the sheet of paper, puzzling over it.

"It's all done," Vinnie said. "You should be so proud of yourself, because we're all proud of you."

"We'd better get you home," Andrew said. "You've had a long morning."

Andrew's role with Mamie was nearly complete. Now, he needed to reinforce the need for secrecy in what she had done. "Hannah's birthday is next month. That's when you should tell her about the fund you've created for her college needs. If you tell her before, it will spoil the surprise, plus it won't be a present." Andrew repeated that message multiple times on the drive back to Westborough.

His true reason, though was to ensure no one had the opportunity to exercise Mamie's 'right of rescission'. Under

Federal law, consumers have three business days to call off, without penalty, a mortgage refinancing, cash-out, or home equity line of credit. While a reverse mortgage is not technically one of those transactions, there is no clear case law it is not.

As a result, one of the first papers placed in front of Mamie was a statement describing her right of rescission. She, of course, signed the document and it was soon shuffled to the back of the growing sheaf of papers. While Mamie lived alone, and her son and grandchildren lived out of state, Andrew needed to make certain no mention of the reverse mortgage leaked out before it became an event capable of being undone only by incurring horrendous fees (and Mamie had signed a document saying she understood those fees).

When Mamie McCoy was safely back in her home, Andrew raced northeast toward the town of Sudbury to collect yet another soon-to-be-fleeced elderly homeowner for an eleven o'clock appointment.

* * * * *

Ryan collected the paperwork from the Mamie McCoy closing. He felt sick to his stomach, which he reckoned to be a good sign because it meant he wasn't yet inured to what he was part of. The woman was 78 and her mental faculties were failing. She had been moderately alert at the start of the process but, halfway through, she was mentally exhausted. Only the 'sugar high' got her through the final documents.

As an officer of the court, Ryan was duty-bound to ensure Mrs. McCoy was competent to execute the documents he had witnessed, and one of the forms in the file bore his signature attesting that, in his judgment, Mamie McCoy knew what she was signing. He had effectively lied under oath.

Further, the trust documents attached to the reverse mortgage made it nearly impossible to extricate Mrs. McCoy from the agreement. Irrevocable trusts bore that name because they were intended to be binding on all parties. While he had not drafted the trust, his processing of the document was a tacit admission he believed its purpose was aboveboard.

One of the documents he initiated said Mrs. McCoy understood her rights to walk away from the agreement if she did so within three business days. The blank look on her face as he explained her rights told him she had no comprehension of what he had said. Because no client had ever exercised those rights, it meant Andrew, or one of Andrew's cohorts, had done something to ensure Mrs. McCoy would never send the necessary letter.

And, in all likelihood, in six or eight months, Mrs. McCoy would do something to violate the terms of the mortgage, such as adding her granddaughter's name to the home's deed. And three months later, Senior Equity would foreclose. Little Hannah McCoy would get her college fund (assuming she even planned to go to college), but her grandmother would lose her house.

He knew beyond question he was a cog in a money laundering scheme, and he knew Chad and Vinnie were doing something causing Senior Equity's clientele to do stupid things. He also knew, based on the number of foreclosures settled from probate court, an uncomfortable percentage of Senior Equity's clients died between the time foreclosure notices were issued and when actions were completed. A fair percentage took their own lives, possibly out of shame for what they had done.

And he knew he was trapped.

Chad paid him just enough to keep The Walpole Law Group in business yet kept them so busy they could not diversify their client base. And, by paying in cash, Chad made Ryan and his partners an active participant in laundering funds. The $16,200 he would collect from Chad this evening was above the $10,000 limit imposed by federal law for cash deposits.

As a result, Ryan divided each week's proceeds into three parts. Each partner deposited half the funds into his or her personal checking account, and half into the firm's business account. He knew his bank manager eyed the deposits with suspicion. It was always hundred-dollar bills and never checks.

From reading U.S. Treasury website notices, Ryan knew banking officials were encouraged to ask questions about suspicious deposits, to pass along those suspicions if warranted, and to request suspicious customers close their accounts if they were unable to satisfactorily explain the continuing inflow of large cash deposits. Perhaps it was his imagination, but in the past few weeks, the tellers who handled his deposits seemed increasingly nervous. Last week, one had periodically looked to a point behind him and subtly nodded at some unseen person.

Now, the $2,000 payments from foreclosure were rising at an alarming rate. For these, he established personal accounts at two banks and spent several hours a week traveling between them to make deposits. Personal checks on those banks fed into the law firm's account in order to pay filing fees (the first time he had attempted to pay a court fee with cash, he had been met with any icy stare).

Something had to change. And it had to happen while he still had the courage to act. He was fully aware he would likely be disbarred, and prison was a distinct possibility. His only confidantes were his law partners and they were, if anything, even more frightened. They huddled in the evening, drinking beer in the office and making macabre jokes.

"It's like that John Grisham book about the law firm that fronted for the mob," his partner Lisa had said just last week. "Except instead of everyone in the firm selling their soul to get wealthy, be given great houses, and fly back and forth to the Caribbean to make deposits, we can't afford to give ourselves a raise. Where's Tom Cruise when you need him?"

Yes, Ryan thought. *Something has to change.*

* * * * *

At 7:30 a.m., Martin was investigating a small dumpster.

He had made his way down to the unfamiliar town of Walpole, some 25 miles south of Boston. The Walpole Law Center lay along Route 1A which, until a new four-lane road built in the 1950s usurped the designation, was Route 1. If you squinted, it was still 1935, with widely spaced, small frame houses lining the road. Many had been converted to businesses, and one such house now was home to the law firm.

A relatively new wooden sign along the road announced its presence, and the driveway ended in a parking pad for six cars, but the house seemed little changed from the time when a family lived here. No cars were in evidence, which was good. Martin's goal wasn't to confront anyone. He was here to look around.

As a law enforcement official, he knew under Massachusetts law that unless trash was on the curb for pickup, it was considered private property and, moreover, he could be cited for trespass. But he intended to remove nothing; just see what was there.

The contents of the dumpster revealed The Walpole Law Group to be a small group of people who subsisted on pizza and Chinese takeout. It also showed they either did not own a shredder or else neglected to use one. Hundreds of discarded documents were in tied garbage bags. Roughly half of the documents related to the issuing of mortgages, the other half to motions to seize properties for having failed to follow the rules set down in those mortgages.

This was a one-product shop and it apparently had one client. Ryan Herndon, Lisa Watts, and Steve Curbow were its lawyers. Surprisingly, there seemed to be no evidence of any other employees, though there were printouts of résumés in one garbage bag.

Martin took a walk around the building. A few desultory shrubs, long overgrown, hid part of the foundation. His lone peek inside was to step onto the front porch and look into the windows on either side of the door. One showed an office, the other a conference room of sorts. The furniture was purely utilitarian; the type that might have been purchased on sale at a Staples.

Martin went back to his car, satisfied with what he saw. The lawyers here weren't part of the Senior Equity gravy train. Rather, they were the conscripts. The State Police were right: here was where you'd find the soft underbelly.

* * * * *

George Waters read the email and laughed aloud. He tried to imagine the earnestness with which the sender had composed her note, and her complete lack of understanding of how the customs business worked.

Dear Mr. Waters, the email read, *At 08:37 EDT this morning, an Air France freighter is due to land at Logan Airport. It contains two pallets of decorative napkins from Provence for your customer, Provençal Home Décor of New England. Madame Winters is much anxious to receive these and the Conseil de Commerce des Tissus Provençaux would greatly appreciate your work to expedite her order. Please let me know if I can help you. Marie Deveraux.*

Waters was a man with six decades of customs brokerage experience. Waters & Company International Services had been his father's and his grandfather's business. He began apprenticing in the office when he was six. Every day after high school he reported to the company's Chelsea offices to handle invoices. There was nothing he had not seen, and he had been on the receiving end of many messages like this one.

What Ms. Deveraux did not understand was air freight had its own rhythm. The plane might well touch down at 8:37, but landing was just the beginning of its content's journey. It was now 9:52. Assuming the craft was an Airbus A330, it would have taxied to the Customs building. If the Air France ground crew wasn't on strike or taking a coffee break, they would open the A deck freight hatch and begin removing the first of 23 containers. Two hours later, they would open the B deck and keep unloading. They would finish offloading the plane sometime early this afternoon.

Somewhere along the line, the first container would be rolled into the Customs area. The Air France ground crew – if they hadn't left early because it was too warm – would begin removing parcels and placing them in the inspections area. Depending on how many planes had landed ahead of it, the Customs inspectors might start getting to the Air France cargo late today. Sometimes, if things were backed up or the Customs unit was short-staffed, it might be a week. When the Customs inspectors finally got around to the Air France cargo, they would first look for things that didn't belong or were otherwise suspicious. Only when they were satisfied everything was in order would he be contacted.

The exception, of course, was time-sensitive or high-priority items, and the expedited service cost a fortune. But, even then, if the item was at the back of Container 23, all bets were off.

Waters was still chuckling over the email when his phone rang.

"This is George," he said.

"How about you drive your sorry ass over here and take charge of these crates," a familiar voice said. "Or should we set out tables and chairs and use these cute French linens for our ten-o'clock tea?"

Ten minutes later, Waters was in the 'cleared' area of the Customs 'shed' – actually an enormous warehouse-sized room.

The Customs agent walked Waters over to the crates. "These things were apparently in Position 1 of Container 1. They were festooned with enough '*la plus haute priorité*' ribbons to paper Fenway Park. The only trick they missed was a diplomatic pouch. If their goal was to get our attention, they did. That, or else whoever ordered this stuff has a fairy godmother watching over them."

Waters marveled at the sight. In six decades he had never seen a package clear Customs so quickly. And these were destined for the lady out in Framingham whose fumbling with words had clearly marked her as someone who had never done any international shipping.

"I'll be damned," was all he could say as he stared at crates that had defied every rule in the book.

"So, why don't you wave your own magic wand and get one of your trucks over here?" the Customs agent suggested.

Still bewildered, Waters obediently reached for his phone.

* * * * *

Forty-five minutes after the lapel mic was first attached to her blouse, Paula was finally told it was OK to remove it.

She was utterly drained.

Adriane Miranda had arrived with NPR's full audio and video resources. What Paula had initially thought would be a young woman with a hand-held recording device was instead a three-person crew for lighting, audio and video. The theme was empowerment: how a woman-owned business thrived and what lessons could be learned when multiple, comparable businesses found a common roof under which to share ideas.

Paula had tried to adhere to the truth as much as possible, but she thought saying the business has been in operation for less than a week was probably unwise. She adhered, instead to the notion of a 'kitchen-table business spreading its wings'.

There was even a lucky break. Adriane had noted the tiny logo at the bottom of Provençal Home Décor of New England's website and the legend, *'designed and created by Austinplex, Austin Texas'*. Earlier that morning, Adriane had called the firm and had been delighted to learn Austinplex, too, was woman-owned and, as a bonus, the website was the handiwork of one of the firm's award-winning designers – also a woman. Paula knew none of this but smiled and nodded as her interviewer complimented her on choosing to keep gender in mind when shopping for resources.

As the crew was packing up, Alice raced into the workroom

and excitedly began pointing in the direction of the elevator. She was mouthing words and showed facial expressions that could be interpreted as either glee or imminent peril.

A moment later, two men appeared. They wore Waters & Company coveralls and each pulled a cart bearing a crate measuring four feet on a side.

"Where do you want these?" asked the first man to reach the doorway.

Adriane took one look at the crates and yelled to her crew, "Stop packing! The visuals on this story just got even better!"

* * * * *

Joyce O'Quinn sat with her office door closed, trying to make sense of the call. Hers was an information-age business in a digital economy. In theory as well as in practice, she relied upon networking and a wealth of web-based resources to introduce herself to prospective customers. 'Old media', and especially radio, occupied no mind space.

But she was, herself, an NPR listener, especially of what she thought of as the 'weekend' shows like 'The Moth', 'Wait Wait', and 'Says You'.

An hour earlier she had fielded a phone call from a reporter in Boston asking what it was like to work with Provençal Home Décor of New England and its woman owner.

Joyce had first suspected the call might be a ruse, perpetrated by whomever needed to be convinced Paula Winters' business was real. As a result, her answers to the reporter's questions were somewhat guarded, and stuck to the sketchy cover story she had been given by Lucy McClellan less than a week earlier.

As the call progressed, though, it became evident to Joyce the call was bona fide; she was speaking to a real reporter who, in an hour, would have 'a crew' at Paula Winters' place of business to interview her about women-owned enterprises.

Joyce began to extemporize. She spoke of the special pride in helping such an enterprise succeed. As they spoke, Joyce rapped on the glass of a wall and passed a note to an intern that Summer Copeland needed to come right away. Soon, the young designer was part of the discussion, which wandered into creating a harassment-free environment with sensitivity to women's needs.

By the time the inevitable question was asked of how a Texas-based web firm came to be doing a project for a Massachusetts company, Joyce's answer was automatic: "I've ordered from her because I loved the products, but I always thought her website – which had to have been designed by a man who dined only from takeout cartons – was terrible. Summer had the site you see now up and running in a matter of days."

Now, an hour later, Joyce wondered how, in a matter of a few days, Provençal Home Décor of New England has gone from a nonexistent company to one worthy of a reporter's time.

Should she call Lucy and ask for instructions?

Joyce instead walked over to Summer's office. "How's the traffic on our house project?" she asked.

Summer didn't need to log in to provide the answer. "There were seven people on the site as of fifteen minutes ago," she said. "They logged over two thousand visits yesterday and more than two hundred spent time on the 'order' page." Summer paused. "Is that enough traffic?"

Joyce shook her head. "Let's not do any tinkering for right now. Keep it steady and ask me again tomorrow."

* * * * *

Bree was having a productive day. Attired and made up as 'granny', she had arranged to encounter a 77-year-old woman outside of her hair salon in Burlington and convince her paying her homeowners' insurance was no longer her responsibility. In nearby Woburn, she arrived five minutes before the mail truck at a home that was already six months delinquent in property taxes. As soon as the truck was out of sight, she removed the most recent tax deficiency notice; thus ensuring a month hence, an 81-year-old widower would find himself unable to explain to a judge why the company holding his mortgage should not be able to foreclose.

A few miles away in Stoneham, Bree followed a 69-year-old woman to an area drugstore where, while they both waited on a bench while their prescriptions were filled, Bree extolled her freedom to be able to spend just the months of July and August in New England while living the other ten months with her daughter and grandchildren in Sarasota. It was their third such encounter in two weeks and, this time, Bree whispered the additional information that she had just rented her home to a university professor for the upcoming school year, giving her an additional bundle of money to lavish on presents for her beautiful granddaughter.

This was how Bree spent most of her days. She kept a spreadsheet and detailed notes on each Senior Equity client noting his or her weaknesses and relative mental acuity. She knew the times of their mail deliveries, where they had their hair done, which days they visited the Council on Aging, and which supermarkets they frequented. She always was alone with the clients. There was never a time when a third party witnessed their conversations.

She was a sufficiently keen judge of human frailty to know when her work was done. This one was going to add a child to her home's deed. That one was going to stop paying taxes. All this information was relayed once a week to Jordan Wells, a man she had never met but who, based on his voice, she assumed was an oily-faced nerd.

Chad's need for secrecy was a royal pain. Other than Chad and Vinnie, Bree wasn't supposed to know anyone else in the Senior Equity structure. Everyone did their job in a vacuum: Wells was hired to keep updating Chad's client dossier. The pilot fish found the easy marks. Bree put the wheels in motion to begin foreclosures on up to two dozen homes a week.

Bree could and did tell herself she was doing this for the huge payoff. The Burlington woman owned a half-million-dollar home and the Woburn widower's home sat on a parcel of land adjacent to commercial zoning.

But Bree was long past needing more money. Had she been willing to engage in introspection, she would understand this was a recurring act of revenge. She was getting even with her mother, who either couldn't or wouldn't accept her twelve-year-old daughter was being groomed for molestation. And she was repaying the six years of hell inflicted on her by a grandmother and great aunt who daily called Bree a slut and a whore, and then evicted her a week after her high school graduation.

The grandmother and great aunt were no longer around to hate. During Bree's sophomore year at Iowa Central Community College, the two women had perished due to a poorly maintained flue which filled their home with carbon monoxide on a cold winter night. This happened a decade before CO detectors were common, let alone mandatory. The investigation was brief and superficial. Bree not only was not interviewed; she learned of the tragedy from reading about it in the *Fort Dodge Messenger*. She was disappointed the Mason City Fire Department had run such a slipshod operation because her alibi for the days leading up to the tragedy, excusing the gallows humor, was airtight.

That she was not mentioned in the two women's wills was not unexpected and it made little difference. She had, six weeks earlier, removed the $3,500 kept in a metal Band-Aid canister in her great aunt's bottom dresser drawer.

* * * * *

It was after 7:30. Ryan had told his partners to go home, get something to eat and have a good weekend. He would collect the documents and ensure they got back to the office.

There now remained the final, distasteful task of collecting the firm's payment.

Chad and Vinnie were in Chad's office, interrupting one another's conversation with laughter. Ryan tapped on the door frame.

"Come on in, Lawyer Herndon," Chad said, adding an exaggerated hand motion. "Let us buy you a drink." There was a half-finished bottle of Macallan Rare Cask on the glass table.

"I'll have to take a pass," Ryan said. "I've got a couple of hours of work ahead of me." He said this in a voice conveying a sense that, under different circumstances, he would have been pleased to accept his offer. Of course, Ryan also knew no such offer would have been made had they not known he was anxious to leave.

"A great day for all of us," Vinnie said, his voice slightly slurred. Ryan noted just twenty minutes earlier, Vinnie had presented someone with their mortgage payout check. Had anyone noticed his condition?

"A *fantastic* day for all of us," Chad added, nodding. "Too bad we get to do this just one day a week. Of course, the way we're writing business, we'll have to start a second closing day pretty soon." He tossed back a shot glass of the Scotch.

"Two closing days a week," Vinnie nodded, speaking to no one in particular. "Won't that be great?"

Ryan said nothing.

"You missed the old bag from Sudbury," Vinnie said. "What was she? Eighty-something and barely able to stay awake. Tomorrow morning she'll wake up and say, 'what check?'" He said those last words in a high, squeaky voice. There was more laughter.

"I need to collect the cash," Ryan said. He was careful not to call it the law firm's payment. To do so would complete the illusion of groveling.

"Ah, cash," Chad said, holding up a finger as an exclamation point. "What would we do without lawyers and what would lawyers do without cash?"

"For one thing, they wouldn't be able to register deeds

Monday," Ryan said dryly.

Vinnie gave out a whoop and laughed. "Got you on that one, Chad baby!"

Chad retrieved a fat manila envelope from a briefcase. He started to hand it to Ryan, then pulled it back. "Are you unhappy, Lawyer Herndon?" he asked, cocking his head and holding the envelope to his chest.

"Tired," Ryan replied. "I've been here for over twelve hours and I've had to be mentally alert every minute of that time. Please excuse me if my being bone-weary is a downer. I've also got a lot to do this weekend." He hoped there was just enough of a hint of an apology to satisfy Chad.

Chad handed him the envelope. "We've all got a great thing going here. Especially you. Have you ever wondered how many of your Western New England Law School classmates are actually working as attorneys, much less have their own practice grossing more than two million a year? And how many will do three or four million next year? That's what you and your buddies are going to take in."

Chad added, "I worked just as hard as you when I was your age. Probably harder because I didn't have your educational advantages. We're all in this together, Ryan. I know you have some personnel issues right now, but you'll work those out. This will get easier when you can start spreading the load. Maybe you could start with a junior associate. I could…"

"Thanks, Chad," Ryan said, placing the envelope under his arm. "Right now, what I need is something to eat and to get a few hours' sleep. I'll take care of all of this over the weekend."

He did not give Chad an opportunity to rebut. Ryan did not want him to see the emotion on his face. It was not until twenty minutes later and he was out of the building, the two bankers' boxes packed and loaded in his car, that he allowed himself to express the rage he felt.

"Bastards!" he said aloud, and then pounded the steering wheel. He pulled out of the One Broadmoor Hill parking lot and made his way toward Route 9. He did not notice that, at the other end of the parking lot, another car pulled out, its lights dimmed.

A few minutes later, close to tears and unable to focus on driving, Ryan pulled into a restaurant parking lot and turn off his car engine. *I can't do this anymore. I won't be a party to it. I won't throw away my...*

There was a tap at his window. Ryan looked up and saw a fifty-ish man in a polo shirt and slacks. He indicated for Ryan to roll down his window. The man did not look dangerous, but he also did not look familiar. Ryan lowered the window a few inches.

"You're Ryan Herndon," the man said. He was smiling.

"And what if I am?" he answered cautiously.

"I'm the guy who is going to get you out of this mess. My name is Martin Hoffman. I'd like to start by buying you dinner and a beer."

Chapter Fourteen
Friday evening

Paula was exhausted. This had been one of the longest days of her life. She had winged her way through an interview and then been inundated with products – all while being videoed. She had spent the entire afternoon sorting inventory and then filling orders; stuffing boxes and JiffyPaks with merchandise. Fifteen minutes earlier, she had sent home Alice and Jean. One hundred and sixty-two web purchases had been fulfilled.

The first amazing thing was an additional 117 orders had come in during the day, and one was for nearly a thousand dollars of merchandise. Those, they would take care of on Monday.

The second amazing thing was Provençal Home Décor of New England was profitable. Paula had only a rudimentary understanding of 'cost of goods sold', 'selling, general and administrative expense', and 'variable cost of sales' but, half an hour earlier, Alice had walked Paula through the spreadsheet she had prepared.

The first days' business produced a loss. Of course it had: Paula had purchased goods at retail from other web sites. Then, she had paid for overnight shipping of those goods, and paid to ship those same goods back out again. "The good news is you didn't go overboard on buying," Alice explained. "If you had insisted on shipping every order, we'd be in deep trouble."

The $40,000 of inventory that had arrived this morning changed everything. "While I don't know what to put down for labor because you never discussed paying us, I used fifteen dollars an hour," Alice said, pointing to another line of the spreadsheet. "We shipped out almost $5,000 of product today. The inventory cost was just over $2,000. Even with our overhead, we cleared more than $2,000, which erased your losses from those first few days."

Alice tapped a line on the spreadsheet. "We know two things. The first is today's orders will chew up at least another $2,000 of inventory. It will also generate another $2,000 of real profits. The second thing we know is you only get lucky once with an order sailing through customs. At the rate we're going, we're going to burn through our inventory in less than three weeks. You need to think about re-ordering."

Paula looked at Alice with admiration. This wonderful, silver-haired woman had just thrown out the phrase 'burn through our inventory' as though she had been saying it all her life. "For now," Paula said, "go home and get some rest. Over the weekend, you and Jean decide how much you're worth and plug those numbers into the spreadsheet."

Now, Paula was left to tidy up and wait for UPS. She had watched throughout the day from the corner of her eye as a parade of people went into and out of Senior Equity's offices; mostly elderly women accompanied by smartly-dressed men and women in their thirties. The last of those odd couples had left an hour earlier.

Fifteen minutes later, a younger man and woman Paula did not recognize and had not seen earlier left the offices. They carried briefcases. Both looked tired and they did not speak to one another as they walked.

After the passage of another fifteen minutes, Chad and another man left the office. They were talking loudly and, if Paula was any judge, they were tipsy. They did not acknowledge her, though Paula was certain Chad had glanced at her out of the corner of his eye as they passed.

Twenty minutes later, another man, probably in his late twenties, left the offices pushing a dolly weighed down by two hefty boxes of the kind containing files and paperwork. The look on his face was one of weariness and defeat. Paula noted the lights were now off at Senior Equity.

The time was nearly eight o'clock. Sometime in the next fifteen minutes, a cleaning crew would come up the elevator to service the lone occupied area of the building. Paula had only minutes to act.

With the floor quiet, Paula walked over to the Senior Equity office entrance. Not surprisingly, the door was unlocked.

She went inside the three conference rooms and saw plates of uneaten Danish and boxes of coffee. The waste baskets overflowed with paper coffee cups. Paula poked through the baskets but saw nothing that was not food-related. She then went to what she thought was likely Chad's office. That door was locked. Another office was being used as storage and contained nothing of interest.

There was one final office; a twin of Chad's by the size of it. This one was open. It must belong to the man who had left the building with Chad. The desk was clean but the waste basket contained a wadded-up ball of what turned out to be six note-sized sheets of paper. All contained writing.

Like most offices, waste baskets held a plastic liner. Paula removed the liner and its contents. In the bottom of the wastebasket was a pile of additional liners. She replaced the liner she was taking with a fresh one.

Though she was alone in the building, she tiptoed back to her own office, turned off all lights, carefully closing and locking all doors. Three minutes later, the elevator chimed and a three-person cleaning crew appeared with vacuum cleaners, rolling waste bins, and cleaning supplies. Seeing Paula standing by the pile of outgoing packages, they nodded and went first to Senior Equity.

A few moments later, the elevator again chimed. This time it was UPS. A man in his forties took a look at the hundred-plus packages and grinned. "You ladies seem to be onto something," he said. "I'm going back down for a cart. There's no need for you to stick around."

When he went down the elevator, Paula gingerly removed the wad of notes from the plastic liner, taking care to leave no fingerprints. She looked at the cryptic notes on them and made the decision Samantha needed to see these.

* * * * *

Chad and Bree relaxed in his bed. An empty bottle of Armand de Brignac Brut lay on the bed with them. Another, partial bottle was on the nightstand in an ice bucket. They were pleasantly tipsy; an evening like this had become a post-closing-day ritual in the past six months.

Chad was, with glee, recounting his encounter with Ryan. "He thought he had popped me a zinger with his crack about being the linchpin because he had to file all the paperwork. I cut him off at his knees, though. Told him I had his career in my hands. Reminded him graduates of cow-college law schools have to pay their dues if they don't want to be bagging groceries at Walmart."

Bree rose to rest her weight on an elbow and showed a look of concern. "You used those words?" she asked.

Chad shook his head. "Naw, it wasn't that brutal. I just told him how lucky he is; he's probably the only guy in his law school class who has his own firm with a couple of million in billings. I also sweetened it by saying he could be grossing five mil next year." Thinking it over, Chad added, "He went away satisfied."

Bree shook her head. "I thought you told me he can't keep people because of the atmosphere at the firm – it's all tearful phone calls and threats."

Chad shrugged. "I suggested he bring in another attorney or two. Pay 'em what it takes to put up with the crying widows. Ryan is smart. He'll figure it out."

Bree didn't accept the answer. "What would happen if he didn't file the mortgages? Did he make a threat?"

"No," Chad scowled. "I said something like, 'where would we

be without lawyers and money', and he said, 'there wouldn't be anyone to register the deeds'. He was tired. He apologized."

Bree pressed. "But what would happen if he and his partners didn't register the mortgages?"

Chad laughed. "For one thing, the three of them would disappear without a trace, and it wouldn't be because they made a run for it. I'd make certain of that."

Bree again pressed. "But what about the mortgage papers? You've already given everyone their money."

For the first time that evening, Chad's face and voice showed annoyance. "I'd figure it out. I'd tell everyone they had to re-submit the paperwork. I'd make it work."

Bree lowered her tone. "How much did you do this week? Dollar-wise?"

Chad reached for the Champagne bottle. "Just shy of seven million." He poured them both a glass. "I love this work."

He fell silent as he sipped. But in his mind he replayed a somewhat different conversation he had with his partner, Vinnie, just a few hours earlier. *Could this operation function just as well without Bree? And, if that became necessary, how could he make that happen?*

Bree, too, silently sipped from her glass and her face showed a smile. But her mind was forming a frightening question: *What would they do if you told them you had just lost seven million dollars of their money?*

"Hey," Chad said, lightly slapping Bree's thigh. "We have company coming in half an hour. We ought to get dressed and I need a shower."

* * * * *

Wearing latex gloves, Samantha carefully smoothed out the sheets of paper. They appeared to be hurried summaries, as though someone was taking down points being made during a telephone conversation. They were the kind of fragmentary records she often made when she wanted something to stick in memory by having been both heard and written, then read. Like the author of these notes, she generally threw hers away after she used them as talking points in relaying information to another person.

The pages were not easy to decipher. The writer knew what they said and it made no difference if they were gibberish to the rest of the world. She looked for the easiest words, then used those letters and words as a Rosetta Stone to translate the others.

They had been handed to her half an hour earlier by Paula, who made the twenty-mile drive from One Broadmoor Hill to her Shrewsbury apartment for the sole purpose of ensuring their safe arrival. Paula accepted a cup of coffee, then pleaded weariness and departed for home.

Paula said the notes' author was apparently in the office all day and left with Chad. From Senior Equity's incorporation papers, the most likely candidate would be Vincent Malone, Senior Equity's President. Samantha asked Paula for the man's description. After Paula left, Samantha called Eleanor Strong, who had been at Senior Equity's 'retirement seminar' just a few days earlier, and asked her to describe the man who gave the closing remarks. The two accounts tied. These notes were the handiwork of Malone.

As the scribbled notes began to reveal themselves, Samantha concluded they were notes from a telephone conversation with someone known by the shorthand, 'R'.

R concerned distb nowhere nr $10M.   Remems conversation w/ C $10M/wk 'piece of cake by Sept'

OK, Samantha thought, *this 'R' is 'concerned' – an ambiguous word – that Senior Equity is disbursing less than $10 million a week. 'R' was reminding Malone of a conversation with Chad in which Chad apparently said Senior Equity would be writing reverse mortgages for at least $10 million a week 'by September'.*

'R', then is *Senior Equity's funding source*, she concluded.

The next part of the note read, *'can we bump mtg amts? told R formula dict by law – don't want draw attn. R: more sems? Adv? Me: considering Need plan + uni front'*

Samantha translated: *'R' is suggesting ways to get to that $10 million a week. Senior Equity can increase the size of each reverse mortgage, it can hold more seminars, or it can have more aggressive advertising. To the first suggestion, Malone responded the maximum amount that can be taken out of a home's value is dictated by law and Senior Equity doesn't want to draw attention to itself. To the latter suggestions, Malone apparently said he was already considering them, as well as making a note to himself that he and Chad needed a plan and had to present it with a united front.*

The second and third sheets of paper were a series of circles, numbers and letters: on one, a circle with *'PRO'* at its center and six lines radiating from it. At the end of those lines were *'CitzB 78 w/5 dwntn wk dis Crn 4'* and *'3x2000x6 22 BAs 16 NH BAs 7x3000x4 <2%*. The second sheet contained a circle with *'MAN'* and similar spokes with *'PU2', 'TD2'* and *'CB2'*, under it, *'all wk dist!'*.

Samantha reserved judgment on those sheets and went onto the next.

The fourth sheet read, *'R unhap w/ forclose split why B 10%? Tried 2 jstfy nd ur help sms to be stick pt w/ R xprs 'unhapnes' svrl tms thinks u&B run sep con did not off rev split Greed? Sol: Dif bks for R?'*

The fifth and sixth sheets held lines of numbers that were neither a formula nor a spreadsheet entry. It wasn't clear if Malone had been taking down information from 'R' or these were his own musings. Samantha sighed and set them aside for further study.

Samantha focused on the fourth sheet, poring over the cryptic abbreviations and trying different interpretations. Finally, she settled on, *'R' is unhappy with the current split in the financial proceedings from foreclosures. Someone named 'B' is receiving 10% of the money and 'R' thinks it is too much, or perhaps he thinks 'B' is unnecessary to the operation. Malone did his best to justify Senior Equity's payments to 'B' but 'R' was having none of it and repeatedly expressed his unhappiness. 'R' also apparently advanced the theory that Chad and 'B' are running a separate con on 'R' inside the larger con that is Senior Equity. Malone didn't offer a revised division of proceeds, maybe because he's unsure whether 'R' is asking out of his own greed or some other reason. Malone's proposed solution, though, was as chilling as it was dangerous: keep two sets of books. One for themselves and one to show to 'R'.*

Samantha looked at her own notes and began to write new questions. First, who is 'B'? The most logical answer was that 'B' was the woman whom Eleanor had encountered in Senior Equity's lobby, and who was also the woman who, in various disguises, had come into Paula's operation and spent much of her day getting Senior Equity's clients to violate their lending agreements.

'B' would seem to be an indispensable part of Senior Equity, but 'R' apparently felt otherwise. Whatever the current split of the proceeds of foreclosures between 'R' and Senior Equity's managers, the 10% allotted to 'B' was a sticking point.

But that discussion paled beside the broader revelation: 'R' was no passive investor, providing long-term funding for reverse mortgages with the goal of earning a stable rate of return. Rather, 'R' was fully aware of the foreclosure side of the business, benefited from those foreclosures, and wanted more of the income stream they produced.

'R' did not work for an insurance company, bank, or investment firm. 'R' represented dirty money. It might be from organized crime or it might be from drugs. Whatever its source, it was a huge and continuing flow of funds. Ten million dollars a week was half a billion dollars a year.

Which made Senior Equity part of a money laundering operation. Since it did not distribute mortgage proceeds in sacks full of money, that half a billion dollars was converted from paper money to bank account deposits elsewhere in the pipeline... unless Malone's math scribblings were intended to convey the depth of a problem he faced. '*16 NH BAs 7x3000x4 <2%*' could mean seven people each depositing $3,000 four times a day among sixteen bank accounts... half a million dollars a week converted from hundred-dollar bills to 'clean' bank accounts on which checks could be drawn or sent via electronic funds transfers.

But half a million dollars was only a fraction of the liquidity required to fund Senior Equity. Were these circles and lines the beginnings of a plan to expand the money laundering network to Providence and Manchester to get to that $10 million per week goal? The letters and numbers at the end of the lines emanating from the circle could be names of banks and numbers of branches. 'all wk dist' could mean the banks were within walking distance of one another.

Samantha paused with another realization. Her four friends had come to her seeking to find a way to get information on what seemed to be a legitimate company that was systematically cheating its elderly customers. What she now realized was this was much larger and infinitely more sinister.

I have placed in harm's way four people about whom I care a great deal. I have to get them out of there before suspicion falls on them, she thought.

She glanced at a clock. It was just after nine o'clock. She tapped in Eleanor Strong's number. Eleanor picked up immediately.

"Eleanor," Samantha said, "refresh my memory. When is your next meeting with anyone from Senior Equity?"

Eleanor's response was prompt. "Chad is going to try to expedite approval for my mortgage. I had a call this afternoon from Andrew telling me everything looked great for that to happen."

"I think your work may be done, Eleanor," Samantha said, keeping her voice as neutral as possible. "If I told you there was no longer any need to have dealings with them, could you disentangle yourself? Tell them you've changed your mind?"

"Is something wrong?" Eleanor asked.

"No," Samantha said, and then realized she had spoken too quickly. "Well, I'm not sure. What I know is you've provided important information and it may be all I need. Maybe the most important thing you've given me is the woman who spoke to you in the lobby is some kind of a chameleon who can pass for almost any age she chooses. That's huge."

"Something has gone wrong," Eleanor said. "What? And what can I do to help?"

Samantha grimaced and gripped her phone tightly. "I have some new information provided by Paula. I'm just starting to digest it, but what I realize is, the idea of your going through with a mortgage may no longer be necessary. When things start to happen, I don't want anyone at Senior Equity wondering if you had something to do with it."

"What do I do?" Eleanor asked.

"For now, just put them off," Samantha replied. "Tell them you're going in for more tests. Tell them you've had a setback."

"Are you pulling out Paula and the others?" Eleanor asked.

"I don't know," Samantha said. "It might look too suspicious if they suddenly don't show up. I just got this from Paula a little while ago. You were the first person I thought of."

Which was the truth, Samantha realized.

"OK," Eleanor said. "I'll come up with something. I'll be listening hard for anything sounding like skepticism on their part."

Samantha closed the call, reasonably certain Eleanor would do what she said. She looked again at the notes provided by Paula. They would have no bearing in a court of law. They were scribbled fragments of words. Malone could disclaim authorship. He could explain them away in a hundred different ways. Samantha was certain of her interpretation; it all made sense. But no judge would ever issue a wiretap based on such flimsy evidence.

She would, of course, take her story to the Attorney General's office. This was far outside of her area of competence now. Maybe the AG's office would pursue it or maybe they would consider it too tenuous.

Samantha suddenly felt bone-weary tired. Her vision of helping her friends was effectively dashed by the revelation of huge sums of illegal money being involved. Six months earlier she had confronted an extremely bad man with evidence of an illegal car parts business generating maybe ten or fifteen million dollars a year in revenues. That man had been ready to kill her – he had a gun in his hands and was ready to use it – because of her knowledge. She had extricated herself from that predicament only because of Paula and Jean's willingness to place their own lives in jeopardy on her behalf.

She needed sleep. She would awaken early and come up with a plan.

* * * * *

It was now after 9 p.m. Martin Hoffman and Ryan Herndon had each downed a meal of steak tips and potatoes at a chain restaurant professing to be an English beer hall. Seated in the quietest corner of the restaurant – something made more difficult by the fact this was Trivia Night – they were downing their third brown ale.

Martin realized this was likely the first time in three years Ryan was able to speak with complete honesty about what he had gotten himself into, and his fears for where this was inevitably headed. For more than an hour, Ryan had provided every particular about his involvement with Senior Equity.

It was a tale Martin had heard many times before. Someone young, hungry, and staring at a mountain of debt accepted an offer that sounded too good to be true. At first, everything seemed fine. Then, little by little, the crooks reeled in the basically honest guy. And kept reeling him in until it was too late.

"Why didn't you just quit that first year?" Martin asked.

Ryan shook his head. "Everything seemed on the up and up." He paused, "Except for getting paid in cash. And that was just an annoyance; something I put down to eccentricity. It wasn't until I was told about the first foreclosure that an alarm went off."

"You could still have quit," Martin said.

"Yeah," Ryan replied. "And hindsight is twenty-twenty. But I had two partners and the firm was going well. We had bought the building as an investment." His voice had a bitterness to it. "Then, I started seeing clients at closing who had no business being there. Old men and women who didn't understand the paperwork. All they knew was, we were their only hope. Some were desperate for the money."

"Speaking of money, how did homeowners get paid?" Martin asked.

Ryan shrugged. "Nothing out of the ordinary. Funds transfer or certified check. There was never anything funky about the disbursements."

"Do you remember which bank?" Martin asked.

"Sure," Ryan said. That hasn't changed from the beginning. It has always been the Nahant Union Bank."

"Ever meet anyone from the bank?"

"No," Ryan said. "But that's not unusual. Chad and Vinnie always had the checks and the congratulatory letters."

"You know you could have gone to the feds," Martin offered.

Ryan nodded slowly. "Yeah, I could have gone to the feds. I *should* have gone to the feds. But I figured I was in too deep. I'd lose my license as well as my practice."

"That's hard," Martin said softly.

"It isn't just me," Ryan said, sadness permeating his voice. "I have two people I consider friends who are in just as deep. And I'm the guy who brought them in."

"I take it you're kind of sweet on Lisa," Martin said, taking another sip of ale.

Ryan gave a wan smile and nodded. "It's hard not to be. She's like me, or maybe what I like to think is me. She has a first-class mind, but she went to the UMass School of Law in Dartmouth, which ranks as the 199th best law school in the country." He added, "Western New England, by contrast, occupies the coveted Number

165 slot. She also passed the bar on her first try and, unlike me, didn't even bother with a prep course. Just went in and aced it. Then she discovered her degree was radioactive."

"Were you both bitter about it?" Martin asked.

Ryan shook his head. "No. All three of us figured out somewhere in first-year law we had chosen poorly. We knew we were good. We also knew WilmerHale would never touch us. So we banded together. And look where it got us." He took a long pull of his ale.

"My goal is to get you out of this with your careers intact," Martin said. "I don't promise it, but I have some good ideas."

"You're a detective in Brookfield," Ryan said. "You're probably a nice guy, but this is definitely out of your league."

"I also used to be a detective in Cambridge," Martin said. "Does that elevate my status?"

"It's a start," Ryan replied and, for the first time all evening, grinned.

"I have friends in high places," Martin said. "How I got them isn't important, but people listen to me. A group of people who want to see justice done have figured out what's going on at Senior Equity. They want to take down the bad guys and leave the innocent bystanders out of it."

"We're hardly innocent," Ryan said, a glum look on his face. "Depending on whether you want to call it misfeasance, malfeasance or nonfeasance, we've been a party to a criminal activity."

"And, when you help bring down bad guys, a lot of things can get overlooked," Martin replied. "I went by your office this morning. No one can make the claim you're getting wealthy off this. You look like you got that office furniture from a swap meet."

For the second time that evening, Ryan smiled. "It does have something of an air of hopelessness about it."

Martin leaned in. "The missing link to getting this wrapped up is a woman. She's close to Chad. She apparently goes by lots of names. She can look seventy or she can look thirty. Do you know who she is?"

Ryan shook his head. "I know who you're talking about. Black hair, slim build. She's been in Chad's office once or twice when I was there. The times I've seen her, she looked to be about thirty. I was rather pointedly never introduced."

"Dead end," Martin said, grimacing.

"If it's helpful, I also saw her once at Chad's condo," Ryan added. "I was dropping off papers."

"Would you happen to remember where that condo is?"

"About a mile from here," Ryan said. "It's that apartment building on top of the Natick Mall. He's in unit 772."

Martin nodded his appreciation. "Here's what you're going to do," he said. "You're going to go home and get a good night's sleep. Monday, you're probably supposed to file those mortgage documents." Martin nodded with his chin at the two bankers' boxes.

Ryan nodded. "We each take sets for the counties where the property is located."

"Do this instead," Martin said. "Settle on a place for the three of you to meet tomorrow that isn't your office. Tell them everything about the conversation we've had tonight. Tell them your own thoughts. Talk it out and take as long as needed because tomorrow may be the most important day of your lives. If you're all on the same page, go back to your office and start copying everything."

"What about filing the mortgages?" Ryan asked.

"You're not going to file those mortgages," Martin added. "You should consider those as evidence. They may also become your leverage."

"I usually get a call from Chad around midday Monday asking how everything is going," Ryan said.

"Tell him it's all going just fine. Use whatever words you normally say. Don't let him suspect a thing."

* * * * *

The Nouvelle at Natick Luxury Condominium was a 'can't miss' idea when it was proposed in 2005. The economy was strong, shopping malls were the unshakeable anchors and profit engines of regional commerce, and Amazon was a money-losing $8 billion internet company selling mostly books and music.

The condominium project was pitched as the perfect lifestyle choice for affluent, empty-nest suburbanites downsizing from too-large homes. The pitch was rather than moving into Boston or some 'active over-55' community on Cape Cod, a select group could reside in 215 condominiums atop a newly-built addition to the newly-renamed 'Natick Collection' containing a Neiman Marcus, Nordstrom, and Tiffany's. For a while, it worked. The first few units were sold for top dollar even before construction began.

Then the world changed. The economy tanked, Amazon boomed and shopping malls became endangered species. The project formally opened in 2008 but, by 2009, just 37 units had sold and, late that year, the developer auctioned a group of units at discounts as steep as 64%.

Three months after that event, Chad Pannett walked into the Nouvelle sales office, placed a cashier's check on the desk of the receptionist, and told the woman to take it to the sales manager. He said the check was for Unit 772, a two-bedroom, two-bath unit. The receptionist summoned the sales manager who looked at the check, noted it represented a 70% discount from the original price of the unit and a 17% discount from the lowest price offered for a comparable unit at the auction.

The sales manager told Chad the auction prices represented the new floor and, in any event, the buzz created by the auction had generated such traffic that prices were now ten to fifteen percent higher than what Chad had read in the press.

"That's my offer," Chad said. "All cash and no sales commission. Take it or leave it."

A week later, he moved into his new condo.

It was a story Chad never tired of telling and, this evening, his audience was two prospective 'shepherds'. Both men laughed and grinned at 'take it or leave it' and nodded their appreciation at what cash can do in a negotiation.

"I'm offering you the opportunity to make a stunning amount of money," Chad told them. "This makes an initial coin offering look like chump change. There's no boiler room because the customer comes to you, and no one is going to tell you they just heard the story from another guy last week." Chad paused for effect. "And, best of all, it's all legal. Stick to the script and you are completely clean."

Chad noted he had their full attention.

"You are here because you have a reputation as good spotters," Chad continued. "You've got a short amount of time to choose your mark. They've signed up for the seminar. You're the table host. You're looking them over while my people talk. Rule out the tanned couple in their sixties and the man or woman with what looks like a son or daughter accompanying them. They're not who you want. Neither is anyone with five carats of diamonds on their hands or arm. You can bet they've got a lawyer."

"Who do you want? You want the woman in her seventies or eighties. You want anyone with obvious health issues. But also be listening: there may be someone with a spouse in an expensive nursing home. There may be someone with medical conditions that don't seem so obvious."

"Talk to them. Because they pre-registered, you should already know where they live. Don't waste time with someone from Chelsea or who lives in a condo in Malden. You're looking for the person who is house-rich and cash-poor. If you can Google their house ahead of time, that's great, but you'll learn more about their situation by asking questions."

"Where do their kids live? If they live in the same small town, walk away because adult children always get involved. You want ungrateful kids who moved to California and never call. And, remember you don't work for Senior Equity. You're an independent advisor. That's going to increase their trust in you and make them more likely to open up."

Chad shifted his stance to show a change of topic. "And here's what you don't do: you don't promise *anything*. You say you'll explore all options on their behalf. You tell them they should use their own judgment. You never say, 'maybe you should consult a lawyer' or 'talk to your kids'. This is an emotional sell: they're taking out a reverse mortgage to pay the nursing home bills. They're doing this to pay for little Bridgette's education. I've got a prospect right now who is paying for her own, long-shot cancer treatment. Your job is to keep reinforcing they're doing the noble thing."

"And then your job is to get them to closing. Help them fill out the paperwork. Stay on them. Call them or, better yet, visit them. Reassure them. Push the lump sum payout. Answer their questions because, if you don't allay their concerns, they're going to call someone else."

"Finally, remember you get paid only if they close. Your goal is one closing from each seminar, and next month we're going from three seminars a week to at least five. This week we closed 27 mortgages and one especially skillful guy had four fish in the pan. For one week's work he netted thirty grand up front with a back-end opportunity for that much again. You could be that guy in a month. On the other hand, if you come up empty-handed two weeks in a row, you're off the team."

One of the two men asked, "How does the back-end work?"

Chad shook his head. "That isn't your problem. It belongs to the attractive lady on the sofa over there." He indicated Bree, who had been carefully studying the two men's body language for half an hour. "You close them, then you go on to the next candidate."

* * * * *

From his vantage point from the seventh level of a nearby parking garage, Martin peered through high-resolution binoculars into the window of Chad's living room. It was a superb view made possible by a Google image search yielding a building floor plan, coupled with the natural tendency of con men to flaunt their physical possessions by throwing back all curtains or altogether dispensing with them.

Martin's original objective was to get some sense of Chad's living arrangement with the faint hope the elusive woman might be there. To his delight, every light in the unit was on and two 'guests' were in evidence. The woman, who seemed to be in her late twenties or early thirties, sat on a sofa off to the side, saying nothing, but keenly observing the two men. Martin's guess was the men were being interviewed as they wore suits and ties while Chad was attired in a polo shirt and chinos.

Martin had ascertained that, if the woman did not spend the night, she would leave via the condominium's dedicated parking garage. The minute the two men departed, Martin was ready to follow her, get a license plate number and, with luck, discover where she lived. He was prepared for a long night.

* * * * *

Vinnie Malone tried to focus on the Red Sox game but found he couldn't concentrate. He couldn't get his mind off the palpable shift in Ramon's attitude. He had tried to convey the seriousness of the change to Chad but to no avail. Chad said he had everything under control. Chad was going to make Ramon do handsprings of happiness.

Chad is going to get us both killed, he thought grimly.

There had never been such a thing as 'smooth sailing' with Ramon. From the beginning there was mistrust that two men could not only launder huge sums of money, but do so with what amounted to a guaranteed rate of return.

The first year, of course, saw hugely negative cash flow. Money went out in the form of mortgages with no return other than liens on properties still occupied by their ancient former owners, plus an imputed interest rate on those loans but no actual payments. It was only when the first mortgages went into foreclosure and ten houses were flipped for a $2 million profit Ramon's skepticism turned to appreciation.

That equilibrium lasted for a year. Then, Ramon pressed Vinnie to take *more* money and turn it into mortgages. Vinnie explained there were only so many potential targets. The Boston region was special because it had hyper-appreciated homes in established neighborhoods. Just about everywhere else in New England, the house that sold for $125,000 in 1980 was worth about the same amount today. It took Ramon some time to wrap his head about that idea.

As the rate of foreclosures began to equal the issuance rate of new mortgages, the full profit potential of the scam became apparent. Ramon's tacit approval turned to glee. A money laundering operation that, in any other circumstance would have been considered a rousing success if it managed to convert 95% of cash to untainted bank deposits, was earning a 20% return. That alone ought to have earned Vinnie a huge bonus.

Instead, today Ramon was on a new tear. Why were Senior Equity's expenses so high? Why did the closers get paid such a large percentage of the loan, and was Bree really necessary to this operation at all? Why couldn't Vinnie expand his network of money mules to New Hampshire and Rhode Island? Didn't they have banks, too? Whatever happened to Chad's brash promise he could be both laundering and investing $10 million a week by now?

Those questions were more difficult to answer because Vinnie had not always been exactly truthful with Ramon about the profits on those houses. Everything was aboveboard with regard to the initial mortgage. If Mrs. McGillicutty's house was appraised at half a million and the old lady had been given $300,000 before the foreclosure, Ramon was guaranteed a twenty percent rate of return. He got a funds transfer for $360,000, and any loss on the actual money laundering was absorbed by Senior Equity. It was a sweet return for a wait of twelve to eighteen months.

The problem was Vinnie neglected to mention the subsequent 'flip' of Mrs. McGillicutty's home. The set of books Vinnie showed him conveyed the impression the final sale of the home was for around that half-million-dollar figure, leaving $140,000 for Senior Equity to pay all its expenses. The ledger showed Vinnie and Chad each took about $25,000 for each foreclosure.

Including a second sale, the actual proceeds from Mrs. McGillicutty's house was closer to $700,000 with Vinnie and Chad each taking $100,000 for themselves. That figure appeared only on a spreadsheet in a laptop which never left Vinnie's home.

Even notes related to division of proceeds were burned in Vinnie's fireplace, which reminded Vinnie he needed to dispose of the notes he made on his conversation that afternoon with Ramon. Vinnie opened his briefcase and looked for them.

They weren't there. *OK,* he thought. *I left them in my suit jacket.* Vinnie went to his bedroom and its capacious closet, where today's suit was airing on a special, jacket-shaped pedestal.

They weren't there, either.

Vinnie began reconstructing the events of the afternoon. The call from Ramon had come at about two o'clock and lasted half an hour. The conversation with Chad in which Vinnie relayed the change of tone in Ramon's voice had taken place at five. Vinnie used those notes to ensure he got all the nuance of Ramon's questions.

And then he remembered. He had gotten so angry after Chad left his office with his 'no problem, amigo' attitude, he wadded up the notes and threw them into the trash can in his office.

You don't leave incriminating stuff lying around, he thought. *Those mistakes can kill.*

Muttering obscenities for his lapse, Vinnie gathered his wallet and keys and drove the fifteen minutes from his home in Weston to One Broadmoor Hill. He used his master key to unlock the building entrance and his passcode to access the elevator.

The entrance to Senior Equity's suite was unlocked, which ought not to have been the case, but Vinnie remembered the lawyer – Ryan something – was still collating papers. He would not have had a key because you don't trust outsiders with access. OK, so Ryan left the door unlocked.

He went to his office and that door, too, was unlocked. Since Vinnie kept absolutely nothing in his office, there was no need to lock the door. He went to the waste basket beside his desk.

It was empty.

Vinnie did not panic. He sat down at his desk and reconstructed the afternoon's events. The call, the notes on… probably five or six sheets of paper. The fruitless one-on-one talk with Chad. The anger over Chad not getting it. That anger translating itself into Vinnie crumpling the small sheets of paper into a ball and throwing them – hard – into the waste basket.

There was a liner in the basket, like always. So, maybe the cleaning crew had come through. Vinnie rose and walked through the office suite to the conference rooms used for the closings.

He breathed a sigh of relief. The detritus of today's activities had vanished. Rooms that had been messy three hours earlier after successive closings were now pristine. He looked down and saw evidence of a vacuum cleaner's work.

Close call, he thought, and added, *sloppy on my part*. Fortunately, cleaning crews emptied waste baskets into bins and bins into dumpsters where everything disappeared under the weight of other waste, including liquids that turned everything to a putrid, waterlogged pulp. Those notes were never going to surface.

But Vinnie also realized Chad had effectively blown off Ramon's call and all-too-real issues it raised. Further, they would not see one another until next week's closing. If there was going to be a united front on this thing, it had to be agreed on now – tonight, in fact.

Vinnie went to Chad's office, which was locked. He entered using his master key and looked around. The man was oblivious. Papers were stacked everywhere. A computer containing God-knows-what was on his desk.

He had an idea. Vinnie took out his phone and called Chad, who took his sweet time about answering,

"It's late," Chad said. "What's so important?"

"I'm at the office, Vinnie said. "I had another call from Ramon. This one was even more intense. If Bree is with you, she ought to be in on this, too."

"We can't do this tomorrow?" Chad asked.

Vinnie could sense Chad's reticence. He needed to create a story to convey the sense of urgency. Vinnie said, "Ramon told me some things that gave me the distinct impression someone who works for him might have been in your office. I can't tell if someone had been in here. I need you to do that. I couldn't be more serious."

Vinnie could hear Bree's voice in the background and Chad's sigh. "Give us fifteen minutes."

* * * * *

Martin watched as Chad spoke to someone on his phone, then saw him talk to the woman, whose face showed concern. He then watched as Chad and the woman left the condo. Martin sprinted down the garage stairs and jumped into his car. With his headlights off, he waited at one of the mall's internal traffic circles. The mall had long since closed for the evening and the condo building had its own garage. Thirty seconds later, two cars exited the condo garage and turned right. Martin pulled down the access road, staying at a safe distance. Only when the two cars were on Route 9 did Martin turn on his own lights.

Ten minutes later, Chad's and the woman's car turned into the entrance for One Broadmoor Hill. Just one other vehicle was in the lot. Chad and the woman entered the building. When they were inside and out of sight, Martin approached the building, first making note of the three license plate numbers. He could run the plates in the morning from the comfort of his office.

Martin circled the building on foot. On the third floor, a single office light showed, and Martin assumed it was part of Senior Equity's suite. He had no angle to view what was going on in the office, and so he returned to his car to wait for the meeting's end. He glanced at his phone for the time: 10:37.

Crap, he thought. There was a call he ought to have made this morning after he went through the dumpster at the law firm. No, not the one to Paula. Yes, of course, he should have told her what he was going to do but she would have only forbidden him to get involved. He had replayed that imaginary conversation in his mind and, every time, it ended with her saying this was her problem to solve and she would let him know if she needed help. Which she wouldn't do.

No, this was the other call. Paula told him Samantha Ayers was more or less 'coordinating' everyone's efforts. He owed it to Samantha to let her know his own involvement.

He met Samantha when he first investigated the Brookfield Fair robbery. Her employer insured the armored car company. Publicity about the robbery caused the State Police to take over the investigation, leaving Martin with no official connection to the arrests which followed. As he got to know Paula in the following months, he began to piece together what really happened at the Fairgrounds that day.

Samantha's role, though, was a surprise. That an insurance

investigator would have such a strong sense of justice tempered with an equally malleable idea of what 'legal' and 'illegal' meant was eye-opening. After Martin's alerting the State Police led to the arrest of a serial killer at Cavendish Woods, he called Samantha and invited her to lunch. They had now met half a dozen times. He retrieved her number from his cell phone's memory and placed the call.

"I think we may need to compare notes," Martin said after introductions. "I just had dinner with the head of Senior Equity's captive law firm. He told me a number of fascinating things I think you ought to know. And, right now, I'm standing outside Senior Equity's office building, where Pannett and your mystery woman just went inside in a big hurry. It makes me wonder if everything isn't quite right in their little world."

* * * * *

Bree watched with a combination of growing anger and contempt as Chad and Vinnie traded blame for Ramon's belief Senior Equity had promised to be issuing two to three million more in mortgages every week. It was like watching two little boys sparring over who lied to Mom first, except her livelihood was also at stake.

She quickly deduced Vinnie had brought them here on a pretext. It was evident from the moment she walked into Chad's office nothing was out of place. It was a ruse designed to get Chad to come face to face with the fact that Ramon – whom she had never met – was holding their feet to the fire for empty promises made under the influence of alcohol or drugs, or probably both.

Bree was especially livid that neither man had bothered to mention to her Ramon had singled her out as being unnecessary to the operation. She still would not have known this critical piece of information except Vinnie had let it slip in an especially heated moment a few minutes earlier.

Listening to this conversation made her realize how fragile

things really were. Boiled down to its simplest, Vinnie's lone talent was understanding how to put together a set of money mules and prevent them from running off with a stack of hundred-dollar bills. He knew exactly how much – or how little – he needed to pay those mules to keep making endless rounds of deposits every day. She had also thought, at least until now, Vinnie's skill set extended to knowing how to deal with Ramon and keep him happy.

Now, she understood these two idiots had systematically hidden money from someone who would kill on a whim. You didn't lie to a guy like Ramon and you didn't – as Chad and Vinnie were doing now – discuss creating yet another fictitious set of books to hide your past sins. What they were talking about doing verged on suicide, except there was no escape for her, and she could be easily caught in the crossfire.

Chad, she had long known, was nothing but a con man. He was convinced both of his own immortality and his ability to extract himself from any situation, no matter how dire. He lived in the moment; ready to concoct another lie, any lie, to free himself from whatever danger he faced.

The two men, at least, had met Ramon. She, on the other hand, was just an expense line. And when it came time to pare costs, she would be the most expendable part of the operation. She knew full well, without her, Senior Equity would have collapsed after a year or been closed down by the state. Her role was the magic ingredient keeping the business legal. Yet, apparently, Ramon knew only she was getting paid a lot of money for no good reason.

As the argument between the two men dragged on without resolution, Bree began to entertain the thought, *maybe it is time for me to disappear.*

* * * * *

"You really know how to throw a can of gasoline on a fire," Samantha said after listening to Martin's summary of his conversation with Ryan Herndon.

Martin shook his head in disagreement. "When I met Ryan this evening, he was at the end of his rope. This was a guy in his late twenties – an attorney – and he was crying. Reading between the lines, he and his partners have been verbally and emotionally abused by Pannett for years, but they're trapped. They can't attract or keep new employees, they can't bring in new business. Senior Equity is all they've got. They know it's a scam and they're part of it, and it's killing them. It doesn't matter if they're caught or they walk away; they're convinced they're going to be disbarred and end up in jail."

Samantha was unconvinced. "If they're just getting around to figuring out what's going on, maybe they're not as smart as you think they are."

"This isn't some discussion they just started today," Martin countered. "It has been going on for months, which is how long it has been since they had either a receptionist or a paralegal. When they're not doing the grunt work of preparing for closings, they're in court explaining why old people ought to have their house yanked out from underneath them. It's relentless and it has taken an emotional toll."

"What I've done is throw them a lifeline," he continued. "They've been frozen by indecision. Tomorrow morning they'll talk it through."

"Or not," Samantha said. "To me, it sounds like a sorry bunch of people who made some bad choices. It's a little late to be getting religion."

"What if they're willing to turn over everything they've got?" Martin asked.

"Which is mostly solid evidence they've been crooked lawyers," Samantha shot back. "If you're quoting them accurately, they said it themselves. They signed the affidavits saying the people taking out these loans were aware of what they were doing. That takes Pannett and Malone off the hook. All they have to say is, 'we were relying on counsel'."

Frustrated, Martin asked, "But taken together with those notes Paula found…"

Samantha shook her head in frustration. She retrieved the six pieces of note paper from the plastic sleeve. Pushing aside case folders and assorted detritus, she carefully arranged them on her dining table.

"Let's assume Malone's fingerprints are on these sheets of paper," Samantha said. "Let's also assume a handwriting expert can testify this is Malone's handwriting. What do we have? Scribbles, not sentences. I interpreted them one way – and I think I'm right. But a defense attorney will show six other plausible interpretations. We both know these aren't going to sway a judge."

"And those sheets of paper tell me we've got an even more serious problem," Samantha continued. "Until a few hours ago, I was going on the assumption all we were dealing with was a predatory scam on the elderly. Pannett and Malone sold mortgages with every intention of foreclosing on them as quickly as possible. Their special twist was a partner – who we now know as 'B', whose job was to talk people who took out those reverse mortgages into doing things which would violate their agreements. I never considered where the money came from."

"Taking them down was going to be as easy as showing intent. Eleanor already has Pannett acknowledging he knows she isn't going to read the paperwork. Once she signed papers for a mortgage, we'd have him dead to rights. And, coupled with their sorry history of quick foreclosures, Senior Equity would be shut down inside a week."

Samantha's voice began to rise in a combustible combination of anger and concern. "Now, we know the source of the money is as dirty as the scheme itself. Pannett and Malone get their funding from 'R' as cash. Malone's job is to launder it; Pannett's is to put it to work. When you're dealing with that much cash, lives become incredibly cheap. So, I don't dare send Eleanor back in there. And I'm not sure I even want Paula and her crew back in on Monday."

Samantha continued, her anger showing. "You just told me these guys are already nervous because things aren't right in their little world, and they're probably talking strategy up there in Senior Equity's office. Now, let's say your lawyers don't show up at courthouses on Monday morning to file paperwork. Suddenly, this whole thing blows up. Pannett and Malone are going to start asking themselves, 'what's different from last week?' and the answer staring them right in the face is three women moved into the offices next door. You can't tell me they'll assume it's just a coincidence."

Martin slowly nodded. Yes, she was right.

Samantha saw the recognition in his face. Her next words were conciliatory. "None of us knew. It all started with an old lady getting a foreclosure notice and we all wanted to help. Neither you nor I nor Paula could possibly have guessed what was really going on."

"I think these people are worried," Samantha continued. "Not about what we're doing; they have no idea; at least not yet. They're worried about 'R' and promises they made to him they haven't kept. They're worried about money they're probably hiding from 'R'. If I were them, I'd be wondering if this weekend might be the perfect time to fold their tent and get out of Dodge before 'R' shows up."

"The problem is they have a bunch of money belonging to 'R', and 'R' probably isn't the forgiving type. Whoever 'R' works for will want their money and they'll want to mete out some old-fashioned punishment. And they won't want witnesses."

Martin again nodded his agreement. "So, tomorrow, my job is to go to Paula and tell her why she has to close up shop."

Samantha nodded. "I don't envy you."

"And the lawyers are on their own," Martin added.

"You may want to give them a 'heads up' it's all about to get messy," Samantha said.

Martin shook his head. "I can't believe how this turned out."

"You and me both," Samantha said. "You and me both."

Chapter Fifteen
Saturday, 7 a.m.

Paula awakened with a feeling of exhilaration. Provençal Home Décor of New England was a profitable business with real orders arriving hourly. Instead of counterfeit products, she had a showroom overflowing with beautiful napkins and placemats available for shipment. She had been interviewed for a news program. It was all so unexpected because, despite the monumental headaches, she *enjoyed* what she was doing.

Moreover, she had found a crucial piece of evidence to help solve the mystery of the inner workings of Senior Equity. Samantha's excitement had been intense when Paula showed her Vinnie Malone's handwritten notes.

She was in no mood to dampen this feeling by working in the garden or cleaning house. The garden could take care of itself this week and she hadn't been home enough to dirty any rooms.

Paula opened the refrigerator to take out the makings of breakfast and saw the remnants of the containers of food brought by Martin a few evenings earlier – back when she most felt everything was hopeless. She did not know what she had done to deserve this man, but she was not going to question providence or whatever force had attracted him to her.

Over breakfast, Paula made a brief list of things to do:

> *Check new orders, see what else we need to get from France*
> *Get into Chad's office, find additional evidence*

After breakfast, though, she knew she had one more thing to do. She opened her computer and composed a brief note:

Cher Marie,

I cannot thank you enough for expediting the shipment of tissus *from Provence to Boston yesterday. They arrived late morning while a news crew was here interviewing me. I hope you don't mind I gave them your name and contact information for follow-up questions on the work of the Council.*

By way of thanking you, I invite you to come to Boston as my guest so I can repay, in a small way, some part of the kindness you have shown me in the last week. To paraphrase Humphrey Bogart in 'Casablanca', I hope this the beginning of a beautiful friendship.

Sincerely yours,

Paula Winters

By nine o'clock, Paula was on her way to One Broadmoor Hill.

* * * * *

Jordan Wells looked over the final version of his two weekly reports for Chad. He had to admire what the guy was doing. It was sheer malevolent genius. Get the geezers to take out a mortgage they may or may not need, keep them in the dark until it was too late to back out of it, and set Bree to work on generating a default. Then, pull the rug out from under those stupid people and pocket a ton of money.

Over the last three years, Jordan had come to realize the elaborate secrecy demanded by Chad made perfect sense. By design, he spoke to everyone associated with Senior Equity over a throwaway phone that changed each month. Each week he grilled Chad's six-person, snake-charming geezer squad; the attorneys who filed foreclosure notices, and Bree. In all that time he had never met any of the players other than Chad and Vinnie; and he could not be certain he knew their real names. His payment was $2,000 a week in cash.

To ensure there was no email trail or 'cloud' copy of his reports to be retrieved by law enforcement agencies, he created his documents on a dedicated computer and printer with no internet connection. Next to the computer was a bottle of sulfuric acid. In the event of something happening, the computer's hard drive took a bath in the acid. In the event of his arrest, he knew no one and no one knew him. He was a ghost.

He proofread and checked the information in the reports, in awe of the audacious scheme he was memorializing and jealous of the minds that perpetrated it. The first document listed mortgage prospects and enumerated everything known about the geezers. The beauty of this report was he had Chad's permission to assume the geezer's identity once Senior Equity was through with them. He had already stripped twenty bank accounts of their remaining cash. It was so easy.

The second report detailed Bree's steps to get them to default, and the lawyers' filing of paperwork to push the properties into foreclosure. Bree was his kind of go-getter; a woman with no conscience who loved what she did. He could only imagine what kind of payday she got from each default. She must be worth millions. He fantasized about her appearance and her ability to pass as a broad in her sixties or seventies when she was probably in her thirties. A few months back he had tried a little phone flirtation with her. She had cut him off in a heartbeat and said, "You're a little young for me. Try again in ten years." All right. So maybe she was in her forties.

Satisfied, he printed out the documents. Now, had had only to deliver them.

* * * * *

Martin Hoffman sat, staring at the phone in his hand, dreading the call he had to make. After fifteen minutes of rehearsing his lines, he realized he needed to do this in person.

Paula, Samantha thinks it's best you shut down your business and stay away from One Broadmoor Hill…

His anxiety was heightened by running the three license plates from his surveillance of Pannett's apartment and the meeting at the office building. Two – those for Pannett and Malone – had come up as expected. He now knew Malone lived in the toney exurban town of Weston, and a quick look at Google maps told him Malone had done exceedingly well. While not one of the biggest houses in town, it was a Colonial on a multi-acre spread which had to be worth a couple of million dollars.

The third vehicle was registered to Emily Colwin. The first problem was neither name began with a 'B', so who was the 'B' in Malone's notes? 'Emily Colwin' lived at a condominium in Boston's South End. It was a rather nice 19th Century townhouse on a street out of the main traffic flow. Zillow's 'make me move' estimate for her unit was over a million.

The second problem was, as a living, breathing human being, 'Emily Colwin' began and ended with that condo and car. No other person by that name came even close to matching her credentials; not in age and not in location. In his professional estimation, 'Emily Colwin' was a one-use cover; a creation devised to have ownership of certain assets and an identity the real woman could slip into if needed.

This meant 'Emily Colwin' was smart. She was intelligent enough to have created multiple identities for herself. It also meant that, underneath those identities, there probably was a woman with a criminal record to hide. Such people, he had learned many times, tended to be extremely dangerous and not predictable.

Martin sighed, collected his car keys, and left his apartment for the drive to Hardington and a difficult conversation with Paula.

* * * * *

Chad's head hurt and it was all Vinnie's fault. Vinnie had kept up his fearmongering until nearly midnight. It was as though Ramon, backed by an armed goon squad, was about to come busting down the door, demanding all his money back with interest.

Chad's logical counterargument was the three of them – he had been careful to include Bree in the proceedings – held the undisputable upper hand. Ramon's money was tied up in a couple of hundred mortgages. Disemboweling the only people who had the paperwork on those mortgages was a poor way to get his money back. At worst, Senior Equity could stop writing mortgages and accelerate the process of pushing existing loans into default. That would take a minimum of a year. In the meantime, Ramon still had to find a way to launder up to ten million bucks a week and starting from scratch made no sense.

The right approach, Chad said from the outset, was to create another set of books. This one could show a slightly better resale on foreclosed homes so Ramon's take could be upped by five points. Even the best money launderers gave back just ninety or ninety-five cents on the dollars they washed. Senior Equity was already giving a twenty percent return on Ramon's money, and he was about to be offered an additional five percent. What wasn't to like?

And, as for going to $10 million a week, well, sure, they could bump up the recruiting effort. Direct mail and radio already filled three or four seminars each week. Why not try internet ads as well?

Vinnie wasn't hearing any of it. He must have said fifty times there was a new tone in Ramon's voice and it was 'dangerous'. Well, that was Vinnie's end of the arrangement: make and keep Ramon happy. Slicing into their income wasn't part of the deal.

He was also annoyed Bree hadn't come back to his condo after that endless, worthless meeting. Spending the night made sense. Instead, she didn't even offer an excuse; just said it was late. That wasn't like her.

After two cups of coffee, Chad finally acknowledged he was in a foul mood and it wasn't going to change on its own. Yeah, he ought to be in the office reviewing Jordan's report. But he just didn't feel like it, and it was Vinnie's fault.

Chad did the one thing guaranteed to take his mind off his bad mood. From the bar in his 'entertaining space', he found his baggie of the white powder with the magical ability to take his mind off of everything. Two lines of coke later, he lay down on his exquisite leather sofa and closed his eyes. He now had a broad smile on his face.

* * * * *

Vinnie, too, awakened in a rotten mood on Saturday morning. Once again, Chad had proven himself to be a moron. They needed a plan; a united front. And his 'plan' was to cook the books.

Worse, Bree had sat through the meeting with her eyes boring a hole through his head. All right, that was partly his fault. He had let slip that Ramon singled out Bree as expendable, and Bree assumed, rightly, that he had not disagreed with Ramon's assessment.

Well, the fact was Bree could easily be replaced with someone who would work for a fixed fee rather than a percentage cut of every damn foreclosure. As Ramon pointed out, the entire foreclosure thing was an unnecessary charade. Why not just have the mortgage holders meet with an 'accident'? They're old. They have coronaries. Their cars go out of control. They walk in front of buses. They fall down escalators. All these contrived meetings in drug stores just dragged out the inevitable.

And Vinnie couldn't disagree. Hell, you didn't disagree with Ramon. You did the sensible thing: you figured out how to make him happy. Well, if Bree was the sticking point, then get Bree out of the picture. Better yet, shift the blame for everything Ramon thought was going wrong to Bree. Let her take the fall.

In his gut, though, Vinnie was coming to realize Senior Equity was nearing the end of its run. Even the longest con seldom went on for more than six months, and Senior Equity was about to wrap up its third year. The last two had made them wealthy. Why not fold the table and quit while everyone was ahead?

The problem, of course, was Ramon. Guys like him usually stayed on top a few years, then got murdered by whatever group most coveted their territory. When the bloodshed stopped, no one knew where all the money was and so they started over, forgetting about tens of millions of dollars stashed somewhere because more money was rolling in every day.

Ramon seemed to be immune to all that. It was uncanny. He treated it as though he thought it was a real business.

Vinnie's head hurt. But it was a big race day at Saratoga and he had bets to get down. He turned to his computer and began examining morning workout times for the horses in the first three races.

* * * * *

In spite of not getting home until 1 a.m., Bree was awake and alert. As was her practice, she checked her brokerage statement. Most mornings it was a perfunctory thing; she looked at the balance, smiled at what she saw, and her brain generated a healthy shot of dopamine to her system.

This morning was completely different. She analyzed the account for cash and cash flow. She also made certain the debit cards tying to the account were current and active.

Sometime in the night, her mind made the decision to implement an escape plan she constructed over the past two years. It all came down to Vinnie's inadvertent blurting out she had been fingered by Ramon as being 'expendable' in Senior Equity's cost equation.

The statement made everything irreversible and necessary to her safety. It was time to become Emily Colwin. It was time to disappear for at least six months somewhere no one would think to look for her.

Her disappearing feat would require a few other actions, and the sooner they were taken care of, the better. The first was to eliminate every tangible trace of 'Bree Fleming'. Her fingerprints were on door handles and other surfaces at One Broadmoor Hill. Those needed to be eradicated this morning. That was the easiest thing she had to do.

The others were a bit messy. She needed to kill Chad and Vinnie. They, alone, knew what she looked like and where she lived. Her condo was in the name of Emily Colwin. There must be no one left alive who could say Emily and Bree were the same woman.

Was there anyone else who had seen her and could describe her? Senior Equity's clients met only an elderly woman who went by names plucked from the air. The noxious guy who grilled her every week was just a voice on the phone. She stayed away from the office when the lawyers were there. By design, she steered clear of the 'shepherds' who corralled the clients.

No, wait. There was Thursday's encounter with the sixty-something woman with pancreatic cancer. Bree had gone to Senior Equity's offices armed with nothing more than a wig because she was playing the role of an adult daughter. One of those shepherds, Andrew Douglas, had seen her and, together, they had met with Chad, where Chad called her 'Bree'. Were Andrew to be arrested, would he be smart enough to remember he had met Senior Equity's 'secret weapon'?

Thinking harder, she remembered she had met one of Chad's lawyers on two occasions. Ryan something. They had not been introduced, but Bree remembered the lawyer eyeing her, memorizing her appearance. There was even the woman with the cancer. If everything hit the fan, it wouldn't be far-fetched for the cops to ask her for a description of the mystery woman.

No. She didn't have time to take out everyone. But Chad and Vinnie had to go. Only then could she safely disappear.

* * * * *

The look of relief on everyone's face was one Ryan would never forget. He had expected opposition or at least concern. Instead, Lisa's and Steve's faces had shown relief this was finally over.

They met Saturday morning at a coffee-and-donut shop in Walpole, commandeering a booth in the back where they were unlikely to be heard. Ryan recounted his meeting with Martin Hoffman and Ryan's assessment of the detective.

"He's the real deal," Ryan said. "I trust him."

To Ryan's surprise, his two partners agreed it was time – in fact, long past time – for all this to end. The crop of mortgagees they had processed the day before was appalling. Lisa Watts admitted she had cried all the way home. Steve Curbow said the look of greed was unmistakable on the faces of the men and women who accompanied their elderly clients.

Thirty minutes later they were at their office, printing out and copying everything they had worked on over the past three years. There would be three printed sets of every record, from initial application to foreclosure on accounts already closed. When they were finished copying and indexing everything, the computers themselves would be boxed up and preserved. By this afternoon, if all went as planned, The Walpole Law Group would exist only as an empty building on Route 1A.

The question, as they printed and packed, was where they would go, and whether they should travel as a group or individually. Funding was not an issue; Ryan had already distributed the $19,000 in cash he received from Chad Friday evening. They had all agreed using credit cards would make tracking them too easy.

"Airlines won't let you pay for a flight with cash," Steve said. "I don't even think you can take a train. It's all about security. I imagine hotels are the same. If someone walks up to the front desk with a wad of hundred-dollar bills, it's going to set off alarm bells."

"I'll ask Detective Hoffman's his advice when I call him," Ryan said. "He'll know what to do."

Despite Ryan's voiced confidence, the three realized the next few days or weeks promised nothing but uncertainty.

Chapter Sixteen
Saturday, 9 a.m.

Jordan Wells pulled into the parking lot of One Broadmoor Hill. A lone car was parked by the front entrance, but it was not the one he associated with Chad. But the front entrance was unlocked, and the elevator was working. He got off on the third floor and walked through darkened hallways to the entrance to Senior Equity. That door, too, was unlocked.

Chad almost always met Jordan here on Saturday mornings to personally receive the two reports and turn over twenty, one-hundred-dollar bills. On the few times Chad was unable to make it, Jordan would find the front entrance unlocked and the elevator working. Jordan was instructed to slide the reports under Chad's office door, where he would also be able to feel the envelope with his cash. Today, though, there was only darkness.

Once inside Senior Equity's suite, though, he thought he heard noises.

"Hey!" Jordan yelled out. "Anyone want to turn on the lights?"

For several seconds there was only silence. Then he heard the sound of light footsteps on the carpeting. Another few seconds later, a woman appeared, looking at him with great caution and apprehension.

The woman was in shadow, but Jordan could make out enough of her to know she was slender, maybe five-eight, with dark hair. Her age might be anywhere from forty to fifty… *Omigod*, he thought.

"Are you Bree?" he asked.

The woman looked startled. She cocked her head to one side, apparently trying to figure out who he was and why he was here. He also saw now why she had said, *'You're a little young for me. Come back in ten years.'* He had pictured her young with the ability to play old.

"Who wants to know?" the woman said. The voice was husky. Just like Bree's.

"We've been talking on the phone for three years. I'm Jordan. Jordan Wells. The guy you call the 'grand inquisitor'."

"Jordan?" the woman said. "I pictured someone…"

"Younger?" Jordan said, finishing her sentence. "Everyone says I sound 'mature'. Although you apparently saw through my façade when you told me to come back in ten years. It hurt, you know."

The woman smiled. "I was a bit of a bitch that day."

It was Jordan's turn to smile. "I have Chad's weekly report." He held it up for her to see. "He usually calls me if he isn't going to be here."

"I'm supposed to meet him here, too," the woman said. "He said he'd be here at nine. I was just… cleaning up some things."

"Looks like he stood both of us up," Jordan said. "But if he left *my* envelope under his door, I'll just leave the report and be on my way."

"Let's check," the woman said. She went to Chad's office, got on her hands and knees, and felt under the door. As she did, Jordan smelled an expensive, floral perfume.

"You don't have a key?" Jordan asked.

"No one has a key to Chad Pannett's office," the woman said. "That's the way he wants it. But I don't feel an envelope."

Jordan was uncertain of what to do.

"Look," the woman said. "Chad is almost never late. Do the two of you usually have a long conversation or is it just exchange envelopes and be on your way to do something more fun on a Saturday morning?"

Jordan grinned. "It's summer and it's a beautiful day."

"Well, I have no choice," the woman said. "This is a command performance. I have to stay no matter what, and I know from long experience if I call and tell him he's late, it will just piss him off. I can have him call you to discuss how he gets your envelope to you." She cocked her head, awaiting a reply.

"Fine," Jordan said, handing her the envelope.

"It's great finally meeting my 'grand inquisitor'," the woman said, smiling and tucking the envelope under her arm. "Have a terrific summer day."

Jordan turned and left, pausing only to turn back to look over his shoulder as he opened the door to Senior Equity's suite. The woman was turning to go back to whatever office she had been in.

Bree was pretty much what he expected: slim, stylish. When he left the building, he glanced over at her car. A bright red, top-of-the-line Tesla Model S. Definitely a Bree kind of car.

* * * * *

Paula did not stop shaking for more than a minute. She had never felt more vulnerable or afraid in her life. At any moment, Jordan Wells could have pulled out his phone and called Chad. Or he could have pulled out a gun or a knife.

She now knew the 'B' in Vinnie Malone's notes was Bree. Where Wells fit into the scheme of things she did not know, but the thick report in her hands was something key; and of sufficient importance he delivered it by hand every Saturday morning.

What she had done had worked only because, in Chad's paranoia, players were not supposed to meet one another in person. Wells spoke by phone to Bree – apparently to extract information – every week. He knew only Bree's voice, and there was just enough similarity to allow Jordan to jump to the conclusion.

She had to get out of the building. Chad could be here at any moment if Jordan was expecting to meet him. He might be coming up the elevator.

Paula raced to the other side of the building to a window with a view of the front of the building. To her relief, her Tesla was the only car in the parking lot. Not daring to wait for the elevator, she ran for the stairwell and down the two flights.

Her heart racing, she raced out the door, taking the time neither to lock it or deactivate the elevator. She jumped into her car and accelerated out of the parking lot, grateful no car passed her until she was safely on Route 9.

She had to get this envelope to Samantha. Whatever its contents, it contained Jordan Well's fingerprints so he could be found.

Paula pulled into a liquor store's empty parking lot and called Samantha.

Pick up. Pick up. Pick up, she thought.

Samantha answered. Caller ID apparently let her know who was on the other end of the line, because Samantha's first words were, "Paula, I'm so sorry…"

"Sorry for what?" Paula asked.

"Martin hasn't called you?"

"Martin? Has something happened…"

Samantha cut Paula off. "Martin and I met last night and agreed this has gotten too dangerous. We don't have anything. Nothing will stick and…"

"I have something that will stick," Paula said. "Or at least I think I do. I was just handed a thick report meant for Chad Pannett."

There was silence on the other end of the line. Finally, Samantha said, "Where are you?"

"On Route 9, about a mile west of One Broadmoor Hill."

Don't break any laws, but get here as fast as you can," Samantha said. "I'll get hold of Martin." ·

* * * * *

Martin and Samantha took turns shaking their heads and saying 'Jesus Christ' as they carefully turned the pages of the two reports, which totaled more than 40, single-spaced sheets.

Martin looked at Paula with fresh appreciation and wonder. This incredible woman had just handed them a current snapshot of an horrific scam, and proof the scheme was a deliberate effort to steal the homes of the elderly.

Every current reverse mortgage applicant was shown, with an assessment of those applicants' mental or physical frailty and the likelihood of their home being flipped for a substantial profit. Every name of every current mortgage holder was listed, with efforts by 'Bree' to throw those mortgages into foreclosure. Every mortgage now, however technically, in default, was being tracked for court dates and notifications.

"What do we do next?" Samantha said softly. Her question, though addressed to both Paula and Martin, was clearly meant for Martin.

Martin, looking at Paula, said, "I start by offering an apology. After dinner the other night, I started poking around. I called a friend with the State Police to ask if he knew anything about Senior Equity. He didn't, but he said I'd find their 'weak underbelly' by looking for anyone associated with it who wasn't raking in the big dollars. I visited their lawyers' dump of an office yesterday morning and concluded they were definitely outsiders."

"I wish you hadn't, but it isn't…" Paula started to say.

Martin held up his hand. "There's more. So, last night, I staked out One Broadmoor Hill and followed the head lawyer when everyone went home. I bought him dinner and spoke with him at length. The firm wants out. They were supposed to meet this morning to make certain they all agreed and if they did, they should be in their offices printing out their files."

"You really know how to take a request to not get involved with something seriously," Paula said.

"You'd better hear the rest," Martin said sheepishly. "At dinner, the lawyer – Ryan Herndon – said he knew where Chad lives. It was less than a mile away, so I decided to stake out the building from a parking garage. I got a good look at Bree in the process…"

"Was she wearing any clothes?" Paula asked.

Martin's face turned red. "It was all business. But Chad got a call from Vinnie Malone, and the three of them met at the Senior Equity office. It gave me an opportunity to collect license plate numbers. I have an address for Malone in Weston. The problem is Bree. The license plate on the car she was driving ties to a woman named Emily Colwin at an address in Boston's South End. Colwin owns a unit in the building."

"So, her real name is Emily Colwin," Paula said.

Martin shook his head. "Emily Colwin's existence begins and ends at her car and condo, and likely a bank account. It's a cover identity; the kind of thing someone creates if they need to have a backup plan and are smart enough to know how to pull it off. People who do those things usually have a record. They're dangerous."

Paula raised an eyebrow. "And you didn't tell me this until now because…"

"Because fairly late last evening, I came out to see Samantha and get her thoughts," Martin said. "Based on the papers you brought yesterday – which, coupled with the late-night, all-crooks-on-deck meeting which was probably a lengthy discussion of what was in those notes – Samantha and I think the wheels are coming off the bus at Senior Equity."

Martin continued. "I agree with Samantha's interpretation: this 'R' guy isn't happy with how Chad and Vinnie are running things, and Chad apparently made some promises he hasn't kept. You don't want to be around a situation like that. I *have* been around those situations. People start shooting one another and they don't care who gets hit in the crossfire."

"So, why didn't you call me?" Paula asked. Her tone was

forthright and her gaze was steady. Martin saw she was on the verge of anger. "Were you afraid…"

"There are things you don't say over the phone," Martin snapped. "There are conversations you need to have in person. I drove down to your home this morning. I was there at 8:15. You were already gone."

He saw Paula start to say something, then reconsider.

After a few moment's silence in the room, Paula said, "So, like Samantha asked, what do *we* do now?"

Martin felt an inner relief. "I find out what the lawyers decided to do. If they're making paper copies, we get a set over here for safekeeping. I think we also find a way to keep them out of sight. Samantha calls her buddies in the Attorney General's office and I do the same with my State Police contacts."

"But in the meantime, we have another problem – two problems actually," Martin said. "The first is Chad is going to go over to his office, if he hasn't already. He's going to be expecting to find his report. When it isn't there, he's going to call Jordan Wells, and he's going to say he gave it to Bree. Chad is going to call Bree. That's when all hell breaks loose."

Samantha said, "I can make and print PDFs of the report. In fact, I'm going to anyway. We can put a report under Chad Pannett's door which looks just like the original and have it there in under thirty minutes."

"If Chad hasn't gone to his office," Paula said, worry in her voice. "And if he catches me…"

"I'll take the report," Samantha said. "If he tries to mess with me, he's going to find he picked on the wrong woman."

"The second problem is what we call the 'silver platter standard'," Martin continued. "You and Samantha are civilians in the eyes of the law. You can do illegal things and they're still admissible in court for purposes of prosecuting bad guys because no one put you up to doing those things. I can't."

Samantha asked, "Why not?"

"Because I'm an officer of the law. A defense attorney would argue the State Police put me up to meeting with Ryan Herndon. If the attorney makes a convincing case that my stumbling into this evidence is too convenient, everything I touch becomes 'tainted fruit'."

"What do we do?" Paula asked.

"You and Samantha become the go-betweens, starting with going to meet with them this morning," Martin said. "You convince them it's in their best interests to say *you* were the person who met with Ryan. I can't be involved with them. All I can do is take all the material you've collected and turn it over to the State Police. It worked well enough at Cavendish Woods."

"When do I start?" Paula asked.

"I'm going to call Ryan while Samantha makes those copies of the report and spoils someone's weekend at the AG's office."

Martin reached for his phone as Samantha took the report and her briefcase to the bedroom she used as an office. Martin placed a call.

"Ryan? This is Martin Hoffman. For reasons that will become clear in just a moment, I'm going to turn the phone over to a fantastically smart lady by the name of Paula Winters." He handed her the phone.

"Ryan?" Paula said. "My name is Paula Winters. When you were at One Broadmoor Hill yesterday, you probably noticed another suite of offices on the third floor were occupied. You probably saw lots of brightly colored napkins and placemats. If you looked really carefully, you may have seen three little old ladies packing boxes. I was one of those little old ladies, except what I've really been doing is keeping a close eye on Chad Pannett…"

Chapter Seventeen
Saturday 9:30 a.m.

"I don't suppose you dropped by to apologize for not coming back here last night?"

Chad sniffled, and his eyes were still bloodshot from the lines of coke. But it was obvious to Bree he could care less about apologies. Chad was in the woozy twilight between a cocaine high and the real world. He could be jolted into the real world or he could be pushed back into those proverbial arms of Morpheus.

They were standing in the entryway to Chad's condo. He was in a loosely wrapped robe, she was in tight jeans and a tank top. She also wore a blonde wig.

She smiled. "It depends on what I get as a reward for apologizing."

He returned the smile and threw back one arm to indicate the apartment. "I think we can negotiate something."

She entered the apartment. "I was so mad at Vinnie. He wouldn't listen to you." She said this in a small voice making her sound helpless.

"Vinnie is rapidly outliving his usefulness to our little organization," Chad said. "Do you want to soak first?"

Bree smiled and began taking off her clothes. Chad stumbled into the master bath and began running water into the whirlpool tub. Bree removed a small tube from her purse and, carefully wrapping a tissue around it, followed him in.

Seconds later, Chad was at one end of the tub, making happy noises. Bree leaned over him, her bare breasts a few inches from his face. "I've got something special for us," she said.

"I'm up for special," he grinned.

She opened the tube, which contained a white powder. "Rub

this across your gums." She held if out for him. He took it without questions. Bree always had new, kinky things.

He smeared the powder on his upper gum. He frowned. "Tastes awful. Now it's your turn."

Instead, Bree smiled and turned around, heading back into the living area and her clothes.

Chad gasped, his mouth burning. He splashed water into his mouth, but the burning would not go away. And where the hell was Bree? He tried to yell out, but his jaw was rapidly turning numb. What kind of a high was this?

He could not turn his head and the numbness spread to his shoulders and chest. He was having trouble sitting up, and his vision was blurring as the muscles in his eyes failed to follow the direction of his brain.

Unable to maintain muscle control, he found himself slipping further into the tub. Soon only his face was above the surface and then, his entire body was submerged. His mind felt terror but his body refused to do anything about it.

A minute later, Bree, now fully dressed, returned to the tub. She now also wore surgical gloves on both hands. She picked up Chad's lifeless left hand and placed his fingers around the vial, which had contained just five milligrams of fentanyl mixed into a like amount of baking soda.

Three milligrams of the powerful synthetic opioid would have been enough to kill him, but Bree really didn't have time to wait around ten or fifteen minutes watching him die. She had other places to go.

She went to his bar where his baggie of cocaine was not too cleverly hidden inside an ice bucket. The baggie already had his prints on it. With her gloved hand, she lifted the lid of the ice bucket and dropped the vial containing the microscopic residue of fentanyl beside the cocaine. The police could draw their own conclusions.

Now, with a damp bar mop, she cleaned areas she knew she had touched in recent days. Chad's extravagances extended to the employment of a twice-a-week cleaning service, and the service would have been in on Thursday. After fifteen minutes, she was satisfied all fingerprint or DNA evidence of Bree Fleming had been removed.

There was, of course, the desk manager who had nodded salaciously whenever she entered the lobby of the condo. He could describe Bree Fleming. But the likelihood was remote Chad's body would be discovered before the cleaning crew next entered the apartment on Monday. She would be long gone by then and, if she needed more time, Bree could always call the service and ask they skip the first cleaning.

She was about to leave when she thought of Chad's phone. If there was some kind of investigation into Chad's death, his phone would be examined for calls close to the time of his demise. It lay on a glass-topped table in his living room. Still wearing surgical gloves, she turned on the phone.

There were two unretrieved phone mail messages. One was from Vinnie early this morning suggesting they get together to 'pin all our problems on Bree'. Bree listened to it dispassionately. It confirmed what she already knew. Vinnie would do whatever Ramon demanded and would have badgered Chad until he came around to Vinnie's position. Well, Vinnie, with his fancy sports car and diamond pinkie ring, had a surprise coming to him.

She deleted the message.

The other message had been sent less than an hour ago.

"Hey, man, this is Jordan. You weren't there when I was at the office a little while ago. I just want you to know I left the report with Bree and I wanted to make sure it got to you. I'll swing by the office a little later to pick up my cash. If you don't have time to talk, just leave it under the door. That's it. Give me a call back to let me know you got the message."

Her hand shaking, Bree replayed the message twice. '...*I left the report with Bree...'.* There was no mistaking the words. Wells had encountered someone at the office this morning. Either the person convinced Wells she was Bree, or Wells had assumed the person was Bree.

She knew what 'the report' was. She spent two hours on the phone with Jordan every week detailing what she had done, and Chad often asked her questions based on it.

And the idiot, Wells, had handed this woman the latest copy of the report.

She erased the message, deleted herself from Chad's contacts, and returned the phone to where she had found it.

Think, she said to herself. *Who could have been in the office?* Law enforcement was one likely answer but the other, more ominous possibility was one of Ramon's people.

If it was law enforcement, it should have been half a dozen agents rather than a lone woman. On the other hand, Ramon's agents were not known for their subtlety. If surprised in the process of going through Chad's office, their first instinct would have been to leave Wells in a pool of his own blood. The tone of the message sounded as though it was a casual encounter.

But the woman knew who 'Bree' was and had successfully masqueraded as her.

Bree had intended to go directly from Chad's apartment to Vinnie's home. She needed to erase fingerprints and other evidence from One Broadmoor Hill. Fine, she would go there first.

* * * * *

Samantha carefully drove up a parallel road to the one leading to One Broadmoor Hill. She parked in an adjacent building's lot amid half a dozen cars probably belonging to employees working the weekend.

One Broadmoor Hill occupied the top of a small knoll, and Samantha had to scale a landscaped berm to reach the side of the building. There, she had an unobstructed view of the parking lot serving the building. No cars were in evidence.

She was about to scramble up the last few feet of the hill and make a dash for the building when she saw a glint of sunlight on metal. She retreated to the shrubbery.

A late-model gray Toyota Camry pulled up the driveway and parked in one of the handicapped spaces directly in front of the entrance. A woman with blonde hair in tight jeans and a white tank top jumped out of the car and raced into the building. In his call Friday evening, Martin had indicated Senior Equity's offices were at the rear of the building. Samantha had no idea how long she would be inside, but the speed of her entry left the impression her return would be just as unexpected.

Samantha quickly moved through the shrubbery to get a view of the auto's license plate. She memorized it and moved back to the base of the hill. She pulled out her phone and called Martin's cell. He answered immediately.

"What was the license plate you got for Bree last night?" Samantha asked. She heard the answer and said, "She just got here and ran into the building. She looks a lot younger than you described her, and she's blonde today."

"I have no way of knowing if Chad has already been here or if he's coming," Samantha added. "I'll wait for Bree to leave and then I'll leave the report."

Samantha saw another glint of light. "Just a minute," she said. "There's another car."

* * * * *

As Bree wiped surfaces around the office she might have touched, she tried, unsuccessfully, to picture the encounter between Wells and the woman posing as her.

There was no evidence of a search, much less a ransacking. No drawers were opened, and nothing was out of place. Moreover, Chad's door was locked. Anyone in the building searching for evidence would have broken down the door of the one office certain to have incriminating evidence in it.

And, from Wells' breezy phone mail message, the encounter had been low-key and friendly. It just didn't make sense.

Unless…

The woman – the phony 'Bree' – was already in the building when Jordan arrived. How did she get in? The entry door to the building was kept locked. Chad and Vinnie had the only keys, and the door did not appear to have been forced. She had just used the elevator. Activating the elevator in the morning required a proximity card. Chad and Vinnie had the lone cards.

But now there was a second tenant.

It was possible Vinnie or Chad had failed to deactivate the elevator or lock the door. She tried to reconstruct the end-of-the-evening events. It was nearly midnight. They all rode down in the elevator together, the tension evident. They had gotten off the elevator in the small lobby.

And Vinnie had taken out his wallet and held a card to the elevator bank.

And, when they exited the building, Vinnie had crouched down to lock the door. The act seemed to have a certain ominous finality to it, as though a chapter was ending.

It was unlikely Vinnie would have come back to the office this morning. Preoccupied with his money mules, he usually visited only on closing day.

Which left the new tenant. The old ladies with their napkins. There were three of them, she thought. Two were in their sixties or seventies. There was no way they could have been accepted by Wells as Bree. The third one, though, was younger; fifty or so. Could she have passed herself off?

She heard a noise in the building; the sound of the elevator moving. Then, the distinctive 'ding' of it arriving on the third floor.

Bree looked around her in the dim light for a weapon. She found a pair of scissors. She put them in her back pocket.

A male voice said, "Anybody up here?"

Bree remained silent. She listened as someone came into the Senior Equity lobby.

"Hello?" the male voice said.

A figure of a man strode toward Chad's office and promptly dropped to his knees. He was feeling under the door.

"Damn," he said and got back on his feet.

Bree stepped out of the shadow. "I was thinking the same thing. If we could just get into his office." She smiled.

The man seemed startled by the presence of someone else in the building.

"Uh, who are you?" the man asked.

"Ashley Moore, and I'm prepared to identify myself," Bree said, seeming to reach into the back pocket of her jeans for a wallet but, in reality, getting a grip on the scissors. "And you?"

"Jordan Wells," he said, reaching for his own wallet.

"It's OK," Bree said. "Bree said you might be coming back later to pick up your payment."

Wells looked at her with caution. "Maybe you want to tell me why you're here, without any lights on."

"I thought I'd be here for about three minutes. I'm Bree's friend. I'm also Chad's girlfriend, for what it's worth. I came here to pick up some paperwork – your report, in fact – from Chad's office. He said he had left the door unlocked. He didn't. He also said the envelope with your money was on his desk, and I was supposed to leave it just under the door when I left. I wonder if he fibbed about that, too."

"I think I can get in the door," Wells said, a sly look on his face. "I know a few tricks."

"Well, I don't, and I really don't want to go back to Natick to get the key. Chad would think I'm stupid, which I'm not."

"Do you have a couple of ballpoint pens?" Wells asked.

Bree threw a glance behind her. "There's a bunch of office

supplies in the closet to the right."

Bree had an idea. While Wells rummaged through cabinets in the supply room, she pulled her phone from her pocket and did a Google search. When the site she wanted appeared, she began scrolling until she found the right item. She enlarged it to full screen size.

Wells returned and pulled apart the pens. He began fiddling with the door. Fifteen seconds later it swung open.

"You are good," Bree said with admiration. "But before we go in, I have one last test for you." She raised the phone to his face. "If you're so smart, who is this woman?"

Wells looked at the image. "It's Bree."

"You pass with flying colors," Bree said. "Let's go in and find your money and get the report." She waited outside while he went into the office.

"There's the envelope," he said.

With his back turned to her, Bree took the scissors from her pocket. It would be so easy to plunge them into the side of his neck. She could sever his carotid artery and he would be dead in two minutes or less. Besides, the kid was stupid. He accepted the word of women far too easily. He tried showing off for them in hopes they would reciprocate his trust by going to bed with him. He didn't deserve to live.

But it would also be messy and obviously a case of murder. A body with scissors in its neck had to be thoroughly investigated. Police would come, and everyone associated with Senior Equity would be under suspicion. With Chad, conversely, it was a simple, self-inflicted drug overdose.

Bree put the scissors back into her pocket.

"I don't see the report, though," Wells said.

"I'll find it," Bree said, smiling and standing by the doorway. "I know Chad's hiding places pretty well. I'll let him know you picked up your payment."

Oblivious to how close he had come to death, she watched as Wells stuffed the envelope into his jeans. A minute later, she heard the 'ding' of the elevator.

She immediately raced to a window facing the parking lot and got there just as Jordan exited the building. His was the only other vehicle in the parking lot, a black BMW. She made careful note of the license plate number, then returned to her examination of Chad's office.

Opening drawers, she found $4,000 in hundred-dollar bills. She put them into her purse. It would increase the time before she needed to make an ATM withdrawal or use her debit card.

She thoroughly wiped down surfaces she had touched. As she did, she thought through her next steps. Wells' visit had been fortuitous. He had saved her the messy trouble of breaking down a door, and he had solved the mystery of the other 'Bree'. She tapped her phone back to life and looked at the image on her screen and decreased its size slightly. Now there was a photo of the woman she had briefly met earlier in the week, together with a caption.

Paula Winters, Founder and President, Provençal Home Décor of New England.

Bree had hoped to depart Boston as soon as she took care of Vinnie. She had convinced herself tracking down Eleanor Strong was unnecessary. But now there was a serious complication. Paula Winters was investigating Senior Equity. Her employer – some government agency, probably – had gone to the trouble and expense of setting up a company in order to be in proximity to Senior Equity. And, now this Paula Winters had a copy of Wells' current report; an explosive piece of evidence showing Bree's central role in the scam.

As the author of that report and all the ones he created before it, Wells needed to die. He was in a position to say far too much to anyone who pressured him for information. He had shown himself to be stupid but, given time to reflect, he might well realize it was the second woman he encountered this morning who was the 'real' Bree. Well, she had his license plate number. Finding him would be easy.

Bree also knew she had to find Paula Winters before she turned the report over to whomever she worked for. Winters must be made to tell how many people were involved and how much they knew. Then, of course, the woman would die. She reached into her purse and retrieved the business card given to her a few days earlier by the older woman. She had something about it still having the president's address...

Bree smiled to herself as she studied the card. It was going to be a busy day.

* * * * *

Less than ten minutes after the twenty-something man went into the office building, Samantha watched him come back out of the building, get into his car, and leave the parking lot. Though she was probably two hundred feet from him, she was convinced he was smiling.

Samantha had already relayed his license plate information to Martin. In a short while, she would know his name and how he figured into Senior Equity.

Ten minutes later, Bree also exited the building. The look on her face was anything but a smile. After a few minutes, Samantha came out of the shrubbery and went into the building.

She turned on the lights in Senior Equity's offices and tried to deduce, from the amount of time each person had spent in the office, what events had transpired. Bree had perhaps five minutes alone before the second man arrived. The man had been in the office less than ten minutes. Using Paula's hand-drawn layout of the office, Samantha oriented herself to her surroundings.

Pannett's office door showed evidence of an amateur and messy lock-picking effort. Scratches and ink stains on the door indicated they had used whatever was at hand rather than bringing in lock-picking tools. So much for the idea the man had come as a result of a call for help.

Chad's door was now unlocked. Paula had said it was locked when she left. Inside the office, all seemed normal. Given Bree was close to Chad, why wouldn't she use his key? She was pondering this question when her phone chimed.

"Brace yourself," Martin said. "The second car belongs to Jordan Wells."

Samantha heard herself gasp.

"Tell me what you see," Martin asked.

"Chad's door has been jimmied open," Samantha said. "An amateur effort, but it worked. Chad's office hasn't been tossed. Here's the problem: less than three hours ago, Jordan Wells met a woman he accepted as Bree. A few minutes ago, he met the *real* Bree. What happened?"

"How did Jordan look when you saw him leave?" Martin asked.

"He was smiling. He looked happy."

"Then Bree didn't tell him who she was," Martin said. "Let's say he was returning to the building thinking Chad would be there and he could get his money…"

"And Bree was there trying to get into Chad's office," Samantha added. "Sometime during their ten minutes together, Jordan would have to say he left the report…"

"But he would have said he left it with a woman he thought was Bree," Martin said. "It only makes sense if Jordan called Chad and said 'Bree' had the report. Chad could have sent Bree to meet him at the office to find out who the other woman was…"

"Except Bree didn't have a key," Samantha said. "Give me a second to see if it makes sense." She placed her eyes level with Chad's desk. It confirmed her worst suspicion.

"There's one other scenario where Jordan comes walking out of the building both alive and smiling," Samantha continued. "Bree somehow overheard the phone call between Chad and Jordan. She realized someone had successfully impersonated her because Chad doesn't allow his people to get to know one another. Bree was here on her own. And she has an exit strategy. Chad's desk has been rubbed clean of prints, and I'll bet every other surface in this office has been wiped."

"That's more than just plausible. So, where's Chad in all of this?" Martin asked.

"The best case is, Chad is drugged or drunk," Samantha replied. "Bree went home last night but could have gone back to his place this morning to party. She left Chad when Jordan called."

Samantha continued. "The worst case is whatever went down between Chad, Bree, and Malone in this office last night made Bree realize she has to get out. And hearing Wells willingly turned over his latest report to an imposter; well, it lit a fuse. Chad and Vinnie could be dead."

This time, it was Samantha who heard Martin's sharp intake of breath. "Could she have coaxed a description out of Wells?"

I don't think we want to chance it," Samantha said. "Get hold of Paula and tell her to get back over to my apartment, with or without the lawyers. Bree has had time to think. She's going to wonder who would have been in the office. Paula would have to be a suspect. In the meantime, give me Wells' address."

* * * * *

The look on their faces wavered between determination and desperation, Paula thought. These were three kids just a few years older than her son and daughter, and they were caught in the kind of existential crisis no one at any age should ever have to go through.

The young woman, Lisa Watts, seemed to have weighed and accepted the odds of coming out of this with her career intact. The head of the law firm, Ryan Herndon, was still uncertain.

"You're not with any law enforcement agency and you're not a private investigator," he said. "Why should we trust you?"

"Let's just say I've been effective doing what I do," Paula said, trying to keep her voice calm.

"How do we know?" Ryan asked. There wasn't any cynicism in his question. It was fear.

"Do you remember what happened at Pokrovsky Motors back in January?" Paula asked. "The guy who was about to torch…"

"Yeah, torch the cars he couldn't sell," Ryan said. "The State Police were there."

"The State Police were there because my friends and I told them where to be and at what time. And a month later, we told them where they could find 'Smilin' Al'." Paula smiled at the thought.

"The counterfeit parts ring?" Ryan asked, incredulous.

"That was us," Paula said with satisfaction. "I could tell you how we caught a serial killer in a nursing home and brought down a crooked town official, but I haven't got time. Just know we set up a real-looking business for the specific purpose of getting next to Senior Equity. And, this morning, their computer guy freely handed over a copy of his weekly report to me…"

"Jordan Wells?" Ryan asked.

Paula nodded. "His report, coupled with your files, is going to shut down Senior Equity and, I imagine, send its principals to prison."

"And what about us?" Ryan asked, his voice betraying his nervousness.

Paula paused before answering. "I can say with complete honesty the people who have helped us were treated fairly. I think the State Police and the Attorney General's office will recognize the three of you got pulled into this so gradually you didn't realize what was happening until it was too late. But you're doing something now…"

Paula's phone indicated an incoming call from Martin. She

answered it.

"It's Martin, and this is serious," he said. "Wrap it up with the lawyers. Get everyone over here to Samantha's as quickly and quietly as possible. Bree almost certainly knows Jordan Wells gave his report to an imposter this morning. She's probably trying to figure out who. You need to stay out of sight, and this is the best place. I'll tell you more when you get here."

Paula kept her face impassive. "I see," she said, and closed the call.

"How much longer do we need?" She asked Ryan.

He looked around the room. The others had heard the question and gave him a 'thumbs up' gesture.

"Let's start packing it in boxes," Ryan said. "I'd say ten minutes."

* * * * *

Samantha had never paused to consider how many black BMWs there were in eastern Massachusetts. To her, BMWs were a 'white boy's toy'; a sign of affluence and ostentation, and the Boston area abounded in both. Now, though, she was searching the parking area of an upscale apartment complex in Foxborough for signs Jordan Wells was in residence.

It seemed as though every sixth or seventh auto was a BMW and almost all of them were black. Finally, she found the right license plate. On the drive from Framingham, Martin had read from Wells' arrest record seven years earlier. It was frat boy stuff, selling Extasy to party animals and getting caught. Wells' conviction was ultimately overturned because of the nefarious deeds of one Annie Dookhan, a lab technician who seldom bothered to test the samples given to her by the State Police. As a result, more than 40,000 cases had been expunged, including Wells'.

To judge by the Lodge at Foxborough, being convicted of selling drugs and getting tossed out of college had not been an impediment to Wells' financial success. Even assuming he had a one-bedroom apartment, he was paying at least two thousand a month. Either Chad was paying Wells exceptionally well, or else Wells had something else going on the side, and it, too, was likely illegal.

Samantha reckoned Wells was likely her own age, and she hoped it would work to her advantage. She parked her own car, found Wells' apartment, and buzzed his door.

Knowing people her age were wary of visitors who didn't call or text ahead, Samantha harbored no illusions getting into his apartment would be easy. She had a few seconds to get his attention. She also knew, before opening the door, he would be peering at her through whatever security system the complex employed.

She saw the door handle turn and the door open slightly.

"There's no solicitation allowed here," Wells said.

"Believe me, Mr. Wells," Samantha replied. "This isn't a solicitation. You work for Chad Pannett at Senior Equity, and I'm here to warn you your life is in danger."

Wells blinked. "Who are you?"

"My name is Samantha Ayers, although that's not important. You met with Bree this morning at Senior Equity's office. If you'll let me in, I'll tell you everything you need to know. If you won't, then I'll leave right now, and you can regret it later."

Wells continued to look at her through the crack in the door. Samantha could have forced her way in. There was no chain on the door and she could have easily thrown a shoulder into it which would have sent him sprawling backwards. But if she did so, he would never cooperate. His mind was likely recoiling with the shock of a stranger uttering three names at him in the space of a few seconds, and he was weighing the odds she was law enforcement.

"Are you a cop?" he asked.

Samantha shook her head. "I said I'd tell you everything you need to know if you let me in. Good luck. You're going to need it." She turned to leave.

"Come in," he said quickly.

* * * * *

Jordan Wells eyed the tall, black woman. Her face betrayed nothing – no smile, no hint of why she had chosen this moment to come to his home.

But the truth was he had spent the last hour worrying about what had happened at One Broadmoor Hill. His first encounter, the one he had assumed was with Bree Fleming, seemed to have been innocuous enough on the surface. It was only afterwards he noticed the odd inconsistency: Bree was always 'all business' and frequently brusque. The woman at Senior Equity was much friendlier. And, while she had quickly and easily dropped Chad's name into the conversation, she mostly parroted back his own words in responding to questions.

Fifteen minutes after leaving the building he had called Chad to verify the woman was in fact Bree, but his call went to voicemail. Moreover, Chad had neither called him back nor been in the office. He went back an hour and a half later only to find a different woman in the darkened office. This one claimed to be Chad's girlfriend but had no key to his office. He retrieved his money but, ten minutes later, felt sufficiently uncomfortable he phoned Chad a second time, asking in the most urgent terms for Chad return his call. Now, an hour later, there was still silence.

"You're inside now," Jordan said. "So, my question is, are you law enforcement of any kind?"

The woman smiled and shook her head. "No," she said. "Like I said earlier, my name is Samantha Ayers. I'm not a cop though, in the interest of full disclosure, I was one for a couple of years, and there are police officers in my family going back two generations. I'm here because I need information. In return for your information, I'm going to tell you what you need to do to save your life. And, because I'm standing here, I have a suspicion you're having some doubts of your own about Senior Equity's stability."

"But who do you work for?" Jordan asked. Everything she said was logical, but he needed to know *how* she knew *what* she knew. "Do you have a card? A website?"

The woman shook her head in exasperation. "I work as an insurance investigator. As a favor for a friend, I began looking at Senior Equity. I realized it's a money-laundering front and it's out to steal seniors' homes. That's everything you need to know about me right now."

His face must have betrayed the shock he felt, because he sensed the woman's change of facial expression. Yes, he knew Chad and Vinnie were now driving mortgages into default as quickly as Bree could cause them to trip up. It had been obvious after the first year. But the money laundering was new information. All he knew was Vinnie brought in the funding and he had a seemingly endless source of investors. But money laundering? Money laundering meant drugs, and drugs meant violence. He didn't sign up for bloodshed.

"I take it you didn't know you were helping to launder a couple of hundred million of drug money," the woman said.

"Yeah, I knew," he said, hoping it was convincing. "I just didn't know anyone else knew."

"Let's get started with what I need to know" she said. "Have you spoken to Chad this morning?"

Jordan shook his head. "No, just left a couple of messages."

The woman said, "I've already heard what went down at your first meeting this morning. What I need to know is what was said at the second one."

His mind was still reeling. He needed time to think. He said, "Not much. I was inside only a few minutes. A woman was there. She said her name was Ashley something. She was Chad's girlfriend. I got my money and I left."

The woman smiled and shook her head. "Nice try, Jordan. Now let's take it minute by minute. You went up the elevator. What happened next?"

"I walked into the offices," he said. "It was dark. Then this Ashley came out of nowhere. She asked me who I was and I told her. She said she was there to pick up some of Chad's papers."

"Then why did you have to pick the lock on Chad's office?"

He stood there, open mouthed. This woman had apparently gone into the office just after he left. It couldn't have been more than an hour ago.

"Ashley said she didn't have a key and didn't want to drive back to Chad's."

"So you volunteered to pick the lock with a couple of ballpoint pens."

Jordan felt sheepish as he answered. "Yeah."

"And what was Ashley looking for?" she asked.

"Umm, just some papers," Jordan said, knowing as he said it the woman would sense the lie.

"We're so close," the woman sighed. "What papers?"

Jordan waved his hands. "I do a report for Chad. I deliver it to his office every Saturday. We usually talk for a few minutes."

"You mean this report?" The woman reached into her large purse and took out his report; the one dated this morning. She fanned the pages to let him know she had the whole thing.

His eyes bulged. "How the hell did you get that?"

"Because the woman you gave it to this morning wasn't Bree. It was someone who works with me. You willingly handed over Senior Equity's private property to someone outside the business."

Jordan was breathless. "But Ashley showed me Bree's photo on her phone."

"What do you mean?" the woman asked. "Give it to me in detail."

"As we were walking into Chad's office, Ashley had a picture on her phone, full screen. It was Bree Fleming, or at least the woman who said it was her name. Ashley asked me to identify her. I did."

The woman took out her own phone and began tapping screens. She scrolled for a few moments, then used her fingers to expand something on a screen. She held the phone out for him to see.

"Is this what she showed you?"

He looked at it. The photo was identical. "Yeah. That's the picture I saw."

This time it was the woman whose face showed concern.

"And Bree let you live," the woman said, almost to herself.

"Who is she?" Jordan asked anxiously.

"Someone whose life you've put in danger," the woman said, placing her phone back in her purse. "The woman who gave you the name 'Ashley' was really Bree. She and Chad and Vinnie had a long meeting at Broadmoor Hill last night. Someone named 'R' is pressuring Vinnie to step up the pace of mortgages and cut expenses."

"I've heard Vinnie mention the name 'Ramon' a few times," Jordan said. "It was always in the context of 'Ramon will like it' or 'I'd like to get Ramon's take first'."

"Well, Ramon is on a tear," she said. "And last night it all may have come to a head. The fact you can't get through to Chad means Chad may be on the run. It could also mean he's dead…"

The woman paused, thinking. "Bree knew you gave the report to my agent. What did you say in your first message to Chad?"

Jordan tried to remember the exact words. "I said I had just been at the office, I had given the report to Bree, and I wanted to make certain Chad received the report. I said I would go back by the office later to collect the money he always gives me. I asked him to call me back."

"Bree wiped down Chad's office after you left," the woman said. "She probably wiped down every place she thought she might leave fingerprints. I'm betting she's getting ready to disappear. I'm also betting she doesn't want to leave behind any witnesses. I know she had at least one false identity. My guess is she has others."

The woman turned her gaze directly on Jordan. "You have two options. You can cooperate or you can run. If you stay here and do nothing, Bree is going to come after you as a loose end. I suspect the only reason you walked out of the building alive is you surprised her and she didn't have the right weapon handy. You may not know this, but women don't like to leave behind a lot of mess when they kill someone."

"If you run, you better have a lot of cash because you're going to need to be off the grid for a couple of months at least. And running means getting as far away from here as possible. If you cooperate, you'll be safe. But unless you've got something really good to offer whoever prosecutes this, they're going to look at you as someone who was deep on the inside. They're going to want to throw the book at you."

Jordan had an immediate answer. "I have Chad's reports going back to the beginning of Senior Equity. It's dynamite."

The woman nodded. "Unless you want to give them to me, find a place to stash them where no one will think of looking." She paused and added, "But also think about Bree or someone else pointing a gun at your head. Maybe they've already shot you in the foot or cut off a finger. And they want to know where you stashed the computer. You know they're going to kill you anyway, but telling them lets you live a little while longer, and you think it gives the Feds time to bust down the door. It isn't going to happen. It only works in the movies."

"You also want an insurance policy. If they've taken you out, you want to make certain they go down. I know it's hard to think about, but it's the truth. Can you give me anything to take now to protect you later?"

The words stung. They were like a swarm of wasps: Bree or Vinnie or Ramon getting ready to kill him and making him give them everything they wanted.

"Will a thumb drive help?"

The woman smiled and nodded. "A thumb drive would be perfect."

While he downloaded the documents onto the drive, she took a business card from her purse and added her cell phone to the reverse side.

"If you decide you want to come in from all this, or if you just need to talk, call me on this number."

He handed her the thumb drive and accepted the business card, which he placed in his shirt pocket.

* * * * *

Bree looked dispassionately around the brownstone she had called home for the past three years. No, on second thought, a 'home' implied fond memories or a place to which she would long to return someday. The second floor of the 19th Century townhouse was just an investment, and a damned expensive one. She had a million dollars wrapped up in this building in Boston's South End and liquidating it might be tricky unless everything went perfectly.

Her goal this afternoon was to ensure everything did, indeed, go perfectly.

Once before, she had walked away from a similar building. That had been in Chicago; a fashionable apartment on the Near North Side. The traveling company of con artists of which she had been a part was breaking up, and an FBI team had Bree on its radar. She didn't know then what she knew now and had watched helplessly as her investment was seized by the government. She would never again make such a mistake.

There was almost nothing she felt she could or should take with her. Everything could be replaced, and she would need to travel light.

There were certain things she could not leave here, though she had no intention of taking them further than an unobserved dumpster in any town at least twenty miles distant. Chief among the items targeted for disposal was her theatrical makeup kit. She spent upwards of half an hour transforming herself into the parts she played and, should an enterprising law enforcement investigator study what items had been used most heavily, her various personas could be reconstructed. Her 'old lady' wigs were expensive but they, too, needed to disappear along with the commensurate clothes and costume jewelry she wore when meeting with mortgagees. She wanted nothing left behind connecting Emily Colwin to Bree Fleming and Senior Equity.

She would deal with the disposal of all of these items this evening, when there were fewer people on the street to notice her comings and goings. For now, all she needed was half a dozen syringes filled with a clear liquid, a pair of latex kitchen gloves, and a fresh wig.

Bree was not much of a reader but, a year earlier, she chanced upon a magazine article about the near-unbelievable potency of a pharmaceutical called Wildnil, a sedative for elephants and other large animals. The story caused her to begin researching the so-called 'designer fentanyl' drugs. She settled on one called carfenatil citrate. It was so toxic the mere handling of it was potentially fatal. Naturally, it was readily available in the darker corners of the internet.

She had amassed a supply sufficient for a 'getaway' package. Now, wearing the gloves, Bree carefully placed those syringes in a small padded cloth bag. Donning a black wig, she returned to her car and set out to clean up the loose ends of her existence as Bree Fleming.

Twenty minutes later she was driving the narrow roads of

Weston, the wealthiest town in the wealthy state of Massachusetts. Just 15 miles from Boston, Weston's seventeen square miles of land held a population of fewer than 12,000 people, almost all of them living on multi-acre lots.

Having been to Vinnie's home on a dozen occasions, Bree knew there was no gate to the property and the house and garage were set three hundred feet back from the street. Vinnie's lone interest was privacy. What landscaping there was served the purpose of screening the house from prying eyes. All this would work to her advantage.

She parked her own car among rhododendrons 100 feet up the driveway; out of sight of both the road and Vinnie's home. Taking only the padded cloth bag, she set out on foot for the house. Ahead of her was a three-car garage.

Vinnie owned two vehicles, she knew, but his pride and joy was his new Audi R8 Spyder convertible. Since taking delivery of it two months earlier he had driven it exclusively. She also knew something else about Vinnie: he hated fumbling with keys and, as a result, just like his office door, the side door to his garage would be unlocked. She opened it and let herself inside. As she suspected, it being August, the convertible top was already down.

From the padded bag, Bree first took out and donned a pair of thick, latex dishwashing gloves. She next took out a syringe and silently began applying carfenatil citrate to the leather-wrapped steering wheel of Vinnie car. In all, three syringes of the drug were applied to surfaces Vinnie was likely to touch. She then returned to her car to set her plan in motion.

* * * * *

Vinnie Malone had ended the tense, half-hour-long call with Ramon ten minutes earlier, but even the glass of Balvenie did not relieve the tenseness and sense of doom he felt as he read the scribbled notes he had made.

Ramon was out of control. He was flying to Boston to 'take

personal control of the situation'. And, by coming to Boston, Ramon did not mean waiting for a first-class sleeper seat on the next available American Airlines flight. He would be here in a few hours courtesy of his own Gulfstream G650.

Vinnie had been ordered to assemble everyone associated with Senior Equity at his home at 6 p.m. Ramon made it clear he was bringing 'his own people' and the meeting would end only when 'all questions were answered' to Ramon's satisfaction.

Vinnie had tried logic: money was tied up in mortgages and you couldn't demand it all back at once. And his laundering network already in place worked smoothly. You needn't replace it overnight. The words disappeared into the ether, unheard. Instead, there was the repetition of Ramon's 'knowing' millions of dollars of his money had disappeared because he had people on the 'inside' who reported back to him.

In short, it was the terrifying end of a good thing. And despite Ramon's cool assurance he had already confirmed Vinnie was not the responsible party and would emerge from the meeting with 'complete authority' and 'everyone's respect', Vinnie didn't believe a word of it.

Vinnie crumped up the notes and threw them in a waste basket. He wasn't going to need these notes for reference because there wasn't going to be a meeting because he wasn't going to call anyone. It was, in short, time to get out, and it was every man for himself.

Vinnie did not lack for cash. His house was overflowing with hundred-dollar bills representing the $7 million he was expected to deposit next week. Cash, though, was almost useless. You couldn't purchase a plane ticket with it, buy or rent a car, or even rent a hotel room. Flashing a roll of hundreds was the equivalent of a blinking neon sign announcing you were involved with the drug trade.

Vinnie poured another finger of Scotch and considered his bleak options. He was a smart guy. Why didn't he have an escape plan? Despite Chad's continuing assertions Senior Equity was good for at least five or six years, Vinnie was certain his partner had a safe place all picked out. And Bree... Bree was the master of disguise and secretive as all hell. Bree could take care of herself.

All Vinnie had was cash. Lots and lots of cash. Because they were so easily traceable, the debit and credit cards linked to his brokerage account wouldn't do him a damn bit of good. But he *could* purchase prepaid debit cards with cash.

So, he began gathering rolls of hundred-dollar bills and placing them in a large Louis Vuitton suitcase. In another, somewhat smaller suitcase he packed some clothes and toiletries. In an overnight bag he packed his collection of watches, deciding he would wear the Rolex Submariner. Seeing there was ample room in the bag, he added another dozen rolls of bills.

His goal was to be across the New York border before 5 p.m. Somewhere between Springfield and the border, he would call Chad and Bree to give them a warning Ramon was on his way. Once in, say, Albany, he could start buying debit cards. From there, he could decide which way to go.

He took his three bags through the house to the garage and paused at the door. He was bidding goodbye to one life, but he had all the funds he needed to start a new one. For now, he needed to go somewhere he was unlikely to know anyone. Texas sounded just right. He would find a way to keep in touch with acquaintances who would, in turn, let him know when Ramon was killed by one of his competitors in one of the unending drug wars.

He paused in front of the two cars. The Mercedes was certainly the less conspicuous vehicle in which to make his escape, but the Audi had set him back $185,000, and he was damned if he was going to walk away from such a large investment.

He threw the suitcases into the trunk, got into the car, opened the garage door and started the engine. He eased out of the garage and tapped the button to close the door for a final time. He looked at his watch: it was just a few minutes after two. The Mass Pike entrance was less than two miles away and Waze said traffic was light all the way to the New York border. Albany by five was a breeze.

He looked at his house in the rearview mirror, giving it a final goodbye until he could safely put it on the market. In doing so, he did not pay attention to the inconspicuous sedan parked back in among the rhododendrons.

But he did notice his hands were numb; as though he had gripped the steering wheel too tightly for hours on end. He took one hand off the steering wheel and flexed his fingers. It didn't help. Also, the numbness was quickly creeping up his left arm and his vision was blurred. He stopped at the end of the driveway in case a car was passing. He legs felt like rubber. He also realized he was having trouble breathing.

He wanted to turn right but the muscles in his arms did not respond and he was increasingly short of breath. In fact, he could not turn his neck to check for traffic. None of this made sense.

Vinnie was gasping for breath, his head pounding. He didn't see Bree approach him with a syringe held in her gloved hand, nor did he feel a needle prick his scalp just above the nape of his neck. After a few moments he felt nothing at all.

* * * * *

Bree had been surprised to see Vinnie's garage door go up. She had been busy rehearsing the fearful and urgent tone she would need to use to get him out of his house and into his car. Her story would involve finding Chad unresponsive in his condo and her need for Vinnie to help go through his papers before... She was still working on that part when she heard the rumble of the garage door.

She had been even more surprised Vinnie had made it only to the end of his driveway before the drugs overwhelmed his system. She had been prepared to follow him for as long as necessary. All in all, she figured this fortunate turn of events put her an hour or more ahead of schedule.

Well, she couldn't leave him where he could be seen by anyone driving by. She pulled his body over to the passenger seat and, donning her gloves, got into the driver's seat and backed his car back up the driveway. Five minutes after departing, the Audi returned to its designated spot in the garage.

As she did this, Bree began to wonder what had prompted Vinnie to leave his home on a Saturday afternoon. There was nothing special about his dress, though she noted he was wearing one of those idiotic watches he was always showing off to anyone unfortunate enough to be in his line of vision.

On a hunch she popped the trunk.

Suitcases. Vinnie was going somewhere. She opened the larger Louis Vuitton case and gasped. Vinnie was making a run for it. Not an especially well-planned run, but then Vinnie was not an especially intelligent man. This looked like a panic response.

Bree retraced Vinnie's path back into the house. After a few minutes she found his notes. She read them, reconstructing the endless diatribe Ramon must have been spewing. Well, Vinnie finally got it through his tiny brain it was time to pull the plug on Senior Equity. If Ramon was demanding a 6 p.m. meeting, he was probably already wheels in the well, likely planning to land at the jet-friendly general aviation facility ten miles away in Bedford.

Had Vinnie planned to call her? Not that it really mattered, but she liked to think he was enough of a friend and a stand-up guy to give her a decent warning. Apart from having just killed him, she had never given him reason to not want to help her.

She mentally shrugged off the question. The only issue was whether any of the money – probably half a million dollars – in the large suitcase was worth taking. It would mean dragging around an extra bag with her, but it might come in handy.

As for Vinnie, he would be found by Ramon's men. She

opened the Audi's door and dragged Vinnie to the rear of the Mercedes. She opened the trunk and placed the smaller suitcase and overnight bag in it. Ramon would find a coward felled in the process of trying to flee and would assume it was a heart attack or a stroke.

When she was satisfied with the tableau she had created, Bree took the large suitcase to her car and heaved it into the trunk. She had two syringes and two more names to cross off her list before the day was over.

Chapter Eighteen
Saturday 3 p.m.

Samantha looked at the piles of documents in her apartment accumulating like snowfall in a blizzard. It was a complete history of deceit and deception costing innocent people their homes and driven more than a few, out of despair, to end their lives.

The lawyers had created an index of every mortgage issued. Paula had printed out all of Jordan Wells' reports – a project requiring so much paper it had necessitated a trip to Staples to pick up two cases of paper and multiple toner cartridges.

Samantha marveled at the willing – in fact, enthusiastic – cooperation of the three lawyers. It was as though a weight had been lifted from their shoulders. In their minds, they had to know it would take extraordinary circumstances for them to emerge from this with their law licenses intact. She knew of attorneys who had been disbarred for far less. But from their overheard conversations as they worked, Samantha knew what they were doing came from their hearts. One word she overheard sent her to a dictionary: *expiation*. They were finally atoning for the harm they had done.

An hour earlier, Samantha had called her contact in the state Attorney General's office and described the trove of documents she was assembling. As the scope of the scam became apparent, the response went from 'we'll talk about it on Monday' to 'let me pull together a crew this afternoon to look at what you have.'

She had not heard from Jordan, an indication he intended to run rather than cooperate. In hindsight, it was to be expected. His was something of a 'lone-wolf' operation, untethered from everything else going on at Senior Equity. But it was also possible he benefitted from the scam in ways other than the weekly payment from Chad.

Given time, Jordan would be tracked down and, when he was, he would face a stiff prison sentence. He had knowingly abetted a major fraud and no jury would look at what he had done with sympathy.

Samantha had two goals right now. The first was to walk the people from the Attorney General's office through the paperwork she had accumulated, and to make certain they knew its origin was untainted. That part was easy.

The second was to shield Paula from the woman Samantha now knew to be Bree Fleming. There was a time – as recently as yesterday – when Samantha believed the key to bringing down Senior Equity was to get the woman to 'flip' on the two principal perpetrators. From reading through Jordan's reports, she now realized Bree was central to the scheme's success. She met and temporarily befriended the vulnerable people she actively pushed into foreclosure. She preyed on those weaknesses and doubtlessly profited handsomely from them.

That Bree had gone to Senior Equity's offices this morning with the specific intention of erasing the physical evidence of her existence – at a minimum, wiping surfaces where she had left fingerprints – indicated her intention to run.

But Bree's escape plan had run into an unexpected obstacle: Paula Winters. Paula had met Jordan Wells, been mistaken for Bree, and now possessed a report documenting Bree's role. She had been smart enough to deduce Paula's identity and, given Bree's cold-blooded tactics and methodical approach to her work, Paula would not be safe until Bree was under arrest.

The lone advantage – a wild card, really – held by Samantha, Paula, and Martin was the knowledge of Bree's alternate identity and where she lived. Samantha could only hope Martin was making as good a headway with the State Police as she had made with the Attorney General's office.

Until then, though, Samantha's goal was to keep Paula out of sight. And this nondescript apartment in an area with multiple, similar complexes seemed tailor-made to keep her safe. Anonymity could be a blessing.

* * * * *

Martin Hoffman's contact at the State Police Detective Bureau in Framingham shook his head with a combination of admiration and disbelief. "I never know what you're going to come walking in here with," he said.

Five Detectives had now gathered to read the weekly reports, and the small conference room was abuzz as they shared the most egregious of the lengths Senior Equity would go to place its mortgage holders in default. Arresting a group of people who preyed on the elderly would be good for weeks of favorable media exposure. Breaking up a drug ring's money laundering organization also held the prospect of promotions.

Martin had two objectives: to get the State Police to act swiftly – meaning today – and to ensure they understood the evidence he brought them would not get tripped up by the Exclusionary Rule.

"All of this was gathered by civilians," Martin stressed. "They brought it to me and I'm bringing it to you. One of those civilians is, right now, coordinating with the Attorney General's office. All I ask is you move on this before Senior Equity folds its tent. There are the three key people plus half dozen con artists who represent themselves as financial advisors but whose entire role is to identify and rope in the most vulnerable seminar attendees. You don't need one person to roll over on the others; the evidence is already overwhelming."

"My fear," Martin continued, "is this 'Ramon' is applying pressure on the group's principals to step up the money laundering effort and issuance of mortgages. The things they're doing tells me they're going to cut and run. Arresting a guy at his condo in Natick today is a lot easier than extraditing him from Luxembourg three months from now."

Martin was satisfied when the discussion turned to the judges most likely to sign off on arrest warrants on a Saturday afternoon.

By 3:30 p.m., Martin was providing addresses for ten warrants. The progress ought to have given him the first reason to relax since hearing Paula's weary summary Wednesday evening. The wheels of justice were in motion. Instead, though, he found himself still on what he considered 'high alert'. He had long since learned to respect a sixth sense telling him seemingly satisfactory progress on a case sometimes masked unknown problems.

* * * * *

Ramon Suarez was inordinately proud of his plane. Cruising at 650 miles per hour, his G- 650 could fly non-stop anywhere in the Americas or western Europe while carrying his 320-pound frame in palatial comfort. The jet had set him back $62 million; not a trifling sum. Fortunately, he alone approved such purchases so there had been no argument about its cost.

He usually slept in the private bedroom occupying the aft section of the plane but, on this three-and-a-half-hour flight, he led a discussion with the four passengers traveling with him.

He had been to Boston four times in the past three years. Each of those other trips had been pleasant affairs. Last year, Vinnie's efficiently-running money laundering operation (his third largest after New York and Los Angeles) turned $350 million of cash into bookkeeping entries and ledger credits. The reverse mortgage idea was brilliant, and the returns had been satisfactory, up to a point.

But word had reached Ramon all was not well in New England. Vinnie and his partner were telling him foreclosed houses sold for one price while public records showed they sold for much more. That extra money – hundreds of thousands of dollars – was being pocketed by Vinnie, his partner, and his partner's girlfriend.

Further, despite being told – *told*, not just advised – not to do so, Vinnie was living ostentatiously. He was now driving a car costing almost two hundred thousand dollars and attracting far too much attention. He was sporting a two- or three-cart diamond pinkie ring.

And, Vinnie's partner had promised he could increase the number and value of mortgages to ten million dollars a week within six months. The promise had been in April, but the weekly mortgage flow – and money laundering – was still just over seven million. This meant a greater burden on New York, Los Angeles, and the fledgling operation in Baltimore.

Changes needed to be made. And an example needed to be set. And so, four men traveled with him today. Two of them spoke little English which, perhaps, was for the best. They would play a role only if things did not go as Ramon wished.

Ramon was not an unreasonable man and he was certainly a prudent businessman within the context of his industry. Thus, the presence of the other two men. Ramon intended to explain they were 'interns'; there to learn the reverse mortgage business so it could be duplicated in Los Angeles. Chad and Vinnie could draw their own conclusions as to what else their presence might entail.

He intended to listen to everyone's explanation before deciding guilt or innocence. As a businessman, he was well aware of the folly of executing too many people all at once.

His discussion with his men was relatively brief and had more to do with the mechanics of disposing of bodies should the occasion arise. And then Ramon's pilot came back to tell him they were descending into Boston, and his limo was already in place.

* * * * *

Jordan Wells was assembling the minimum number of personal belongings he could take with him. It was a painful process because it had only been in the past few years he could afford fine things. There were wines in a rack in the kitchen costing more than a hundred dollars each. How could he leave those behind? Or the Burberry wool cashmere coat? It had set him back eighteen hundred bucks. There was a $700 Babolat tennis racket. How could he not take it?

It was only by sheer chance he happened to glance out the front window of his apartment. There was a woman standing beside his car. Curious, he looked more closely. Then he recoiled and stood out of sight of the window should the woman look toward his apartment.

It was the woman he had encountered at One Broadmoor Hill a few hours earlier. Not the first one; the one who told him she was Bree Fleming. It was the second one. The one Samantha Ayers told him was the real Bree.

He lay on his stomach with only the top of his head visible, peering over the window sill. Bree was trying his car doors and even his trunk. Fortunately, they were locked.

She periodically looked around to see if she was attracting any attention. Apparently, she was not. After failing to gain entry to his car, she stooped over and came back up wearing a pair of yellow gloves; the kind his mother used to wash dishes. She had something in her hand and she was doing something with the driver's side door handle. It was like she was painting the handle. She then did the same to the trunk pull. Then she went back to the driver's side door and applied something to two other areas.

When she appeared satisfied with what she had done, she returned all the materials to a small light-colored bag. She then walked away from the car and out of his line of sight.

Jordan was scared more than he had ever been in his life. Getting arrested didn't begin to approach the anxiety he felt. He felt for the business card in his shirt pocket.

Call Samantha Ayers, he thought.

* * * * *

Samantha's cell phone rang. The caller ID gave no clue as to who was on the other end of the line; a hallmark of a burner phone.

"Talk to me," Samantha said.

The rush of words took more than a minute to coalesce into a coherent narrative. It was Jordan. Wearing rubber gloves, Bree had applied something to several points of his car – places he was likely to touch.

"Wait a second," Jordan said, "I'm getting beeped."

"On a burner phone?" Samantha asked, incredulous.

"I change the phone every month," Jordan said. "Chad's rule. Let me see who it is."

Samantha started to tell him not to answer but he had already placed her on hold.

A minute later, Jordan was back on the phone. "It was Bree – except she said she was Ashley Moore, the name she used this morning. She said Chad needs to see me right away. She said it's an emergency. She said to drop whatever I was doing and drive to his condo in Natick."

"Well, it's obviously a lie, since she's right there at your apartment complex," Samantha said.

"What do I do?" Jordan asked, his voice showing his fear.

Samantha shook her head. This was far beyond anything in her experience. It had to be some kind of poison…

Then she recalled reading about a powerful drug police had encountered. Just handling it sent several officers to the hospital. Some exotic designer drug… But how would someone get hold of it?

"It's a trap, but you already know that," Samantha said. "I'm going to guess she has applied some kind of a poison that works even on contact with your skin. Do you have access to anyone else's car?"

"I don't really know anyone here," Jordan said.

"Friends nearby?"

"I don't really have a lot of friends…"

Samantha had an inspiration. "Order an Uber as soon as we get off the phone. Not the black car service; order the one using everyday cars. Have it take you to Logan. Does your apartment complex have a security office?"

"Well, yeah, I've seen them drive…"

Samantha cut him off. "After you know the Uber's pick-up time, wait until five or six minutes before it arrives and call the security office." Samantha found her notebook and flipped to the last page. "Bree is driving a gray Camry. She's probably in it, waiting for you to go to your car. Tell the security people you saw a woman trying the doors on several cars. You didn't see her get into any of them, but you're certain she isn't a resident." Samantha added the license plate number of Bree's car.

"That should probably distract her while you get into the Uber, and it will probably take her several minutes to figure out you've left the apartment without taking your car. If she calls you once you're in transit – and she will – tell her your car has been acting up and you were afraid of breaking down."

"In other words, make her think you're doing exactly what she asked. As far as Bree is concerned, you're going to Chad's place. Just to make certain she hasn't followed you, you're going to change Ubers at Logan. Call me when you get there, and I'll give you your final destination."

Samantha ended the call. Jordan's voice betrayed a combination of anxiety and stress. People frequently did stupid things in such positions. She hoped she had given him good advice.

She called Martin and repeated what Jordan had said and her instructions to him.

"I'm concerned Bree is stalking a relatively minor player like Wells," Martin said after listening to Samantha's retelling of the two calls. "I couldn't have given him better advice. Let's just hope he follows it."

Martin added, "What I can do from here is have a Hazmat team go down and figure out what Bree applied to his car. I can think of a couple of possibilities, none of them pleasant. This will tell us what tools she has at her disposal."

"How do you stand on the warrants?" Samantha asked.

She heard impatience in his answer. "The Staties are still getting together their teams. They have ten warrants to serve and want two detectives and two armed officers on each one, which is a lot of manpower for a Saturday afternoon. They also want to serve them simultaneously so no one gets advanced warning."

"Are you going with them?" Samantha asked.

"I've asked to go to the one for Vinnie Malone. I want to see the look on his face."

* * * * *

Bree positioned herself just outside the entrance to the apartment complex. A stand of burning bush obscured her car to vehicles coming out of the complex yet allowed her to see everyone exiting.

Had she gained entry to his car, the imbecile might not even make the hundred yards to where she was now. Vinnie's trip had lasted less than two hundred feet. But touching a door handle was iffy. He would have the drug on the fingers and palm of one hand, but how long would it take to have an effect?

Bree planned to follow him as his driving became erratic. It would be nice if he drove into the path of a truck, but she also was prepared to use the last of her syringes to finish him off if he simply stopped. Then, she needed to quickly get his apartment key, find the computer he used to create those reports, and destroy it.

It had now been ten minutes. Three cars had entered the complex. Two held a single female driver and one a male at the wheel with an Uber placard on the dash. Just one car had exited, driven by a woman.

Where was Wells? Her message had been clear: drop what you're doing and come immediately. Might he had collapsed as soon as he touched the door handle?

She placed a call. Wells picked up immediately.

"Are you on your way?" Bree asked.

"Yeah, been having some car trouble, though," Wells said. "Had to call an Uber. But I'm on the road now."

Just then, the vehicle with the Uber placard, a red Prius, pulled in front of her. Wells was in the back seat, his phone to his ear, oblivious to his surroundings.

This is going to require a change of plans, she thought. *OK, I'll trail him at a safe distance and take him out when he gets to Chad's building. A little more public than I'd like, but doable.*

Fifteen minutes later, following five cars behind the Prius, Bree eased into the left lanes on I-95 where the highway joined Route 128 for the final northbound leg of the trip to Natick. Instead, the Uber stubbornly stayed in the right lane. Seconds later, the Prius took the southbound ramp for Boston and Cape Cod. At the last possible second, Bree veered across two lanes of traffic to stay with Wells.

She momentarily considered calling Wells but knew doing so at the exact moment the Uber diverged from the expected route would alert him.

He knows, Bree thought. *He somehow saw me at the apartment complex. He's running.*

* * * * *

Jordan did not begin to relax until the Uber took the ramp onto the Southeast Expressway. Bree was, by now, racing up the wrong highway. She would arrive at Chad's place, and then would wait… and wait.

Samantha Ayers' advice had been good up to a point. Yeah, take the Uber. Smart thinking. But why the hell should he take yet another Uber when he got to the airport? His phone showed the trip was going to cost him more than seventy bucks.

He had a much better idea: hop a plane.

Using his phone, he trolled half a dozen travel sites, looking for something going someplace interesting out of Boston in the next two hours. He turned down Philadelphia, Chicago, Atlanta, and multiple points in Florida. Who wanted to go to Florida in August?

Then he saw a Denver flight with seats available. He quickly booked the last seat in first class. He could just make it…

Which is when traffic on the expressway went from 'heavy but moving' to 'dead stop'. He pulled up Waze and saw his driver was doing the same. The Southeast Expressway was solid red all the way up with a report of an accident at Columbia Road.

"I told you we should have taken the Pike," the driver said, not turning around. "All the side streets are just as bad."

Jordan could see it for himself. Well, at least he was still safe from Bree.

Half an hour later, and too late to make the Denver flight, Jordan exited the Uber at Logan's Terminal D. There was a JetBlue flight to Denver leaving from Terminal A later in the evening, but now he looked at the International Departures board for other possibilities. He had grabbed his passport on the way out of his apartment, so perhaps Paris or Amsterdam might be an even better idea. If he was going to have to lay low, he could be somewhere really cool.

Staring up at the changing times and destinations, he barely felt the pinprick on his hip. He merely rubbed the spot as it began to sting. Thirty seconds later, though, he was lying helpless on the floor, unable to do anything other than open his mouth in a vain attempt to bring air to his lungs.

* * * * *

The whole thing had taken ninety seconds. Bree watched as Wells got out of the Uber. He had no knapsack, much less a suitcase. He was a man on the run who thought he had just made a successful getaway. Wells had seen her outside his apartment and guessed correctly he shouldn't use his car. The Uber was a brilliant stroke and, had she not called when she did, he might have eluded her.

But there he was, standing in a crowd at the base of one of the flight status signs, probably trying to choose where to go. Bree realized she could not don the protective yellow glove, nor could she leave her car in the Departures area for more than a minute or two.

She put her car in park, left the engine running and popped the trunk, just like half a dozen other vehicles. She carried only the inconspicuous cloth bag. Just outside the terminal entrance, she passed a trash receptacle overflowing with the detritus of incoming and outgoing passengers. She spotted an empty plastic bag and grabbed it as she walked by. It would have to do for protection.

She saw him not fifty feet inside the terminal, looking upward, with his back to her. She carefully reached into the bag using the plastic bag as a glove. She found the remaining syringe and removed its safety cap. Slowing her stride, she paused behind him, looking up along with everyone else, and pushed the tip of the syringe through his jeans. He didn't even seem to notice what had happened.

She pulled out the syringe and placed it back in the cloth bag. She turned and retraced her steps back out of the terminal. Only as she reached her car did she glance back at the entrance. She saw and heard nothing unusual. To a casual observer, she was a woman who had walked into the terminal to check on a flight, then returned to her car.

There were almost certainly surveillance cameras recording the event. But police wouldn't know if what happened to Wells was the result of an event ten minutes earlier or an hour. In time, they would look at their security footage frame by frame and, possibly, deduce the blonde woman had injected him. By then, she would be far away.

Bree had hoped to retrieve Wells' keys. Finding them, though, would have required staying in the terminal until he collapsed and would have drawn unwanted attention. She was also miffed she had used her last syringe. Now she would have to return to her apartment for a re-supply.

At least it was a clean getaway. No policeman was inspecting her car. She closed her trunk and drove away. Yes, it was inevitable there would be security footage. Silencing Wells, though, was more important.

Unfortunately, there was no mistaking what had happened for an accident. But, by the time a medical examiner concluded Jordan Wells had died due to the deliberate injection of a lethal quantity of drugs, she would have disappeared.

Winters' business card was in Bree's hand. She weighed driving directly to Hardington to confront Paula Winters against stopping at her apartment for more syringes. Carfenatil ensured no blood or gore and, hence, uncertainty over the cause of Winters' death. Skipping the stop in Boston would save time but entail using a different, messier, weapon when she confronted Winters.

Bree had planned to use the cover of darkness to load her car with those items needing to disappear, but she could make a second trip tonight. Getting the drugs was paramount.

Bree returned Winters' business card to her purse.

Chapter Nineteen
Saturday 5 p.m.

Bree was moments away from making the turn off Tremont Street when her phone sounded an urgent text message informing her of an unauthorized entry into her apartment. Instead of turning, she stopped in a bus zone and tapped the sequence of keys to show the live feed from the security camera inside her unit.

What the hell? she thought.

The building manager was ushering four men – two of them uniformed State Troopers – into her apartment. One man in a coat and tie looked up toward the camera, then pointed and drew the attention of the other three to its presence. They all nodded and said something to one another.

She watched for five minutes, knowing they were conducting a thorough search of her home. She felt sick to her stomach.

Wells had been dead less than twenty minutes. *They couldn't possibly have…*

It had to be Chad. Someone had gone to his apartment and found the body. She hadn't wiped down all her prints… *No, my prints aren't in any database.*

There was just one answer: *Paula Winters.* She had given Wells' report to the State Police… *But how did the police know to come here?*

Bree watched as one State Trooper carried her 'old lady' wigs into the camera's range, set them on a table, and a second Trooper began placing them in evidence bags. Next, her theatrical makeup kit made an appearance.

Bree was in a rage. One block away, her carefully prepared life was being dismembered. She pounded her steering wheel, knowing she had been followed home. And, if they knew about 'Emily Colwin', they would also know about her accounts and her car…

Bree looked up at the EZ-Pass transponder affixed to her windshield. It had told the world she had come through the Ted Williams Tunnel. Her location could be tracked from her phone. And she would have to ditch her car or at least its license plates.

Bree threw her phone and her transponder into a trash can next to the bus stop. The thought of watching Paula Winters die in excruciating pain before her eyes was never so appealing but, first, she needed to vanish. Only a suitcase full of cash in her trunk stood between her and a pair of handcuffs.

* * * * *

Ramon's limo pulled into the long driveway of Vinnie Malone's home. The first thing Ramon noticed was the absence of cars. There ought to be at least eight of them. Instead, there were none. He examined the exterior of the house. This was definitely the place he had visited in the spring.

He told the four men to circle the building and look for evidence of occupancy. Ramon remained in the limo, took out his phone, and called Vinnie's cell. It went to voicemail. He called Chad. That call, too, offered him the opportunity to leave a message. He ended both calls without uttering a word.

The scared little field mice have scattered, he told himself. Now, he would have to hunt them down.

He lifted his bulk out of the limo and went to the locked front door. Three kicks later, the splintered door jamb gave way. Hearing the noise, the four men joined him, and they went inside.

The interior of the first floor was neat and tidy, as though Vinnie had just stepped out for a few minutes. With his chin, Ramon indicated a study off of the living room. "You're looking for a black laptop computer," he said. To the others he said, "Spread out," indicating other rooms.

Ramon went to the second floor. Four bedrooms were empty of any furniture. Only the master suite was used, and Ramon could see the evidence of a man packing in haste. Shirts and slacks had been left on the bed.

He would find Vinnie and kill him slowly.

From downstairs, he heard the excited cry of *'Jefe!'*

At the bottom the stairs, one of his men was pointing toward the garage. Moments later, Ramon stood over the lifeless body of Vinnie Malone. One of his men had opened the suitcases Vinnie had already placed in the truck of the car. One held a few days clothing. A smaller overnight bag was filled with rolls of hundred-dollar bills and expensive watches.

Ramon used his foot to roll over the body. The look on Vinnie's face was one of extreme pain. Seeing no sign of foul play, Ramon assumed it was a stroke or heart attack brought on by fear. Vinnie was overweight. These things happened. At least he had suffered, though not for nearly as long as Ramon would have liked.

Ramon noted the laptop computer was not among the things Vinnie had packed. He remembered Vinnie showing him a safe. "In the study, behind the football jersey," Ramon said to one of his men. He added, pointing to a rack with outdoor tools. "Take the sledge hammer."

He turned his attention to the metallic silver Audi convertible; one of the lesser reasons for his visit. Vinnie had proclaimed himself an astute businessman, but one of the first lessons you learned in *this* business was not to draw attention to yourself. Unless, of course, you owned the local, state, and federal police forces.

It was a shame to let such an expensive car go to waste.

"Check his pocket for keys," Ramon said to another of his men. The man promptly found two fobs and two door keys and handed them to Ramon.

"We need to find Vinnie's other people," Ramon said. "We can't do it in a stretch limo. We'll use these cars." He smiled as he heard the sound of the sledge hammer breaking through plaster and lumber. At least all of the records of the operation were available to him. It would take time, but he had lost only unfaithful and soon to be dead employees, not money.

Which is when Ramon heard a new sound. It was several vehicles coming up the driveway. "It seems Vinnie's compatriots are assembling," Ramon said, and indicated the garage door opener button by the door to the main house.

The man did as he was told. Slowly, both garage doors opened. There were three vehicles.

They were State Police cars.

Ramon judged the gap between the garage and the closest police car. Yes, he could make it. He jumped into the Audi and pressed the 'start' button. The engine roared into life. He put it in gear, clenched the steering wheel, and screamed out of the garage.

He had no idea where he would go but he remembered there were two major highways nearby and the limo had turned left to go into the driveway. He would turn right and let his instincts take him to the highway.

He turned right and realized his hands felt numb. He gripped the steering wheel more tightly but could not feel it. His arms were turning to rubber, he was short of breath, and his vision was blurred.

Angrily, Ramon jammed his foot down on the accelerator and felt the car respond. He could see the winding road only with difficulty. There was a rock wall ahead of him at a turn in the road, but his arms would not respond and he could not feel his feet to hit the brake pedal.

He hit the rock wall at what was later estimated to be well over a hundred miles an hour. The impact ejected him from the car and into the trunk of a stately oak. Two coroners could not agree whether he was already dead when his body smashed into the tree.

* * * * *

Two Massachusetts State Police Detectives and one uniformed State Trooper waited while the Concierge unlocked the entry to Unit 772, A second State Trooper was stationed in the resident's garage next to an automobile registered to Charles Pannett.

Only the State Trooper's weapon was un-holstered. The two detectives assumed they were arresting a non-violent white-collar criminal. And, indeed, the entry way to the apartment spoke of a male resident with money, if not taste. All chairs and sofas were dark leather, all surfaces were glass and chrome.

Were it not for the fact that Pannett's lone auto was in the garage, the three men might have first thought there was no one home. But there were plates in the kitchen sink and an unmade bed. At 5 p.m., such a scene branded Pannett as a slob in the eyes of the men who had come to arrest him.

One of the detectives walked into the master bath expecting, at worst, to see further housecleaning neglect or, at best, encounter Pannett hiding in the shower. What he saw instead was the fully submerged body of a man in a three-quarters-filled spa tub. He shouted for the others to join him.

They did not touch the body. Instead, they compared it to the driver's license photo they carried. They all agreed the body was that of the man whom they had come to arrest.

The second Trooper was called up from the garage and told to bring the full evidence kit. A Medical Examiner was also summoned.

The two Detectives did make an examination of the death scene. They noted there was no blood in the water and the victim's eyes were open. There were also no marks on the body to indicate a struggle.

Five minutes later, one Detective, examining the bar area, lifted the lid from an ice bucket and found a baggie of white powder and a vial. The four men gathered around the bar, speculating on an accidental overdose as the cause of death.

Which was when one of the State Troopers placed his eyes level with the surface of the counter and noted it had been wiped clean of fingerprints.

"I think we can take 'accidental' out of this," one of the Detectives murmured.

* * * * *

Martin Hoffman did not come prepared to be part of a running gun battle. He was an invited guest, although with an unspoken understanding he was strictly an observer of a high-profile arrest.

As at the other nine locations, two Detectives, backed by two State Troopers, went to Vinnie Malone's home in Weston. They were still getting out of their cars when the garage doors opened, and a silver convertible burst out, clipping a hedge as it skirted the third police vehicle. It happened so quickly no guns were drawn.

Almost immediately, though, two shots were heard coming from the house, and one bullet smashed through a windshield. The Detectives and Troopers took cover from behind the vehicles and the black limousine parked in front of the home.

Unarmed, Martin could not aid the fight. He figured his lone option was to make himself as small a target as possible. But then, amid the firing, he heard the distinctive sound of a car crash. Judging the direction of the sound, he backed into the woods, then sprinted to and over a stone wall.

The convertible, or what was left of it, was less than a quarter mile ahead. The vehicle had smashed head-on into a four-foot-high dry stone wall; the kind skilled masons labored over for months. Martin had enough experience investigating fatal traffic accidents to judge that the driver had never applied the brake pedal and was traveling around a hundred miles an hour at the time of impact.

Two tons of German automotive engineering were no match for New England granite. The front of the vehicle had disintegrated, and a large mechanical apparatus that had once been part of the trunk – likely the retractable roof and its motor – had ripped free and was lodged in what had been the well of the driver and passenger area.

The driver had been ejected on impact, traveling at that same hundred miles an hour, but stopped suddenly by a hundred-year-old oak some ten feet behind the wall. Martin did not want to disturb the scene, not the least because he could see the man had not survived.

The rear license plate, virtually the only part of the car remaining intact, tied to the one in the State Police notes as being registered to one Vincent Malone.

He took out his cell phone and dialed 911, calmly instructing the local police on what to do and whom to contact. He also noted the sound of gunfire had ceased.

Martin cautiously returned to the house and saw two civilians, their hands cuffed behind them and with their faces to the wall.

He found the head of the detail and reported what he had found at the accident scene. "It was Malone's car. The body was too mangled to make an identification, but it was a male. Maybe Malone decided to make a break for it."

The Detective motioned with his pen toward the garage. "Malone's in there. He has been dead for a couple of hours."

"Then who was in the car?" Martin asked.

"I think you just witnessed the demise of Ramon Suarez, drug lord." The Detective indicated the handcuffed men. "They flew up with Suarez this afternoon for an all-hands meeting with everyone from Senior Equity. They swear Malone was already dead when they got here."

"So, we're going to be here quite a while," Martin said.

The Detective shook his head. "There's nothing you can do here, and you were just a ride-along. There's one dead and one wounded in the house. They were Suarez's muscle. They were also lousy shots. They put twenty bullets into that limo but there's not a scratch on our guys." The Detective added, "Anyone you can call for a ride?"

* * * * *

Samantha's phone rang with an unexpected Caller ID: 'Troop F'. She answered the phone cautiously.

"Is this the Samantha Ayers who is employed by Massachusetts Casualty Insurance?" a female voice asked.

"Who wants to know?" Samantha replied.

"Please, ma'am," the exasperated voice said. "Can you verify I am speaking with Samantha Ayers who…"

"Yes, this is me," Samantha quickly answered.

"This is Lieutenant Deirdre Dickson of the Massachusetts State Police," the woman said. "Will you also verify your office phone number."

Still bewildered, Samantha provided the number.

"Are you acquainted with a man named Jordan Wells?" Dickson asked.

"I met with him a few hours ago – around noon," Samantha said. "I spoke with him about two hours ago."

Samantha heard the audible sigh of relief on the other end of the line. "Mr. Wells collapsed and died at the airport about an hour ago. Your business card was in his shirt pocket. We're looking for possible information about a next of kin and anything you can tell us about him." Dickson paused and added, "Because you met with him, we also need assistance in identifying the body."

Samantha felt a sharp pang in her chest. *I should have convinced him to come with me…*

"I'm in Shrewsbury, but if there's no traffic, I can be at the airport in under 45 minutes," she said. "I'll call you back while I'm on the road, but here's what you need to know: earlier today, someone made an attempt on his life using some kind of drug or poison, something that may be incredibly fast acting. You want to run a tox screen on him. You also want to pull all the security footage you can find from the time he entered the airport. I know he got there in an Uber."

Samantha got the officer's number. She looked around the room. Four fear-and-horror-filled faces were looking at her. They had heard her end of the call.

"It's Jordan," Samantha said as calmly as she could. "He collapsed and died at the airport. I have to assume Bree got to him – tailed him to the airport.

Ryan spoke. "You talked about security footage. I met Bree at Chad's apartment. I can identify her."

"I can help," Paula added. "I saw her on Monday and, of course, I met Jordan this morning."

Samantha looked at the faces. It wasn't ideal but it solved the problem. "Let's all go," she sighed.

Samantha's phone rang again. She glanced at the Caller ID. "I'm in a hurry, Martin," she said, motioning everyone to follow her.

"I'm looking for a ride," he said. "You wouldn't believe what happened up here. There has been a genuine Old West gunfight here in Weston. Vinnie Malone is dead and – wait for it – so is Ramon, who flew up here to install his own people at Senior Equity…"

"The police shot them?" asked Samantha.

"There were a lot of shots fired, but none of them hit either guy. Malone was already dead when we got here. Ramon – last name Suarez – took off in Malone's hot sports car and promptly ran into a stone wall at something close to warp speed. They're going to have to peel him off a tree."

Samantha spoke as she herded her four charges into her car. "Where did they find Malone's body?"

"On the ground next to one of his cars," Martin said. "He was getting ready to run…"

"Go talk to the Detective in charge," Samantha said, pulling her car out of its parking space. "Remember the call I had from Jordan Wells? He saw Bree 'painting' all the surfaces of his car he would be likely to touch. How about Vinnie's car?"

"A convertible with the top down; the same way I saw it last night when Vinnie, Bree and Chad met at Senior Equity's office."

"They need a tox screen on the doors and steering wheel, and on both bodies," Samantha said. "I think Bree may have some kind of miracle drug."

"Jordan didn't touch the car, did he?" Martin asked. "I haven't heard from the unit that went to arrest him. Is he OK?"

"No," Samantha said. "I'm on my way to the airport to identify his body. If you want to come with us, you'll have to sit on someone's lap, but I'll slow down for you as I go by the old Weston tolls."

* * * * *

Over the next hour, reports filed in on other warrants being served and information obtained from the two men who had accompanied Ramon Suarez. Chad Pannett was dead in his apartment and Bree Fleming's was empty. The team charged with serving Jordan Wells turned, instead, to one keeping vigil over Wells' BMW until the car could be impounded. Only the six 'shepherds' were successfully served, and three of them had been watching a Red Sox game together. All were now in custody.

At Logan Airport, Samantha and Paula made the identification of Jordan Wells. Samantha could not hold back her tears.

In the airport's security offices, Paula and Ryan identified Bree as the woman getting out of a car in the departures area less than a minute after Wells alighted from the Uber. They also identified her as she walked out of the terminal, got into her car, and drove away. An airport security guard stood twenty feet away, talking to someone. The guard never even glanced in Bree's direction.

They also watched footage from a security camera inside the terminal as Bree entered, took a syringe from her bag, and momentarily stood behind Wells as he looked up at a departures board. She then walked out of the terminal, placing the syringe back into the bag. All of this took place amid a crowd of people. Only by zooming and isolating the camera on Bree was it clear what she had done. Once again, a uniformed State Trooper was observing people as they entered the terminal. Nothing about Bree stood out and so the trooper ignored her. He sprang into action only when Wells collapsed thirty seconds later, by which time Bree was out of the terminal and driving away.

"We would have missed that completely," said Lieutenant Dickson, shaking her head. "Congratulations, you just solved a murder."

Chapter Twenty

By 7 p.m. everyone associated with Senior Equity was accounted for except Bree Fleming, aka Emily Colwin. Three of the ten individuals who were to have been served with warrants were now in morgues, where blood samples were being analyzed to determine what kind of drug was in their system at the time of their deaths.

Also dead were a drug kingpin and an unidentified gunman. A second gunman was hospitalized in serious condition. Additionally, two other Mexican nationals were in custody. They had been unarmed and had taken no part in the gun battle in Weston. They were also in no hurry to return to their home country and were offering information on Ramon Suarez's drug empire in return for sanctuary.

A description of Bree/Emily, together with that of her car, was in the hands of every major law enforcement agency in New England. Airport security cameras traced her as far as the Ted Williams Tunnel where her vehicle disappeared into the Saturday evening flow of traffic.

The story – a heady combination of murder, elder abuse, and drugs – proved to be catnip for the media and coverage was nonstop for three days. All credit accrued to the swift actions and tight coordination of the Massachusetts State Police and State Attorney General's office.

A laptop computer recovered from Malone's home detailed an intricate and interconnected money laundering scheme and reverse mortgage racket that sought to defraud the seniors who applied for them. The money laundering ledger detailed payments to a network of 'mules' who spent their day going from bank to bank making cash deposits. The accounts were frozen, but few of the 'mules' were ever apprehended.

A few bright notes came out of the carnage: all default proceedings on existing Senior Equity mortgages were cancelled, including one against a Hardington resident named Rebecca Cooper. Plans were put in motion to administer the defunct firm's mortgages through an existing, HECM-compliant agency and to adjudicate claims from seniors who had lost their homes. Payment for those claims would come from the seizure of bank and investment accounts for everyone associated with Senior Equity, plus cash found at Malone's home. Left in limbo was a top-of-the-line Gulfstream jet belonging to the late Ramon Suarez, still parked at Hanscom Field. That asset was claimed by both the Commonwealth of Massachusetts and the U.S. Drug Enforcement Agency.

The Walpole Law Group's three partners escaped sanctions. In the official record, they willingly and proactively brought their complete Senior Equity files to the Attorney General and provided the crucial description of the crime being perpetrated. Also part of the record was that the three had convinced Jordan Wells, now deceased, to turn over to them a complete set of the weekly reports he had prepared for Chad Pannett.

* * * * *

But, where was Bree? Her phone and an EZ-Pass transponder were found in a trash receptacle a block from her apartment. Her abandoned car was found four days later in a train station parking garage in Stamford, Connecticut. From there, the trail went cold.

By then, toxicology reports showed four men had died from lethal doses of carfenatil citrate. With video footage showing Bree injecting one victim, four unused syringes filled with the drug found in her apartment, and all four victims having been associated with her in one way or another; no other suspects were considered.

The fingerprints from Bree's apartment were something of a surprise: she had no prior arrest record. Her prints existed only as a 'Jane Doe' in an FBI file relating to a group of con artists working primarily in the Midwest. Surveillance photos from the earlier case showed a woman similar in appearance to Bree. Age-subtracting software applied to archives of college and high school yearbooks showed a strong resemblance to an Iowan named Candace Lockhart who had not been seen since her mid-twenties.

There were periodic Bree sightings, none of which produced the fugitive with multiple murder charges against her. With her bank account seized and her alternative identity exposed, it was assumed Bree had few choices but to find an obscure place to hide.

Samantha continued to be concerned for everyone's safety, including her own. Because of the extensive coverage, her name appeared in several news articles as well as multiple police reports. It was known her business card was found on the body of Jordan Wells and that she made the preliminary identification of his body. She was also listed in the official account by the Office of the Attorney General on how Senior Equity's records came to light. Paula's name appeared as one of two people who identified Bree in airport security footage.

Slowly, though, everything returned to normal. Provençal Home Décor of New England – now relocated to larger quarters on the second floor of the Women's Empowerment Zone at Broadmoor Hill – gained fourteen sister companies to the delight of Realtor Leslie Mullen. WGBH ran its profile on the business and, in turn, the segment aired nationally via NPR and PRX, bringing in still more orders. A nonexistent company at the beginning of August had, by early September, five full-time and four part-time employees fulfilling $35,000 of orders each day. Austinplex received a check from Provençal Home Décor compensating the firm for the cost of the website it created.

* * * * *

In early September, Marie Deveraux boarded a Boston-bound Air France flight. Her protestations that she could book a €129 flight from Nice to Providence on Norwegian Air with only a modest five-hour layover in Dublin were dismissed, and she instead was treated to business class. She carried with her a sample case of Provençal linens never before exported to the United States.

With Paula as her guide, Marie saw one corner of America. Her lone disappointment was so few people she met spoke French. When she departed, though, she also took with her full documentation of the shipment of counterfeit Chinese linens seized two months earlier by Mass Casualty. Samantha provided to Marie the complete chain of custody of the fraudulent wares so French and EU trade officials could find and attempt to close the Keqiao, Shaoxing factory producing them.

At her request, Marie's return flight included a two-day stopover in Montreal, allowing her to experience a city she had visited so many times via the internet. While she thought it a beautiful city, she found the French spoken there to be largely incomprehensible.

In his annual letter to the members of the *Conseil de Commerce des Tissus Provençaux*, Director General Paul Tanguay did not take sole credit for landing the largest new account in two decades for the Council, nor for producing the smoking-gun evidence of Chinese counterfeit goods leading to a promise by that country to cease mislabeling its products as Provence-made. Instead, Tanguay charitably acknowledged the 'helpful assistance' of Ms. Deveraux.

* * * * *

On a mid-September Saturday morning, Eleanor Strong's doorbell rang. Standing on her front step was a gray-haired woman of about her age wearing thick glasses. The woman held a moderate-sized box with UPS markings on it. Eleanor did not recognize the woman, but she could tell by the way the woman was standing the box must be heavy. She opened the door.

"Hi," the woman said. "This got left at my house by mistake."

Eleanor stepped back to allow the woman in, thinking a cup of coffee was the minimum way she could show her appreciation.

The woman took one step inside, threw the box aside, and shoulder-slammed Eleanor into a stair railing. Eleanor fell backwards onto the stairs with a cry of pain as the woman slammed shut the front door.

The woman, now holding a ten-inch-long boning knife, kneeled over Eleanor.

"Whether you live to see this afternoon is going to depend on what you do and say over the next few minutes," the woman hissed, pressing the point of the knife into Eleanor's neck.

"You're Bree Fleming," Eleanor said, still in considerable pain.

"Yes, I am," she said. "And you're Eleanor Strong, who seems to have made a remarkable recovery from Stage Four pancreatic cancer."

Eleanor did not reply.

"By which I conclude you were sent in by Paula Winters. Is that true?" Bree increased the pressure on the knife blade.

Eleanor nodded. "Yes."

"And who does Paula Winters work for? Certainly not for the State Police."

"No," Eleanor said, shaking her head. "Senior Equity sent a friend of ours a foreclosure notice – Rebecca Cooper. We decided to investigate…"

Bree slapped Eleanor hard in the face with her free hand. "You didn't *'decide'* to investigate."

"We did," Eleanor said through the pain. "It isn't our first time."

"You just moved a business next door to Senior Equity." The knife point dimpled Eleanor's neck.

"Paula set up the company," Eleanor said. "She can afford to do things like that."

"Then who is Samantha Ayers?"

Eleanor gulped. "She's an investigator for an insurance

company."

"She works with you or you work for her?"

"You don't really have to hold a knife to my neck," Eleanor said. "I've told you the truth."

Bree slapped Eleanor again and repeated her question. "She works with you or you work for her?"

"It isn't like that," Eleanor said. "Last summer she caught us doing something we shouldn't have done. Instead of turning us in…"

"What did she catch you doing?" Bree demanded.

"We robbed the Brookfield Fair."

"You what?" Eleanor felt the knife point.

"We robbed the Brookfield Fair last August. Four of us. We did it out of friendship for Paula."

The pressure on Eleanor's neck stayed constant. "I remember the robbery," Bree said. "But they recovered the money and people were arrested and convicted."

"The people who were arrested deserved it," Eleanor said. "They were laundering money through the Fair."

Bree snickered. "Just like Senior Equity. Why didn't she turn you in?"

"Because Paula saved her life. Then we went undercover for Samantha at a car dealership and, after that, at a nursing home. We were trying to make amends for the Fair robbery."

"And where does Samantha Ayers live?"

"Somewhere out near Worcester," Eleanor said.

The knife point pressed more deeply. "Somewhere out Route 9," Eleanor gasped. "I've never been there."

"And which one of them put you up to applying for a reverse mortgage?"

"Samantha," Eleanor said. "She was trying to gather the evidence to get Senior Equity shut down. After you and I met in the lobby, I recorded Chad telling me he would give me a mortgage even though I told him I hadn't read any of the material."

"That was Chad," Bree said. "As stupid and greedy as any man ever born. How did you find out where I lived?"

"On Friday night, the three of you met," Eleanor said. "It must have been some kind of an emergency…"

"I was being followed?"

"Chad was being followed," Eleanor said. She almost added, 'by Martin' but stopped herself. "Samantha must have followed you into Boston afterward."

Bree looked at Eleanor. *She's looking for a lie*, Eleanor thought.

"Then let's call Samantha and Paula and get them to come here," Bree said. "If you can get them to do that, you get to live. If you don't, then I'll kill you now. I already know where Ms. Winters lives. I can probably figure out where Ms. Ayers lives based on what you've told me."

"Why are you doing this?" Eleanor asked.

Bree gave Eleanor a pitying look. "I knew Senior Equity couldn't last. I knew Ramon was so full of his own coke that he had to explode sooner or later. That's what that meeting was about Friday night. Ramon had been told Chad and Vinnie were cheating him. Well, after that meeting I knew it was over, but I was prepared. I had my escape plan in place. Or, I thought I did. Your two friends cost me everything I had. And they're going to pay the price for it."

Bree must have seen the fear in Eleanor's face because she added, "You were incidental to all this. You don't deserve to die. But they do. But, if you warn them, you'll die, too."

She pulled Eleanor to her feet. "Let's go make those calls."

"I need to have a reason," Eleanor reasoned. "I can't just say, 'you've got to come here right now'.

"Well, then, think of one." Bree handed Eleanor the phone, keeping the knife at Eleanor's neck.

Eleanor dialed a number and, with Bree listening closely, heard

Paula quickly pick up and say, "Hey, Eleanor, I was just thinking about you."

"And I was thinking about you, too," Eleanor said. "I went to the nursery this morning and found all the plants you were looking for. I have the oleander, the monkshood, and the castor bean. The nursery says they're perfect for planting right now. I'd appreciate you coming over to pick them up. Right now, if you can."

"Right now?" Paula asked.

"The sooner the better. I'm going out."

"I'm up at Garden in the Woods but I can be there in under thirty minutes," Paula said.

Eleanor looked at Bree for approval. She nodded.

"See you then," Eleanor said and hung up.

"Plants were good," Bree said. "Now Ms. Ayers."

* * * * *

Walking into her kitchen, Paula put down her cellphone with her hand shaking. Martin, drying dishes, asked, "What's wrong?"

"Eleanor is in trouble," Paula said. "She just named three of the most poisonous plants on the face of the earth and said she had found them for me. She wants me to come right over and pick them up. I said I was at Garden in the Woods and it would take me about half an hour to get there."

"Good answer," Martin said, nodding. "You're thinking what I'm thinking…"

"Bree is there," Paula said, "and she's looking for me. I've got half an hour to come up with a plan…"

"Which gives *us* half an hour to come up with a plan," Martin added. "I'm glad I stayed over."

* * * * *

"Hi, Samantha, it's Eleanor."

"To what do I owe the pleasure?" Samantha asked.

"I need your help and you're the only person I can talk to," Eleanor said. "Can you drop whatever you're doing and come over? I know it's a hike, but this is really important."

"Can you give me any idea of what it's about?" Samantha asked.

"No. We really need to discuss it in person," Eleanor said. "But I can make it worth your while. I know how much you love aconitum tea. I can put on a big pot of it, double strength."

"Aconitum tea? Well, in that case, give me, say, forty minutes and I'll be there."

"Thank you so much, Samantha," Eleanor said and hung up.

"I've never heard of it," Bree said. "Do you actually have aconitum tea?"

"No," Eleanor said, shaking her head. "I wish I did. It's an herbal tea and Samantha loves it."

Bree lowered the knife. "I have some preparations to make. I'm going to tie you up while I make them."

* * * * *

Samantha thought to herself, *Sweet mother of Jesus. Bree is back.*

Aconitum tea, brewed from the leaves and flowers of the monkshood plant, was the poison that had been planned to silence Alice Beauchamp at Cavendish Woods, the high-end retirement home where the Garden Club Gang had gone to catch a serial killer.

Samantha immediately called Paula. "Eleanor is in trouble," Samantha said.

"She just called here, too," Paula said. "I guess Bree wants revenge and figured Eleanor was the perfect way to get us in the same place at the same time. I should tell you Martin is here with me. We were about to call you."

"I'm getting in my car," Samantha said. "I said I'd be there in forty minutes, which is about five minutes less than it will take me to get there if I run every red light."

"I'm putting you on speaker," Paula said. "Martin said we can also use the Hardington Police. He knows John Flynn, the town detective. Should Martin call him?"

"Definitely," Samantha said. "I hope he's the kind of guy who works Saturdays. Have Martin bring him up to speed and then we can all talk." She waited while Paula relayed the instructions to Martin, running her first red light in the interim.

"It has been just four weeks since Bree took off," Samantha said. "She obviously has a car – probably stolen – but I don't see how she could have established a new identity in such a short period of time. Given background checks, the chance she has a gun is fairly remote."

"Also, the Medical Examiner in Boston said the drug she used came out of China and is available only on the dark web," Samantha added. You have to be able to supply a credit card and a place to have it shipped. Unless Bree had two backup identities, she's living on cash and staying in motels that don't ask questions."

"How could she have cash?" Paula asked. "I thought all her accounts were frozen."

"They were," Samantha said, running a second light. "But when the State Police tallied up the cash Vinnie was supposed to have according to his computer, and counted the cash they found in his house, they came up almost half a million short. Bree probably caught Vinnie in the process of making his own escape and scooped up most of the cash Vinnie was planning to take with him."

"So, we're probably looking at a weapon you can walk into a sporting goods store and buy without a permit," Samantha concluded. "Hunting knife, machete, maybe a crossbow. But I don't think we're up against a gun. She could have more of the drug, though. She had a small bag at the airport and there could have been additional syringes in it."

Martin came on the phone. "John Flynn is going to do a drive-by in his car and tell us what he sees. He also suggested we call anyone else we think Eleanor may have been forced to contact and warn them off. He'll have a pair of police cars set up a quarter mile from her house – out of the line of sight from the house – so if

Bree tries to make a run for it, she won't get far." Martin paused before adding, "He also thinks he ought to position paramedics and an ambulance in case they're needed."

"I'll call Alice and Jean," Paula said.

"I overheard what you said about weapons," Martin said. "I think you're spot on. Police psychologists say women don't usually gravitate to guns though, in Bree's case, I wouldn't rule it out. But it's hard for someone without contacts to buy a gun on the street, and Bree is fresh out of connections."

Samantha ran another red light. "Has anyone had a bright idea yet of how to get Eleanor out of that house alive?"

"Flash-bangs would be nice," Martin said, "but they're not part of your usual local police department's arsenal. The Boston PD and State Police keep them under lock and key, and it would take a couple of hours to go through that chain of command. I know because I asked. One of my calls was to the State Police and two detectives are on their way. We've got twenty-five minutes before Paula is supposed to appear in Eleanor's driveway."

"I was thinking about a decoy event," Samantha said, pushing her car to 70 as it approached I-495. "A brush fire on the street behind Eleanor's house."

"I think Bree would see through that, though smoke is a good idea," Martin replied. "I thought about a Fed Ex or Amazon truck. They're all around on a Saturday morning, and Bree has never seen me."

"It could come to that," Samantha said. "And Bree has never seen me, either. She would be less on guard with another woman, and some people see a woman of color and automatically dismiss the idea of any threat. And, as to guns, please remember I was Worcester PD for three years. I'm fully qualified with any standard-issue police weapon." She added, "I'm getting on 495. I should be there in under twenty minutes."

* * * * *

Eleanor could hear noises from the basement. Things were being scraped along the basement's concrete floor and there were metal-on-metal sounds.

Her hands and feet were secured to a kitchen chair with plastic zip ties. She could have, with great effort, tipped over the chair, but to what purpose? The chair wasn't going to break apart; she would only have betrayed her attempt to escape.

Eleanor, of course, did not believe for a moment that Bree intended to allow her to live. But she did take Bree at her word when she said she could track down Samantha and Paula and surprise them just as she had done to Eleanor a few minutes earlier.

Eleanor further understood her usefulness ended as soon as Samantha and Paula said they were on their way. *Why, then, am I still alive?* she thought. The question was not hard to answer.

She wants us to die together, and to die at the same time.

Eleanor was certain both women understood the clues she gave in the brief time she had to speak. They would certainly come prepared.

And their coming prepared was the only way she was going to remain alive.

Bree was now on the second floor, going from room to room but spending just a few seconds in each one. She was checking something.

Now she was on the first floor in the family room. For the first time she heard a distinct sound she recognized.

It was the sequential, seconds-long, wood-on-wood squeal of casement windows closing.

* * * * *

Detective John Flynn of the Hardington Police Department phoned from his car to report just one vehicle parked in front of Eleanor Strong's house: a white Chevrolet Equinox with Rhode Island plates.

"You couldn't pick a more forgettable car," he said. "Small

SUV in its most popular color. I've called Rhode Island to ask them to run the plates." Flynn added, "We have Kevlar vests in women's sizes. Do you want me to bring them over?"

Martin looked at Paula, who shook her head. She whispered, "It's 70 outside. It would be obvious from 50 feet away."

"We'll pass," Martin said. "How are you on wireless transmitters?"

"I wish," Flynn replied. "I was thinking along those lines. Would you consider using a second phone? It would accomplish the same thing."

For several minutes, Paula, Martin, Detective Flynn, and Samantha discussed the grim reality and limited options of the situation. The appearance of any law enforcement official – whether a SWAT team or a hostage negotiator – would tell Bree that Eleanor had managed to include a coded message with her two brief calls. Having already murdered three people and been responsible for a fourth death. Bree would not hesitate to add Eleanor to the tally.

They discussed and rejected not showing up. That would infuriate Bree. Eleanor would suffer the consequences.

In a standard – if there was such a thing – hostage standoff, a marksman could be positioned to play a pivotal role. However, it would take an hour or more to get such a person into place and there was no discreet position in a suburban neighborhood.

Whatever was going to happen would take place in the next half hour. Nothing they knew about Bree lent itself to extended drama. There might come a time when one or more policemen could approach the house, but it would not be until Bree was preoccupied by whatever was going on inside and, by then, it might be too late.

"Let me throw out one other tidbit of information," Martin said. Mass State Police have determined from fingerprint records that Bree is the same women – never identified – who ran with a

Midwest-based con artist ring for several years. The photos of that woman, in turn, bear a strong resemblance to an Iowa actress and model named Candace Lockhart."

Martin continued. "The interesting thing about Ms. Lockhart is, at the age of twelve, her mother sent her to live with relatives – Candace's grandmother and great aunt. Lockhart stayed with them until she graduated high school, then was more or less tossed out, according to neighbors. Candace enrolled at a community college two hours away and never returned for a visit. One night eighteen months later, Grandma and Great Aunt Whatever died of carbon monoxide poisoning when a furnace vent broke."

"It was an old house and those things happen, but two things stuck with the Fire Marshal who investigated. The first was the furnace had been serviced three months earlier and a broken flue should have been noticed. The second was Candace didn't go to the funerals. If the neighbors are to be believed, there was no love lost between Candace and her family, and she apparently was left nothing. But skipping the funerals of the ladies who raised you is a social no-no in the Midwest. The Fire Marshal wanted to investigate but the police overruled him. Candace graduated, got work with an acting company, and then disappeared after a few years."

"If Candace were Bree, then Bree would be 42 and, based on what Eleanor says, that's not inconsistent. Everyone agrees Bree isn't 28. But it's a leap of faith to assume the two are the same person. Age-shifting software is art, not science. But *if* we take that leap of faith, it may give us some insight into what's going on inside Eleanor's house."

"We'll take whatever we can get," Samantha said, now off the expressway and making her way along the state highway toward Hardington. "Paula is supposed to be at the house in fifteen minutes."

"This is what I think," Martin said. "This isn't Bree's version of Custer's Last Stand. She has no intention of going out in a blaze of glory. Everything we know about her says she's a survivor. Had she not been ID'ed at Logan, no one may ever have known who killed Jordan Wells. Chad's death might have been chalked up as an accidental overdose and Vinnie Malone a heart attack – or the work of Ramon Suarez. Had I not run her license and discovered Emily Colwin, we'd be looking for a woman who, like Candace Lockhart two decades ago, vanished into thin air."

Martin added, "I think Bree sniffed out Samantha's existence from a careful reading of news reports – her name did get mentioned several times. Paula and Eleanor were out to bring down Senior Equity and, with it, Bree's golden egg. The State Police seized more than $3 million from her account. Think what another year or two might have brought her."

Martin continued. "So, this is an act of vengeance for ruining her life, just like her grandmother and great aunt. She has every intention of getting away with this – *driving* away with no one being able to prove a thing, and maybe not even suspecting. Here's the question: how can three people die and have it look like an accident?"

"Scratch the malfunctioning furnace idea," Samantha said. "Wrong time of year, plus everyone has CO detectors now."

Paula, silent until now, gasped. "Every year in New England, there are a couple of gas explosions – houses literally blow up. Everything burns and there's debris everywhere."

Everyone was silent.

"What does it take to turn off the gas to a house?" Samantha asked. "Can it be done from outside, or do we have to turn off gas to the entire town?"

"I guess my assignment is to get the answer to that question," Martin replied.

"We could get lucky," Paula said. "If Eleanor is allowed to open the door, we yank her out and run."

Samantha said, "Bree is too smart for that. She may not think Eleanor warned us, but she would definitely expect Eleanor to run if she had the opportunity." She added, "I'm five minutes away from your house, Paula."

Detective Flynn broke in. "Can I say how uncomfortable I am with two unarmed people walking into a trap set by someone who has killed at least three people? Hardington is my patch and, from what I hear, this is a case of two intelligent women rolling the dice that everything will go their way when they get inside. I don't like the odds."

"No one said anything about going in unarmed," Samantha replied. "Our first advantage is, we know what we're getting into. Our second is you'll know what's being said in the house. One of us ought to walk in with a plant and, buried in that plant's foliage, will be a phone ready to provide a play-by-play. Finally, I'm wearing slacks. My hope is Paula can loan me a nice, sharp knife I can strap to my leg. Oh, and Paula, can you find a large potato for your two detective friends?"

* * * * *

Bree made a final inspection of the house. Everything was as it should be and the door to the basement was closed firmly. The kitchen clock indicated it was 27 minutes since the call to Paula Winters. She hadn't called to say she would be late. *It's polite to be on time, even if it is for your own funeral,* she thought. As for Samantha Ayers, the information Eleanor Strong had provided made this woman all the more culpable. Ayers, if not the brains of the group, was definitely its behind-the-scenes force.

There were just two final tasks. Bree took some never-used candles she found in the dining room and matches from the kitchen. She went into the farthest bedroom, placed them on the dresser, and lit them. The first task was completed.

As if on cue, the doorbell rang.

Bree walked quickly into the kitchen, where Eleanor was still secured firmly to the chair. Two other chairs were arranged nearby, ready for their occupants.

"I want you to yell, 'It's open. Come on in. I'm in the kitchen,'" Bree said, the knife at Eleanor's neck.

Eleanor did exactly as she was told.

Bree did not expect a rescue attempt but, if there was to be one, it would come now. Perhaps Paula would rush in, or there would be a policeman with gun drawn. They would confront a scene of Bree with a knife, ready to cut the throat of a helpless victim. It would stop them in their tracks and, if not, they would live out their days with the memory of their 'heroism' costing a woman her life.

Instead, the surprise was hearing two women's voices, talking and laughing. Bree moved the knife to Eleanor's throat. "If you warned them, you die," Bree whispered.

The two women continued talking until they came around the corner to the kitchen. Then they saw Bree and they screamed.

"Shut up!" Bree yelled. She made certain the look on her face was one of grim determination.

The two women immediately stopped.

Bree recognized Paula from her website photo. Incongruously, she held a plant – some kind of fern, apparently. She now held it tightly, as for protection. The look on her face was one of abject fear.

The second woman was something of a surprise. Samantha Ayers was young, dark-skinned, and tall with an athletic build. But she, too, appeared fearful. But why would this twenty-something African-American woman be on such friendly terms with two people who were likely twice her age?

With her chin, Bree indicated the kitchen counter. "Put the plant down."

Paula did as she was told.

"Ms. Ayers has a purse," Bree said. "Take it from her and empty it on the table. Just turn it upside down."

In small, tentative steps, Paula did as Bree demanded. The small purse contained just half a dozen items, none of them a weapon.

"Open her wallet and take out her driver's license," Bree demanded.

Thirty seconds later, Paula, with shaking hands, held out the license. The photo and name matched. The address was in Shrewsbury, a town just east of Worcester.

Now, your own purse," Bree said to Paula. "Empty it."

Paula did as she was told. Again, nothing that could be used as a weapon.

Indicating Samantha with her chin, Bree said, "Ms. Strong called you separately. How did you come to drive here together?"

"If I tell you, will you take that knife away from Eleanor's neck?" Samantha said.

"If you don't tell me, or if I don't like the answer, this knife will sever Ms. Strong's throat and jugular," Bree replied, her voice cold.

"If you look out the front window," Samantha said, "you'll see two cars. Paula was halfway up the sidewalk when she saw me pull up. We were surprised to see one another. You heard us talking about it as we came in."

Bree accepted the explanation. In one way, it made things easier.

"Ms. Ayers, take a seat in that chair." Bree indicated one of the kitchen chairs and Samantha carefully walked to it. As she did, Bree took further note of her athletic build. If anyone was going to try a 'rescue', it was this young woman.

"Ms. Winters, there is a box of zip ties on the counter. Starting with her arms, I want you to secure Ms. Ayers to the chair in at least three places for each limb. Pull the ties tight. If I don't like the way the ties are done, Ms. Strong will be in a great deal of pain."

Bree watched carefully as Paula did as she was told.

"Now, her legs," Bree said.

Three minutes later, the job was done. *So far, so good,* Bree thought.

"Now you have a seat, Ms. Winters. Secure your left arm and your feet. I'll do your right arm, and then we're going to have a talk."

"I smell gas," Samantha said.

"I do as well," Bree said. "But you see the burners on Ms. Strong's range are off." She shifted her attention to Paula. "Ms. Winters, you should be done by now. You don't want to hear your friend in pain, do you?"

Paula quickly finished. With the boning knife now held under Paula's chin, Bree secured three ties to Paula's right arm. Bree then checked Samantha's ties and found them satisfactory.

"I'll be back in a moment," Bree said. "I want to make certain there are two cars out there. If there aren't, blood will be shed."

"So, here we are," Samantha said. "Three ladies, tied up with zip ties in a kitchen, waiting to learn our fate. I don't care if Bree isn't worried, I smell gas in here. But she's right; the burners on the stove are off."

Bree returned to the kitchen. She now held the knife in her hand, but it no longer menaced anyone in particular. "We have just a few minutes left and then I have to go," she said. "I thought I would have many questions of you, but Ms. Strong gave me the highlights and I've pieced together the rest. You have this 'noble cause' thing going on and it has worked a few times. Along comes Rebecca Cooper begging for your help. I had her figured for an overdose. Go join her dear-departed husband. Instead, the three of you decided to intervene on her behalf."

Bree went to the range, knelt down and opened the cabinet underneath it. She reached in and pulled out a plug. She then opened one of the gas jets and was satisfied to see no pilot light.

"Excuse me," Samantha said. "Are you turning on the range?"

"What a bright young thing you are," Bree replied. "Yes, I am.

You see, the basement has been filling with gas for almost half an hour. Now, we add gas upstairs. When it reaches the bedroom, there are half a dozen candles waiting. I've always wanted to see a house explode." Bree smiled at them.

"And here's what you get to think about in your last few minutes of your pitiful lives: you brought this on yourselves. You decided to get involved in something that didn't concern you, never thinking that it might annoy someone. You cost me $3 million and a very nice apartment worth at least another million."

"The generous thing to do would be to kill you now. But, after all that money you cost me, I don't feel generous anymore. So, you're just going to sit here and wonder if the gas will render you unconscious before the house explodes. The answer, according to my research is that it won't. You'll see and feel the flames. And, the wonderful part is the fire will burn away the plastic ties. Three dumb ladies sitting in a house died in a preventable accident. How tragic."

And, with that, Bree turned and made her exit through the front door.

Her plan was to watch the spectacle from a safe distance, which she figured to be about five hundred feet. As soon as she saw the explosion, she would make her way out of Hardington, her vengeance complete.

She turned the key in the ignition and took the car out of park. Fifty feet down the street, the engine sputtered and died. She pressed the gas pedal and turned the key. The engine would not turn over.

She looked over her shoulder. The house was set back 50 feet from the street, but she was well within the blast zone. She turned the key and heard the starter groan from the effort, but without result.

I'm going to have to walk out of this, she thought. She momentarily thought of racing in the house and taking one of the women's set of keys but dismissed it as too dangerous. The house could blow at any second.

She pulled the lever to open the car door and felt resistance. She looked over. Incongruously, there was a man standing at her door. He seemed to have come out of nowhere.

She pressed the button to roll down the window. "I need to get out of this car," she said through gritted teeth. "I don't need any help from Good Samaritans right now."

The man laughed. "You need all the help you can get."

Three other men had appeared. Two were in suits; two, including the man at her car door, were dressed casually.

"Hi," the man said, leaning down to peer in the window. "My name is Martin. You just tried to kill the three bravest women I have ever known, one of whom is my lady love. That's not a nice thing to do. These two men are with the State Police and they're going to arrest you for attempted murder of those three women, plus four other murders, plus a whole bunch of other things."

He added, "I learned two amazing things today. Did you know a simple crescent wrench will turn off the gas to a house from the outside riser pipe? Even more interesting, when applied to the tailpipe, the most powerful internal combustion engine is no match for the common potato."

Bree looked to her right, back at the house. The front door was open and the three women were walking out, arm in arm, escorted by two uniformed officers. They looked in Bree's direction.

Bree could see them smiling.

Acknowledgements

Most of my books have defining 'aha' moments when seeing or hearing something causes a bell in my head to announce, 'that's an idea for a book'. Not so, this one. It took a steady drumbeat of ads from aging celebrities on cable channels to pound into my consciousness that retirement is one of the scariest decisions a person can make.

Once I started kicking over rocks, I found all the fodder I needed for this book. If you Google 'reverse mortgage horror stories' and you'll see what I mean. Everything in Senior Equity Lending Solutions' nefarious bag of tricks has been pulled on vulnerable elderly. I am indebted to Cheryl O'Donnell for indulging me with multiple conversations on the topic from a banker's point of view.

The genesis of the Provençal linens subplot, on the other hand, has stared me in the face multiple times each day for five years. They are the bounty of one of those 'pop-up' sales described in the book. As to the *Conseil de Commerce des Tissus Provençaux*, I have no idea if such an organization exists. If it does, I hope its real-life equivalent of Marie Deveraux is properly appreciated and financially compensated.

My biggest 'thank-you' goes to my wife, Betty, who has now put up with me for 42 years. Hers is the first (and sometimes last) reality check on my plot and characters. Second on the 'thank-you' list is my group of 'first readers', whose candid comments and sharp eyes make up for my continuing inattention to grammar, punctuation, and plot plausibility. They include Jan Martin, Faith Clunie, Connie Stolow, and Linda Jean Smith. Your assistance shines throughout the book. Another tip of the hat goes to David Robson for suggesting the book's title.

Finally, to all the libraries, garden clubs, COAs, senior centers, women's clubs, and book clubs who continue to invite me to speak, I say, 'please keep the requests coming'. My three talks, 'Gardening Is Murder', 'Gardening Will Kill You', and 'Strong Independent Women' allow me to meet and hear from my readers. Because of that interaction, I can continue to say with complete honesty that I still look forward to every presentation.

Other books by Neal Sanders

All titles are available in print and Kindle formats

Murder Imperfect. A Wellesley Hills housewife plots to kill her philandering husband before the SEC can arrest him for securities fraud. She succeeds, but the police suspect foul play, the SEC wants to know where she's hiding millions of dollars, and her husband's pregnant mistress wants half of his estate.

The Accidental Spy. In 1967, a Pan American stewardess' attempt to deliver a misdirected bag to its owner results in a cross-country chase to outrun multiple intelligence services that want the bag's contents: plans for what may be the first microprocessor. She will be aided by a handsome Mossad agent.

Deal Killer. A young investment banker is perceived by a corporate executive as the lone impediment to his stealing millions of dollars as a failing company is acquired by its larger rival. When her car is run off the road, the banker understands she must determine which executive is the potential murderer.

How to Murder Your Contractor. An exceptionally resourceful suburban Boston housewife and her husband want to build their retirement dream home. What stands in their way is the world's worst contractor who sees the couple as his ticket to riches. Aided by friends with unusual areas of expertise, a battle of wits ensues between the couple and the contractor. *Also available in audio through iTunes or Audible.*

The Garden Club Gang. Four 'women of a certain age' devise and carry out the perfect crime: robbing a large New England fair. Complications ensue when they discover they've stolen far more money than they should have, and some very bad people want their money back.

Deadly Deeds. To atone for robbing a fair, the four ladies of *The Garden Club Gang* help an insurance investigator bring down an unscrupulous car dealer and investigate the death of an elderly friend in an upscale nursing home. Neither good deed goes unpunished.

A Murder at the Flower Show. When the head of a major Boston cultural institution is found dead, his identity unravels; leading to a search not just for his killer, but for priceless artifacts he has stolen. A young Chinese-American Detective and her about-to-retire partner are in a race against time to find his killer.

Murder in Negative Space. A prominent but universally disliked Russian floral designer is murdered at an international floral design conference in Boston. A young Chinese-American detective and a garden club president must sort out the multiple motives.

A Murder in the Garden Club. A suburban Boston garden club president discovers the body of a close friend. The town's Detective thinks it is an accident. It will be up to the club president to prove otherwise.

Murder for a Worthy Cause. The body of a suburban Boston town selectman is found dead at the site of a home being built by a popular TV show. Was the selectman murdered because he was in the wrong place at the wrong time, or was he involved in something criminal?

A Whiff of Revenge. The distinguished head of a venerable New England conservation organization is in truth a liar, crook, and a cheat. Six women, some of them close to him, some of them strangers, band together to bring him down.